The Waxing Queen Part I
The Moon Cycle Series Book I
A. F. Schreiber

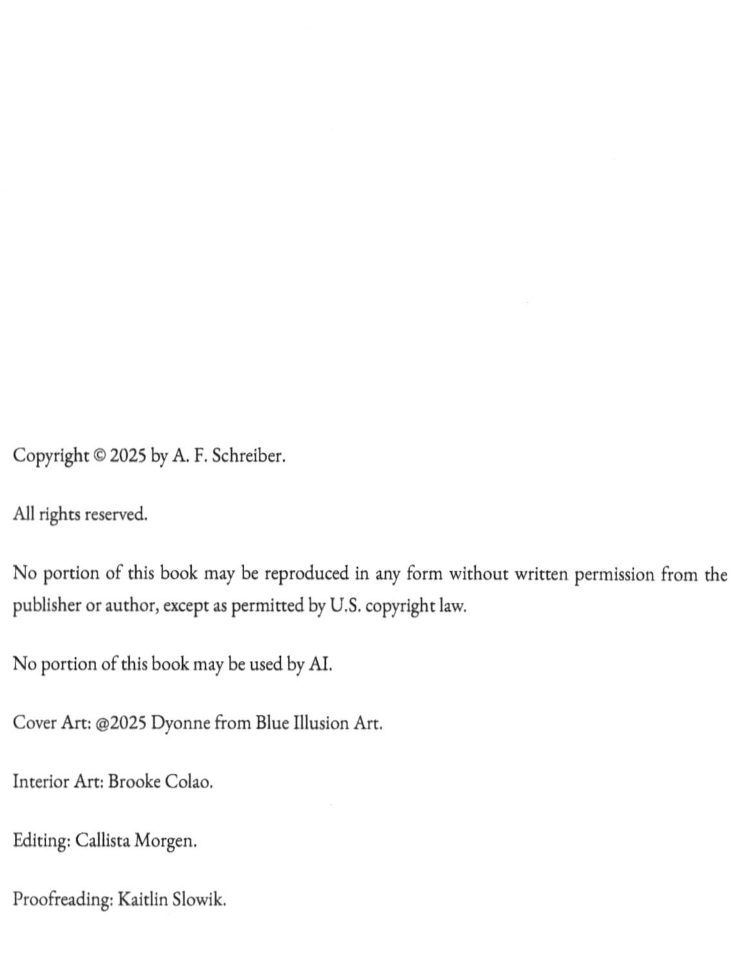

Welcome to the world of The Waxing Queen

Alanna: Ah-la-na

Alaric: Ah-lar-rick

Apolina: Ah-poe-leena

Lord Arel: Lord Air-el

Cerdwin: Ser-dwin

Cethin: Seth-in

The Dark King: refers to the "big bad."

Elana: El-ah-na

Eleonora: El-eh-oh-nora

Eldwyn: El-dwin

Lord Evaliel: Lord Ev-ale-ee-el

First Commander: refers to the highest leader of Aviva's military forces.

The Gods: refers to the eight gods who created the world.

The human king: refers to the king of the mortal continent; also referred to as the mortal king or the Southern King.

The human queen: refers to the queen of the human continent; also referred to as the mortal queen or the Southern Queen.

King Ewan: King Eh-wan

The Night Queen: refers to the "big bad's" other half.

Queen Serenity: refers to the former queen of Aviva.

Satrara: Sah-trar-ah, a surname.

Second Commander: refers to the secondary leader of Aviva's military forces.

Sonia: Son-ya

Welcome to the world of The Waxing Queen

Places

Aviva: Ah-vee-vah, the Elvish kingdom.

Catonia: Ca-toe-nia, a town in the Riverlands.

The Endurnal Mountains: The En-dur-nal Mountains, the mountain range separating Aviva from the Dark King's territory.

The Eridanos: The Error-ee-dah-nos, a river in the Riverlands.

The Elvish continent: refers to Aviva, the Endurnal Mountains, and the Dark King's lands.

The Healer's Quarters: refers to a specific place in Aviva's palace where the Healers live and work.

The human continent: refers to the continent south of Aviva and includes the city of Ozul, the Riverlands, and the Southern Kingdom. Also referred to as the mortal continent.

The Islands: refers to the archipelago east of Aviva.

The Meadows: refers to the gardens in Aviva where the dead are laid to rest.

The Otherworld: refers to the purgatory created by the Battle of the Breaking.

Ozul: Oh-zule, refers to a city at the north of the human continent.

The Realm of Blessings: refers to the heavenly realm where the Gods rule, and those deemed worthy pass on to after death.

The Riverlands: refers to the lands between Ozul and the Southern Kingdom.

The Royal Archives: refers to where Histories are housed in Aviva.

The Rusty Rose: refers to a pub in Ozul.

The Southern Kingdom: refers to the capital of the mortal continent.

Tymer's Pub: refers to a pub in Ozul.

Welcome to the world of The Waxing Queen

Animal form: refers to the animal forms all Elvish males can take.

The Annor: refers to the elders who take care of Aviva's Histories.

The Battle of the Breaking: refers to the day the Darkness spread over Aviva and the Light of Aviva was created; sometimes referred to as the Breaking.

dianaflora: diana-flora. Refers to a flower.

Elemental magic: refers to the magic wielded by Elvish males, as well as Elvish females of the royal bloodline, with earth, water, air, and fire being the most common.

Essence: refers to everything that encompasses a person, their soul.

Fake day: refers to the endless days in Aviva.

Fake night: refers to the faux nights in Aviva.

The Fire Folk: refers to an ancient race of Elves who existed millennia before the events of The Waxing Queen Part I; includes dragons, phoenix, etc.

The First Guard: refers to the unit of eight guards who protect Aviva's royal family.

Half-Elf: refers to someone of half-Elvish and half-human lineage.

Healer: what Elves call their doctors/nurses because they are magically gifted.

High Healer: refers to the most exceptionally gifted Healers.

Historian: refers to what Elves call their historians and scribes.

History: refers to Elvish history, stories, lore, etc.

Human body: refers to the form all Elves can take should they choose; also referred to as human form, mortal body, or mortal form.

The life oath: refers to the oath sworn between an Elf and an Elf, or half-Elf, when one has saved the life of the other; offered by the one who was saved, and can be denied by the savior; once accepted, both parties must exchange blood and vows; the saved is then in service to defend the savior with his or her life, until they pass on.

Life-sworn: refers to the two parties of the life oath.

The Light of Aviva: refers to the never-ending light over the city of Aviva.

The Lord's Council: refers to the body of nobility that serves Aviva; typically appointed by the royal family.

Mate: refers to the bond between two Elves that connects them mind, body, and essence; a blessing that can only be bestowed by the Gods.

mutatio: moo-tah-she-oh. Refers to a creature that can change its skin to impersonate any being and use their memories. Also referred to as a changeling.

The Noir: Refers to creatures of Darkness who serve the Night Queen.

Sandsnakes: refers to poisonous vipers that live in the Southern Kingdom.

syrena: refers to a type of Water Folk.

True day: refers to what Elves call daytime outside of Aviva.

True night: refers to what Elves call nighttime outside of Aviva.

The Water Folk: refers to an ancient race of Elves who existed millennia before the events of The Waxing Queen Part I take place; includes the *synera*, mer, sprites, etc.

A note from the author

This book is set in a fantasy world, and contains elements of romance that are generally suitable for readers ages 18 and older.

Additionally, although the story is set in a fictional place, some of the themes and content are very, very real. These include: foul language; memory loss/amnesia; physical and emotional abuse; domestic violence (off page); attempted sexual assault; trauma surrounding death, grief, and loss of family and friends; blood and gore related to battle; physical and psychological torture; and characters who struggle with their sexual orientation due to social/familial constraints.

Please protect your heart and mind.

To the readers who jump into a book and find themselves.
Welcome home.

Prologue

Eleonora

The sweet, tranquil scent of *dianaflora* was heavy in the air. The blessed aroma mingled with the smoke looming in the palace walls—smoke from fires that'd been lit three days prior to cleanse the halls of death.

The young princess was reading in her chambers, for what else was there to do in times of sorrow and uncertainty, but lose oneself in reading? Though, what she was reading wasn't exactly uplifting: an account of the Battle of the Breaking. Five years prior, Darkness had swept from the Endurnal Mountains into the Elvish kingdom of Aviva, turning the once fertile lands outside the city to sand—and killing her father, King Ewan, during the conflict.

It wasn't his essence the *dianaflora* had been left for this time, nor were the fires lit for his death.

They were for her mother.

And now that the three days of observed mourning were over, the young princess would be crowned queen: no longer Princess Eleonora, daughter of Queen Serenity and heir to the throne, but Queen Eleonora, ruler of Aviva. The one who would save their kingdom from the Darkness and re-Bind the Balance. Even though it was a role she'd prepared for her whole life, the young princess felt wholly unprepared.

A knock sounded at her door.

"Eleonora."

Not a question, but a statement from Queen Serenity's head lady's maid, Sonia, as the old, mortal woman entered the chamber. The young princess rose from where she sat at her table and walked to her full-length mirror to give her reflection a final evaluation.

Her coronation gown was the deep blue of the royal house, the silver locket her parents had gifted her for her birthday glittering against it; her full red lips stood out in a solemn line across her pale face; her blue-gray eyes—similar to her mother's, but with none of Serenity's sunlight—were dry of tears; her long, curly dark hair—which Sonia had managed to wrangle into a respectable style earlier—remained undecorated. She wouldn't receive her mother's crown until the official ceremony in the throne room. The crown was a work of art: gold and silver filigree woven together with images of the sun, stars, and moon within. It was studded to near-blinding with diamonds and sapphires, and a larger diamond—carved into a *dianaflora*—sat at its peak.

That ceremony would take place once she greeted her people as their queen—a people she'd rarely seen in her fifteen years. Her mother had kept her sequestered in the castle, far from the reach of those who sought to destroy the royal family, their lives, and their magic—those driven to malice by promises from the Dark King and his Night Queen.

Eleonora glanced to her window, where the Light of Aviva—created by her mother's magic—lit up the city. Her mother's elemental magic—rare in females, except those of the royal bloodline—had been strong and intertwined with the sun. Her own magic hadn't manifested yet, though she'd learned about both elemental and Healing magic from her tutors. They'd also taught her about her people: the Elves, half-Elves, and humans who called Aviva home; History from the wisest Elves, the Annor; courtly topics like music and dancing; and what little they told her about the rest of their world outside of Aviva.

The Light reflected off her locket, catching the young princess's attention. She prayed to the long-lost Gods that the Light remained beyond her mother's passing. Without it...

"Eleonora." She turned to see her mother's lady's maid—now her lady's maid—shaking her head affectionately. "Away from the window with you, child."

Eleonora smiled: child. Only Sonia would call her—the soon-to-be queen—anything other than *Your Majesty*. The young princess didn't begrudge her for it, though. The older woman was blunt for a lady's maid, but Sonia was a good person, beloved—or, rather, slightly feared—by those she was in charge of. Eleonora included.

"It's just one day," the lady's maid told her. "You'll make it through."

"One day." Eleanora sighed. "And how many after that?"

The old woman's still-sharp blue eyes met hers. "Be grateful, Eleonora, that you have been blessed with more days than most could ever hope to wish for, and many more beyond that."

Eleonora's throat tightened, but she nodded all the same.

"You look so much like your father," the woman said, her gaze softening. "And you will rule better than either your mother or father. Make us proud."

Eleonora opened her mouth to reply when another knock sounded at her door.

Sonia opened it, revealing Lord Evailel in his First Guard uniform. The lord—younger than most of the other nobles—was known as a quiet and prudent male who served the royal family with honor. Rumor was he'd been life-sworn to Queen Serenity, but Eleonora had never seen the life-oath scar on her mother's or the lord's hands.

"Your Highness," the lord said in the elegant courtier's voice all lords and ladies of the court were well trained in. "I am here to escort you to the procession."

He nodded to Sonia, who'd given him a small curtsy—something the lady's maid rarely did for anyone. The woman's mouth pursed. "I am to walk with the princess."

He shook his head. "Change of plans." The male strode forward and offered the young princess his hand, but not before he leaned over to whisper something in Sonia's ear. Not that it mattered—Eleonora's keen Elvish hearing picked up every word: the city guards—though the city itself was not yet in the Dark King's grasp—had an updated report on things. That was just it, though: *things*. Nothing more specific than that, shadows with no form lurking about. It was nothing new. Rumors had run amok for years since the Battle of the Breaking. But with her coronation, the crowds...Eleonora shook her head to clear it. *It would be fine.* She took Lord Evailel's hand, and together, they made their way down the hall.

Eleonora loved the palace, a stone behemoth that rose over the city proper with spiraling towers, balconies, gardens, pools—though she'd avoided those ever since she'd almost drowned in one—and waterfalls placed throughout. It was the most beautiful place the young princess knew. Now, it was a spectacle. She and the lord passed yards upon yards of blue velvet and silk hanging from the walls as they descended toward the throne room. Every banner and flag was branded with the royal sigil. The design itself was so simple Eleonora sometimes found it difficult to believe it *was* the royal sigil: two diamonds with lines from all eight points—representative of the eight Gods—that joined in the center, where a *dianaflora* blossomed into its five-petal starburst.

She took a deep breath as they approached the throne room. It was still appointed with her mother's and father's marble thrones; both were covered with black mourning cloth. She walked past, brushing her hand against the fabric with a tightness in her chest.

"Are you ready?" the lord asked, voice gentle, as they paused in front of the doors that would lead them outside. She nodded, but he was staring at her as though he were seeing someone else.

"My lord?" He shook his head, as if clearing away a memory, and pushed the doors open. The act revealed the rest of the First Guard lined up the steps and the golden carriage waiting at the bottom. From there, the palace gates, the city—and her people.

"There you are." Another male, another lord to accompany her.

Lord Arel Satrara was a cunning, shrewd, and ancient male whom Eleonora didn't care for. She knew the male had children of his own—twins, one male and one female—a few years older than her. She'd heard rumors the lord didn't spend much time with them because they looked too much like their lady mother, who'd died before the Breaking. The daughter was rumored to be a striking beauty with a sharp tongue and a Healing gift she'd levied to join the Healers instead of bowing to the whims of her lord father. The son had been sent to the human continent around the time of the Breaking, as far as she knew. The lord hadn't wanted to risk his only male child, the heir to his seat—especially since the lordling was in line to become Eleonora's betrothed.

Suddenly, one of the accompanying captains stepped up to them. She scented the unease on the male as he tried to discreetly whisper something in Lord Evailel's ear. The lord grasped her arm.

"We need to get you back inside the palace. Now," he murmured. Eleonora opened her mouth to ask why, but the lord cut her off. "Go—stay in the palace until I come for you."

She nodded and took the captain's hand. "What is it?" she asked as he opened the door. Some of the males had already shifted into their animal forms, a silver wolf and a giant dog catching her attention, and then—

She felt it—the otherworldly *wrongness* permeating the castle, the city.

"She's here," the captain said curtly, unsheathing his sword and drawing Eleonora inside and behind him. She didn't need to ask who he meant.

The Night Queen had come for her.

Screams of terror rang from outside, and a loud thundering sound cracked through the city. The noises came closer, and closer, until the fear Eleonora had sworn she wouldn't let grip her took hold. The captain turned back to her.

"I must help them defend the city." Anger and frustration shone in his eyes. "You need to get out. Out of the palace—out of the city. The gates will not hold much longer. Go. *GO!*" he shouted again when Eleonora didn't move.

But go where? Where could she go? How could she escape?

Eleonora ran out of the throne room and into a side hall. Steps spiraled above her. No, going up would only ensure her demise if the Night Queen had brought the Noir with her—dark and twisted bird-like creatures with talons strong enough to cleave a fully grown male in two.

The other hall would lead her farther into the castle—to the Healer's quarters at the heart of the mountain, leaving her trapped. Eleonora looked left and right, desperate for something, any instinct that might tell her what to do or where to go.

"Princess." A male's voice. She whirled toward it, pulling out one of the pins in her hair to use as a weapon if need be. But he was a male of the royal household, one of the Elves who worked in the stables, by the look and smell of him. His skin was a deep tan that contrasted with the light blue of his tunic, and his sharp amber eyes were wide as he took her in. He motioned her toward him with large, callused hands. "This way."

Eleonora hesitated. She didn't recognize him, but she'd met so few of the palace staff outside of her lady's maids. Then, she felt it—a kiss of cool air against her skin, the feel of it reassuring, as if letting her know she could trust him. So she followed the stablehand—pin still tucked in her sleeve—as they made their way through doors and chambers she hadn't known existed: servant's corridors, hidden passageways connecting to the main hallways, chambers, and rooms. She didn't know how long they'd been running when—

The outdoor air hit her first—then the smell. The same smell of horses she'd scented on him. They were on the south side of the palace: the stables. The male quickly saddled a white mare and tossed a pack of bread and cheese and a water skin into the proud horse's saddle bag. Then, he brought out a light gray stallion—already saddled, and already laden with provisions.

His caramel eyes returned to Eleonora as he spoke in a low voice. "We ride hard and fast. We do not stop. We do not look back. We do not go back. When we reach the shore, there will be a boat waiting for us at the dock. If I fall on the way," he said, eyes glittering as he stared into hers, "*you* do not stop. *You* do not look back. *You* do not go back. You get to the shore, you board that ship, and you go. You run, you hide, and you stay hidden. Do you understand?" She nodded, too dazed to do anything else. "That settles it, then," the male said. He picked her up as though she weighed nothing and set her on the mare, gathering a blue cloak around her shoulders and tugging the hood over her head. He mounted the stallion. "Let's go."

They rode hard and fast, exiting the city walls through the stable's personnel entrance. Eleonora tried to block out the cacophony of sounds: the screams, the pleas, the cries of fear and heartbreak. They threatened to break her own heart.

She looked at the male who'd given her a way out, who was pushing his horse faster and faster. He caught her eye. "Keep going!" he shouted over the din. "Do not stop."

Tears streamed down her face as they rode away from the walls. Her city. Her kingdom. Her people. A royal legacy she'd been about to pledge herself to entirely, prepared or not.

She looked back, just once. Dark shapes moved through the skies.

The Noir had come.

A sharp pain took root in her chest. The dark creatures hurtled toward them. The city had become smaller behind them, but she'd seen the maps; there were still miles between them and the ports to the human continent, and all that lay between them and those ports was crisp, flat land—like the desert that lay between Aviva's city walls and the Endurnal Mountains. There would be nowhere to hide, no place to take shelter from the beasts who hunted them—hunted *her*—like dark birds of prey.

Eleonora paused and heard the male who'd been next to her—and was now ahead of her—yell for her to keep going. But she couldn't—couldn't take her eyes off the terrifying creatures, the gathering storm of feathers, talons, and beaks.

"GO!" the male shouted as the creatures picked up speed, carried by some unnatural wind made of shadow. "RUN!"

Still, Eleonora couldn't. She could only sit on that beautiful horse and stare as the Noir descended for them—for her. The male made to position himself, his horse, and a sword Eleonora didn't remember him having on his person between her and the Night Queen's creatures.

She heard them as they approached, the hissing and cawing noises they made grating along her skin, her bones, her essence—sounds that sent shiver after shiver down her spine while the pressure in her chest grew and expanded. Echoing even deeper was a sense of dread—a dread that she'd already failed: failed her mother, her father, her people, her kingdom, their world. She was utterly defenseless against the servants of the Night Queen. She had no magic to defend herself or the male at her side with.

Eleonora sobbed, the sound drowning out the Noir. She'd promised herself at her mother's funeral that she wouldn't be afraid—but here she was, fleeing her home, giving up, allowing herself to be swept away by the Darkness before she was ever crowned queen.

The feeling in her chest tightened, then cracked, as if some part of her had broken open. She gritted her teeth as the winged beasts grew closer, her disquiet now coming not only from their certain victory over her and the male with her, but from that feeling, that pull, deep within her. Something rich and velvety pooled in her chest. No—in her heart. Something calming. Something cool. Something soothing.

She cried out as a silver light flared at her heart, then flowed from her chest into her belly, down her legs and into her feet, her arms and hands, her neck and face. All of her panic, all of her heartache, all of her despair came alive inside of her with the force of a thousand shooting stars.

A wave of pale light erupted from her whole being and speared for the Noir. The Dark creatures hesitated, wary, then pulled away from her and her companion.

Toward the city. The light that'd come from inside of her wrestled with the Darkness over the city, then pushed it back toward the Endurnal Mountains until that Darkness was gone from her home and only the Light of Aviva remained.

The remaining glimmers of silvery light flowed back into her body, into her heart. She heard her companion curse—

Eleonora slumped forward on her horse, feeling the weight of a heavy exhaustion she'd never known hit her like a stone sinking to the bottom of the sea.

She opened her eyes. She was atop a white horse. She was alone. No, not alone. A male with dark hair and eyes the color of honey rode next to her. And they were riding...toward a port. A human woman walked next to them. The woman and the male murmured together in soft whispers she couldn't hear. The woman looked familiar. *But why?*

She looked around, taking in the harbor, then looked back toward...a city. Had they traveled from it?

"Come, child," the woman said in a voice that sounded both familiar and foreign.

"I have to go back," she said, trying to sift through her memories to determine *why* she needed to go back, and *where* she needed to go back to. It was as difficult as wading through soft sand.

"No, child," the woman said. "Not now. Not yet."

She wasn't a child, she thought indignantly. But...who was she? She panicked, searching her mind for that sense of self, her hand reaching for...a necklace. She twisted the silver chain.

"Come, Elana," the woman said.

So Elana let the woman lead her onto the waiting ship.

49 years later...

Elana

It was the end of another long day at Tymer's Pub. Elana stared out the tavern window as a sleepy pink and gold dusk made its way across the town square in Ozul, the place she'd chosen to call home for the past nine years.

It was almost time to move on again.

She barely remembered where she'd grown up—those memories were like the faded wine stains on the bartop. All she had left of her childhood was a silver necklace she couldn't bear to part with. She knew she'd been born an Elf, but Elana lived in her human form to integrate with the humans who made up the majority of the mortal continent's population. But others could still tell she wasn't entirely human—she never showed signs of aging, even as the years passed by—which made relocating every ten years or so sensible.

Most days, though, people only saw the same human woman reflected back at her as she turned toward the glass behind the bar: an almost too-thin body covered by a simple brown dress; mousy brown hair woven into a messy braid; gray eyes, and a plain nose and mouth. Her human life was just as ordinary as she was.

Elana worked at the tavern and rented a room in a nearby hovel that was barely worth her pay. But it was worth enough to be there, in that place close to the sea, to listen to the whispers of sailors and merchants—and some Elves—as they made their way in and out of the bar, to and from the shores of Ozul and the land across the sea: the Elvish kingdom of Aviva.

Elana assumed that's where she was originally from, though she had no memory of the place. It was where most Elves were born, though many had fled from their homeland under the threat of the Darkness. She assumed that's what had urged her own parents to send her to the human continent alone.

But how long would it be until the Darkness spread? For reasons Elana couldn't explain or ignore, that question haunted her, occupying her mind during work as she refilled tankards of ale and served dishes of sea fish, stews, hearty breads, and smelly cheeses to both humans and hidden Elves like her.

She wondered what the owner of the pub had thought of her when she'd first arrived. Jack Tymer was a human man without the innate ability to sense her Elvish lineage—but the decision to take her in hadn't been his, anyways. His wife, Lydia, had taken one look at her travel-worn appearance—Elana had left her home in the Southern Kingdom, the capital of the human continent, quickly for the north—and ordered her to where the couple lived above their business for a bath. Not out of any sort of pity, the woman had said, but because the smell of her would scare away their more well-to-do customers.

At first, Elana had stayed in the spare room next to the human couple's. The lodging was part of her pay, along with the scraps of food she ate after the customers left for the night—at least, until Lydia passed away. Not that Jack was an unkind man—no, he was like a father figure to her—but Elana didn't want to impose. He solemnly accepted her offer to do more around the tavern and earn coin to stay nearby instead.

Elana remembered the day of Lydia's funeral clearly: the weight of emotion had been thick in the air—as thick as the smoke from the fires burning around the town to cleanse it of death. Lydia had been revered as highly as any queen, a pillar in Ozul's community as an upstanding businesswoman and a loving wife, caring for each and every person she encountered—like she had Elana. Elana visited the woman's grave once a year on the anniversary of her passing, and the pub was always closed that day—unlike the rest of the year when it remained open, even on holidays.

Elana's counterpart—a young human girl named Amy, blonde haired and blue eyed with a well-rounded figure—took the morning shifts, so their work only crossed over briefly before the tavern reopened for breakfast. Phillip—the cook—worked longer hours, though he didn't live at the bar like people often assumed; he simply had a burgeoning family to take care of. Jack still made appearances, though his jovial air had diminished since Lydia's death.

What it was like to love someone so deeply, only to lose them?

Elana returned the glass she'd been cleaning to the oaken shelf behind the bar, right next to a dozen others just like it. It was almost nighttime—when the less-than-respectable crowd came in. Still, she liked to make sure things were as clean and presentable as they were for her sunset regulars, like the sweet young newlywed couple—human—who always dined together; the older gentleman who always tipped her well at dinner—an Elf, she sensed from him, and likely he about her; and a few others—some traders and merchants she eavesdropped for information about the blockade from.

The Dark King had kept Aviva under a blockade for almost fifty years, controlling all trade between Ozul and the Elvish continent. People feared he would drop his hand one day and spread Darkness throughout their entire world. Then, there was the Night Queen, who bore her own dark host of hideous, bird-like demons that hadn't been seen since the princess of Aviva had disappeared.

But some people whispered of hope—hope that the lost princess would return and re-Bind the Darkness and the Light, restoring the Balance.

Elana swept the sticky, crumb-covered floor of the bar as she brushed those thoughts away. She rewove her braid to include strands of dark hair that'd escaped throughout the early evening, gazing at the rounded ears of her human form as she restocked the cheap ale and more expensive liquors.

Had this always been her parents' plan for her? To live out her days in a mortal body, having to move every decade? Would it not have been better to stay in Aviva and fight? There was little she could've done on that front, though. Unlike on the mortal continent, females weren't allowed to join the military in Aviva—the only exception was the queen.

Elana straightened her apron and looked behind her to where Phillip stood, ready and waiting for the orders that would soon come throughout the night, and nodded. He nodded back. She couldn't think of the what-ifs of the past when there was work to do in the present.

It was almost early morning when Elana made her way home. The night had gone as it was prone to: a laughing, raucous crowd, whose singing grew worse as the night went on; a few life threats amongst the clientele over debts owed; a new gambling game running rampant at the tables; drinks spilled, and the whole pub in desperate need of another round of cleaning when Phillip finally yelled for last call.

Elana didn't mind the late hours, or walking home in the dark—especially when Cerdwin joined her on his way to work. The male—now a man in his human form—was apprenticed to the local blacksmith and taught her self-defense. Their first lesson had come when she'd passed by the forge one morning sporting a blossoming bruise on her cheek from a late-night customer who hadn't understood the word *no*.

"Who marked you?" he'd demanded when he'd stopped her, pure menace lacing each word. Something buried deep within Elana's Elvish instincts had told her to trust the kind, if not somewhat melancholy, apprentice—so she had.

Elana considered Cerdwin a fixed presence in her life, as she likely was in his, she supposed, though the two had never become a couple like Paul—the blacksmith—teased. It wasn't that Cerdwin was unattractive—the male had curly, sandy blond hair; unique blue eyes that looked almost purple; and strong muscles cut from the hours he worked at the forge—but he was more like a brother to her.

He'd taught her how to defend herself using her own body—or the weight of the other person—to her advantage. His lessons had served her well: she'd made it out of additional situations with no more than a few bumps—while her assailants hadn't. After she'd mastered using her body, he'd taught her how to fight and spar with the weapons he made. He'd even promised to make her a blade or two of her own in his spare time. Given that Cerdwin worked even longer hours than she did, Elana was grateful for the time he gave her.

She felt something as they walked together under the light of the waxing moon. Something unfamiliar—yet not. A strange tug in her chest.

Elana rubbed at the spot over her heart, hoping it wasn't some insufferable human issue, like indigestion, something Tymer's customers regularly complained about. But this felt *different*. Older—almost primordial. She scanned the street behind them. The businesses on either side were still closed, and she didn't see anyone in the gloom. If Cerdwin noticed her distractedness, he didn't say. Yet she couldn't shake the feeling that *something* was in the city—and it was watching her.

She bid Cerdwin farewell as she unlocked the door to her lodgings, closing and bolting it behind her. Leaning against the rough wood, she sighed. It would be harder to leave this place than the others. She wasn't just leaving the town, but its people: her closest friend, the kind man who still mourned his wife. While she thought Cerdwin might understand, Jack was a different matter. It would be best to leave in the night without a word to the man.

Rubbing her hands over her face, Elana pushed away from the doorframe and packed what few belongings she owned: undergarments, several sets of pants and tunics, grooming tools, a box of herbs, various travel supplies, and a blue cloak she hadn't been able to part with all these years. Then, she sank onto her bed, mattress groaning with the motion, the sound grating against her senses as she willed herself into a restless sleep.

Everything began according to Elana's plan—everything except for one thing.

When she stopped by the forge, Cerdwin wasn't there—at least, not outside like he normally was. Guilt bit at her. She wanted to say goodbye to her friend.

Elana slipped into the shop's storage room while Paul hammered loudly in another one of the outdoor spaces. Cerdwin wasn't inside, either, but she spotted a fresh piece of parchment tilting out of a box on the top shelf—their secret communication spot. She found an empty box, turned it upside down, and stood on it to reach the paper.

Elana read his note once—twice, blinking in surprise: he'd left, and wouldn't return any time soon. *Where had he gone?* She flipped the paper over—nothing more written there, but he'd drawn something akin to a maker's marker. She peered back into the basket.

Cerdwin had left her more than a note. Inside the box was a beautifully engraved leather belt with two cases on either side, and within those sheaths...Elana's breath caught as she pulled a blade free. It was beautiful, a deadly, sharpened steel, and—

Her mouth dropped open, eyes wide as she ran her fingers over the hilt decorated with silver and *real* gold—not just gold plating. The two precious metals wound around the wicked steel to form elegant whorls and flowers. Not only would it've taken most of Cerdwin's already limited spare time to create the design and craft it, it also would've taken a decent chunk of his pay to afford the gold. Elana drew the other blade and palmed both by the hilt, feeling the perfection of their fit in her hands, flipping them as he'd once shown her how to do. They usually worked with one knife or a sword. Two blades would take some getting used to.

Beneath the belt were two additional sheaths she realized would fit snugly around her thighs if she didn't want the weapons on display. She fit them under her dress and slid the daggers into place, the metal cool against her skin. Breathing deeply, Elana placed the belt in her bag and quietly slipped out of the room.

Walking to Tymer's, she sent a silent word to the lost Gods for their patience—and to ask them to watch over her friend, wherever he might be.

Her shift went smoothly. The tavern was less crowded than usual due to the prognostication of a late winter storm. Winter in Ozul hadn't been as brutal as some Elana had experienced, though winters in ocean or riverside towns were normally colder and brought heavier snows than winters in the south. While some believed the incoming storm would be the first and last real sign of winter they'd see for the year—besides the chilly nights and mornings, and the frost-coated plants and flowers that dared poke through the small gardens of the wealthier townsfolk—others whispered it was a sign.

Phillip passed her a warm cup of tea while she finished cleaning the last of the evening's merry drinking companions' cups. The winds outside whipped against the tavern door. She offered the cook a quiet smile as he headed back into the kitchen to cool the stoves before shouting his farewell. With a wife, three little ones, and another on the way—and now the threat of the snowstorm—he needed to get home quickly. Jack had come downstairs earlier in the evening to ask if she wanted to spend the night in her old room. Though grateful, she'd declined his invitation, guilt pooling in her gut. Perhaps Jack would catch wind of Cerdwin's departure and think she'd chased after him.

A dull ache began pulsing behind her temples as she dried her hands. She'd had terrible headaches over the years, some so bad she stayed in bed for days—and they always brought on strange dreams.

Folding her apron and setting it on the countertop, Elana paused, taking in the wooden room around her: the tables, stools, and benches; the variety of alcohols and liquors; the place she'd worked in—Hell, practically finished growing up in. She thought of the man upstairs and his wife who was now in the Otherworld. Her friend who'd left her behind. Then, Elana pulled her travel satchel from under the bar. She rummaged through it until she found the heavy blue cloak. It'd kept well over the years: the fabric still sturdy, the blue not even a little bit faded. She gathered it around her shoulders and pulled the hood up, sealed the bag and swung it onto her back, and walked out of the tavern.

The freezing wind hit her instantly, even with the cloak, whipping strands of hair that'd come free of her braid across her face. She shivered as she watched the clouds shift in front of the moon and stars. That was another reason she didn't mind walking home at night: she could see the sky, the stars, and the moon. Something always stirred in her chest at the sight of them—a strange, powerful pulsing leading from her heart to her fingertips. She felt that tingling now, but it didn't feel whimsical—it felt like a warning.

Elana kept a steady pace as she made her way to the outskirts of the town, toward the open, rolling hills that swept down to the riverside miles beyond. She hadn't lived there in quite some time, but the richer humans always needed people to tend their beautiful manors, care for their gardens, and serve the guests at their lavish parties. She'd mainly avoided the area because of who lived close by.

It would be a long, cold trek. She wished whatever she sensed could've waited until summer. Goose bumps broke out across her skin as she moved forward, darting down different streets and alleyways to change direction as she went, should anyone be following her—something else Cerdwin had taught her.

She glanced up at the sky again. There was something else there, something darker than any cloud. *Drip, drip.* She looked down as freezing rain fell, then glanced left to right. The streets were empty, the homes lining them lit from within by roaring fires as people fended off the cold while they slept.

So there was no one to hear Elana cry out at the sudden movement from an alley to her left—as a large, dark shape barreled into her.

Chapter 2

Elana

Her bones reverberated as her body hit the cobblestone street, teeth singing with the impact. It was a man—or male—she surmised, taller and heavier than she was. He pinned her to the ground, slamming one of his forearms across her chest. He caught her hands with his other hand, and secured them above her head, wedging his knee between her legs. His features were hidden by a heavy black cloak. Between that cloak, the darkness of the evening, and the clouds dumping buckets of freezing water—which now dripped from his cloak onto her face—she couldn't see him clearly. She also couldn't reach her daggers.

Elana refused to let panic take hold. He was probably just a common thief looking for an easy mark.

He was about to learn she wasn't one.

Use his weight against him, she heard Cerdwin's voice say. She gritted her teeth against the headache pulsing through her shoulders, neck, and face. Her attacker might be stronger, but, thanks to Cerdwin, she knew strength didn't always equate to speed.

She heard her assailant's ragged breathing from beneath his hood. She'd learn who he was by the end of all this—and make sure the town guards did, too. But, if he were a common thief, why hadn't he begun searching her for coin? Other than money, the silver pendant around her neck was the only thing she had of value, and even that was likely only of value to her. Elana tensed her muscles in preparation, feeling that familiar tightness in her chest, that tingling in her hands.

Before she could execute a maneuver Cerdwin would've been proud of, another shape that was definitely *not* a cloud caught her attention over his shoulder. Every one of her senses choked at the *wrongness* of it. The shape cut through the rain like a knife. Above her, the man stiffened. Not a man then—not if he felt that creeping sensation as strongly as she did. An Elvish male in a human body.

Or a half-Elf.

He pivoted as the dark, bird-like shape swooped over where they'd toppled into the center of the alleyway. The male loosed a shout as two of the creature's long talons ripped into the shoulder of the arm he'd raised above his head, the wicked-looking curved knife he'd drawn clattering to the ground.

The creature retreated skyward and disappeared, but instinct told Elana it would make another pass. She moved in front of the male now clutching his wounded arm, his blood mixing with the freezing water that coated the stones beneath them. She heard him cry out again—this time more likely in shock than from pain or fear—as pale light erupted from her body.

The pulse of light was brief—but it sent the menacing creature coming back for them high into the sky again. It shrieked in pain as it went. The sound froze Elana's blood faster than the bitterly cold rain biting at her face. She stood as she watched it flap away—north—then looked down and stared at her hands.

Where had that light come from?

Female Elves didn't have magic beyond the Healing gift. That couldn't have been what she'd used against the creature, could it?

Another more human groan of pain reminded Elana that her original assailant was still there. She whirled, drawing her blades—

But the male was on the ground, sitting upright, still clutching his shoulder where talons had ripped through cloth and skin. She could leave him there and let someone else find him and deal with him. Let him bleed out and freeze in the streets. She should, for whatever he'd been about to do to her.

But some sense urged her not to. Pulling the dark blue hood back over her head, Elana picked up his blade and put it in her bag. She pulled out the leather belt Cerdwin had made for her, sheathed the daggers, and approached the wounded male.

She squatted next to him and pulled his hood back. He looked older than she would've guessed, appearing to be in the middle of his thirtieth year of life—though with the half-Elvish blood her senses confirmed ran through his veins, he could be much older. While half-Elves didn't have the same essentially immortal lifespans as fully-blooded Elves, they did live extraordinarily long lives compared to humans. His eyes were caramel, the same color as the sinfully sweet treat she'd tasted in the Southern Kingdom; his brown hair was so dark it was almost black; and rugged, tanned skin suggested he spent time outdoors. A light scar ran down the right side of his jaw, and the stunted ears of the half-Elves poked up from beneath where his hair gracefully fell around them—hair not as long as most fully-blooded

Elvish males like Cerdwin kept theirs, but long enough that it touched that scar.

Under different circumstances, she supposed she might've found him attractive.

His eyes were glazed with pain. He opened his mouth as if he were going to speak—

Elana punched him directly in the jaw, rendering him unconscious. She needed time to think about what to do with him next. She slung the unconscious male over one shoulder, her traveling bag over the other, and wound her way nimbly back to her home—the ease with which she did so telling her she had shifted into her Elvish form at some point.

She sighed—she hadn't intended to do that. She also hadn't intended to return to her room; no, she'd intended to leave the city until she determined *what,* exactly, she sensed—preferably in a locale far away from those she cared for. Now, she knew: this male and that creature, though it was clear they weren't working together.

Was it because of her and whatever that light had been?

She tied the half-Elf to the lone chair in her room with the length of rope she kept in her bag—an odd accessory to most, but she'd found it handy in her previous travels. She shifted back into her human form before he regained consciousness, wincing at the brief flash of pain and confusion the transition brought on—and the headache that pounded more intensely against her temples in that body.

Elana grabbed a cup, opened the window, and leaned out, filling it with freezing rain. Returning to the male, she tossed the cup at his face. He sputtered, then took her in with what she deduced was a mixture of irritation and...amusement?

"Who are you?" she demanded, quietly but steadily, hands within casual reach of her daggers.

He opened his mouth but didn't speak. Elana watched a shudder roll through his body—not from the cold, but from the pain lining his face, which shifted from tan to pale to green as she eyed him. That's when she recognized what it was: poison. The creature's talons must've been tipped in it.

She went back to her satchel, hands steady as she retrieved and opened the small wooden box she'd found in a shop years before. It was divided into sections, the interior two levels deep, despite its size. It housed all manner of herbs and plants she'd identified as capable of human healing.

There it was—the yellow flower she was searching for. She bit into its petals. Keeping a slight distance between herself and the male, Elana pressed them into the cut that was turning black. He was lucky: the wound wasn't as deep as she'd originally thought and was on his right side, high up on his shoulder. Had it been on his left—anywhere near his heart—he'd already be dead. The yellow flower she'd selected could suck poison from surface wounds like his—so he'd live—but it wouldn't have been able to handle anything more severe. Anything worse would've required *actual* Elvish Healing magic—something she'd never learned.

The male hissed when the petals made contact with his flesh, the yellow turning black. When there was nothing but the red of blood, Elana fished a spool of bandages from her bag and wrapped it around his shoulder. He was panting.

Amber eyes found hers, flickering, as though they were searching for something. "You saved my life." His voice was deep, lower than Cerdwin's rich tenor—yet somehow more *alive*. It struck something in Elana, like a musical note she'd heard before but would forever struggle to recall.

"Who are you?" she demanded again, unsheathing a dagger as she moved to stand right in front of him. She lowered the dagger to his throat. The male's gaze slid from hers, to the dagger, then back again.

"*That's* a fancy weapon for a barmaid," he remarked, tilting his head to one side. She pressed the blade firmly against his throat and watched as a trickle of blood ran down his neck.

"That doesn't mean I don't know how to use it," Elana threw back at him. He let out a low chuckle, and the sound sent a pulsing rush of blood through her veins. She inwardly cursed her body, which apparently *did* find him attractive—even in this situation.

"I could think of another use for that blade right about now," he said.

"You mean besides killing you and dumping your body for the local guard to find?" she sweetly replied, forcing a smile that was more confident than she felt to her mouth. His lips quirked to one side.

"That would be a waste of my potential," he advised, "considering I now owe you the life oath."

Elana sucked in a breath. His Elvish heritage must be strong for him to know about the life oath. It was only offered in the gravest of circumstances: when an Elf—or half-Elf—saved the life of another of their kind, Cerdwin had told her, it was the obligation of the rescued party to offer their life's blood in return, swearing lifelong protection to their savior. However, the receiving party was not required to accept it.

She hummed and put on the air of considering it to buy time. "And why would I accept the life oath from a common thief?" she asked. "And, honestly, not a very good one?"

He let out that dark chuckle, the amusement in his eyes sparking her irritation. "Because I am no common thief." She raised a brow, and he let out a long-suffering sigh. "I can't believe you would think that of me," he said in mock disbelief, shaking his head, hair damp from the rain. She pressed the dagger deeper into his flesh, and his lips tugged up again. "I'm not here to rob you. I'm here *for* you."

Elana's heart stuttered, then started beating wildly in her chest. "Who sent you?" she demanded, willing her suddenly trembling hand to steady.

"I don't know." Even though she didn't want to believe him, she did. "I'm often hired through back channels, you know. People of higher stations not wanting to get their hands dirty and all." He shrugged.

"So you're a mercenary," Elana ground out. And he had the nerve to *smile*.

"You say that like it's a bad thing." She grunted in disgust. "A mercenary who was sent for you, for what purpose he doesn't even know, who now offers you the life oath."

She took a deep breath and *really* considered him. "Why?"

His gaze bore into hers, and she noticed his amber eyes were ringed around the pupils in a color that was lighter, giving them an almost golden hue. She inhaled sharply as some invisible instinct brushed against the nape of her neck—the same sensation she'd felt with Cerdwin.

"Because I honor my oaths," the half-Elf said, voice softer now, "even more than my coin." He winked.

Elana sank back onto her heels, head spinning. On the one hand, he was a mercenary, a blade for hire who'd *attacked her*. On the other hand, she was armed but minimally trained, traveling alone, right when something else had come for her and she'd, well, glowed. And she still wasn't exactly sure where she was going to go or what she was going to do next.

She exhaled through her nose. "I accept."

An emotion she couldn't quite place crossed the male's face, and then he nodded. Elana stood and walked around the chair to work just his left hand free from where she'd bound it behind him—just in case he changed his mind or this was some trick. She glanced back up at him, and he nodded again, so she dragged the dagger across his open palm, blood leaking in its wake.

"I, Cethin"—so that was his name—"swear my blood, blade, and protection to..." He raised a dark brow.

"You don't even know who I am, but you offered to *take* me?" He shrugged, but those warm eyes never left hers. "Cad," she spat at him. Was she really going through with this? "I'm...El." Apparently so, though she wasn't sure why she didn't give her full name, but the nickname she used sparingly.

"El." That amusement returned to his eyes. "Interesting name." His gaze turned serious. "I, Cethin, swear my blood, blade, and protection, to you, El."

Elana hissed as she pulled the dagger across her left palm. She clasped it to his bloodied, blistered, callused hand.

"And I, El, accept your oath, Cethin."

"Till my death severs our bond," he finished, voice low.

"Till your death severs our bond," she whispered, fully drawn into his gaze. She could've sworn images flashed in his eyes, images of...

The pain that'd receded to a slight pulsing behind her eyes reemerged against her temples with full force—

Elana gasped as those images—not images, but memories—flooded her mind.

The young princess stepped into the empty hall, pausing to take in how perfectly beautiful everything was: the Light of Aviva shone through the open windows of the space, delicate blue and purple flowers climbed the pillars, and the pool cut into the marble floor shimmered.

She'd managed to escape the head lady's maid, if only for a little while. The mortal woman and her mother were always pressing upon her the importance of her studies, her courtly interactions—minimal though they were—and her duties as a princess. She just wanted to escape for a moment, to be by herself, to have something *for herself.*

She stepped out of her amethyst-colored dress and approached the glittering pool. The Light and water danced together, making the room look as though it were from another place, another time, as all colors illuminated the walls.

She sighed in relief as she dipped her toe in the water: it was a shallow pool, same as the others she frequented. Sonia knew those, but the woman wouldn't find her here, in what was technically part of the lord's wing. The lords were currently in a council meeting, discussing something regarding the Breaking with her mother. She tried to avoid her mother whenever those meetings took place—meetings that reminded everyone that the king—the young princess's father—was dead.

She took another step into the water, then another, the coolness of it beckoning as it came up around her ankles, her thighs. Farther, and farther until—

The young princess gasped as she took another step and her foot touched nothing. This wasn't a shallow pool. There was nothing there but water.

There was no one there to help her.

And she didn't know how to swim.

Arms flailing, feet kicking, she thrashed in the water, limbs trying to find purchase somewhere, anywhere, breath choking as cool water filled her lungs. She couldn't cry out.

Finally, her arms made contact with smooth marble. She clung to it, pulled her entire body toward it, until she was hauling herself up and over the edge of the pool, coughing up water as she went.

As she tried to catch her breath, her eyes found the open window and the gloomy mountains looming in the distance—mountains that seemed to mock her near death. She wouldn't give them that satisfaction. She wouldn't give him—the Dark King—that satisfaction.

But she certainly wouldn't ever try swimming again.

"Eleonora!"

Chapter 3

"**A**re you going to untie me now?"

The attractive—and apparently brave, or maybe stupid, he hadn't decided yet—woman blinked, her cheeks flushed and breath unsteady as if *just* realizing she still held his bleeding hand. She promptly dropped it. But those flushed cheeks, that hitched breath—Cethin couldn't help himself.

"I typically like to get to know a lady better before I let her bind me up." He grinned wolfishly at the additional heat the comment brought to her cheeks, staining them a faint red. He rubbed his free hand over where she'd sunk her fine blade into his skin, and casually added, "Or torture me, although it's typically not all blades and blood and pain." He gave her a wink that normally made the local ladies of wherever he was swoon. But not her—though that red remained splashed across her delicate features. She had gumption, he'd give her that. *Brave it was.*

"As you've already stated," she said flatly, though he detected a slight shake to her voice that hadn't been there before, "I'm just a barmaid." She used her now-bloodied dagger to finish undoing his bonds. Rubbing his wrists, Cethin stood, watching her do the same, though he towered a good few inches over her. He rotated his injured shoulder; the creature's wound was already healing thanks to this interesting woman who called herself El.

"And why would someone pay a mercenary to find and abduct a barmaid?" he asked, circling his wrists.

The blush disappeared from her cheeks as she paled. Then, lips curling, she said, "Perhaps they were displeased with their tab."

Cethin laughed—not the low, wicked laugh he typically gave in more *intense* situations, but an actual laugh at the words this fascinating woman he'd been sent to...he didn't let himself finish that thought.

He wasn't entirely sure what he'd been thinking, offering her the life oath. But it was an inherent part of him, that Elvish heritage he buried deep—unless it gave him an advantage. And right now, his advantage was being linked to this otherwise seemingly plain barmaid who'd somehow saved him from an attack from—well, Cethin wasn't sure what. But it'd interfered with his plans and his job.

He'd ditched jobs before when he decided they weren't worth his time or skill, or the coin offered. But this job was different. *She* was the job, this El. But why? As her life-sworn, now would be a good time to find out. Actually, *prior* to becoming her life-sworn would've been a good time. Cethin shook himself out of his thoughts and cleared his throat. She flinched, as though the sound had pulled her from her own.

"Who are you?" Cethin asked, crossing his arms and taking in her small frame. She wore a brown wool dress partially hidden by a rich blue cloak, the color of which brought out the blue in her gray eyes. They reminded him of the middle of the sea under the full moon. *Exquisite.* And she had a locket that looked to be made of silver tucked beneath the cloak.

He dropped his gaze to the Elvish make of the beautifully crafted leather belt at her waist that had held twin daggers, the hilts crafted from silver and *real* gold, he noted. It was a set of weaponry far richer than she should be able to afford, though he'd gathered from tracking her the past few days and nights that she often frequented the local blacksmith's shop. *Was that where she'd learned how to defend herself?*

She wore brown shoes that'd seen better days and had her hair in a brown braid that'd become slightly unbound during their skirmish, wisps of hair shifting around her face. He wanted to reach out a hand to brush one away, but stilled as he watched her assess him in return.

"I told you," she said, though a haunted look clouded those beautiful eyes. "I'm a barmaid. My name is El."

He clucked his tongue. "And why would a mercenary be hired to...?"

"I told you," she said again, frustration edging her tone. "Perhaps someone was unhappy with their bill."

"Seems rather extreme," he dryly observed, keeping his laugh to himself this time. Whoever she was, she was certainly unexpected—and he was intrigued.

El shrugged. "You would be surprised by what men think they're entitled to when it comes to beer, money, and women."

Cethin uncrossed his arms and took a step closer. She stiffened. "I suppose that's why you learned those skills," he said, lifting his right hand to his jaw that was now bruised where she'd punched him. Again, that rosy color appeared on her cheeks. He rather liked that color.

"A woman should know how to take care of herself," she said. "Now, who are you?"

"I told you," he intoned mockingly. "I'm Cethin. And you decided the rest, the mercenary bit," he added, waving his hand between them. She hesitated, biting her lower lip. It was distracting.

"And you were sent...for me," she said slowly, as though working through some mind puzzle he couldn't see.

He nodded. "And you are...?"

She rolled her eyes at his repeated question. "We need to leave this town."

"Well," Cethin said, throwing his hands up, "I'd say that's the first thing you and I agree on." He looked at the bag next to the chair. "Although, I'd say it looks like you were already in the process of leaving?"

She sank down on the bed behind her, rubbing her face with her hands. "I need to think," she whispered. "To figure out..."

Cethin sat in the chair again and crossed his leg over his knee. "May I offer a suggestion?" El looked up at him, expression wary, so he leaned forward until she met his eyes. "Take this as you will, but as your life-sworn, consider that keeping you alive is now in my best interest. And, in order for us both to survive tomorrow, I suggest you get some rest while I take watch. We'll depart before first light, then learn from the local gossip what that *thing* was, and decide what to do from there. Unless you're aiming to chase after that male from the forge—"

"You've been watching me," she said sharply.

He leaned back in the chair, grin tight as an unexplained ball of jealousy gripped his chest. "Part of the job, El."

Frustration warred with exhaustion on her face. Then—

"First light," she said, that drawn, tired look on her face winning out.

"First light it is, then," he agreed, pulling a knife from his boot and heading toward the open window to observe the night sky. He heard the small noise she made as the dagger flashed in the moonlight, the clouds and rain apparently having cleared while they'd spoken.

"What?" He turned back to her with a grin as he shut the window. "You didn't think you'd completely disarmed me, did you?" She stared at him with those weary blue-gray eyes, then curled up on her side on the bed.

But he saw her hand was still tightly curled around her blade.

Elana

She couldn't sleep.

Flashes of what she'd seen in Cethin's eyes—through her *own* eyes—as she'd held his hand to complete the life oath haunted her.

Memories. Memories of someone's life.

Memories of *her* life.

She startled awake at the light touch to her hair.

The room was cast in soft shadows by the moonlight and starlight streaming through the open windows of her bedchamber.

"Father?"

The male smiled down at her. "Hello, love."

"It is late," she said with a yawn.

"It is," he agreed.

"You do not sleep?"

He sighed. "Sleep eludes me tonight, love. I thought I would come hear about your day, since mine have been so busy as of late."

She rolled onto her side to look at him. His hand never left her hair. "Well, today I had lessons with some of the lords' younglings. But they all seemed afraid of me."

"Afraid of you?"

"They would not talk to me or sit too close to me."

"Why do you think that is?"

She thought for a moment. "One of them called me princess. Are princesses scary?"

He let out a laugh. "I suppose they can be. Are you?"

"What? A princess?" She wrinkled her nose.

He chuckled. "Of course you are a princess, love. But are you a scary one?"

She giggled. "Of course I am not scary, Father. But what does it mean? To be a princess?"

"It means that you were born of a queen and a king. You understand that is who your mother and I are, yes?"

She nodded. "But it is just a title, right? It is not who I am?"

Something flickered across her father's face, but perhaps it was just a trick of the light. "It will mean whatever you decide it means." They lapsed into a peaceful silence. She reveled in the hand that stroked her hair. He was right, they hadn't spent much time together as of late.

"And what of your magic, love?"

"Magic?"

"Any hint of it? Moonlight? Starlight?" She shook her head. He sighed in what she was sure was disapproval, but she wasn't sure what he expected. She was still far too young to possess any magic of her own, princess or not.

"Will I see you tomorrow? Later in the week?" She missed him.

His hand paused, then continued its soft movement. "Of course, love. Who am I to deny the princess of Aviva?" She giggled as he stood and pretended to curtsy.

He pulled the blankets snugly around her. "Sleep well, love."

She was the one people whispered about.

The lost princess of Aviva, Queen Serenity's heir, the one who would wipe away the Darkness from their world with...

Her hands trembled as she recalled the burst of silvery light—*moonlight*—that had erupted from her and sent the winged creature flying away from her and Cethin in the alley.

The creature had been one of the Noir.

Elana—Gods, she couldn't bring herself to even *think* her real name—squeezed her eyes shut as the memories sped up in a blur of color and motion behind her eyelids, then slowed, replaying her parents handing her the locket she still wore; her mother's funeral; what should've been her coronation day; her escape from the palace; stepping into the arms of someone who'd seemed like Sonia, yet not; a male urging her onto a ship, a male—

A male with caramel-colored eyes and dark hair.

She opened her eyes and looked at the half-Elf partially illuminated by the candle he'd lit after she'd feigned falling asleep. He was studying the door, flipping a dagger over and over again in his hand.

As her life-sworn, he couldn't hurt her. It was his duty to protect her.

But that didn't mean she trusted him.

"El."

She started as rough hands shook her awake. Her body automatically coiled into a defensive position, dagger poised to strike. The male—Cethin, she repeated his name over and over in her mind like some sort of puzzle—stood there, hands and knife raised.

"Not a morning person, are we?" he said, amusement coating his rich voice. She let out a low, tired sound, and he chuckled.

He may have interrupted her plan to leave, but her decision remained the same: leave the town, make her way to the riverside city, and determine what to do and where to go from there. Now, with the caveat of having a trained killer—sworn to defend her life, whom she did not know or trust, despite what her senses told her—at her side.

And her, a princess, heir to the throne of Aviva, a female who supposedly possessed a moonlit magic that would bring the Darkness to its knees, thinking about returning to a kingdom she wasn't quite sure would receive her with open hearts because it'd been—dear Gods, it'd been almost fifty years since she left.

"Are you alright?" It was a softer and certainly unexpected question from the male who'd slammed her into the ground with the intent of abducting her. Elana touched the back of her head and glared at him.

"Just a bump," she said through her teeth. She pushed off the bed and made her way to the bag she'd left on the floor. He fixed her with those intense eyes, and she paused. "What?" Cethin shook his head, so she pulled the bag onto her back.

"You want to tell me where we're going?" he asked, running a hand through his now dry hair.

"There's a tavern two quarters south of here," she said, quickly unbraiding and rebraiding her hair. "We travel until we reach it."

"And learn from the townsfolk what they witnessed last night." She fought back a grimace. She knew what had happened. Cethin, of course, completely misread her.

"I have a plan," he announced.

Chapter 4

Elana

E lana hated his plan.

She'd assumed it would include posing as travelers passing through the area—which they technically would be. Whoever, or whatever, was looking for her—and now him, Cethin said, which gave her no amount of guilt—would be looking for a male and a woman traveling together. So they needed to pretend they didn't know each other. That's where her interest in his plan dissolved.

Cethin would enter the tavern first. The building included guest houses on the upper level—rented rooms used for more than just shelter and sleep. He'd secure a room for the week to give the impression he was in town on business. Elana would remain in the main barroom as a lady of the streets looking for *business*, as he'd called it. She'd known ladies like that at Tymer's: ones who escorted drunk men tossing coin at them off to dark alcoves and alleys to do what only the Gods would witness. She'd almost stabbed Cethin for the suggestion. But she'd given in to his master plan in the end. It was likely he had practice with such schemes—something she'd dryly observed, which made him smirk. She hated that smirk.

"What else?" He was staring at her.

"Ladies like that aren't usually dressed so..." He waved a hand toward her.

"So what?"

"So modestly," he said, his amber eyes lingering a bit longer than she would've liked on her high neckline, before meeting hers.

"This is the only dress I own." His brows rose. It was true, though: the rest of her pack was all tunics and leggings.

"I could...*modify* it." Her attention snapped back to Cethin. He'd come to a stop directly in front of her, and his knife—which he must've stolen back from her bag—was in his hand. He smirked again. She glared at him as he angled the blade between them. "I can either do it while you're wearing it, or..." His smirk turned into a full grin.

Like Hell *would that ever happen.* Besides, as her life-sworn, it wasn't like he could stab her.

Elana stood perfectly still, every muscle tensed, barely breathing as Cethin made his alterations to the neckline of her dress. His knife and hands were a startling contrast of cool and warm, and she felt his breath against her neck as he worked, raising goose bumps on her skin. She could almost scent him—even in her human form—that half-Elvish essence in him, and something else, something that reminded her of her time in the Southern City, by the sea.

"There we are," he murmured a few minutes later as he pulled away.

The sudden absence of his warmth hit her like freezing rain. Elana looked down, slightly self-conscious, though not embarrassed by the curve of the material over the swell of her breasts. He'd cut the V lower than she usually wore, exposing her skin and necklace. Cethin flipped the blade one more time, then sheathed it at his side. *How many other weapons did he have on him?* she wondered.

"You're rather talented at this," she said instead.

"At what?" He tilted his head to one side. The movement sent a curl of dark hair over his brow. Her hand itched to brush it away. She tightened her fist.

"Ruining a woman's clothing."

Cethin laughed. It was the same laugh he'd given her bar tab comment—not the dark one he'd growled when she'd had him contained with her dagger at his throat; no, this one felt wild and *real*, like the wind on the sea.

"You should see what I can do with some ribbon and a few buttons." He winked.

Gods help her. Elana rolled her eyes in exasperation, wondering if, at some point while traveling with the insufferable male, they would become permanently lodged in her forehead.

"Truth?" It was more of a statement than a question, but she looked back at him. His expression showed an openness she hadn't seen from him before. She nodded.

"I've had to cut all manner of clothing apart—usually my own," he added when she narrowed her eyes. "To wrap wounds, strained muscles, cuts..."

"Your own self-inflicted injuries?" she asked, smiling sweetly.

"If I weren't skilled with my own blade, El, I wouldn't be a very good mercenary, now would I?" was his equally cheeky reply as he smirked again.

She'd watched Cethin's eyes track every person as they traveled; his half-Elf ears probably noted every word or sound he heard over the sloshing of their feet in the slushy, ice cold muck the freezing rain had left on the streets. She wondered what would've happened to her—what he would've done—if the Noir hadn't made its entrance. What would've happened if they hadn't made the life oath. If she'd never remembered...

Elana shuddered and tried to keep from wrapping her arms around herself, chillier than usual with the *modified* neckline of her dress. She pulled the black cloak she now wore—one of Cethin's—around her. He'd taken her blue one, along with her bag, into the establishment—a place called The Rusty Rose—ten minutes ago. She lingered in a nearby alley, counting the seconds until her entrance. She would float through the bar, sit with the local men, listen to their chatter, and attempt to pick up on anything they'd seen or heard the night before.

A shiver skittered down her spine as a new thought blossomed: what if someone *had* seen her? Cethin hadn't said a word about her shifting or her magic. She was certain that if he'd been stable enough to see or comprehend any of it, he would've known exactly what—who—she was. A small blessing his wound had ended up poisoned. He likely either didn't remember, or, if he did, brushed it off as some venom-soaked dream. *Good.*

Finished with her countdown, Elana took a steadying breath and pressed into the warmth of the tavern. She scanned the tables, chairs, and stools, took in the smell of the space—it reeked of booze, smoke, and greasy food. *Not much different from Tymer's.* It was just past dinnertime, so it was likely the tavern's more *questionable* clientele hadn't arrived yet. She pulled off Cethin's cloak and hung it on a nearby peg in the wall. Her eyes immediately found the male.

Cethin was lounging on a barstool near the main counter. A red-haired, freckled, young barmaid was filling up a cup in front of him. He gave the girl a lazy smile. She blushed and retreated to the bar. Elana sighed in irritation. But he was scanning the room as well, she noticed. At least he hadn't lost sight of the reason they were there: his own Godsdamned plan.

As if he sensed her presence, those caramel-colored eyes narrowed on her and scanned her from head to toe. Elana forced herself to hold her chin high under that assessing gaze. When Cethin's eyes connected with hers, they no longer held any sign of teasing amusement. No, those golden eyes were blazing, but with...

Her stomach flipped as he lifted his cup and raised it to her, then drained its contents. She gave him a small nod. He twisted back to the counter and waved his hand to a man also working behind the high top.

But Elana was frozen in place.

"Have you ever been in love?"

"That is not a ladylike question," her lady's maid chided.

"It is a good thing I am not a lady then—ouch!" the young princess exclaimed as the woman brushed a knotted mass in her hair.

"Oh hush, we both know it would not be this messy if you were not always running about."

"I am not always running about," she gritted out.

"And you are right, child—you are not a lady. You are a princess. It is about time you started acting like one." The woman set the brush on the vanity.

"I do everything you and Mother tell me to do," the young princess said.

"Being a princess is not about acting a certain way, and definitely *not about listening to what others tell you to do, or who you should be."*

The young princess opened her mouth to argue. *Hadn't she just said she shouldn't ask—*

"But I have been in love before." The lady's maid's blue eyes winked with mischief as they met hers in the mirror. *"Many times, in fact."*

"Ew, Sonia, gross!" The young princess sank back into her chair and ran her hands over her face. This *was unladylike conversation.*

The woman laughed, but the young princess thought she heard a note of sadness in it.

"You will learn, child, that there are different ways to love, and to be loved. Different types of love to experience."

"It was a dragon!"

The sudden noise of patrons snapped Elana out of whatever trance she'd fallen into. She peered at a young man to her right who sat with a group wearing town guard uniforms. "I swear it to the Gods!" A few men at the table sniggered.

"Dragons are a myth," snorted an older man seated toward the end of the table. He looked down at what Elana recognized as playing cards. *Gamblers.* Men who might be interested in the company of a woman for luck. She made her way through what was quickly becoming a crowded bar area, heading toward their table.

"They might be legends now, old man," the younger one countered as his arrogant face flashed with anger, "but they were once as real as the *syrena*." He also wore a guard's uniform—not that she believed that made any of them noble or brave. She'd learned that most guards had no sense of propriety the first time she'd reported being injured by one of her bar's *livelier* patrons. Shaking her head clear of the past, Elana sauntered up to the table.

"Do you also believe in luck, soldier?" she asked with a smile, trying to emanate some of the insufferable flirtation that came oh so naturally to Cethin. She placed her hands on the table and leaned forward to meet the man's eyes, feeling utterly exposed in the neckline Cethin had cut in her dress. The young man dragged his attention from the older guard sitting on their far left—his eyes not meeting hers, instead roving over her exposed chest. He licked his lips, and Elana tried not to shake her head in disgust.

"That I do," he replied, patting his lap. "Why don't you come over here and be my good luck charm for the evening? Though," he went on, finally tearing his gaze from the tops of her breasts to look at the older guard again, "he likely needs luck more than I do."

"I doubt you could afford her, anyway," the older man retorted, his gaze, too, now firmly on her chest.

"I accept forms of payment besides coin," Elana said, willing a lightness to her eyes. Her eyes always gave her away. She remembered someone—a lady's maid—had told her that once when she'd given what she'd thought was a brilliant lie for sneaking into a palace event unattended.

A low rumble of desire dragged her back to the present. She hadn't been paying enough attention. The older man had kicked the younger one out of his seat—and his hand now palmed her backside. "Oh?" The older man raised a gray brow, his mouth twisting to one side. "And what might that be?"

She wanted to punch his bearded face for the entitlement written all over it, but willed hers into neutrality as she said, "I've always loved stories, sir, and his"—she looked back to the younger guard, who scowled from where he'd been moved to—"I find his intriguing. Those kinds of stories deserve more attention." The older man tugged at her—

She was sitting in his lap. His voice was greasy, and alcohol and smoke coated every inch of his breath as he said into her ear, "I could offer you more attention than that knave." Elana reined in her shudder as he leaned into the side of her neck, inhaling the scent of her hair. She resisted the urge to punch him as he licked up the column of her throat. His hardness poked into her thigh, and she'd just decided it might be worth punching him when—

"Please don't spoil her for me."

Elana had never been so grateful to hear Cethin's voice. She and the man both looked up in time to see him plunk a bag of what clinked like coin—*her* coin, the sum she'd saved and hidden away her travel bag, she noted with no small amount of irritation—onto the gambling table.

"Here to play for her?" the man remarked.

Cethin gave him a cold smile. "From what I overheard, she only offered to join your game for luck and stories. And anyways"—he waved a hand back to the man at the bar—"the owner of this establishment and I have come to an agreement regarding the *ladies* who work here." A pointed glance at Elana. "And I am willing to offer her additional payment for whatever she would've made from you." That lazy smile returned as he looked at her, and she offered him one in return. Cethin winked.

Then, without another word, he hauled her up out of the man's lap and over his own shoulder, walked them toward the steps behind the card table, and carried her to the second level. She barely had time to register her body's position over his shoulder as her skirts rose ever so slightly—though not so high that they revealed anything particularly salacious—or to stop her cry of surprise. Apparently no one heard or cared if they did.

Cethin didn't put her down until he'd unlocked and opened one of the doors in the hall. It led to a small, cramped room, barely big enough for the large, single bed it held. No fireplace. One window.

"Was that necessary?" she demanded, her body shaking with barely contained rage.

"Seemed like a good idea at the time," he said, sliding onto the bed. She traversed the room and looked out the window, crossing her arms. It was colder in the room than it'd been the tavern; though quieter, it didn't smell much better. "Learn anything interesting?"

"Besides that you are, and continue to be, insufferable?" she muttered, earning another one of his laughs.

"I'll take that as a no, so let me tell you what I overheard. I overheard that more and more people are leaving this town. Some headed south. Others, east."

Elana let his words sink in. Likely Elves or half-Elves making their way to the Southern Kingdom. And east...The Islands.

Elana didn't know much about the wild archipelago beyond the stories someone had told her about the Water Folk who'd made it their own home over the centuries. Maybe...maybe it'd been her lady's maid, the one named Sonia. She sighed, memories still not entirely clear.

"That means that the Darkness is spreading across the sea," she said. "And"—she caught herself from saying *my*—"the people are afraid."

"As they should be," Cethin noted, then said, somewhat more quietly, "though I also heard some are returning to Aviva." She remained silent. "I also heard someone mention something about a dragon," he added. She snorted. "I would assume they were talking about the creature who attacked us last night," he observed. Elana's mouth went dry. "A large, winged beast, and a bright light. Tell me something, El." She heard him rise from the bed, and then he was beside her. She kept her eyes fixed to the glass, though she felt his on her. "Why would a dragon—a creature that, as far as we know, is mere legend—attack a barmaid and a mercenary in the streets of Ozul, in the middle of the night, only to retreat before it did any real damage?"

Forcing a calm expression onto her face, Elana turned to him. She held his questioning gaze, lifted her hand, and poked his arm. "I wouldn't say it didn't do *any* damage," she remarked when he flinched at her touch.

He was quiet for a moment, then, "At some point, you will have to tell me *something* about yourself, you know."

She ignored him. How could she tell him something about herself when she was still processing what *she* knew about herself?

"Does it still hurt?" she asked.

That amused spark returned to his eyes, though his expression remained appraising. "So concerned about my well-being," he said, voice teasing, but containing a darker undercurrent that rolled over her like a wave. She swallowed, then, irritated with both him and herself, rolled her eyes. He laughed again, and she watched him retreat to the bed.

One bed—not two.

She narrowed her eyes. He lifted his brows in an innocent expression. "A single male—a traveling investor—here for the week couldn't be expected to request a room with two beds, now could he?" She glared at him. "And, as the injured party," he continued, at which she snorted, "I will be sleeping on the bed. Besides," he added, laying back and gazing up at the ceiling, "I have an old back injury that bothers me whenever I sleep on the ground." His eyes flicked back to hers and he shrugged. "You're welcome to sleep wherever you wish, of course."

Elana gave him her coldest stare—the same one she used when the men at Tymer's got a little too close. He arched a brow. "What? Never been in bed with a male?" His tone was light but contained that darker undercurrent she felt in her bones.

"I—" she sputtered, then fell silent. She'd been with a *human* man. Had been with two different mortal men, actually. One, a woodworker in a small village settlement by the riverside. She'd been working in a neighboring village as what the mortals called a nurse. He'd cut his hand, she'd bandaged his wound, and there was just *something* between them. An ease and understanding she'd needed then. The other, a hot-tempered young man she'd met as a serving girl in one of the Southern Kingdom's more opulent establishments. Their fierce passion—often kindled more from hate than love—would've burned the whole city down had his father—a noble lord, she'd found out later—not caught them one night and promptly thrown her out on the street. A whore, he'd called her, and his son a fool for debasing himself with someone as lowly as she.

Elana banished the shame threatening to work its way to her face as the memory resurfaced. "I have been with a *man*."

An emotion she couldn't quite place flickered across Cethin's face.

"But not a male?" It was a technicality, she supposed, but as she sifted through memories that were far older, she confirmed—for herself—that she'd never been with an Elvish male. As Princess of Aviva, she hadn't been around many males; and she'd barely blossomed into an adult female before...

"Interesting," she heard Cethin say in a quiet voice.

Elana shook her head and looked at him again. He was picking at his fingernails with another knife. She let out a sigh she hoped sounded full of haughty disapproval as she curled up into a ball on the floor at the foot of the bed.

Chapter 5

Elana

The Darkness was everywhere.

Not the darkness of night on the human continent, but true, cruel, unyielding Darkness. The Darkness of the King and his bride of Night. The Darkness of those he'd turned to his cause. The Darkness of the Noir. The Darkness of him.

The hairs on her arms rose at the sounds of skittering and hissing noises pressing in, closer, and closer.

Then pain, pain she'd never felt before hit her chest.

She screamed.

Pale morning sunlight danced in front of Elana's eyes. She groaned and swiped a hand over her face, rolling onto her side on—

She wasn't on the floor anymore.

She was on the bed. Icy panic settled in her gut as she recalled the guard from the gambling table. Heat rose to her cheeks as she thought of her conversation with Cethin. She quickly inspected herself and the bed: clothes still on, and no sign of the guard—or her life-sworn.

She looked to the foot of the bed and found the half-Elf curled up exactly where she'd fallen into a restless sleep. Cautiously, she kicked back the sheets.

"Morning," the male drawled from his spot on the floor. *So he was awake.*

"Why am I in the bed?" she demanded.

Cethin pulled himself into a sitting position, groaning and rubbing at a spot on his lower back. Had he spent the whole night sleeping on the floor?

"You were screaming," he said. "And not the kind of screaming I'd like the owner and other patrons of this establishment to hear." He gave her a crooked grin that didn't quite meet his eyes.

Elana rose and went to the window. The sun was breaking over the horizon. Light, like her mother's—not Darkness. But if she'd been screaming, that meant old dreams—dreams that had left her awake, haunted, angry, and full of guilt—were back. The dreams that had made her seek out the merchant's son in the south in the first place; anything to pour all of that restless energy, those *feelings*, into.

"You want to talk about it?"

"No," she said, and meant it.

There were no seers amongst the Elves, hadn't been in a long time—just like there hadn't been dragons, *syrena*, or any of the original Folk besides the mer of the Water Folk. But some Elves still claimed they could sense things—*feel* things—before they happened. Elana had written it off as

Annor nonsense. Besides, they'd already seen the catalyst for this particular nightmare: the Noir. That's all this was.

She needed to get back to Aviva, but she wasn't ready to tell Cethin why.

And she certainly wasn't ready to tell him about the memories and dreams that haunted her.

Cethin

They continued southeast—per El's request, and for reasons she wouldn't give him—working their same routine to elicit information from townsfolk.

The answers were always the same: dragons. Darkness. The lost princess.

All of it utter nonsense, in Cethin's opinion.

But he continued to yield the bed, if there was only one, to El every night—because he didn't want her screams to wake the other customers, he told himself. Not because she appeared softer, more relaxed in a bed. Not because he was trying to be a gentleman—none of the women he'd ever bedded would call him that.

No, he told himself it was the life oath going beyond waking hours—not because, ever since those screams had hit her that first night, his emotions toward El had gone to a place he didn't want to acknowledge. Besides, sleeping on the floor also meant he had to deal with his Godsdamned back, which ached more every day.

They reached the outskirts of Ozul in a few days, then proceeded through open countryside on horses he noted El pointedly deigned not to ask how he'd procured, much to his amusement. Light blue flowers poked their heads up through the frost-covered ground one morning, which made her grin. He tried not to smile at her smile, the first positive spark of emotion he'd seen from her.

He'd studied her before as a target, a job. Now, he studied her as both a traveling companion and the person he'd sworn to protect with his life. From the information he'd gathered so far, he knew she was skilled with her fists and blades, had a knowledge of Healing plants, and was talented at serving drinks...and that she'd been with two men, a fact that made him burn with a dangerous emotion.

And blue flowers made her smile.

The weather had taken a turn for the warmer, so Cethin halted them under a great oak tree for the evening. They would save their coin—her coin, really—and spend the night camping under the shelter of its long, budding branches. They both needed the fresh night air—and to bathe and clean their clothing in the nearby stream before they entered the Riverlands.

The bathing part earned him a warning look, but then El sniffed and sweetly said, "You do smell." She ordered him off to find some random weed he guessed was meant for his back while she dipped in the stream, since he insisted she smelled worse and should go first. Her returning glare had him moving quickly toward a small grove.

Beyond directions, El had kept her mouth shut and her eyes on the road during their journey. She was someone used to keeping things to herself, he surmised, as he searched for the pale, leafy green plant she'd described. His mysterious employer hadn't given him any information about her, not even her age. She appeared in her twentieth or early in her thirtieth decade of life, but she *felt* older. Perhaps she was—there was no way to tell for sure when she obviously had Elvish heritage but hid in a mortal body.

Spotting the plant, Cethin knelt to cut the leaves and shove them into his pockets.

That's when he heard her scream.

He whipped around, heart pounding as that scream sounded again, sending waves of pain through his hand, up his arm, and along his spine.

This wasn't the same scream that accompanied her dreams.

He ran back, the life oath tugging at him to hurry, *hurry*. Each breath he took echoed in his ears—not just his breaths, but hers, too, the life oath stretching taut between them. He willed his legs to go faster, the very world around him seeming frozen in time as he left the entrance of the glade, and—

There were three of them—all men, he determined. Two of them held El—half dressed and with her back against the tree—while the third examined their horses, packs, and belongings. *Likely common thieves.* But he'd seen the hunger that lingered in the eyes of the men who pinned her to the tree before. A cool, killing calm settled in Cethin as he strode forward to greet their unwelcome guests.

"Evening, gentlemen," he drawled, casually walking toward the edge of their makeshift camp. Three heads whipped toward him, though it seemed an effort for one who'd been staring at El. Cethin cocked his head to one side. He'd take his time killing that one.

"Is there something my lady wife and I might assist you with?" He kept his voice even and controlled. He was the calm before the storm.

"She don't look like no lady to me," the hungry-looking one said. The man's eyes returned to El, drinking in every inch of exposed skin.

Cethin took a moment to scan El for any sign of injury: nothing obvious. And her breathing…he stilled, listening to the sounds around him. Her breathing was even. Steady.

But she'd screamed.

Stuffing his hands into his pockets, Cethin paced the outer edge of their campsite. "That's no way to speak about a man's wife."

The one ransacking their supplies stood and pointed a sword at him. "You are no man."

Cethin rolled his eyes. *So original.* As a half-Elf, he'd lost count of how many times people had hurled similar insults.

And they were the last words the man spoke.

Cethin drew his knife and threw it. The blade struck dead through the man's heart. Then, Cethin became the storm, a blur of motion and death as he moved forward and pulled the knife from the man's chest. He went to the tree where the two men held his life-sworn. But as he closed that small distance, a movement that only took seconds—

His half-Elvish senses barely registered the grunts of surprise from the men as El moved, fast as the wind. She kicked her foot out and stepped on the one of the man to her left. He dropped her arm. His friend let out a small noise of surprise as she drew one of her beautiful blades up from a place Cethin tried not to think about for too long, then sliced it across the disgusting man's throat. The light had scarcely left his eyes when the man she'd injured whirled back to her—

And ended up with her other blade in his gut. Blood splattered the grass in front of her, the tall tree behind her; the gray britches she wore; her face, hands, and exposed belly and shoulders; and the band of linen covering her breasts. She was breathing heavily, hands still clutching the now-bloody daggers that went *drip, drip, drip.* The only sound as the sun set.

"Took you long enough to get back," she said, and dammit if her voice didn't send goose bumps along his arms.

He closed the distance between them. "Are you alright?" He reached out a hand and cupped her cheek. She nodded, and though her eyes were wary, her lips formed a small smile. "What?"

"No quips about the long-suffering of the life-sworn?"

"None," he replied, a bit more gruffly than he'd intended, and withdrew his hand.

Because he was her life-sworn. And if that's all he was to her—not someone she trusted, just someone she shared an archaic bond with—that's all she was to him.

Elana

They packed the campsite quickly. Cethin washed the blood from their weapons while she scrubbed it from her face, hands, and body, and changed into another set of clothes. She didn't argue when Cethin led them to a town on the other side of the grove.

He paid the innkeeper handsomely with some of her coin for a room—a room with two beds and an adjoining bathing chamber—along with the man's discretion. Elana didn't object. They hadn't said a word to each other since the wood.

She took in the room, the beds, and immediately headed for the washing room. She vaguely heard Cethin mutter something about getting them some food.

Elana sank into the cold water of the tub, not caring that its temperature was just above freezing. She allowed it to numb her, to wash away the blood and dirt she hadn't been able to scrub clean in the stream.

She couldn't stop seeing the looks on the men's faces as they'd crept into the clearing, faster than she could've anticipated. As fast as Cethin had leapt on her that night in the alley. But there'd been something different about these men, something uglier about their intentions that had made her skin crawl.

She scrubbed with layers and layers of soap. They wouldn't have killed her—they would've just left her desiring death. And Cethin, who'd been sent to take her the Gods only knew where for the Gods only knew what purpose, had been there. Had helped her. Not saved her—a flicker of rebellious fire settled under her skin despite the chill of the water. It would've been challenging to escape three men on her own, but she could've done it—would've done it. She'd taken care of herself alone so far.

So why had she screamed for him?

Elana heard the door to their room unlock and click open, then shut, interrupting her thoughts. She stilled in the water, listening as Cethin knocked on the door to the washroom.

"Almost done in there?"

She rose from the tub, dried off with the holey towel that'd been tossed over a wicker chair, pulled on her spare leggings and tunic, and opened the door. Cethin's brows knitted as he took her in. She walked to one of the beds and laid down, not touching the bread he'd brought up.

"I could have handled it myself," she finally said. She heard him pause at the bathing chamber door.

"Then why did you scream?"

"I don't know." Silence fell between them again, like a blanket of fresh snow that quieted the sounds of even the busiest cities.

"How did you get that scar on your back?" he asked, breaking it.

"It happened when I came to the Riverlands." He must've seen it when she'd changed at the stream. A flash of guilt and pain squeezed in her gut. "I was working as a nurse, helping with daily tasks, running errands, delivering messages regarding medicines. One of the men—a butcher—didn't appreciate a particular message, the physician's feedback, really, on how much of a specific medicine he requested." The memory flashed in front of her eyes, as if she were living in both the past and present at once. "He did not take it well," she finished quietly. She watched Cethin's shoulders tense.

"What did he do to you."

"He told me that if the doctor didn't understand the level of pain he was in, he would give him an example." Cethin swore, but she continued, proud of the steadiness in her voice as she finished the story of her first experience with real pain. "He carved a single line down my back with one of his tools." Cethin swore again. "That's when I asked to learn more about medicine." The reason she'd known about the plant she'd used the night they'd met to save him. The reason their lives were now eternally entangled.

Elana lay awake quietly, listening to water rise, fall, and splash in the bathing chamber. A gnawing feeling had settled into her stomach, growing as she allowed herself to dwell on her past, her people, her kingdom.

She'd failed them all. She'd run off. But worst of all, she'd forgotten.

She didn't know how to lead armies to defend her people against the Dark King's forces or the Night Queen's unholy terrors. She could only protect herself—and barely, at that. Those men in the clearing...she'd wounded, bound, tied, and gagged bad men before, but she'd never killed anyone. Not until then. Elana had a feeling those kills wouldn't be her last, regardless of how the future played out. *Shouldn't it have been a world-altering experience?* She just felt empty. Disconnected. Unfeeling. She took a deep, shuddering breath and closed her eyes.

She didn't hear Cethin return from the washing room until she caught a masculine grunt. Her eyes flicked open to find the male sitting on the edge of the other bed, freshly washed and cleanly dressed in cream-colored pants. He was in the process of pulling on a brown tunic.

"Your back," she remembered, sitting up.

He twisted toward her, face distorted with pain. "I thought you were asleep."

"It seems wounded males will forever keep me from sleep," she said, earning an exasperated—if not tired—smile. "Did you find it, before—" Cethin reached into the pocket of his original pants and dug out some leaves of the small plant. He extended them to her, and she sat up, accepting them.

She bit a leaf and chewed on it until it turned into mush in her mouth. Then, she spat it out into her hand and patted the space in front of her. "Sit."

Cethin's eyes were wary, but he sat on the edge of her bed. His tanned back was a web of toned muscle, evidence of the strength and skill he'd built over the years. Elana ran her hand from the center of the golden skin down, gently poking and prodding until he flinched. *There.* She pressed the leafy mush into his warm skin and felt the balm send a cool tingle into the muscle beneath. The muscle relaxed, and he sighed.

"You're skilled with your blades," he said as she worked. "I could teach you more."

She paused, then, "Tomorrow," she said.

"Tomorrow." His voice was low now, rough with an emotion she didn't understand, though she attributed it to the life oath. He didn't actually care about her beyond that...did he? *Could* he?

And if he did, what did it mean?

Out of the healing paste, she chewed on another leaf, pressing it into another tender segment. "I suppose if I weren't half-man, half-Elf," he said softly, the muscle relaxing under her touch, "this wouldn't be an issue." She continued moving her hands, making small swirls along the planes of his lower back. "I'd either be dead or paralyzed—or fully Healed." She suspected he was right. He'd told her what had happened as they'd traveled: he'd briefly been a horse messenger in the Southern Kingdom. The job had ended with him flat on his back in the sands.

"Do you know anything? About your parents? Who they were?" He turned to her, muscles flexing but more relaxed than they'd been. She wasn't sure he'd say anything—not when she'd barely spoken a word about herself.

"I don't remember much about them," he finally said, voice soft. "I think my mother was human." Elana nodded. His eyes met hers, searching. "And you?" She broke his gaze, and Cethin let out a raspy laugh. "Still don't trust me?"

She met his eyes again. "Insofar as your oath goes."

He turned away, standing and grunting as he pulled his shirt back over his head. Like he couldn't bear to look at her.

"They were wealthy trading merchants," she blurted. It was the closest thing to the *not*-so-truth she was willing to give him, and she needed some excuse to return to Aviva and—and what? Exact vengeance? It sounded ridiculous, but she couldn't stop herself. "Between Aviva and here. They died in a border skirmish, so Jack took me in."

Cethin turned back to her. She held his assessing gaze, watched his mouth form a thin line. "I'm sorry for your loss," was all he said as he got up and returned to the other bed.

He didn't believe her, and she wasn't sure why she cared. He was a half-Elf. She would outlive him by decades, maybe more. And not only was he a half-Elf, he was a mercenary. A mercenary—even one who honored his oaths more than his coin—could never fall for a queen. Nor she for him.

Queens seldom made their own choices.

Regardless of whether he believed her, Cethin kept his promise. After a quick and silent breakfast of a rather disgusting but hot oatmeal, he brought her to another part of the woods that separated the oceanside and riverside towns. They spent the early part of the day sparring. He corrected her form, added new techniques she hadn't learned from Cerdwin, and offered praise when she followed through correctly. He was a decent teacher, much to her surprise. The male even went so far as to cut down branches for them to use as makeshift swords. It took Elana time to get used to their heavier weight—her speed of attack or defense was slower than it was with the light blades Cerdwin had crafted for her. Cethin also mentioned teaching her archery, though there was nothing around for them to use as a makeshift bow and arrow; he showed her the proper stance and how to aim by throwing rocks at larger rocks.

That was how they continued on for the next week, their afternoons spent traveling roads that weren't quite roads, as there were fewer towns between the cities now. But Cethin still found somewhere for them to sleep every night. Neither of them had suggested making camp since the attack. They also didn't try to pry information from the few people they came across. Elana was relieved that Cethin seemed resigned to the fact that he wouldn't find out what had happened the night they met.

But would that last?

Chapter 6

Each path brought them closer to the Riverlands—and every step brought Elana closer to needing to make a choice about where she would go and what she would do next.

It seemed to be on Cethin's mind, too, as they hunkered down in a small inn and restaurant. The male had become restless, his eyes scanning the space more often than usual while they ate their evening meal at a table in the seated area. The dining room wasn't overly crowded, and, at least to Elana, no one appeared to be a threat. She observed her traveling companion.

It almost looked like Cethin was...*waiting* for someone?

Even flames from a nearby fire couldn't keep away the cool tingling sensation that ran down her spine at the idea. He was her life-sworn, yes. He could do her no harm, was obligated to save her from any danger.

But did that mean he also couldn't abandon her to a later danger?

She was imagining things, Elana told herself. He wouldn't have come this far and taught her further skill with a blade only to break his oath—although she couldn't recall what happened to those who did.

She shook her head and took a deep drink of the golden ale the serving girl placed in front of her. It went well with their meal of river fish, the taste of the pesce richer and less salty than that caught in Ozul.

I honor my oaths. Even more than my coin. Cethin's words rolled over and over again in her mind as the pair made their way up to their room for the night. It was a small space with no bathing chamber and one bed, although there was a small couch. She immediately took up the space on the couch. Ever since she'd kneaded the herb into his back—ever since she'd lied about her parents—being in close proximity with Cethin made her nervous. The male sank into a seated position on the mattress, ran a hand through his dark hair, and let out a sharp breath through his nose.

"Was something wrong with your meal?" she asked, partly joking, partly bracing herself for the question she knew was coming. He turned his head, amber eyes as golden as the ale they'd had with their supper threatening to drown her as he fixed her with them.

"What's the plan from here, El?" He leaned forward and braced his elbows on his knees. "When we get to Brookland"—the name of the closest Riverside town she'd noted from a small map tucked in with their supplies—"what's the plan from there?"

She brushed a stray hair away from her face, hand shaking. She'd figured they'd reach this conversation, but she wasn't sure of her answer. While they'd heard nothing further about dragon sightings, or—to her immense relief—magical moonlight, there were other rumors: whispers of hidden Elves and half-Elves fleeing farther south, as if that would keep the Darkness from finding them. Even more alarming were the softer whispers about random disappearances from larger and smaller towns alike of those who hadn't been suspected as fully-blooded Elves.

Those were the hardest accounts for Elana to digest: that people had been taken and were being turned into minions of the Dark King and Night Queen.

Before, those rumors had been contained to Aviva. Now, they'd spread to the mortal continent—to the humans.

She was running out of time—her people were running out of time—and she needed to get back to them before things got worse for everyone. No matter how long it'd been; no matter the shame and grief she harbored over fleeing in the first place, and those years of hiding; no matter how untrained she was in the art of war and with her magic. She had to go back and aid them.

She had to re-Bind the Balance, even if she couldn't begin to fathom how.

She would go back. She would help. And she would earn her people's trust and respect without her crown, her title, or her throne.

Not until she deserved it.

She swallowed. "We need to find passage to Aviva."

Cethin was quiet for a moment, eyes boring into her.

"Shit, El," he said, standing up, hands flexing as he ran one through his hair. "Was this your plan from the start? To go back—and what? Avenge your parents against the Darkness that took them from you?" He let out a harsh laugh that stung as she thought of her lie. "You should know that's impossible."

It still didn't feel like the right time to tell him the truth. She stared back at him, held her chin high, and said, "Yes."

Cethin let out an exasperated sound—one she was becoming all too familiar with—and sat back down on the bed, facing away from her.

"I know you don't trust me," he said. "I can even respect your decision to not tell me anything until absolutely necessary. But if I'm going to protect you—"

"I don't need you to protect—"

"Damnit, El!" he growled, twisting toward her as he stood and closed the distance between them. He lifted his hand. "Don't you understand what this is, what this means?" He pointed to the scar there, then grabbed her hand.

"I am bound to you—*for the rest of my Godsdamned life*—to defend yours with my own. So, whether you like it or not, you're not alone in whatever this is." Cethin dropped her hand and Elana let it fall limply to her side.

"I'm going for a walk," he announced and headed for the door.

She didn't try to stop him.

Cethin

He opened the tavern door and immediately gave up on the idea of a walk: it was pouring down rain. Not that weather usually stopped him—but tonight it did. He opted for a drink instead.

Cethin sat at the bar counter, half-Elf ears taking in the chatter flitting throughout the dining area. Rumors dotted the louder conversations of weather, spring crops, trade, and the upcoming wedding of the Southern King to a young woman from the Riverlands—*Imagine! What a fairytale!*

they said in a way that made Cethin want to choke on his drink. Rumors of a shadow creeping closer to Ozul from across the strait, of Elves in human forms, of half-Elves scattering in all directions—or being taken. Of humans being taken.

"I hear she's rallying her armies," came a woman's voice, followed by the laughter of her companions. Cethin looked in that direction.

"Of course she is, beautiful," said the man whose lap the woman occupied. "The Night Queen has been creating soldiers for years."

"Not the Night Queen," the woman said, lowering her voice. "The lost princess."

Cethin twisted in his seat, not failing to notice it pained him less to do so. It'd been a long time since he'd heard *that* particular gossip: that Queen Serenity's daughter had escaped the attack on her coronation day, remained hidden, silently built her strength over the years, and would bring an end to the Darkness.

Horseshit. While it was true the princess's body had never been discovered, the Night Queen's attacks typically didn't leave a trail of bodies behind. No, if rumor were true, the Night Queen delighted in breaking those she abducted, in bending them to the will of her Dark King, in turning them against friends and family.

It'd been chaos during the Battle of the Breaking: Avivan soldiers had turned on one another in seconds; friends and comrades hadn't registered what had happened—until they were being cut down by someone they knew and had fought beside moments earlier. That's what was whispered about the queen's husband, though gossip couldn't decide if King Ewan had been turned or killed by a trusted friend who had been. And *that* was something Queen Serenity had worked hard to keep out of the History books he'd learned from the master mercenaries who'd traveled the entirety of their world. Aviva's Archives were amiss with distorted History.

"It's true!" the woman exclaimed as her companions roared with laughter again, drawing Cethin back to their conversation. "I have a friend in the Elvish city who swears Princess Eleonora has been secretly raising an army from across the world this whole time!"

Her partner gave her a consoling pat on the shoulder. "Who knows, she may even be among us now!" he said, and they all laughed again as the woman blushed. But the hairs on Cethin's arms rose at the man's words, despite the heat of the crowded room. A sign he typically didn't ignore but chose to for the moment. He had enough on his mind.

And when the pretty barmaid brought him another mug of ale, her pale-blue eyes looking him up and down, Cethin smiled.

He'd found a different distraction for his frustrations.

Elana

She didn't hear Cethin return from his walk, but she decided he'd returned to the room at some point while she'd slept. That he hadn't stayed out all night. A ball of jealousy formed in her chest as her mind combed over memories of the women in the bar. Jealousy she had no right to claim.

"Where are we going?" she asked the next morning while Cethin saddled their horses to lead them away from the town—and not in the direction she'd indicated on the map over breakfast.

"To get supplies," he answered gruffly, mounting his horse and urging it forward.

"In another town?" Elana hauled herself up on her horse and brought it to a trot beside him. "Besides this one?" She pulled on the reins to sidestep a particularly large puddle, squinting into the heavy mist that accompanied the now partially risen sun. There must've been a heavy rain during the night.

"In a manner of speaking," was all the male said. Elana opened her mouth, closed it, opened it again, then decided *this* particular mood was one she didn't want to push; she fell into line behind the male as they followed a path only he seemed able to see, through brush and under trees dripping with excess rain. It was a wonder their horses didn't sink into the mud.

The sun had reached its midday peak when Cethin stopped them for a light lunch of fruit and fish outside a wooded area. The male had become more alert the farther they'd traveled, she'd noticed. But the shade beneath the trees was peaceful—

Not for long. The sound of a bowstring being drawn was the only warning before a lilting feminine voice spoke.

"Better watch next time, traveler."

Elana sat perfectly still and stared at the green-cloaked figure with a hood over their head. They were aiming an arrow directly at Cethin, not two feet from the male.

"Who said I wasn't watching, Apolina?"

Elana's mouth popped open as the archer threw back her hood. Dark brown curls went flying. Green eyes that matched the forest coloring of her cloak scanned Cethin's face. Dark, freckled skin glowed in the sunlight. She was beautiful. Cethin knew her—and she knew him.

That ball of jealousy expanded.

The female—a half-Elf like Cethin, Elana noted—reached out a hand, drawing the male to his feet with a broad grin that only widened as she hugged him tightly.

"What in the name of the Gods are you doing here?" Apolina demanded as she stepped out of their embrace. "I thought you were on a job."

Elana flinched. The female's eyes flicked to her, then back to Cethin. "Decide to become an honest male since last I saw you?" Apolina asked, dark brows lifting. Elana and Cethin snorted simultaneously. Apolina's face turned wary.

"Don't tell me..." The female's eyes went back to Elana. Elana tried not to balk under their piercing gaze as Apolina pointed the tip of the bow at her. "*She* was the job, wasn't she?"

"Yes," Cethin replied, voice low with warning.

Apolina's attention snapped back to him. "Cethin," she hissed, "you should know better. Hell, I *know* you know better. What were you thinking?"

To Elana's surprise, Cethin didn't offer his left hand to the pretty female, nor did he speak a word about their life oath. He simply smirked at his...*colleague*? Elana guessed, noting the various weapons the female had on her person.

He shrugged. "You know what a pretty face does to my senses."

Apolina sniggered, then turned back to her. "Meaning no offense, of course," she said in a way that told Elana she definitely did. For a moment, Elana wondered what she'd looked like the night she'd shifted and pushed the Noir back. She hadn't seen herself in her Elvish form since childhood, and now, as an adult...would she at least be as pretty as the half-Elvish female? Cethin's...*friend*?

"I'm assuming you're here because you need something from me, then?" Apolina directed at Cethin, a hint of frost flickering in her pine-green eyes. His amber ones were wary as he looked right back at her and said, "Yes." The two half-Elves stood there, staring each other down. Finally, Apolina's shoulder twitched.

"And what, exactly, might that be?" Her voice, though sweet, had taken on a crisp edge.

"Weapons and supplies," Cethin said, rolling his neck from shoulder to shoulder. "And passage to Aviva."

The female paled at his last request. "Shit, shit, *shit!*" she exclaimed, pacing the clearing. "Why?" Those eyes threatened to cut through Elana like emeralds.

"I have my reasons," Cethin replied, seeming more interested in picking a stray piece of grass from his pants.

"Always the same with you. Come on," Apolina huffed, motioning for Cethin and Elana to follow her into the woods.

The outside of the large maple tree appeared normal enough. It was likely due to her keener half-Elvish eyes that Apolina was able to see the door that led to a hollowed-out space where swords, bows, arrows, knives, and other assorted weapons Elana couldn't begin to name—but the female and Cethin likely could—were laid out, along with coins of all known kinds, food, and clothing.

"Take what you need," was all the female said before she disappeared back outside, the entrance to the tree swinging shut behind her.

"What is this place?" Elana asked Cethin as he inspected a particularly nasty looking blade, ribbed to the point—a brother to the one he favored.

"A sanctuary, of sorts," was his short answer. Elana found herself drawn to a longsword hanging on the far wall. The handle was polished silver inlaid with all manner of sea creature. Something about it felt familiar. She reached out a hand—

"Don't. Touch. Anything." Cethin came to a halt in front of her, dissuading her reach.

"Aren't we supposed to take what we need?" she said, crossing her arms defiantly.

"Not *we*. *Me*." She watched Cethin add a few extra daggers—along with the sword she'd been staring at—some extra cloaks, and what looked to be additional loaves of bread to a new bag, tossing their original belongings in as he went—minus her daggers, which remained strapped to her thighs under the light brown cloak she wore.

"My contact needs more time to arrange travel," Apolina said as she rejoined them, focusing on Cethin and wholly ignoring her, which Elana didn't fail to observe.

Cethin sat on the moss-covered ground. "Then we'll rest here." Elana sank down next to him. The male rested his head against the tree-bark wall and closed his eyes.

She didn't trust their safety *that* much, but what else could she do?

With a final suspicious glance to where Apolina settled on his other side, Elana closed her eyes.

Cethin

"What in the Otherworld, Ceth?"

Cethin sighed. He knew Apolina had been waiting for El's breathing to even out—proof that she'd fallen asleep—to prod him. His mind raced, because the truth was, he still had no explanation for why he'd done what he had. It went against everything he—everything they—was trained to do.

"Is that the phrase people are using these days, instead of 'what the Hell'?" he asked with a smirk. After the Breaking, after the Balance of Light and Dark had been broken, the Realm of Blessings had been obstructed by the Otherworld. Now, Elves, half-Elves, and mortals alike entered the Otherworld upon their deaths—or Hell. No one was sure which was worse.

Apolina's eyes narrowed on him. "You might use that charm to avoid speaking with most people, but I am not most people."

Cethin sighed and rubbed at his lower back. She wasn't wrong. In all the years he'd been working for the mercenary masters, Apolina was the closest thing he had to a friend. Not that they could ever *really* be friends. They weren't meant to—their masters had seen to that—even though sometimes it seemed like that wasn't what Apolina wanted. She knew the effect she had on men and males, which was partly what made her so effective. Cethin recognized that she was attractive, but he'd never seen her that way. Plus, mixing business with pleasure was never a good idea.

Something he'd well and gone fucked up now. He sighed again and rubbed his temples. "I can't explain it, Poly. It's just a feeling."

Her eyes turned incredulous. "You blew a job based on a *fucking feeling*? And what happens when the employer finds out? You know just as well as I do that when people want someone gone, they'll go to great lengths to make it happen. And when they find out that you got her away—"

"They didn't want her gone," Cethin interrupted. "They wanted her found and brought to them."

Apolina scowled. "That's not any better. And when word gets out you screwed this up—Gods, you'll lose your other contracts, Ceth."

"I know," he gritted out between his teeth—but Apolina wasn't done.

"Not to mention lose payment for this one." Cethin looked her directly in the eye. It'd been months since they'd last run into each other. In that time, Apolina had become colder, even more desensitized to the nature of their work. Not that he didn't understand exactly what the nature of their work was. But Cethin had always thought he felt differently about it than she did. He hadn't asked for this life—he'd been tossed into it by parents he barely remembered. He did what he needed to do to survive in their world as a half-Elf.

Apolina had chosen it on purpose. It wasn't something they'd discussed more than once—but Cethin had been there the night she'd killed the men who'd raped her. He'd hoped that, afterward, she would be able to move on. But their deaths hadn't satisfied her.

He wondered if any death ever would.

"Some things are more important than money," he said—a bit more sharply than he'd intended.

Apolina sighed. "I know, I just..."

"You're worried about me?" he said, casually bumping her shoulder in an attempt to course-correct the conversation and the mood.

She laughed, a sound he rarely heard. "I don't think anyone ever needs to worry about you. You've always been a survivor." Her brows bunched. "Is that why…?" He heard her unspoken question; knew that—even though he'd tried to hide it—she'd seen the life-oath scar on his palm.

"Yes."

"You know I'm also someone you can't lie to."

"What do you want me to say, Poly?" he snapped, struggling to keep his voice low. "That the night she saved my life I had some sort of eye-opening revelation? That I know exactly what sounds she makes when she's in danger? That I've memorized every detail I can about her, beyond what protocol deems necessary? That I find her attractive?" He snapped his mouth shut. He hadn't meant to say that last bit.

Apolina's mouth formed a small O shape.

"What?" he demanded, training the only thing keeping him from throwing his hands in the air.

"You care for her."

"I'm a mercenary. I care for no one and nothing but myself. You should understand that."

It was quiet for a few moments, then:

"I was wrong," Apolina said.

"About what?"

"I am worried about you."

Elana

"El."

Elana pretended his voice had roused her from sleep, but she hadn't slept at all—hadn't been able to, not with the conversation between the mercenary and his friend, who'd left minutes ago. Elana wasn't sure what to make of his words, but they left her feeling warm and tingly—something she *shouldn't* be feeling about someone who'd tried to kidnap her. But she couldn't help it. Things between her and Cethin had changed—slowly and then quickly all at once—in a way she'd never known with anyone else.

"Come on," Cethin said over his shoulder as he made his way out of the tree.

"Now what?" she asked, following him to where he sank into a low squat on the ground outside.

"Now, we wait."

Cethin

Two whistles rang through the twilight—his and Apolina's signal. Cethin rose and motioned for El to do the same. She'd looked lost in her own mind while they'd waited for Apolina to return, and he hadn't wanted to break that silence, not when he was still pissed off about what was to come—the voyage to Aviva, and whatever mess awaited them there. Half-Elves were second-class citizens in the city—even more so in the years since the Darkness had spread. Some fully-blooded Elves actually blamed the half-Elves for it—*more horseshit.*

They quietly followed Apolina to the edge of a small river—a brook Cethin knew connected to the Eridanos, the large river that cut through the Riverlands and eventually spilled into the strait that divided the human and Elvish continents. A small riverboat waited at the water's edge, its lights dim. Apolina motioned for them to board as two men—the captain and first mate, Cethin guessed—walked up to the railing, hands raised to Apolina in greeting.

Behind him, Cethin heard El pause and inhale sharply.

They weren't waving.

Two arrows came at them from above, a third from their left. Cethin tossed El to the ground, cursing as he landed on top of her. He shot back to his feet, daggers in hand. Even in the dark, his vision was still better than a mortal man's, and the first two daggers he threw found their marks on the false captain and first mate. Both men fell into the water with soft splashes.

He heard El's warning shout as the third man moved in closer on their left. The man didn't have the chance to loose his arrow—Cethin's third dagger landed in the center of his forehead. Cethin heard another arrow nock, and—finally out of daggers—drew the ribbed blade from his side.

Apolina's eyes were an eerie shade of green in the dark as he watched her train her arrow on El.

"What is this," he growled, trying to buy time—for who, he didn't know. He had to make a choice: his life-sworn or his oldest friend.

Apolina's gaze never left his as she spoke. "I'm finishing the job you didn't. And earning far more for it."

Red exploded in Cethin's vision as he watched her draw the arrow back. Time slowed as he ran forward—

—and plunged his blade into Apolina's chest.

Blood, warm and red, flowed onto his hand, the blade only stopping when it struck bone.

Something like shock and relief flashed in Apolina's eyes as they both looked down at the wound. Her arrow slackened in her grip as she looked back up at him. Cethin withdrew the blade, and she slumped to the ground.

He could've sworn her mouth formed the words *thank you*, though there was no sound. There was a soft buzzing in his ears, ringing, ringing, *ringing*. Somewhere, far off in the distance, he heard El's voice.

"We need to go," she was saying, shaking his shoulders as he knelt over the female bleeding out before him.

"Cethin." Something was different in her tone this time. "We need to go."

Cethin let her pull him away.

Chapter 7

Apolina had betrayed them. It had happened so fast, and Elana thanked whatever Gods still watched over her for the brief opening in the clouds that had allowed the moon to peek through and show her what the men on the boat had held in their hands.

Cethin was in shock—possibly for only the second time in the male's entire life—as she half tugged, half dragged him east. *East.* Elana saw the lake through the reeds as they approached. She knew that lake well—knew who lived at its edge.

For all of Bron's passion for woodworking, that excitement was unmatched by his complete lack of enthusiasm for tending the plants that occupied his dozen or so acres of land—which meant the small structure that had served as the previous owner's potting shed was always empty. Following the thread of a more recent memory, Elana brought Cethin to the dilapidated shack.

"Halt." The familiar voice cut through the chilly night air, warming Elana's bones. Cethin had the opposite reaction—the male snapped out of his shock enough to shove her behind him, bloodied knife raised. Elana peered out from around him to take in the owner of the voice: the dark hair that had always had a mind of its own; the lightly tanned skin covered in bumps, bruises, scrapes, and calluses from his work; and the kind sapphire-blue eyes that hadn't aged like the rest of him had. Bron held a scythe in one hand, and Elana cursed herself for forgetting that, while the shed was far enough from the main house, it wasn't far from the barn. The man's eyes widened as he took her in.

"Elana?" Bron lowered the scythe, and Elana stepped out from behind Cethin, placing a hand on his shoulder as she did so.

"It's okay," she whispered to the male. "He won't hurt me." The look in Cethin's eyes told her was ready to attack Bron for so much as breathing in her direction.

"What are you doing here?" Bron's eyes tracked from her—her travel-worn clothes, their satchel of supplies—to Cethin and the blood coating the male's tunic and hands and the blade he still held between them. Something flickered in the man's eyes.

"I'm sorry," she said, motioning again for Cethin to drop his weapon and showing Bron her own weaponless hands. "We mean no trouble." That blue gaze went from her to Cethin and back again, as though he were trying to put a puzzle together. "And I vouch for my companion," she added, willing confidence into her voice. She wasn't sure what had been racing through Cethin's mind since they'd left those bodies—including Apolina's—bleeding and cold in the river. Part of her wasn't sure she wanted to know, but she now recognized the look of a male willing to kill.

Bron paused for a moment, then apparently made his mind up about something—her or Cethin, she wasn't quite sure. It'd been years since the woodworker had seen her.

"This way," he said, jerking his chin toward the barn. "You can wash up and rest in there." Elana moved to pull Cethin forward, but he brushed her off. His eyes were clear of rage, now assessing Bron as the man led them to the barn. "Water barrels here," Bron said as he lit a small torch and pointed to the looming shadows against one wall, "and you can spend the remaining hours of tonight in the loft." He pointed to the ladder Elana knew ran to the barn's second level.

"You can wash up first," Bron said pointedly to Cethin. The man tugged gently on Elana's arm. "We need to talk."

She turned to Cethin, who'd opened his mouth, probably to disagree. "It's fine," she promised. "I'll be right back." The dark shadows swirling in Cethin's amber eyes said he *definitely* disagreed, but the male turned away and began cleaning his hands and arms in the nearest water barrel.

Elana let Bron pull her outside. He'd left the torch with Cethin and was now barely more than a shadow in the moonlight, the stars hidden behind clouds and fog once more.

"Are you okay?" It was likely only his first question, Elana presumed. She nodded. "And that...male?"

"I'm fine. He's fine."

Bron was shaking his head. "No, Elana, he's not. Are you in trouble?" Concern overtook his beautiful eyes, and Elana's chest tightened at the gentle warmth that'd drawn her to Bron so many years ago. He looked older, of course, but still handsome; that understanding hadn't dulled either, even with the time that had passed. She felt that understanding from Cethin sometimes, under all of his layers of sarcasm and dry humor. *Gods.* She was in trouble if that's what she was thinking about.

"I'm fine," she said softly, but firmly. "It's a long story, but it's okay. I'm okay. It was just a misunderstanding."

Doubt flickered in Bron's eyes. "Will that misunderstanding follow you here?"

Elana stared at the ground. "I'm not sure," she answered honestly, letting out a long breath before she met his eyes again. "I'm sorry, I didn't mean to bring trouble to you." She watched his jaw tense. "We can go if—"

"No," Bron interjected. "You're already here. That part is done. But I need you gone come morning." She nodded and made to walk past him, back to the barn, exhaustion weighing on her mind and heart. "I have a family now." She halted and turned back to the man she'd once cared for so deeply but couldn't fall in love with. "A wife." She watched his cheeks pinken, even in the dim light. "And we expect to be with child soon." Elana closed her eyes and let his words sink in.

There'd never been a real future—not with him. She'd known that, even before she'd remembered who she was, when she'd left him all those years ago. Bron had let her go. And now...now Elana wasn't sure how she felt. Not jealousy over whomever his wife was—the woman who would one day carry his child—but a deeper twinge of sadness, mourning the loss of something she wasn't sure she would—or could—have: love, happiness, companionship, family, a life.

For she was a queen, and a queen's life was never her own.

She forced a smile. "Congratulations," she offered. "I'm happy for you."

Bron inclined his head toward her. "And are you...?" His gaze lifted to the barn as his question lingered between them.

Her smile faltered. "I'm not sure things like happiness or love are written in the stars for me, Bron."

Cethin was in the loft when she returned. *How much had he heard of with those half-Elf ears?* She splashed cold water on her face, arms, and hands, then climbed up the ladder and hauled herself onto the floor. One half of the loft held miscellaneous tools, feed, and objects she couldn't identify. Of the many jobs she'd held over the past half century, farming hadn't been one of them. The other half had been cleared out save for a few hay bales, chairs, blankets, and a small table. It looked like Cethin had dragged some hay across the floor to create makeshift bedding for the night. Her pile had a blanket across it.

Though weariness crept over Elana's bones, her mind was racing—not because of the personal news that Bron had shared, or what their presence meant for him and his family, though she hoped they hadn't been followed and that Bron would be sharp enough to leave should any threat manifest.

It was because of Cethin.

He was lying on the other makeshift bed, arms stretched above his head, legs crossed, head facing the ceiling, eyes closed. She considered him—all of his words and actions since they'd met. He would never make her a comfortable home like Bron. He would also never push her emotions like the merchant's son had, though he'd figured out how to get under her skin. With Cethin, things were different. He wasn't at all the mercenary she'd thought she'd met. He'd sworn his life to defend hers, trained with her, talked to her. Flirted with her.

Killed someone he cared about for her.

"One of your human lovers?"

Elana started, but the male's eyes remained closed. Out of all of the conversations they could be having—that they *should* be having—this wasn't one of them. Temper flared under her fatigue.

"And did you find one at the inn? Or was your charming *friend* who betrayed us one of yours?" she challenged.

Cethin's eyes flicked open, an eyebrow rising. "Jealous?"

She snorted. "Of what? Your deadly passion for each other?"

That sent the half-Elf shooting to his feet. "For your information," he said, voice low and threatening, "Apolina"—she didn't miss his wince when he said her name—"was not my lover. Or my friend. She was my training partner and my oldest companion." Elana's anger dulled, turning into sorrow for the male. Apolina hadn't been his lover—not even his friend. Cethin let out that low, wicked laugh.

"I'm surprised you thought I had friends," he continued, stalking closer and closer. Elana rested her hand on the loft railing, steeling herself against the pillar behind her. "We're trained from the beginning in *our line of work* to know that there are no friends. No one we can trust. Even our lovers—numerous as they may be." Elana's jaw tightened at the emphasis he put on the second part of his sentence.

Cethin smirked, and her rage rallied again. "So while I may be fazed by what happened tonight," he went on, stopping two feet away from where she'd braced herself against the railing, "it was what we are trained to do. What *she* was trained to do." He crossed his arms.

Elana swallowed. "And you?"

Cethin looked her up and down, his gaze sending a chilling and simultaneously thrilling sensation straight through her body. "I broke protocol that night, when I swore the life oath to you—even if it was in my best interests." He took one step forward, then another. "But some things run deeper than protocol, El."

She wondered if he'd admit what he'd said to Apolina under the tree—wasn't sure she was breathing as he halted right in front of her and braced his hands on the railing behind her. He leaned in close enough that she smelled the river water he'd washed up with.

"Now that we've established how *I* am handling the events of this fine evening," Cethin said, "why don't you tell me what we can expect from your gentleman friend." His last words dripped with distaste.

"Bron is a good man," she snapped. "You will leave him, his family, and his home untouched."

Those caramel eyes narrowed on her. "A wife—and a child someday," Cethin purred. "But not you. Not *with* you." He tilted his head to one side, his relentless focus pinning her to the spot. "If he is as good a man as you say he is, why did you leave? Why not make all this"—a mocking sweep of his hands to the barn—"your life?"

Cethin's words to Apolina—about finding her attractive, about the little details he'd memorized about her, the idea that he *did* care for her—hit Elana with full force. She was sure he could hear her heart beating wildly in her chest as he leaned forward and grasped a loose curl of her hair, moving it behind her ear.

"Do you want to know what I think?" he asked.

"Not particularly," she replied with enough bite in her words that the gold in his eyes flared. He leaned forward farther, every inch of his muscled body aligning with hers as he lowered his head.

"I think," he said, moving a hand under her chin and gently running his thumb over her bottom lip, "that something unique hides beneath this skin. Something that wouldn't be content with a simple life."

Elana tried to slow the rapid beating of her heart; the breaths that threatened to come out too tightly, too quickly; the panic he was sure to read on her body at just how close he was to figuring it all out—not about how she felt, but who she was.

Would he be even more furious than he already was about returning to Aviva when he discovered who she was—the lost princess of Aviva, heir to Queen Serenity's throne, the female who would re-Bind the Balance?

Would he hand her right back—oath be damned—to whomever had hired him?

Or—her stomach flipped—would he stand by her side?

"Maybe I just wanted a *man*." The words came out with the intent of keeping him from digging any deeper, but...

Elana swallowed at the surprise that glowed in Cethin's eyes. She felt the arm he'd braced on the railing slide around her waist. He pulled her tighter to him, and she lost her grip on the railing. Her breathing was ragged as he pushed them both against the support beam.

It was a distraction, she told herself. For him—for both of them—from this incredibly messy situation they'd wound up in.

And yet she also wasn't sure she cared, not as his other hand slid from her chin to the nape of her neck. He tugged at her braid. She could see that his eyes were closed as he bent and brushed his lips against her neck, the contact sending a tingling sensation through her entire body.

"Just say the word, El," he whispered, his mouth trailing from her neck to stop right before her lips. Starlight raced through her blood at his touch. Her choice, to stop their dangerous, distracting flirtation, or...

"What is it you want now?"

Cethin

A loud boom broke through the sounds of their breathing. He whirled from El—from her suddenly overwhelming and intoxicating scent.

Fucking Hell, what was *that*? Cethin lunged for the scythe he'd seen next to the hay bales. "Stay here," he ordered her without looking back, tempering his desire and steadying his breathing. He'd regretted his night with the barmaid as soon as it'd ended. It'd done nothing to quell the desire for the one person his body wanted: El.

Later. He'd think about it—they'd talk about it—later. Whatever *it* was. If it was anything more than the despair and passion of two people desperately clinging to some semblance of light in their own dark worlds. A world he wished El would share with him—those dreams that haunted her sleep.

Exiting the barn, Cethin caught the shapes of three winged creatures. They were flying over the main river—the one that cut through the Riverlands and ran to Ozul, then out to sea. The river they needed to travel on and the sea they needed to cross if they were actually going to follow through with El's insane plan to go to Aviva.

Cethin's eyes tracked those shapes as they wheeled around overhead, their unearthly voices shrieking, sending shivers down his spine, awakening senses in him that were more Elf than human. Something about the creatures wasn't right. He should run from them, a primal instinct warned him. They definitely weren't dragons. But whatever the creatures were, they didn't stop, didn't touch down. They turned and continued farther south. He exhaled and lowered the scythe to his side.

A rustling noise behind him had him lifting it again. Cethin whirled around. The woodworker was walking toward him slowly, hands raised.

"What was that?" the man demanded, jaw rigid. Cethin didn't fail to note the knife strapped to his leg—similar to the wicked hunting blade he carried at his own side.

"I'm not sure." He looked back to the sky.

"What were they doing here?" the man asked. Cethin met Bron's gaze again. The male's eyes were assessing him more thoroughly than he would've thought possible for a human.

"I'm not sure about that either," Cethin said.

But wasn't it ironic they'd come near him and El twice now?

The woodworker brushed one hand through his hair and looked down as he said, "I think you need to leave." It wasn't anything against them, Cethin acknowledged—it was for the sake of his family.

"We'll leave immediately," Cethin said. "Catch a boat to Aviva from farther in the Riverlands." He turned away, eyes back on the sky.

"There's a group." Cethin turned back to Bron. "They meet every midweek morning, five miles southeast from here. They take groups from the Blue Dock to"—the man lowered his voice—"Aviva. They could provide safe passage—for both of you, if that's where you are looking to go."

Cethin stared long and hard at the man. Exhaustion lined Bron's face, and those tired eyes regarded him even more warily now. But there was honesty there—more honesty than Cethin had ever seen in Apolina. More honesty than he'd even seen in El. Maybe that was what made humans so...*human*. Cethin tucked the thought away.

"I think," Bron continued, swallowing, "I think she needs you." Cethin again took the measure of the woodcutter. "And from what I saw earlier...I think you need her, too."

The man held Cethin's stare for a few moments, then turned away, immediately swallowed up by the reeds. Silence, broken only by those murmuring grasses, filled the world as Cethin stared after him. The man who dared speak truths he wasn't ready to hear.

Elana

She sagged against the pillar, the only thing keeping her body—her *Elvish body*, which was currently glowing, Gods save her—upright and wrapped her arms around herself at the sudden chill that'd crept in without Cethin's body pressed to hers.

Elana closed her eyes and tried to calm her pounding heart and wild breathing. What had she been about to say to him? Would it've been a confirmation, or a damnation of them both? She hadn't even argued to go out there with him, emotions and heat clouding everything.

But those beating wings only meant one thing.

She unwrapped her arms and pushed away from the pillar, heading for the ladder. She could feel her magic coiling inside of her, ready to strike the Noir and send them scattering to the ends of their world. She heard them flying overhead, their strong wings booming, their hideous sounds sending her blood chilling further.

They had to be tracking her, just as they had that final day in Aviva and the night Cethin had found her.

But how?

Elana paused for a moment, considering. Then, she tried to envision her Elvish form, her beautiful silver moonlight and starlight, and drew them in deep, into the very depths of her heart and essence. She returned to her mortal form, a body that left her unable to access that magic—

The wings stopped then started again. But the sound was moving away—leaving the riverside towns.

Well, that was good to know.

Elana descended the ladder to intercept Cethin before they ended up back in that loft—back to whatever had been about to happen. She wasn't even sure what she was going to say when he slipped back through the barn's doors, scythe in one hand, breath sending tendrils of wispy air around him.

"We need to leave," he said by way of greeting, then headed to the ladder behind her and climbed up. She followed him, watching as he returned the scythe and repacked their bag.

"Now?" she asked, though the answer was obvious as he tossed her her blue cloak and donned his black one.

"It seems," he said, tightening the hunting blade at his thigh and adjusting a few places she assumed hid more weapons, "our host isn't keen on us lingering."

Her heart paused. "You spoke to him?"

"Briefly," Cethin replied, tightening a lace on his boot, swinging the pack across his shoulders, and motioning for her to start back down the ladder. She followed.

"What did he say?"

The male jumped from a higher rung and grabbed her arm, forcing her to face him as her feet hit the floor. "He has a family."

Elana shook out of his grip and made for the barn door. "I know," she said as she walked out into the night.

"He can't protect you."

"*I know.*"

A strong, callused hand gripped hers, and she paused, the scar that crossed at an angle on his hand scraping against hers.

"El." Cethin was quiet long enough that she turned back to him.

"Where do we go from here?" she asked—a question with different meanings, and many possible answers.

"Five miles that way," he said, jerking his chin to their left. He'd picked the least dangerous one. "Your man was kind enough to share that there are people there who provide transportation to Aviva."

"I thought you didn't trust anyone."

He ran his thumb—the thumb that'd been at her lips not so long ago—across the scar on her palm.

"I said I was *trained* not to trust anyone."

Chapter 8

The five miles passed by agonizingly slowly—not just because of the uncomfortable silence between them as they walked, crouched, and darted between grasses and trees, and over and under the bridges that popped up across the small streams that foretold of the mighty river ahead, the heart of the Riverlands—but also because of the exhaustion taking over Elana's human body.

How long had it been since she'd slept? Ate?

A day? Longer?

Cethin still had energy. What kind of energy would she have if she returned to her Elvish body? But if the Noir felt her shift or her magic like some sort of beacon that wasn't an option.

Cethin paused suddenly, and she almost walked right into him and the pack. Course-correcting, Elana slipped in a small puddle—one of many that dotted the paths of the waterside town.

"What day is it?" he asked.

She stumbled through her brain, trying to remember. "Assuming it's past midnight," she calculated, "it should be the third weekday."

Cethin looked back at her. She saw his raised brows, even in the shadows of his cloak. "You don't say," he murmured, then looked back in front of them. "Finally, a stroke of luck." He crept out of the shadows of the home they'd hidden themselves in. Elana followed him—and his gaze to a red bridge across the street.

"We need to cross there," he said, pointing to it. "Get farther into the city—as close as we can to the river. From there, we need to find the Blue Dock."

The Blue Dock, then passage—passage home.

Cethin

The main riverside city, Catonia, was divided into districts, each defined by a different color. *How human, their need to classify everything.* Cethin shook his head as they crossed the red bridge. He detested his Elvish half somewhat less than his human one. It gave him some value in their world, some advantage over being a mere mortal. His human heritage wasn't something Cethin liked to dwell on. For creatures with such short lifespans, humans tended to be unnecessarily cruel and calculating. But the kindness, compassion—and truth—the woodworker had shown him, had shown El...Cethin shook his head again. People were never as kind as they seemed—and if they were, they always had ulterior motives.

The city's streets and overpasses were illuminated by torches that burned brightly outside of businesses and the homes of wealthier citizens, but

Cethin kept them to the shadows the best he could, El following silently behind him.

There was more to her story—just as there was to his. She would want to tell him in her own time, yet something urged him to ask more, to learn more, as soon as he could. Cethin shoved that feeling down as he pressed them both into a shadowy alcove, picking up on the sounds of revelry from late-night city-goers.

The riverside people passed them, when—faster than Cethin could detect—El was flung from his side to the ground, and he was pinned against the wall of the still-closed pastry shop they'd taken refuge against.

He immediately saw why: the long, pointed ears of a fully-blooded Elf peeked out from beneath their attacker's blue cloak—blue, to blend in with the Blue Quarter.

It seemed their luck had just run out.

Cethin assessed: the Elf was a male and had pinned him to the wall in a position that left him without easy access to his weapons. Not a citizen out for a late-night stroll, then. Cethin took in the distance between where they were and the river with the blue bridge. Not even half a mile. If he could incapacitate the male, they could make a run for the dock, and maybe still make it to meet whomever would be waiting for people like them.

If Bron hadn't betrayed them, too.

Cethin clung to the memory of the truth he'd seen on the man's face, trusting that the human had not and would never do that to El. His gaze shifted to her. She was pulling herself to her feet from where the male had knocked her aside in clear dismissal.

Cethin grinned—that'd been a bad move on the male's part.

"Have we done something to offend you, sir?" Cethin asked, raising his brows and quirking his mouth to the side in a way he knew made most of the people he encountered very, very angry. Anger made people stupid. Anger made people sloppy. But from what he could see of the male's face beneath that blue cloak, his stern expression didn't change. The male had discipline. *Interesting*. A true warrior, then.

But what was an Elvish soldier doing in the Riverlands?

"You tell me," the male said in a voice as rich as velvet. "What is a half-Elvish mercenary doing with..." The wind shifted, and the male's eyes—a stormy silver, Cethin noticed—widened.

The male whirled as El's cape rippled around her, the restless breeze blowing the garment away from her head, face—and sides where her daggers were. She reached for them, and Cethin watched the male's eyes track the movement. But there was no indication of fear from the male. No, instead, there was shock—surprise.

"Where did that come from?" The male motioned toward her cloak, a deep blue color that Cethin found brought out the blue in her gray eyes. He watched her eyes widen as he wrapped his arms around the Elf in a hold the male was unlikely to get out of—and pressed his hunting knife into the male's side to ensure it.

Elana's eyes hardened to steel as she surveyed their attacker-turned-captive. "A friend."

Lie. She was lying. Cerdwin had only given her those daggers, and Cethin could smell that the cloak was old. *But why lie?*

"And where did you get those?" the male questioned. Cethin nudged his blade a little closer. They should be questioning *him*, not the other way around. What game was El playing?

"These?" She unsheathed her blades. Cethin's breath caught at the violent light that sparked from nowhere in her eyes. She would kill the male—and not in the defensive way she'd killed the men in the forest and would carry some degree of guilt about for the rest of her life. No, this would be different. This time, there was a choice.

He'd sworn the life oath to her—but could it run both ways, somehow? He couldn't remember offhand.

Or was it the *other* thing between them? Cethin had assumed he was the only one who sensed it, the gradual shift between them since she'd tended to his back, that connection that'd all but come to fruition in the barn. He wondered again what she would've said if they hadn't been interrupted by the creatures that were apparently following them.

"They were a gift. Also from a friend," she replied nonchalantly, flipping both daggers hilt to blade, and back again, a move that had Cethin thinking about more than just their connection.

Truth. She gave the male the truth this time. Cethin had found the daggers minutes before she had while he'd been tracking her that day. And the apprentice...from his work, Cethin knew he'd jumped on a ship back to Aviva.

Was there a connection? Something he'd missed?

"A gift from a master Elvish blacksmith," the male observed. "It's just as likely that you stole them."

El took a step closer to the male. "She speaks the truth," Cethin heard himself growl at the male. He was out of patience. The male stiffened in his arms, coiling to find a way to spring out of his hold. El's eyes tracked to Cethin, then back to the male.

"They were a gift," she said again, voice even and clear. Her eyes narrowed on the dagger just beyond the male's reach. It was smaller than the twin blades she held, but it had a similar make—and the same markings. "Tell me," she said slowly, "what is one thing you know of this master blacksmith—one thing that he would be unlikely to share with others?"

"That he's an artist," the male answered quietly, "behind all that fire."

Not a particularly detailed answer, but Cethin watched her eyes widen all the same. He bounced his line of vision back to the male, who asked, "And what is his favorite meal?"

"Vegetable stew." El crossed her arms. "No meat."

This was getting ridiculous.

"And how did an Elvish female in a human body come to befriend Cerdwin?" the male asked, voice attempting a casual tone, but Cethin heard the surprise in it. Cerdwin had been the apprentice's name. It was the only confirmation Cethin needed that El was going to trust this male. Was he part of the group Bron had spoken of?

"A story for another time." She shrugged. A spark of pride flared in Cethin's chest. "At the moment we are on our way...farther north."

"Perhaps," the male said, angling his head to her, "I could be of some assistance in that matter."

El smiled coyly. "I was hoping you would be." She sheathed her blades. "Now, are you two done with your male posturing, or do you still need to beat the shit out of each other?" The male glanced up at Cethin, silver eyes flashing, then back to El, who quietly said, "I vouch for my companion."

Cethin released the male from his hold. Gods, was it really so difficult for people to trust mercenaries?

El extended her left hand to the male—the one with their life-oath scar. The male offered her a curt nod in return.

"Follow me, my lady."

Elana

The male didn't bother looking back to make sure they were following him as they approached the main river—the Eridanos.

The trio walked silently down a narrow path, half hidden by the large blue bridge, to the blue dock below. A boat waited there, hidden by the shadows of the bridge.

The boat that would take her home.

Elana's steps became purposeful as she strode after the male. He turned to help her aboard the vessel—no plank or rowboat to help them on...or off. He moved with the fluid grace she vaguely remembered the soldiers of Aviva possessing. She paused.

"Is something wrong, my lady?" the male asked, tilting his head as he looked at her. "What's your name?"

"Elana. And yours?"

"Eldwyn," the male said, inclining his head to her. The hood of his cloak slipped back as he straightened, revealing silver hair cut close to his head—a drastically different cut compared to the longer ones of most Elvish males. The cut accentuated his high, sculpted cheekbones. With his tan coloring and those uncanny silver eyes, he could've been a sculpted statue in one of the many art galleries in Aviva—especially if the strength he'd sent her to the ground and pinned Cethin to the wall with said anything about the body concealed beneath his cloak's folds. A jagged scar ran from his right ear to the side of his neck. *What injury had he sustained that even Elvish Healing hadn't mended it completely?*

Eldwyn gave no indication he'd noticed her eyes slip—he was looking to where Cethin stood behind her. "And your...*companion*?"

Gods save her. That would give Cethin something else to smirk about.

"Cethin," the half-Elf said, stepping closer to her side as they crossed the deck and followed Eldwyn down a set of steps into the interior. She watched Cethin mark all possible exits and escape routes, all the while monitoring for any threats. Yet he'd let her handle Eldwyn in the alcove, let her make the first move.

If she didn't know the half-Elf better, she would've thought he was starting to trust her.

"You'll be on the lower level," Eldwyn said, shadows bouncing off of his head from the torches illuminating the stairwell as they descended another level, "where food and supplies are typically kept." They halted, and Eldwyn opened a small door to a tight, cramped space not much larger than a closet—like the supply closets at Tymer's. The male's mouth tightened at the expression on her face. "While we run a clean operation, my lady, there are always risks." That silver gaze bounced to Cethin and back. "It's why I was wary of your presence." Of Cethin's presence was what the male really meant.

"And with the Noir's appearance on the outskirts of the city last night, we must be doubly careful. Their Dark Majesties don't need to know we're raising an army against them." Elana heard Cethin trip and mutter a curse behind them.

He knew what was hunting them now.

Eldwyn motioned for them to enter the small, dimly lit space. "And I would prefer to deliver the friend of my friend in one piece," he said, offering her a small smile, which she returned. The male glanced back. "As much as I would prefer to travel with you and hear your story," he commented, "I'm afraid I'm needed above. The journey is roughly an hour, and—"

"An hour!?" Elana couldn't stop the question as it burst from her lips. Eldwyn's eyes twinkled in amusement. "How?" she exclaimed.

"Magic," Cethin muttered as he positioned himself between her and the door.

She stared at Eldwyn. "Truly?" The male nodded. "Yours or someone else's?" The question spilled out before she could stop it. She wasn't sure if it was polite to ask.

As if in answer, a whispering breeze brushed against her cheek in the otherwise stagnant space. She gaped. Eldwyn chuckled, and the breeze drifted away as quickly as it'd come.

"I'll open the door after an hour has passed," Eldwyn promised.

There would be no opening the door until then if he locked it from the outside, and there were no windows in the room. Cethin was staring the male down again. It was almost as if some silent conversation passed between the two males, and Eldwyn—to Elana's shock— inclined his head to Cethin.

Then, their new acquaintance was gone, locking the door behind him.

Leaving them alone in a closet.

Eldwyn

He leaned against the starboard side of the boat and watched the early morning fog roll across the river, using his magic to wrap the dense mist around the ship to further conceal them from prying eyes.

Eldwyn had done this for months—years. Most trips were simple: sail from Aviva to the Riverlands, collect anyone who wished to return to Aviva, and return to Aviva.

Those first years, he'd imagined he would find the lost princess. The daydream had worked its way through his mind each time he'd waited at the Blue Dock.

Eldwyn had been a guard at the palace gates on her coronation day—the day she'd disappeared from the city.

The day he'd seen the Noir for the first time.

As a lower-born citizen, he'd never had many options, but Eldwyn was a skilled fighter. He'd worked his way through the Avivan army's ranks quickly—but never forgotten where he'd come from. Never forgotten the fear and terror of the Darkness. Never forgotten how the lower-born Elves, half-Elves, and humans were treated by the lord's regime.

Never forgotten the resilience of others who still believed as he once did: that the lost princess would return one day and save them all.

So he'd waited for the lost princess to return.

That daydream had faded as the years had gone by. He'd continued working through the ranks of Aviva's forces to become First Commander—in part due to his skill as a warrior and in part due to his magic.

Eldwyn still remembered the first time his elemental gift had manifested: he'd been upstairs in his family home and heard his mother's voice as clearly as though she were standing right next to him—but she wasn't, and had been shocked when he'd come downstairs asking why they couldn't afford to send him to the city with his friends for schooling.

His gift had grown from there: in addition to being able to hear others from far away, he could also amplify his voice so that others could hear him—handy when you had a rowdy group of males in the training ring or on the battlefield. It also made a useful shield.

Then, one day the wind had started whispering to him—not just the whispers of what others spoke quietly, but whispers of secrets. That was what made Eldwyn so valuable to the Lord's Council, why they'd overlooked his lower-born status and raised him to the highest position in Aviva's military.

But his talents also made him valuable to his males and the people. He always knew about quarrels in his camp—sometimes before they happened; knew when someone needed extra encouragement or discipline to be the best soldier they could be, or when someone was homesick and needed a week to spend time with their family. Eldwyn had honored as many unspoken requests as possible during his years as First Commander.

And—above all—he wanted to honor the requests from those who wanted to return to Aviva and fight against the Darkness.

Somewhere along the way, though, he'd forgotten who he was fighting for.

Then...there she was.

Eldwyn hadn't immediately known it was her—he threw a flicker of his power at the wind to shower his displeasure, as though it were a corporeal entity. It huffed at him—in laughter, frustration, maybe a little bit of both. Eldwyn sighed and dragged a hand over his face as he recalled throwing the lost princess—the heir to Aviva's throne—to the ground. She'd held her own, though. And when the wind had whipped the cloak from her face, he'd known. It was her. Eleonora. Or Elana, as she was apparently calling herself. She'd managed to hide for the past half a century. His wind had brought him no whispers of her.

Why now?

Did it have something to do with Cerdwin? Something settled low in Eldwyn's gut. Did she know Cerdwin as well as he did?

He let out a deep breath. It didn't matter—none of it did. The only thing that mattered was that he ensured the lost princess made it home safely—*and continued to be safe*, the wind whispered in his ear. Eldwyn took the moment he propelled the ship forward to send a whisper of his power to the storage room she currently occupied and wrapped his magic around her like a shield. It wouldn't protect her from everything, but it would at least keep her secret until she was ready.

He would handle whatever came next—no matter what it was.

Elana

There was only one candle in the supply closet, and it was almost down to its wick. For a moment, Elana imagined what it would be like to light the space with her own power.

Her magic stirred.

She pulled it back deep within her. It'd become harder to contain the moonlight swirling beneath her skin, to resist the urge to shift into her Elvish form and unleash her power. Allowing her power to flow freely would attract unwanted attention—specifically, the Noir—but she also didn't want that power, that *self*, to be who her people met when she returned. She didn't even want them to be *her people* at first; she wanted to be a part of them, one of them. To work with them, for them. To earn their trust without her title. To heal the broken pieces of herself—those pieces that made her feel weak, guilty, and ashamed for having fled to Ozul and spending so many years in hiding, regardless of having no control over or memory of who'd sent her away. She would strengthen those pieces on a new foundation—not one of power, magic, and hierarchy, but of heart, belief, and compassion.

She hadn't been a terrible princess, Elana reflected, but she'd allowed her parents to shield her from the worst of things; she'd been content to remain with her lady's maids, to be sheltered from the brutal realities that confronted not only her people, but their entire world. She'd had a narrow vision as a youngling, had been so naive, with only books to tell her about their world. Even her little rebellions sneaking around the palace hadn't told her much.

Leaving Aviva had changed everything.

Living on the human continent had changed her.

Elana came to the conclusion that she couldn't have done anything for her people if she'd stayed in Aviva—only become a stagnant version of her mother. Her mother had been a wonderful queen, but after the Breaking, the people had needed something else, something different—something new. And while Elana would meet them with the goal of peace and serenity, she would also come armed with reality, truth, and the strength of someone who'd struggled as they did, who'd lost as they had, who was afraid as they were. She would show them what it meant to be strong, to overcome, and to live life free from the threat of the Darkness.

Yes, returning would change everything.

Returning would change her.

Something brushed against her knee, drawing Elana from her thoughts. Cethin had extended his legs out in front of him where he sat next to her on the ground. Her own legs were still drawn to her chest, arms wrapped around them. She closed her eyes and tried not to think too much about what would be their incredibly close quarters for the next...well, it had to be less than an hour now, right?

He nudged her with his elbow. "What's on your mind, *my lady*?" Elana could make out the smug smile on his face, even in the shadows.

Inhaling sharply through her nose, she made up her mind: if she could say more to Eldwyn, this friend of Cerdwin's, she could say more to Cethin, too.

"I'm thinking that I'd like to stay with them when we arrive. I'd like to join"—she tried motioning with her arms in the tight space and ended up bumping Cethin in the head instead—"whatever this is they're doing. To do *something* to fight the Darkness."

She turned her head to look at him. Cethin was staring at her, his face unreadable as he took the hand she'd accidentally whipped into his forehead in his.

Life-oath scar to life-oath scar. A shiver crept up her spine at the contact.

"What-what about you?" she asked, stumbling over her words as he brushed his thumb against the scar on her palm.

"I'm thinking you're full of surprises," he said, expression still unreadable. "You widened your circle of trust quite a bit tonight."

"I trust Cerdwin, and if Eldwyn knows—"

"Not just with him," Cethin said, thumb stopping its path along her palm. "But with me."

Her breath caught. Even in the dim space, she saw the burning intensity in his eyes. Closing hers, she attempted to redirect the conversation. "My trust yes, but what of my bravery?"

He chuckled, a rough sound. "I already knew you were brave," he said after a moment. "I knew it the night you brought me into your home. Well, actually, I thought you were very, very stupid." She opened her eyes and scowled at him, knowing his half-Elvish vision would make her expression clear. His shoulders shook with laughter, causing his hair to fly and brush against her cheek. "But," he continued, "in the weeks I've known you...you are brave, El. Perhaps even braver than I am."

Silence filled the compartment.

"That almost sounded like a compliment," she eventually said, looking in front of her again. She felt his fingers close around hers, the strength and warmth of him leaking into her.

"I don't give them freely."

She snorted. It remained quiet between them for a long while, and then—

"I think, even without the life oath between us, I would still follow you between continents to face the Darkness," he said.

Elana didn't look at him, even though she felt him watching her. She didn't speak, either. But she tilted her head to the side and rested it against his shoulder.

Cethin

Cethin watched the candle sputter and die, the light going out just like it'd gone out of Apolina's eyes when he'd stabbed her.

He winced, then stilled, hoping the movement wouldn't wake up the female dozing against his shoulder. Even in the dark, he could make out El's face: features framed by that unruly brown hair; long dark lashes that swept down over eyes that were sad most times but stunning when they lit with joy, softened with understanding, or narrowed with irritation at his antics;

cheeks that didn't flush when she wielded a blade, but when he made her angry or uncomfortable or aroused, as she had been in the barn; lips that held secrets he wanted to know, and a mouth that could speak so plainly or lie so sweetly.

A mouth Cethin wanted to kiss, to mark, to memorize every detail of.

He looked down at where his hand was wrapped around hers, then flinched again and dropped it. Sighing at himself in frustration, he gently lifted her hand again and arranged it in her lap as best he could in the cramped space.

His hands were covered in blood.

Apolina's blood. The blood of so many others. How could he think to take the innocence of a barmaid who was likely so much more?

But was she so virtuous? He *had* been hired to take her. Maybe she was a mercenary, too, involved with a competing group, and his employer was actually his masters, who wanted to convert her—or, if they couldn't, kill her. He almost laughed at the idea. El had some wildness to her, but she wasn't a trained killer—that'd been obvious with how she'd reacted to dispatching the men under the tree.

Eldwyn had called her *my lady*—perhaps she was a noble lady being used as a pawn between two warring houses, and one had sent him to collect her. *Gods, that would be a headache.* He certainly wasn't worthy of a noblewoman. Thank the Otherworld there was no way she could be the lost princess of their fairy tales. Regardless, there was no going back. He was involved. He'd sworn the life oath to her.

But Apolina had been right—it was more than that.

Cethin resisted the urge to slam his head on the wall behind him.

He'd killed her.

He'd killed Apolina.

Cethin would never forget the hurt and anger he'd felt when he'd realized what she'd done—never forget the fear and dismay radiating from El as he'd shoved her to the ground. He hadn't needed the life oath to guide him then.

He'd never forget the way every muscle in his body had gone as taut as the bowstring Apolina had trained on his life-sworn. Never forget the anger and resentment he'd felt toward the female mercenary for putting him between them.

Never forget stabbing her, watching the life leave her body, her essence leaving their world for the Otherworld.

And she'd *thanked* him.

Like she'd been waiting for someone to end it. Like the only death that could ever satisfy her was her own—and it had to be by his hand. Cethin closed his eyes, bowed his head, and sent a silent prayer to the Gods who could likely no longer hear him for his...his friend.

Opening his eyes, Cethin turned his head back to the female who slept on his shoulder. *I think you need her, too.* The woodworker's words echoed in his mind. Cethin was trained to not need anyone—just as he was trained to not trust anyone. But all of those rules vanished like a sandbar in the sea where El was concerned. He'd needed her to save him from those creatures—the Noir, apparently—that night in the alley. He'd needed her to soothe his back after the skirmish in the clearing. He'd needed her in the barn after...after everything that had happened.

Once would be enough, Cethin decided. He could have her once and let her go.

But in his foolish heart, he knew once wouldn't be enough.

Chapter 9

Elana

"El." Elana lifted her head—she'd fallen asleep.

Fallen asleep *with her head on Cethin's shoulder*.

Heat crept into her cheeks, but the door to the closet was opening, and the crisp sea air that followed cooled her embarrassment. The hand she vaguely remembered Cethin holding was now artfully draped across one of her knees, and Cethin's own hands were at his weapons.

Eldwyn's head popped through the open door. The male glanced down at both of them as they squinted in the sudden light.

"We're here," he announced.

Here.

Aviva.

Home. Elana's heart thumped in her chest so loudly she was sure that both males could hear it, even though they wouldn't understand what this moment meant to her—what it would mean for all of them.

The lost princess was about to set foot in her homeland. Elana's chest constricted, making it difficult to breathe as she and Cethin made their way up the steps behind Eldwyn.

Everything would be different now.

Elana blinked at the brightness that came from everywhere as they emerged onto the main deck—the Light of Aviva.

The light of her mother.

Aviva.

Home. It'd been almost fifty years since she'd seen it, fifty years since she'd lived in the open marble palace that sprawled above them, looking as though it'd been built into the ridge behind it, the rock of the small range displaying hues of white, peach, and cream. It looked so *clean*, so elegant compared to the human towns. Elana had never seen the palace of the human continent up close during the years she'd spent in the Southern Kingdom, but she had a feeling it could never compare to this.

Then again, what could compare to the feeling of being home at last?

She could see the sweeping spirals of the palace more clearly as they moved inland. She recalled the spinning staircases that led between the different levels of the castle, could almost hear the water from the falls that jutted outward and spilled into small pools between those levels. The falling water, with its mist and spray, had always brought a welcome reprieve in the summers—and less perilous to cool herself by than the pools.

The gilded gates that had served as a barrier between her and the outside world—gates between her life as a princess and the freedom of the city, the rooftops of which she could see from the ship: the noble and richer Elvish homes built up high from the same marble as the palace, with curtains to block out the Light of Aviva during the fake nights. While many of the castle's residents chose sleeping chambers deep inside the walls—where the Light couldn't penetrate—that wasn't something the lesser nobility, or even the upper class, could afford to create space for in their homes, so they hung night curtains from their windows—meaning their party had arrived in the fake morning.

Down from the noble houses, the city faded into smaller homes—mostly made of wood and painted in so many brilliant colors and with wild decorations; homes she'd never really seen until the day she'd walked across the kingdom, when every stop had brought her closer to the field and garden at its edge where the dead were laid to rest.

Where her mother and father were laid to rest.

The Meadows.

It wasn't a particularly long walk from the city to The Meadows where gardens grew to house the dead. But that fake day, it felt impossibly long. The young princess kept a measured pace as she and her escort of eight Elvish warriors—the royal First Guard of the former queen—walked the dianaflora-covered streets of Aviva. The open air was filled with the sounds of an Elvish mourning song; Aviva's people were mourning her mother, just as she was—though she had to keep herself contained, a solid symbol of her mother's legacy and her people's future.

The Elves of the city reached out to her from where they lined the roads, voicing their sympathies for her loss—and their allegiance to her, their soon-to-be crowned queen.

Eleonora nodded, waving every few feet, maintaining her cadence as she continued through the different levels of the city. The stone streets wove a *tapestry of everyone who dwelt there: the homes of the nobles who didn't reside within the palace; the merchant's trading centers, inns, restaurants, and taverns; the Healing centers and artist's galleries; the more expensive homes and buildings of marble, and the cheaper buildings of stone and wood—some painted in different shades of whites, grays, blues, and silvers—all with black banners hanging from their windows, reflecting a city united in mourning.*

The Elvish-made streets gave way to dirt paths as Eleonora and her escort neared the city limits. There were more homes than establishments there—simpler builds yet sturdy. Younglings—not just Elvish, but some half and some fully human—darted across the path to offer the young princess flowers. The presence of human children wasn't entirely unexpected: many mortals had once left the human continent with the desire to give their children a better life in the peaceful Elvish kingdom.

Eleonora inclined her head to the bobbed curtsies and little bows before the younglings ran back to the sides of the road to where their families waited.

She missed her mother.

She missed her father.

And the Darkness had dashed any hope of a once-peaceful existence.

Sorrow clouded Elana's vision, reducing the sparkle and shimmer of the city, the Light reflecting off the palace, the golden gates, the marble city, and...the outer wall.

Elana's hand instinctively reached for her locket. There hadn't been a wall before the Battle of the Breaking.

The battle that had ended her father's life.

"Is it true?" Sonia's voice was barely more than a whisper in their family's living area.

It hadn't been the lady's maid's voice that had woken the young princess, though, but the sounds of her mother, finally returned. The battle was over.

"It is," came her mother's weary reply.

The young princess carefully turned the handle of her bedchamber door, opening it a fraction. She could easily see the two women in the light—the light that hadn't gone away at sundown like it should've.

"You must send her away. Immediately. You know he will not stop—"

"You forget your place, Mistress Sonia."

The young princess stiffened. She'd never heard her mother speak to the woman so harshly.

"Of course, Your Grace." Sonia's response didn't sound the least bit apologetic. If anything, the woman sounded angry. The young princess had never heard the lady's maid speak that way to her mother, either.

"I have lost my husband. I will not send my daughter away out of fear."

Splintering pain hit the young princess everywhere at once. She crumpled to the floor. Her right hand hit the ground to catch her fall. Her left reached for the necklace her parents had gifted her for her birthday.

Her mother had lost her husband, which meant...

The young princess's father was dead.

That wall had failed on her coronation day—the day the Noir had come for her for the first time. Towers had been added to the wall, she noted. She supposed that, with Elvish eyes, she'd be able to see archers in those towers, soldiers monitoring every movement in the sky and beyond the city.

And outside of the wall...

The desert.

Elana closed her eyes and summoned memories of maps she'd seen of what that land had looked like before the Battle of the Breaking: in addition to there being no wall, no warriors atop it, there had been no great desert between Aviva and the Endurnal Mountains. That stretch of land had once been as lush and green as The Meadows. After the battle, it was as if the earth had died as so many Avivan soldiers had, becoming nothing more than brittle sand. Some of the older servants, she remembered, had whispered that the withered land was a greater example of what the Dark King would do if he took the city—reducing it to nothing but dust, death, and Darkness.

She opened her eyes and looked west to where the sands ended and the Endurnal Mountains began. The mountains were said to have been beautiful during the time when the Light and Darkness were Balanced: lush green forests and elegant trees, mountains where all manner of flora and fauna had thrived, and a place where Elves blessed with the Earthen gifts had found peace and prosperity amongst the Earth Folk.

Now, those mountains were ensconced in murky shadow—not the Darkness of the eternal night that prospered farther west beyond their jagged cliffs, but a grayer, moodier dullness that gave way to rough brush, jagged bushes, and pine trees that threatened death with their spindly needles—the last bit likely part of an old lady's maid's tale to keep more adventurous younglings away from the assumed boundary between Aviva and the Dark King's realm.

None who'd dwelled in the Endurnal Mountains called it home anymore. The Elves had either retreated to the city—where their gifts were less likely to flourish—or traveled to The Islands. Rumor was those Elves had used their magic to help The Islands become as rich and thriving as their mountains used to be. There was less about their History, as going to The Islands was looked at as betrayal. One did not leave one Elvish kingdom for another. Very few Elves who'd gone to The Islands had ever come back or even visited Aviva once they'd left. But Elana imagined their fates were better than those who'd been caught in the Endurnal Mountains by the Dark King and Night Queen and turned into creatures of Darkness, twisted and mutilated by evil until they'd become predators.

The Earth Folk had simply disappeared, as though they'd been absorbed into the land itself.

Elana wasn't sure about the fates of those who'd remained in the radiant city, the fates of those on the human-ruled continent behind her, or those—like herself—who'd fled to the mortal kingdom and now returned, determined to offer whatever aid they could to their people in their greatest time of need.

Would she be able to save them?

"You look so much like your father." Sonia's words from her coronation day came back to her. *"And you will rule better than either your mother or father. Make us proud."*

A movement to her right caught her eye, and Elana turned to find Cethin watching her. Gods, she would forever be frustrated with the neutral face he maintained so well. She could only imagine what he was reading on hers.

"What?" she demanded, raising a brow. The Light of Aviva gilded his tanned face. Deep shadows played along his cheekbones and jaw—except for the lighter scar and the lines on his forehead, which she imagined were probably from how often he liked to glower. But the Light made him look younger somehow.

And something else...

The half-Elf crossed his arms and looked from her to the city and back to her again.

"It suits you." Elana scrunched her face: could the Light—her mother's Light—bring out something in her, something Cethin could see—*feel*? Who she was, who she would be? Who she *could* be, once she decided to?

"The city, the Light, the way it—" He stopped, and Elana turned around to see Eldwyn a few feet away from them. "It suits you," Cethin repeated, shrugging. "My lady," he added with a wink. Elana snorted and rolled her eyes.

"Are you not one of the returning ladies of nobility?" Eldwyn asked, walking toward her.

It was a fair question: the noble ladies of Aviva were infamous for the strength of their Healing gifts—so much so that those born second or third to their families were given to the High Healers, while the first remained free to marry and bear children; those who gave their life to the Healing arts would have neither. With war likely coming, it would be practical to suss out the former—not that the Healing gift wasn't present in lower-born females as well, but the knowledge and art passed down through the noble houses, along with their penchant for matchmaking, made those ladies especially talented.

Elana shook her head. "I am no lady," she said, binding the lie and truth together.

"Apologies," Eldwyn said, inclining his head to her. "I shouldn't have assumed. I just—since you know..." The male shook his head. "It's of no matter. A friend of our friend is my friend." He winked and gave her a small smile, which Elana returned.

While her lack of noble lineage might not be of any concern to Eldywn or Cerdwin, it would make things that much more difficult for her—and by extension, Cethin—once she sought to establish a foothold with the people. Claiming a false noble lineage would require hours of poring through the Royal Archives, and, even though she was certain Cethin had experience falsifying documents, they didn't have the time for that, nor would she wrap her identity up in something that could so easily be discovered as the lie it was.

Her best option was to return as a simple female who was unable to shift back into her Elvish body. Then, she would put in the work, effort, and training to gain the trust of the people, the soldiers and their leaders, and, possibly—if she was willing to admit it—herself. It was a different risk, but one she was willing to take.

"We will be disembarking shortly—and quickly," Eldwyn said. "Do you have family you can stay with?"

Elana's heart twisted: no family. No friends. No one who would recognize her like this—not even Sonia, though she couldn't imagine the old mortal woman was still alive.

"I don't," she answered quietly.

"And you?" the male asked Cethin.

"No," was the half-Elf's grunted response.

Silence fell amongst them, broken only by the hustle and bustle of the crew and other passengers she hadn't seen earlier disembarking around them, the crash of the waves against the shores of the small settlement at the edge of the strait, and the cries of the gulls overhead.

"I guess that makes you our guests, then," Eldwyn said.

Cethin

While Cethin could admit he'd been attracted to many charming women and females in the past, the tension that had built over El's allure struck him hard as they approached the shores of Aviva. The sight of her gazing in awe toward the city, the Light of Aviva shining on her...it was like he could see her—the real her she hid beneath her mortal facade and limiting beliefs, her fears and distrust.

Not that it mattered—not anymore. Cethin had meant what he'd said in the confines of the ship's closet: life-sworn or otherwise, he'd followed her this far and intended to continue to do so. Not for the adventure, not for the glory of war, not for the mystery she offered, not so he could mark her as another one of his conquests—but for the things she'd shown him that he'd long forgotten: kindness, compassion, friendship, loyalty, bravery—and maybe not complete honesty or trust, but he had the impression that El was exactly who and what she wanted to be right now. And that conviction of self was likely to inspire more than just his devotion.

"I think she needs you. And from what I saw earlier...I think you need her, too."

Perhaps the human woodworker was right.

"Guests?" he asked Eldwyn, the male's statement drawing Cethin from his ruminations.

Eldwyn nodded. "Cerdwin and I will make space for you in his camp. I'm sure he won't mind," the male added—more to himself than to them—with a small smile.

"Camp?" El sounded puzzled.

"Yes," Eldwyn said. "Cerdwin is one of the Commanders of Aviva's armies."

Cethin watched the emotions pass over El's face. "You didn't know." El shook her head, and Eldwyn gave her a curious look. "Come, it's our turn to disembark."

They covered the rocky ground between the cove and mainland in a matter of minutes. Horses waited for them in the small oceanside town that remained far outside the city's walls—a town mainly occupied by humans and half-Elves, of course. The miles of sand stretching between it and the city proper were vast and golden.

From how determined El had been to return, and how palpable her connection to the city was, Cethin saw her sudden change in her demeanor as they mounted their horse.

One horse. For both of them.

Eldwyn mounted the other. "We travel in small groups of two or three, take a formational route through the sands, and enter the city at different points," the male explained. "That way, if enemy eyes are watching, there's too much for them to track at once."

"The Noir!" El interjected. "Do they ever...?"

Eldwyn shook his head. "No. The last time we saw the Noir was the day the princess of Aviva disappeared." Cethin didn't fail to notice the flicker of emotion in El's eyes, the gray and blue surging like a summer storm at the mention of the lost princess. "Well, not until our departure from Ozul," the male continued, blowing out a breath and running a hand over his head. "It seems you've seen them more on the human continent than we have here." Cethin nodded, tucking away the additional nugget of information.

"How long is the ride from the coast to the city itself?" he asked the male.

"About half a day's ride," Eldwyn replied, casting a sidelong glance at El.

"I can manage." She swung herself up—and not gracefully—behind Cethin on their horse. He chuckled when she wrapped her arms around his torso.

"I knew you fancied me," he remarked, earning a flick in the ear, which only made him laugh harder. "All you had to do was ask." Her answering huff in his ear sent his skin thrumming as he urged their horse forward.

Despite the near-death grip El had kept on him when they started—she clearly wasn't used to being a second rider—she relaxed her arms, if only slightly, as the miles went by. Eldwyn kept a steady pace in front of them, and Cerdwin noted the male constantly scanned their open surroundings, including the sky. He did the same.

"Worried about sand monsters?" El asked.

"Not at all. This isn't like the sandy deserts of the Southern Kingdom." Cethin felt her slight shudder against him. The sandsnakes of the mortal continent's capital city were infamous for being quick and poisonous—utterly lethal. "Did you encounter any during your time there?"

"What makes you think I've ever been to the Southern Kingdom?" Cethin heard her unasked question: *how long have you been tracking me?* But he hadn't been—not then; he hadn't even had her as an assignment until a few weeks before he'd tackled her in the alley and she'd punched him in the face.

Cethin shrugged, the light weight of her arms around him a tantalizing restraint. "Most people who've been there and haven't seen them—or never been there—like to tell glorified stories of the Southern King and his legendary snake-fighting contests. Those who *have* been there and have come across them, well, they typically react the way you just did."

"I knew..." El cleared her throat. "Someone." Alright then, that someone was clearly her other former lover. "They loved the snake-fighting rings. Bet loads and loads of silver and gold on them. Sometimes they won. Sometimes they lost—badly. And when they did..."

Cethin stiffened. Something deep in his essence begged him to go to the Southern Kingdom, find that man, get to know him—and end him. *Godsdamned life oath.* He turned his eyes from where they'd slid to her over his shoulder back to the expanse of sand in front of them. Eldwyn had just cleared a small dune, and they were rapidly approaching it.

"Monsters fighting monsters," Cethin said as they cleared the drift.

"The sands here feels different," she said after a few moments. "It's like they're shards of light and darkness, broken and mixed together to fill a void. To remind us."

"Remind us of what?"

"That tipping the Balance—in either direction, light or darkness, love or hate, life or death—comes at a cost."

It was an effort to keep his eyes on the path ahead of them—well, whatever path Eldwyn saw. This woman—this female—speaking wasn't the same one who'd spoken in Ozul. It was as if being in Aviva, with the Light, illuminated another facet of her.

"I assume that's part of the reason we're here," Cethin commented, attempting to sound nonchalant.

A whispered, "Yes" was his only answer as the city wall rose to its full height before them.

Chapter 10

T he wall was bigger than she remembered—but it was more than that. Elana shivered and tightened her arms around Cethin. She could've sworn the male tensed at the change in touch, then relaxed. There was still *that* conversation to look forward to: what had happened—or had been about to happen—in the barn. But first, they needed to find a place to stay.

Eldwyn had mentioned staying with him and Cerdwin in Cerdwin's camp—not just any camp, but one of the top-tier Avivan military camps, if Cerdwin were indeed a Commander. And, while it would be a good place to ingrain herself as a valuable asset, Elana doubted her presence would be welcome—likely only slightly less welcome than Cethin's. A female in a mortal body meant no Healing gift, and no Healing gift made her presence in the camp unwarranted.

It was so different on the mortal continent where both men and women would fight when war came. But in Aviva, the old rules remained as the Elves did, and those rules said only males could join Aviva's military. Just because her people lived longer didn't mean they lived any smarter. While those rules had been bent for females of the royal bloodline—since their magic superseded what was expected—if she were going as just a woman...

The issue of lodging was the first of many she needed to figure out. But she would figure it out.

Cethin nudged their horse to follow where Eldwyn had withdrawn into the wall's shadow. "Smart," she heard him murmur under his breath.

They continued following the male until he came to an abrupt stop. "Here," Eldwyn said quietly. He motioned to what Elana assumed was a door in the wall. Squinting, she could almost see the stone offset only by a thin gray outline. Eldwyn pressed his hand against it. A pale light flared beneath his palm, and that small section of wall swung inward.

"Aren't you concerned that if enemy scouts are watching," Cethin said, "they'll use these doors—doors I'm assuming are placed around the wall—to enter the city?"

Elana didn't hear the male's reply as she peered over Cethin's shoulder at the city. It was like walking through a vivid memory—a winding path through the past—as the door led them to the outskirts of the city, west of the palace. A part of Elana was relieved they hadn't approached from the east and north, where her father and mother were laid to rest. That would've been too much to bear too soon.

"There will be no procession, and she will not *be joining us in The Meadows." Her mother's voice was clear, firm, and direct.*

But that didn't stop the lord. "I understand Your Grace's hesitation, but it is tradition," came Lord Arel's reply.

"Tradition? You speak of tradition now?" her mother seethed. "There is nothing traditional about any of this. Nothing you can look to your Annor or the Gods for now, my lord. Everything has changed, and that is something we must all face."

It was true—the last three days had been a flurry of change in the young princess's life: she was officially forbidden from leaving the castle walls, and she had a detail of First Guard whenever she moved about the palace. Thick black curtains that had nothing to do with mourning hung from the palace windows to block the endlessly brilliant light that flooded the city at all hours. She hadn't seen her mother until now. Sonia wouldn't tell her anything about the battle the servants whispered about, the Battle of the Breaking.

Her father was dead, and she wasn't allowed to go with her mother to lay him to rest. Tears filled the young princess's eyes.

Everything had changed—and she didn't understand why.

Elana blinked back tears and scanned the pathway for the *dianaflora* that had always brought her great comfort.

There were none.

Closing her eyes, she took a deep breath. This was also almost too much to bear: if she tracked their path just a little farther west, a little farther south, she would find the route she'd fled so many years ago.

She opened her eyes. She was atop a white horse. She was alone. No, not alone. A male with dark hair and eyes the color of honey—Gods, he looked so much like Cethin—*rode next to her. And they were riding...toward a port.*

A human woman walked next to them.

Sonia.

"Did anyone see you?" Sonia was asking the male.

"You mean besides the Noir?" the male dryly replied. He even sounded like Cethin.

Sonia's brows pinched together in a manner Elana was all too familiar with. "Now is not the time for your jokes."

The male sighed. "No, no one saw us. They likely believe she's dead."

"Good," Sonia replied. The male gave her a sharp look. Sonia shook her head. "It is best for it to remain that way for now. We will see her safe passage to Ozul." The woman looked at her, and the young princess closed her eyes. "I will bind her memories. Until the time is right."

"How can you be sure—" Elana squinted one eye open. Sonia had cut the male off with a glare. He sighed again. "It's just..."

The lady's maid squeezed the male's hand—a rare sign of affection from the woman. "I worry for him, too," Sonia murmured. "But this is the way it must be. It has been decided."

Sonia's attention returned to Elana. Elana squeezed her eyes shut again, and...

There was a tingling sensation as she felt Sonia place her hands on her face and chest.

Her memories...that must have been it...but why?

Elana pretended to wake up and look around, taking in the harbor, then looked back toward...

"Come, child," Sonia said.

She would remember none of it.

"I have to go back."

"No, child," Sonia said. "Not now. Not yet."

She wasn't a child anymore.

A soft, warm breeze blew through Elana's hair, sending loose curls waving around her face, pulling her from the tangled mess of her past and present. She opened her eyes.

Sonia had sent her away.

Sonia had taken her memories—until the time was right.

What did that even mean?

Elana inhaled deeply and breathed in the scent of her home.

Home.

It was spring in Aviva, the breeze not as cold and biting as it had been in Ozul or the Riverlands. Elana absorbed the scent of earthy vegetables and spring fruits being grown and harvested by those who lived in the furthest reaches of the city, every scent marked with an edge of water, dirt, and horse.

Her attention shifted to the path in front of them as several half-Elvish younglings ran between their horses. Her heart strained as she watched a young mortal man carrying wooden beams over his back to where a new home was being built. Half-Elves and humans were held in low esteem and often relegated to the kingdom's menial roles. It was a shame to not allow these people the opportunity to fight for their homes, she thought, to build different lives than the ones they'd been born into. They had just as much right as anyone else—regardless that they possessed no magic of their own, weren't as physically strong or long-lived as fully-blooded Elves.

To Elana's surprise, Eldwyn shouted greetings to a few of the younglings by name, tossing coin their way. He seemed a kind and noble male, taking two strangers in, helping those who wished to return here to fight for their home, and showing kindness to those younglings, when most fully-blooded Elves would not.

But how did he know Cerdwin?

And what was his role here?

They reached the end of the wooden houses. The path became grassier and rockier, and tents sprung up on either side of them instead of homes.

"This is the Second Commander's Camp," Eldwyn said, slowing his pace. "It runs about five miles long."

Elana started. "Didn't people used to live here?"

Eldwyn nodded, and she could've sworn something like regret passed over his face. "They did," he said quietly. "But the Lord's Council deemed occupation near the wall a necessity. So they were...*displaced*." Cethin stiffened again beneath her touch. That could've been his fate, had he not grown up on the human continent and become...well, who he was.

"And where were those people *displaced* to?" the half-Elf asked sharply. Elana sucked in a breath. This wasn't the place for that conversation—not with Avivan soldiers mingling outside the tents they passed. The soldiers were fully-blooded Elves, which meant their hearing—along with their other senses—was even better than Cethin's.

Eldywn shot Cethin a look that spoke a similar sentiment. "They were well compensated for their relocation," was all the male said.

Elana felt those soldiers' keen Elvish eyes on them—watching, assessing. She supposed the soldiers saw Cethin for the threat he presented—not as much as they could, of course, with no human blood running through their veins. And those eyes on her...mostly curiosity, as far as she could tell. Irritation from a few at the female in a woman's body, riding on a horse with a half-Elf. She and Cethin would be the talk of the camp now. *So much for not attracting unwanted attention.*

Their party halted in front of a pavilion much larger than the tents around it. The sigil of the Lord's Council hung from it; while Elana remembered the design, she didn't remember it in green and gold—the colors of House Satrara.

Her closet was overflowing with dresses fresh from the dressmakers, but the young princess noticed there were more green ones than usual. She took one in her hand and wrinkled her nose as her mother paced behind her impatiently.

"Shouldn't there be more blue?" the young princess asked.

Blue was the color of the royal house. While her mother's blues were often threaded with the finest gold, the young princess's were usually lined with silver.

Her mother halted her pacing in the center of the bedchamber and turned to the young princess with a look that said everything. The young princess wasn't stupid—she'd been eavesdropping outside the doors of the Lord's Hall the day her mother and the lord discussed it.

"It would be a most advantageous match," the lord had said.

"For you," her mother had replied, clearly unimpressed.

"For the royal house, for my house, and for the future of Aviva."

"You think you threaten—"

"This is not a threat, Serenity. This is a fact. Despite your feelings for me"—she'd heard her mother snort—"we both know this is for the best."

"Your son is not even here."

"He will return when it is time for them to wed."

"And you expect them to just accept this?"

The male had let out a harsh laugh. "Come now, Serenity. We both know love matches are not always what they seem."

The young princess shook the memory of the male's tone from her mind.

"When?" she asked her mother, who'd resumed her pacing.

"In three years' time."

"El." Cethin's voice jolted her.

Cerdwin. *Cerdwin* had been her intended.

Elana exhaled deeply and released her grip on Cethin as Eldwyn dismounted and motioned for them to do the same. Cethin climbed down first and offered her a hand. Elana grasped it, that scar across his palm scratching against hers, as if in reassurance.

Eldwyn approached the tent's entrance—and the two males in Avivan military regalia posted outside of it—first. The soldiers nodded and stepped aside to let the male through. Elana followed, Cethin a step behind her.

It took her human eyes a minute to adjust from the brightness of the Light outside to the dim light of the tent.

"Elana?" The voice that spoke was one she hadn't heard in over a month—one she wasn't sure she'd ever hear again.

"Cerdwin," she exhaled, and was pulled into a bone-crushing hug. A small *oomph* escaped her, and her vision was obscured by gold.

"Sorry," Cerdwin loosened his grip and stepped back. "I keep forgetting my strength." An exasperated sigh—Eldwyn, she recognized—came from her left, and Cerdwin's eyes sparkled.

He looked the same, yet so different in his Elvish body: his hair was a mass of golden curls that seemed to spark with an inner flame; his eyes, a vivid purple, were blazing like glittering amethysts; and his face younger—sharper—was even more handsome than it had been in his mortal form. Elvish Cerdwin was nothing short of magical, like a prince of the Goddess of Light. Nothing like the brooding half-Elf who stood with her.

"Well, amongst other things, like manners," Cerdwin added, taking another step back and inclining his head to her. Elana watched his eyes drink in every detail of her as he lifted his chin. Her friend cleared his throat. "Second Commander Cerdwin Satrara, at your service. And..." Cerdwin glanced at the half-Elf behind her.

"A friend—and my life-sworn."

Cerdwin's eyes widened, bouncing from Cethin to her and back again. "Well met," Cerdwin said, extending an arm to Cethin, though there was nothing friendly in the gesture. Elana knew how many blades the male probably had on his person—he always had something tucked up his sleeve in Ozul.

Cethin didn't balk as he met the male's stare and grasped his arm in return. "Well met," the half-Elf replied.

"May I ask," Cerdwin drawled, crossing his arms and drawing himself to his full height, "what you rescued her from that made her feel obligated to offer you the life oath, mercenary?"

Gods, this wasn't going to end well—for a multitude of reasons.

Cethin let out a dark laugh. "I think you need to learn to ask better questions, *Second* Commander."

No, this wasn't going to end well at all.

"I didn't offer him the life oath, Cerdwin," she interjected, attempting to position herself between her life-sworn and her friend. "He offered it to me."

"Is this true?" Cerdwin demanded. Cethin nodded, giving the male his signature smirk. "And what would a female in a human body be able to protect a half-Elf of your *occupation*"—Cethin's mouth tightened at the word—"from?"

"One of the Noir," Cethin said. Silence fell, then, "You trained her," he added.

Cerdwin's laughter warmed Elana's heart as his eyes found hers. "That I did," he said, and she shifted under his gaze. "But the question remains—" His brows slammed together. "You shifted."

Her mouth ran dry, but she nodded. "Yes—but only briefly. It was an accident, and—"

Cerdwin waved a hand. "It is alright. I know that talking about the shift might be challenging right now." His voice was soft—the voice of her friend, not the Second Commander he'd transformed into overnight. She bowed her head, then felt the weight and warmth of his hand on her shoulder. "I have had some trouble, myself," the male said quietly. She lifted her chin to look at him again. "It is no easy thing to settle back into who you were—or are—supposed to be. Even now, sometimes, it is fake-day by fake-day for me." Elana swallowed, nodding and blinking back tears at the kindness that was her friend.

Cerdwin had always known what to say to her in Ozul—he was like an extension of her own heart. They wouldn't have made a terrible match, had her mother and his lord father succeeded in their aim. But her heart now...

"I know who can help you!" Cerdwin was saying excitedly. Elana smiled at the grin blooming on the male's lips. "My sister."

His sister. Elana vaguely remembered Cerdwin mentioning a sibling during one of their training sessions in Ozul. His sister—not just his sister, but his twin, she recalled from the History of House Satrara.

"She is currently away on"—a look from Eldwyn had Cerdwin stiffening as he finished with—"business." *Interesting*. Females were generally prohibited from any sort of service to the kingdom beyond Healing.

"She must be a potent Healer then," Cethin said, earning himself another cutting look from Cerdwin.

"She is," Cerdwin said. "Which makes her the most able to help Elana shift back into her Elvish form and maintain it. She has been helping me with—" Eldwyn cleared his throat again.

"Where are you staying?" Cerdwin asked, abruptly changing topics as he turned to the large oak table behind him. There was a complete map of the city prominently displayed on it, amongst other maps, papers, and weapons. "We shall both pay you a visit once she has returned."

"I—" she started.

"Here," Eldwyn cut in, and Cerdwin whipped toward the male.

"Here," Cerdwin said slowly.

Eldwyn nodded. "I figured it was my duty to ensure your friend received proper lodging. I will also ensure careful word is sent above to smooth over any friction." The candles in the room flared, and Elana watched Cethin's hand reach for his blade. It was nothing short of a miracle that Eldwyn had allowed them to keep their weapons on the ship—and then bring them into a military camp.

Cerdwin's eyes shone as brightly as the flickering flames. The male had dropped his arms to his sides, but his fists were bunched together tightly. Eldwyn walked forward quickly, as if he would shield them all from the roaring, fiery magic that lined the Second Commander's body.

"Cerdwin," Eldwyn said in a voice that was commanding yet gentle. Elana felt the male's own gift of air spread around them. It wasn't quite air now, but almost smoke—no, steam, matching Cerdwin's magic. The candles in the tent resumed their normal cadence, and the fire in Cerdwin's eyes dimmed from a burning maroon to a sparkling amethyst. Eldwyn stepped back to Cerdwin's side, leaned against the table, and crossed his arms.

"If he has a problem with it," Eldwyn said, voice clear and even, "I will handle him."

"Him who?" Cethin demanded.

"My lord father," Cerdwin said quietly. "Lord Arel Satrara—Head of the Lord's Council." One of the lords in service to her mother and father during the Breaking. One of the lords present for her unsuccessful coronation. And now, apparently, the main person responsible for keeping her kingdom together while she'd been gone.

But it wasn't his to rule—not forever.

This was *her* city.

These were *her* people.

"If it's too much trouble," Cethin said, stepping forward, "we can find other accommodations."

"No need," Eldwyn replied. "It's been a while since I've seen something rattle him."

A touch of a smile graced Cerdwin's face. "True," he agreed, if not a bit stiffly. Well, if they were already talking about it...

"If that's the case," Elana said, folding her hands together in front of her, "and we are to stay here, in the camp"—she looked Cerdwin straight in the eye—"I would ask that we train. And that we help with any scouting or sentry work—whatever you need."

Cerdwin sighed. "Elana," he said, and she hated the change to his tone. "I know I taught you in Ozul, and you did well—Hell, really well, if you saved his ass," he said, casting a look in Cethin's direction. The half-Elf's eyes held nothing but spite as he took the jab. "But things are different here. These are all fully-blooded Elvish males—soldiers—who have been training to fight, track, scout, and kill, some since they were younglings. I am sorry, but there is no place for you here. And any help you *could* give..." He exhaled. "Without your Elvish form to wield Healing magic..." He sighed again and ran a hand through his golden mane. "Even as the Second Commander of Aviva's armies, son of the Lord of Aviva, I could not consent to let a—for our purposes right now—basically human woman train alongside my males. There would be too many problems. Too many questions. You have to understand that."

She felt Cethin inch closer to her, knew he sensed the shaking rage she was trying so hard to fight. Elana leveled a flat look at Cerdwin. "Then who is the First Commander of Aviva's armies?"

"That would be me."

Chapter 11

Elana

Elana looked at the male who'd brought them to the shores of Aviva, who'd let them right into the city, right into the camp—armed.

Where Cerdwin appeared to be a constant inferno of calculation, assessment, and discernment—at war between the Second Commander and the lord's son, and the untamed golden flame she believed was her friend at heart—Eldwyn was somehow more and less complex at the same time. Someone more mature, someone—*something*—older. It was like he could see beneath all of the layers, stories, and forms she'd woven around herself—like his power blew them all away and revealed the essence beneath.

"I'll allow it," Eldwyn said. Elana nodded, preparing to thank him, but—

"But I'm not saying it'll be easy," he went on, coming to a stand right in front of her. Cethin took a step toward her. "You—both of you"—Eldwyn nodded to her life-sworn—"will be under constant observation, judgment, derision, and worse. Being in one of Aviva's units is not an easy thing. We make it that way for a reason." Elana hoped her gulp wasn't audible.

"But you survived a Noir attack." Those depthless silver eyes found hers again, and a breeze shifted between them. "That isn't something many of my males could say."

"Until Alanna returns," Cerdwin said firmly. "After that, she helps you shift, and we re-evaluate your position. But, I swear to the Gods, if I hear one word of any distraction, any disruption—"

"It won't be from us." Cethin's voice was pure steel beside her.

It was Cerdwin's turn to smirk. "I am sure."

"It won't," Elana said loudly over the males. She looked back to Eldwyn. "You have my word."

"Then allow me to show you to your tent."

The tent was more spacious than Elana had expected—not as large or elegant as Cerdwin's; no, as Second Commander and Lord Arel's son, he had all of the trappings that came with his title and position. Someday, Elana mused as they entered their quarters, he would be Second Commander of *her* forces. The concept rattled her.

Would she do it?

Could she do it?

And if, once she achieved her aims, the lord still intended his son to be her husband...

In Ozul, Elana had been sure she would never feel anything for Cerdwin beyond friendship—but would it be different here?

Eldwyn pointed out how the tent was divided: the communal space, which they were currently in, and three curtained off additions—two bedrooms and a washing room. Once again, more than she'd anticipated, and Cethin raised an eyebrow at the First Commander. Eldwyn shrugged and said its former occupants weren't expected to return anytime soon—and that, as life-sworn, they may as well share the space. Elana didn't miss the smug smile that briefly touched Cethin's lips as he glanced at her. She fought to keep her eyes on Eldwyn, urging the warm, tingling sensation Cethin's look gave her to stay buried deep down with her magic.

They still hadn't spoken about everything that had happened over the past—what was it, two days now? Time had become a blur since they'd fled the barn, boarded the boat, crossed the strait, and come to the city. Now, they were here; now, the first phase of her plan was so carefully, so luckily sliding into place...

A wave of anxiety washed over Elana as she registered that Eldwyn would soon take his leave, and they would be alone again.

Just say the word, El. What is it you want now? Cethin's words from the night in the barn rang through her head, her heart, her essence. What *did* she want from him? Marrying a half-Elf mercenary would never be an option. She allowed herself a silent laugh—no, that wasn't something either of them would ever want.

"I suggest you wash up, eat, and prepare for the fake night," Eldwyn was saying, his last words recapturing her attention. Fake night, that's what they called it in Aviva, with no true day or night—not while the Light of Aviva shone over the kingdom at all hours. It had been a long time since she'd slept—even with the brief nap she'd taken on the boat. Exhaustion weighed on her as the First Commander added, "We meet at the first hour tomorrow for training." He jerked his head to the right. "Sparring ring is a few tents down. Even if you don't wake up in time, you'll hear it." She caught the meaning behind his words: don't be late. She nodded, as did Cethin, who'd finished surveying the space and turned back to the male.

"Thank you," Elana said, and Eldwyn inclined his head to her.

"Anything for my friend's friend...*lady*," the First Commander tossed in Cethin's direction with a wink. A sly grin appeared on the half-Elf's face. If they started trusting each other, if the two males became *friends...Gods help her*. And if Cethin became friends with Cerdwin...

Elana frowned as she replayed their brief encounter. She'd seen Cerdwin protective and loyal, but never so defensive—so unyielding. Perhaps the fire magic burning beneath his skin had something to do with it, more so now that he was back in his Elvish form. *Males*. One of the many reasons she'd steered clear from any of them lurking in a man's skin in Ozul. Territorial, possessive, domineering—not particularly attractive traits. Except for Cerdwin. He'd always been her exception.

How different would she be once she shifted into her Elvish body? Would she find herself bending toward the wishes of males, even though she outranked them all?

"Something on your mind?" Cethin asked as Eldwyn departed.

"Yes—a bath." It was the first thing that popped into her mind—a way to separate herself from him while she sifted through the multitude of half thoughts piling up in her head, the weight of them collecting into a light pain at the nape of her neck.

Apparently, it was the wrong thing to say. His grin spread, golden light flaring in his rich caramel eyes. "Oh?" he said, stalking a step closer.

"Yes." She balled her hands into fists at her sides—to punch him or restrain herself from doing so, she wasn't sure. "For you." She sniffed delicately. "You stink." Cethin's growl mixed with his rough laugh chased her the remaining steps out of the tent.

Elana let the breeze cool her blood and soothe her head as she caught up with Eldwyn and asked the First Commander for a tour of the rest of the camp. Whether or not the male noticed her flushed cheeks or rushed words, he didn't say.

Cethin

He was more than finished bathing and dressing when El returned. Cethin heard her bid the First Commander farewell outside of their tent as he eased himself onto one of the beds. Heard her step cautiously into the space, then the bathing room. Heard the thud of her clothes and daggers falling to the ground. Then, a splash and a small groan and a contented sigh that had him clenching his teeth together. She'd stepped into the warm water. *Naked.*

He'd planned to dump the muddy, bloody water out and find some fresh, clean, warm water for her before she returned. But the second he'd exited the tub and reached for one of the towels stacked on a nearby table, the water had shuddered, shimmered, and turned clear, steam wafting from its surface. He'd gawked at it and carefully swirled one of his hands through it—*magic.*

Something he'd never have.

Cethin sighed and stared up at the tent ceiling. The canvas wasn't thick enough to block out all of the Light. It would be a change, getting used to being here, in a kingdom he had no memory of being born in—and no real memory of the mother or father who'd left him in Ozul.

Most Elves in Ozul stayed in their human bodies, so they couldn't use their magic—not unless they shifted forms, earning either utter contempt or wondrous praise from nearby humans. Either way, they'd never be looked at the same way by their friends or neighbors—or families, he supposed. Families that produced half-breeds like him.

Half-Elf, half-breed—whatever they decided to call him here, it wouldn't be kind—especially in the training ring. He might have some of the fully-blooded Elves' skills—if not more—but those would be outweighed by their senses, strength, and speed.

And magic.

And El...why had she asked for this? For them to train with the soldiers—*both* of them? And why had she agreed to stay in this tent in the camp? Cethin was well aware of how females had been treated by males over the centuries, regardless of how much time had passed or progress was made. Females of the royal bloodline were lucky in that regard. But when King Ewan had passed, even Queen Serenity—along with her influence—had dwindled. It was easier for people to return to their ways rather than to embrace change. It made a part of him sad. Although women on the human continent weren't held to the same level as the men, they owned their own shops, had their own businesses, and had some say in their marriages. The queen-to-be of the Southern Kingdom even trained, insisted on having her own unit of women in the royal army. But in Aviva...

It wouldn't be easy tomorrow. Not for him, but especially not for El—even if Cerdwin or Eldwyn were present. The others wouldn't take it easy on them. Cethin closed his eyes and released his breath, listening to the sounds of water splashing a mere curtain away.

Whether or not he understood her plan, he trusted her. Trusted that she had gotten them into this jumble of ancient opinions and politics and camp of domineering male warriors for a reason.

And he would raise his blade to anyone who got in her way.

Cerdwin

He closed his eyes and willed himself to not allow the leash on his power to slip again as he watched Eldwyn, Elana, and Cethin exit his tent.

Elana. Cerdwin didn't think he'd ever see her again, yet here she was—and with a half-Elvish mercenary at her side.

He sighed, opened his eyes, walked around the table to a small decanter, and poured himself a glass of whiskey to steady his mind for the conversation that was coming with Eldwyn's return.

Cerdwin had first seen Eldwyn in the Commander's camps. Cerdwin had been barely out of his youngling years, and the male had been a rising member of Aviva's military forces. Though Eldwyn had come from a humble lineage, he was so skilled the Lord's Council had made an exception. Cerdwin had been deemed talented enough by his private instructors that he trained with the soldiers, but his main priority in the camp was to learn from the blacksmith there—his lord father thought it would help him get control of his fire magic. So he'd learned to both fight and forge, to do something besides study or dally with the mindless ladies of the court who had no ambitions beyond becoming a future lord's wife. To do something that actually mattered—something that felt like *him*.

Cerdwin's twin sister, Alanna, had been of the same mind in that area. She'd worked endlessly with her Healing gift—even when their lord father had threatened to force her into her mortal form to make her stop. Alanna had refused and earned the attention of the High Healers. She'd moved out of their family's quarters in the lord's apartments and into the open garden level where the Healers dwelled and kept training. She'd even saved the life of another lord the day the princess of Aviva had disappeared—at least, that's what her letters had said. Cerdwin's lord father had sent him—his only son, heir to his title—to Ozul before that fateful day.

Cerdwin had always listened to his lord father's wisdom. Alanna had always been more spirited. And now, as a High Healer herself, she wasn't held to the lord's standards. Cerdwin smiled thinking about her. While they both looked more like their mother than their father, Alanna had their mother's spirit, too—at least, what Cerdwin remembered of it.

The tent's opening shifted, and Cerdwin threw back the rest of his drink.

"What were you thinking?" he asked as Eldwyn entered. The male ignored him, came around the table, refilled the glass Cerdwin had just emptied, and took a drink of his own.

"I figured I was doing us all a favor." The male shrugged, set the glass down, and faced him.

"A favor?!" Cerdwin demanded.

"Yes. I thought I was doing your friend a favor by helping her leave the human continent to return here, to her home. I thought I was doing you both a favor by bringing her here, to you. And I thought I was doing all of us a favor by allowing them to stay here and train. A female in a mortal body and a half-Elf, both already somewhat skilled. Both having escaped the Noir." Eldwyn shrugged again. "It might be useful to send them about certain activities we do not wish to send our males for."

Cerdwin closed his eyes and willed the rising heat in his blood to calm, breathed deeply like Alanna had taught him. He wasn't sure which part of his magic was more riled: his fire gift or the animal form that'd wanted to rip into the mercenary's neck on sight.

"So you presumed to reunite me with my friend, keep her in this camp, and send her on scouting missions with a bastard mercenary, all to piss off the Lord's Council and keep our own males in line?" Cerdwin opened his eyes and reached for the decanter again. Eldwyn was already holding a full glass out to him. The corners of the First Commander's mouth tugged upward, and he winked.

"This is why I still outrank you," Eldwyn commented, moving to sit in one of the chairs off to the side of the tent. Cerdwin rolled his eyes, but Eldwyn shook his head. "Truly, Cerdwin," he said, gazing at one of the candles on a shelf stacked high with maps, books, and papers. "You could lead this army. You have the fire power. You have your...other form," the male added more quietly. "Your abilities exceed those of any other male in this camp—in this city. If you mastered your emotions...

"I don't mean to cause more trouble between you and your father," Eldwyn continued. "And I don't mean your friend any harm. Quite frankly"—he leaned back in the wooden chair and crossed his ankles on the low lying table across from it—"I have a feeling she can take care of herself."

"Well, I *did* train her," Cerdwin mumbled, and Eldwyn's lips twitched.

"I believe you. And so will the males in the camp. They'll know better than to try and lay their hands on her."

A low growl rose in Cerdwin's throat.

"Although I have a feeling," Eldwyn mused, wholly ignoring him, "that her life-sworn will present a much larger threat to anyone who even gets the idea in his head."

"And what, exactly, is *that* supposed to mean?" Cerdwin said, stalking for the chair facing the male's.

Eldwyn snorted. "You mean to tell me you didn't read what lies between them, beyond the bond of their life oath?" Cerdwin shook his head. "Gods, Cerdwin—"

"Not all of us can speak to the wind," Cerdwin snapped. "And I do not need the details."

Eldwyn's eyes twinkled. "Jealous?"

Cerdwin took another deep breath and closed his eyes for a count of three, then opened them again. "No."

Eldwyn chuckled and ran a thumb over his bottom lip. "I didn't think she was your type."

"Now is not the time for that conversation."

Eldwyn uncrossed his ankles and rose to his feet. "Indeed," he said, eyes frosting over as if he'd been bitten by an icy winter wind. "I will see you at the first hour tomorrow." He strode to the tent's door, and Cerdwin watched him leave.

They were about to be in some serious horseshit.

Elana

Elana sank deeper into the warm water, groaning as the comfort of it wrapped around her tired muscles. While there were problems with the way Aviva was run, she had missed the perks of magic—and it had to be magic heating the water.

She'd peppered Eldwyn with enough questions to keep them away from the tent—away from Cethin—for a long while, long enough that she hoped the male would be asleep when they returned. She hadn't seen Cethin when she'd entered their common area, and he hadn't been in the bathing chamber, either. So Elana had quickly and quietly stripped and entered the tub. Now, she let herself settle into its embrace, watching small wafts of steam trail up and away over her head. Even the ache in the back of her neck faded. Sleep would claim her soon after she finished bathing, and food...when was the last time she'd eaten? Elana couldn't remember, but the debilitating fatigue that gripped her told her enough: food would have to come later—sleep first.

Finding a bar of soap next to a dry towel and a washing cloth next to the metal tub, she picked them up and scrubbed off any remaining dirt and blood from her face and arms. Then, she sank deeper into the tub as she untangled her hair from the braid it had been in for the Gods only knew how long. Her dark hair was as tangled as her own life. It had been a long journey back here—back home. But she'd made it.

Elana smiled to herself as she continued washing her back and neck, the ache there almost completely gone now. If she could make it back, if she could come back, if she could fight through the guilt, the pain, the shadows of memories—she could do anything, become who she was meant to be.

And maybe she wouldn't have to do it alone.

Elana rose from the tub before she drowned at the warm water's behest. Dressing herself in fresh undergarments, loose black leggings, and a slightly large blue tunic, she stumbled blearily through the nearest canvas and dropped onto the cot that rose up to meet her.

Cethin

The sounds of morning birds summoned Cethin from sleep. The animals remained, even though the Light of Aviva persisted. *Fucking Hell, how did they keep track of time here?* He shifted on the cot, preparing to rise, only to find his arm pinned by a heavy object.

Instantly on alert, Cethin tugged at his arm and used his free one to reach for one of the daggers he'd placed under what barely passed as a pillow. But the object...*grunted*?

Blinking sleep from his eyes, the object—or rather, the person—who had him wedged there became clear: El.

They hadn't shared a bed since those early days in Ozul, after she'd suggested she was uninterested in such close contact. But the barn—then the boat. Cethin gazed down at the female clinging to his arm. Her brown hair was slightly damp and flowed around her face, free of the braid she normally wore it in. Her eyes were closed, and her breathing was an even sound through her parted lips. *Lovely.* She looked so lovely, and more peaceful than he'd ever seen her.

Cethin wasn't sure he was breathing as he slid his free arm away from the dagger. Without thinking, he lifted his fingers to brush a stray curl away from her cheek.

Her eyes fluttered open. She stared at him, her face mere inches away.

Then she pushed away from him and the cot, rolling onto the ground.

"What are you doing here?"

Cethin stared at her in shock—shock that quickly transformed into irritation.

"Me?!" he demanded. "This is my space!" She gave him a look of derision, then glanced around the sleeping area—the sleeping area filled with male's clothing, *his* clothing, and his weapons. He enjoyed watching her squirm as she rose to her feet.

Cethin reclined back on the cot and looped his hands behind his head. "Good thing neither of us sleeps in the nude," he said. She threw him a withering stare.

"I-I was tired," she spat back at him, and he smirked.

"Then it's really a good thing neither of us sleeps in the nude. Although," he continued, looking up at the ceiling, "I rather enjoy seeing you dressed in my tunic."

Her snarl had him turning back to her—

El ripped the tunic off over her head and threw it at him. Cethin couldn't help it; he looked over her bare skin until the white linen of a breast band appeared. Her eyes were pure storm as he met her gaze.

"Hoping to see something more?" she demanded and stomped out of the space. Cethin grinned, folding the tunic and placing it on the table next to his cot.

They both knew the answer to that question—whether she'd admit it or not.

Elana

Elana cursed Cethin thoroughly as she yanked a new tunic—a tunic clearly made for a female—over her head in the adjoining sleeping chamber. Then, she cursed *herself* for not paying more attention to where she slept. She'd been so tired, and the cot had been warm and inviting—because she was so exhausted. Not because of Cethin's presence. But she'd slept so easily on the boat to Aviva...

He was her life-sworn, yes, but maybe also her friend?

Something more?

"El." Cethin's voice came from outside the curtain that partitioned off her sleeping area. "If you're done being embarrassed, we're going to be late for training. Not that I need it, but you—"

Cursing again—loudly enough that the half-Elf could hear—Elana tucked her locket into her bag—it would only be a hindrance during training—threw on the new boots neatly lined up by her cot—a perfect fit—and strapped Cerdwin's knives to her hips.

Chapter 12

Elana

Brutal was the least descriptive word Elana could think of to describe their first day of training—not only because of the stretches, exercises, and endless fighting stances Cerdwin made them practice over and over again, but also because of the eyes that were on her.

It was a camp for newer recruits, Eldwyn had explained to her, to see who would be most useful in upcoming conflicts against the Dark King's forces. One of Cerdwin's less glamorous jobs as Second Commander, the male had admitted with a flicker of amusement in his eyes. Eldwyn's own camp was a few miles north, where the Avivan army's elite scouts, spies, and soldiers resided. The rest of the army was spread into camps around the city, at points along the inside of the wall, and at the base of the castle itself, where a small barrack offered residence. Once, Elana remembered, that area had been used as housing for visiting royalty or nobility; that had been before the Battle of the Breaking, before Aviva had been cut off from the rest of the world. But they would need allies before the end.

Elana wondered if it was also worse because the First Commander wasn't there for their initial training day—he softened something in Cerdwin. And she knew she hadn't become *that* sloppy in the time she and Cerdwin had been apart; in fact, she'd learned more during those weeks on the road with Cethin—something Cerdwin had apparently noticed and was displeased with. Not with the techniques, she assumed, but that Cethin had been the one to teach her. When Cerdwin's burning stare wasn't focused on the slight adjustments she'd made to her old techniques under Cethin's instruction, it was on Cethin himself. But Cethin wasn't paying any attention to the Second Commander. No, his gaze was entirely on her as well—and it wasn't the look of a warrior assessing an ally or partner.

Lost in daydreams of golden eyes, Elana swore as she stumbled during an exercise Cerdwin had already made them do three times. Last night had been an honest mistake with the cot—and the tunic. A mistake the male would likely hold over her head for the rest of his life. But waking up in his arms, with him gazing down at her like—like *what*, she wasn't entirely sure—had felt strangely peaceful, so at odds with the constant noise and internal dialogue in her mind; between her body and her magic; the duty she owed her people and this newfound desire to not only reclaim her kingdom, but also claim something for herself. Something that was hers, and hers alone.

A strong hand gripped her shoulder and steadied her. Elana looked up and found a male smiling down at her.

"Alright there?" he asked. She smiled and nodded.

His name was Alaric, she remembered. He seemed like a decent male. After his initial introduction at the beginning of their session, he offered to partner up with her during one of their first training exercises, seemingly unabashed at her being there. Now he, along with most of the other males in the training ring, had taken their shirts off, sweat dripping down their strong warrior's bodies, nothing but flesh and heat—but no steel, not yet, at Cerdwin's behest. That, apparently, would be part of a later lesson.

And no magic. A Healer had come by that morning and erected a barrier against any magic use by the males who resided in the camp. They wouldn't be training with magic for weeks. No, this session—and the ones that followed—was about strength of body and sheer force of will.

There were twenty other males training with them in one of the four training rings in the camp, she recalled from Eldwyn's tour, and Cerdwin would rotate them throughout the week. Elana saw the malice that flickered in the displeased looks those males threw in Cethin's direction, though none would say anything with their commanding officer present—the Second Commander who allowed the half-Elf into their camp.

And a female who couldn't shift. *Would things be worse after she shifted?* She would be a female amongst so many males—and a seemingly useless one at that. Her moonlit power had only manifested a few times under great duress, and she wasn't ready to show anyone that. And Elana hadn't felt a drop of the Healing power all female Elves possessed to some degree.

When the soldiers learned that it was the lost princess who trained alongside them...it might never come to that, though—not if Cerdwin's lord father had anything to say about it, Elana guessed. She would probably be forced behind the palace gates, held there for as long as it took to confirm she was heir to the throne of Aviva and then either celebrated for returning by being joined in a union with whomever the Lord's Council deemed suitable—likely Cerdwin—or tossed into the dungeons for fleeing on her coronation day. But Eldwyn had also mentioned a scouting mission to test them—and Elana had every intention of being a part of that, every intention of proving her worth to them all.

Her foot slipped again. This time, she threw out a hand to steady her balance herself. Cerdwin's eyes weighed on her; Cethin's eyes…

She wouldn't allow herself to be distracted—not in the ring, and not in any upcoming battles. When she was training or fighting, she wasn't the lost princess. She wasn't El—nothing to Cethin. She was Elana, and she was there to serve her kingdom. That grounded her, and she pushed through the next set of exercises flawlessly, if not breathlessly.

"Enough." Cerdwin's voice—harsher than she'd ever heard it in Ozul—clanged through the ring. "Morning training is over. You have an hour to rest, eat, bathe, fuck—whatever you like. We meet back here when that hour is over."

For what? Elana wanted to ask, but kept her mouth shut. The other males splintered off, those who'd removed their shirts tossing them back on as they headed back to the tents—or outside the limits of the camp, to the city beyond.

Cethin had apparently taken his shirt off at some point, too: his abdominal muscles were on display and slick with sweat, defined by the ever-present Light. One side of his mouth kicked up when he caught her eye. She looked away, only to find Cerdwin approaching them.

"My tent. Now," the male said tightly, and stalked off.

Elana started following him—

But her vision swam. She lurched forward. Strong arms grabbed her, and a familiar voice was in her ear—not speaking to her, but about her, as black spots crowded her eyes.

"Food first," Cethin said firmly. She was vaguely aware of Cerdwin turning back to where they still stood in the ring. "We are not like your males," Cethin said. "Least of all her."

Elana wanted to protest, but Cethin was right. She was still in her mortal body and still couldn't remember the last time she'd eaten. Through the haze, she saw Cerdwin's eyes rest on her.

"You have twenty minutes," he said firmly, but his gaze softened.

Cethin

Lunch was quick, but he watched El closely to make sure she had enough—even rationed some of his fare over to her, which she accepted without protest or question. It had been three—maybe four—days since they'd last shared a meal together.

While El took his food, she avoided his gaze. Cethin wondered if it was because of the attention he'd received during training, or some emotion lingering over the change that'd passed between them since they'd arrived. He might tease her—toy with her—but any continuation, any extension of the friendship they'd built, that would be her decision—even if it would shatter something fundamental in him if she walked away.

They were in Cerdwin's tent less than twenty minutes later, Cethin noted with no small amount of satisfaction. He'd picked up on the Second Commander's timekeeping strategy, which involved casting several rocks and sticks in the shade. Rudimentary at best, but better than having to simply *guess* when true sunrise and true sunset were. Cethin missed both after only one day. He'd spent most of his life rising with the sun, traveling, working, and training and then spending coin long past sunset. Real night was what he missed most now: the clear, vast blackness of a night sky with a smattering of stars overhead while he was on the river; the moon, half hidden by clouds on a misty night in the forest; the mysterious, secretive nature of the night itself, and the beauty of the light that touched it. Here, it was nothing but that endless, insufferable Light. How could they stand it, after almost fifty years? Although the alternative, what they might all face someday: complete, unyielding Darkness with the pain, terror, and destruction that followed it...

"What did you make of our first training session?" Cerdwin's question was directed at him.

"No worse than any others I've been a part of." Cethin smirked and enjoyed the spark behind the male's purple eyes. Magic was bound in the camp, but the shield the Healer put in place hadn't been able to contain all of Cerdwin's fire, it seemed.

"It will only become more difficult from here," the male warned. "Especially now that the others have seen you and marked you." As weak or as a threat, the Second Commander didn't say.

"We'll be fine, Cerdwin," El interjected, stepping in front of him, much to his—and Cerdwin's—surprise.

The Second Commander's face became as hard as adamant. "It is not only the physical training I am worried about," he said, sighing and running a hand through his curls. "The others will not make this an easy or pleasant experience for either of you."

"I can only hope they do not." Another shot of surprise—and pride—flickered through Cethin at her words. If Cerdwin's aim had been to scare her—both of them—out of the camp, he'd failed.

"I do not think you understand, Elana," the Second Commander said, voice taking on a rough edge. "Only the strongest and most capable males make it here. They work and train hard. And without an outlet here for their magic, they tend to look for other ways to…let go," he said, voice faltering on the last words. "Fights can break out in the camp, and they go into the city for pleasure, but with you here—"

Cethin couldn't hear anything but the blood roaring in his ears as his brain worked through exactly what the male meant. Didn't hear El's reply before she turned from the Second Commander and left the tent, leaving him and Cerdwin staring at each other.

"Cethin." El's voice came from the entrance of the pavilion where she waited for him.

"I'll be there in a moment," he replied, not breaking Cerdwin's gaze. He heard her sigh, then could've sworn he heard her roll her eyes, too. The tent flap closed.

"I will say this once, and only once," Cethin told the Second Commander, ensuring his tone was low and deadly—the voice of the mercenary he was raised to be. "If any of *your* males in *your* camp lay a hand on her, it will not only be *them* I hold responsible."

A trace of fire appeared in the male's eyes. "Are you threatening me, *half-Elf*?"

"Not threatening, *Second Commander*. Promising."

Elana

An afternoon of additional training passed, and Cerdwin finally announced they were finished for the day.

Their *first* day.

Elana did her best to not let the other trainees see her arms and legs shaking as she made her way back to her and Cethin's tent. Cethin offered her the bath first, and she accepted—then snuck out when he took his turn.

She didn't want to spend the few hours they had between the end of training and the beginning of the fake night with him in their accommodations—no, it would be far too easy for her to do or say something to further embarrass herself. Or something else she'd regret. So Elana dressed quickly, put on her new boots, slung a spare cloak around her shoulders, and left their tent. Cerdwin had requested that they—actually, had demanded that *she*, specifically—not wander the camp unaccompanied after training, lest she run into some sort of trouble with the other males. But she didn't intend to wander the camp.

She intended to wander the city.

It was different from the day she'd walked through the city for her mother's funeral procession, all eyes on her in her black mourning garb: the Princess of Aviva, the heir apparent. No one looked at her twice as she walked the streets now, taking in the sights and smells, the *feel* of the kingdom she'd once called hers—and would again. She passed the wall and its hidden doors, the painted homes of the humans and half-Elves, then wove her way to the streets of the finer homes of the merchants and nobles. At one point, she found herself on a road that led to the palace gates. She wasn't prepared to face that. Not yet.

Turning away, Elana mingled with the crowds, looked through store windows, and spent some of the coin she'd stuffed into her pockets on food from the street vendors—food so delicious she craved more of its flavor. Then, there was the music—even more beautiful than she had remembered; although no longer as charming to her ears as the combined music of the different peoples on the mortal continent. The memory of her time on the mortal continent dimmed something in her, so Elana made her way back to the camp. It had been a few hours, and most of its occupants were probably asleep.

The camp's pathways were as empty as she'd suspected—most of the soldiers were abed or otherwise preparing for another day of training. She was surprised her legs had had the strength and mobility to carry her through the city streets after such a long day. Will had fueled her forward in those hours—will and the desire to see everything. Now, back in the camp, that mortal weariness sank back into her body.

Weariness that meant it took Elana a moment to register what was happening when she was suddenly pressed into the support beam of a tent—one that faced away from the sentries on patrol.

"What an interesting *female* you are," came a rough male voice, followed by a long inhale next to her hair. Elana found herself face-to-face with a male she didn't remember from their training ring. No doubt word of her and Cethin's presence had spread in the hours since then. "I would love to see what lurks beneath this useless facade." A smile twisted the male's features, and there was no kindness in it. "A lone female amongst us all. You must be special."

Elana cringed at the scent of alcohol on his breath and made to move away, but the male struck her right cheek. A splintering noise cracked under the sting of his palm. She'd heard rumors of how males treated females in war camps—unless they were Healers—and this was just a training camp.

You have an hour to rest, eat, bathe, fuck—whatever you like. Cerdwin's words came back to her—so indifferent from the male she'd known in

Ozul. Maybe his warnings hadn't been completely unwarranted. But this would be *her* kingdom, *her* people—*her* army. She wouldn't yield, not to this impetuous male who only saw her as something to claim. Gods above, if he only knew who she really was.

Elana shifted her stance and went for the knife hanging by the male's side, silently cursing herself for leaving Cerdwin's daggers in the tent. This male was a fully-blooded Elf, faster and stronger than she was, but he didn't know her—didn't know her training. She had the element of surprise.

Grasping his blade, Elana kicked out her legs, swept the male's own from underneath him, and landed on top of him. She dragged the dagger lightly—but deep enough to cut—across his chest. He wore no armor—only a light tunic, as she did. A small noise came out of him as she settled the dagger against his skin, shock flaring in his eyes.

"It would seem that—in addition to combat training—some etiquette lessons are also needed in this camp," she hissed. He made to rise, but she pushed the dagger back down—deeper this time, making a line twin to the one above it. He stopped fighting, eyes wary. "You will not touch me without my permission. In fact," she continued, "you will never touch another female or woman without their express permission ever again. If you do"—she gave him a smile—"I will know." Let him decide what that meant about any magic he couldn't feel from her.

Pushing up and away from him, Elana threw his dagger back in the direction she'd come from and strode toward the tent. Her whole body shook with anger—and worry over what Cerdwin would make of what she'd just done. She hoped the trainee's pride was so thoroughly wounded he kept his mouth shut.

She pushed through the tent and toward her personal area to get to the washing room. "El, where the Otherworld have you be—" Cethin's voice came from her right, then stopped. She lingered as he stared at her, stiffened when his nostrils flared and his eyes marked the throbbing spot on her cheek. She stiffened further when he walked over to her, coming to a stop right in front of her. He reached a hand—the hand scarred with their life oath—up and gently explored the mark the male had left. Elana closed her eyes, shuddering beneath his touch. She hadn't thought about Cethin.

"Who?" Cethin's voice was lower and deadlier than it had been that day in the woods.

She opened her eyes and shook her head. "I took care of it."

His eyes narrowed as his hand moved down to grip her chin, tilting her face up to meet his gaze. "Who."

"I took care of it," she repeated, staring into his deep caramel eyes. There wasn't even a slight shine of gold in them now.

They stood there for several moments until Cethin dropped his hand and exited the tent. Elana stared wordlessly after him, hoping he wasn't about to do something incredibly stupid.

Cethin

He stalked silently through the camp, blood howling in his veins, unseen forces urging him to find whoever had marked his life-sworn.

It wouldn't do them any good if he found the male. Cethin would kill whoever it was, which would result in getting himself—and El—kicked out of the camp.

Or worse.

He wouldn't interfere with her plans.

I took care of it.

Cethin trusted her. But still...

He'd felt something through the scar in his palm. The sensation had roused him from the warm water of the bathing tub he'd half dozed off in—he couldn't help it; it was the first time in ages he'd relaxed, even in the middle of a training camp.

But it had cost him—cost *her.*

He hadn't been quick enough.

He hadn't been there for her.

Elana

Elana shrugged off her clothes, sweaty and dusty from walking through the city but not bloodied from the male she'd encountered—at least there was that. A wash would take care of his lingering scent.

She sank into the tub, closed her eyes, and hoped Cethin wasn't doing something that would likely get them both kicked out of the camp—or worse, especially for him. She'd seen the flicker of guilt in his eyes when he'd realized what had happened, but she didn't understand that guilt. Was it because he hadn't been there? He hadn't exactly been there that day in the woods, either; at least, not right away. She'd screamed for him then.

That had been different, though. Their relationship—what they meant to each other—had changed. But they couldn't—she couldn't—let that get in the way of things.

Toweling off and dressing in clothes she had no doubt were hers, Elana decided to ask Cerdwin for access—even if it wasn't direct access—to the Royal Archives to learn more about the life oath. There had to be some explanation about the connection, the emotions—the feelings—that would help.

"El?" Cethin's tone still had an edge to it, but it was also softer, kinder, than it had been before he'd left. Finishing braiding her hair, Elana walked through the flap that connected to his space. He patted the space next to where he sat on his cot. "Sit."

His eyes didn't leave the mark on her face as she made her way to the spot next to him. Her heart was pounding. What would he say? But there was no blood on him—not on his face or hands. There was no sign of any altercation at all.

But there was a small silver tin in his hands. Cethin opened it, and Elana sighed at the scent that wafted from whatever was inside. He reached his hand in, fingers covered in some sort of cream as he withdrew them. "The Healer said this may sting a bit," he murmured. "Is that alright?"

His gaze finally met hers. Elana swallowed but nodded, wincing as he pressed some of the balm to her skin. Her cheek tingled—whatever Healing power the balm possessed soothed her stinging skin.

"She said it will help with any pain and"—Cethin reached back in for more, fingers trailing soft lines down her face—"reduce any mark left behind."

Elana remained silent as he made a third pass across her cheek, then closed the tin and wiped the remnants of the salve on his pants.

"You should get some sleep," he said, placing the tin on his bedside stand. He pulled himself onto the cot. But Elana was frozen—surprised by what he'd just done; not only by leaving well enough alone, by trusting her—but also by caring for her in a way that felt so...*intimate.* His behavior was so at odds with the male she'd met in Ozul: no arrogance, no male swagger, no joking or teasing. Just Cethin. Part of who he was—who he would've been—if he hadn't been cast into the life of a mercenary.

Elana laid down beside him, curled one arm under her head, and tucked her knees into her chest. As she drifted off to sleep, she felt Cethin roll onto his side and tuck her into his body.

Cerdwin

Cerdwin wasn't surprised when the male told him what had happened—that the *female,* the male had practically seethed, *he* had allowed into the camp had stabbed him. Elana could defend herself—Cerdwin had seen to that. The feeling that he was partly to blame for her having to do so here, in the city that would be her home, didn't sit well with him. Hell, stepping back into his role as Lord Arel Satrara's son wasn't comfortable, either. And stepping into his role as Second Commander...Cerdwin sighed and took another drink. It was what was expected of him, though: to be tough on his males and their training, then allow them free range during their breaks and at night. At night, they weren't his problem—nothing was.

Except tonight. Cerdwin hadn't been able to shake the heaviness in his heart after the soldier's report, so he'd gone into the city. It was something he did to escape the pressures of everything about his position—lord's son, heir, commander—and find the part of himself he'd discovered in Ozul, the part that craved freedom. The part that was still there, even though he was back in Aviva. The part he didn't know what to do with.

He kept to whatever shadows the Light cast and made his way to a bar he doubted any of his males frequented in a lower section of the city. He'd been there many times to meet with an old friend. But tonight, he just wanted to be alone. And that's where his other problem came in. *Problems.*

For starters, one of his males *was* there—Alaric. The male was newer to his camp, but Cerdwin had marked him because of his lord father's orders: Alaric was one of the few Elves left—especially one of the few younger Elves left—who possessed Earth magic. Alaric was also skilled with weapons, particularly the sword. Cerdwin had already made a note in his mind to mention it to the First Commander and have Alaric promoted to his camp. Outside of that information, Cerdwin didn't know much about the male. He'd never heard stories about the trainee outside of the camp; then again, Cerdwin didn't sit around the fires with his males the way the First Commander did.

The blond-haired, green-eyed soldier appeared to be alone—not in the company of any other soldiers, at least—which was a relief, nor was he paying any attention to Cerdwin. No, the young male's attention was on a couple *occupied* at the bar. But just because no other males from his camp were there didn't mean Cerdwin didn't recognize anyone else—or, rather, *sense* anyone else.

He would probably always sense Eldwyn: the scent of snow and ice and pine that reminded Cerdwin of the northernmost peaks of the Endurnal Mountains, the light breeze that brushed up against his skin whenever the male was nearby, the tingling sensation that shot up and down his spine at their proximity.

Cerdwin had been attracted to both females and males for as long as he could remember. None gave him the feeling the First Commander did. Not that he'd—*they'd*—ever acted on it. Not outside of that one time...

"Interesting seeing you here," came Eldwyn's light-hearted tone as he sat across from Cerdwin. The male's features were evident in the flickering candlelight: almost-shaved head—but Cerdwin knew the male's hair would be a flowing silver; the scar that Cerdwin had given him when he'd lost control of his magic—a wound so deep that even Alanna hadn't been able to fully Heal it; silver eyes that could swirl with deep thought or humor. Currently, they were full of the latter. "Meeting someone?" the male suggested.

Cerdwin took another drink and leveled Eldwyn a look that said he wasn't in the mood to be fucked with. "Not tonight."

"Shame," the First Commander said, scanning Cerdwin's face with the accuracy that'd helped him earn his position. "You look like you could use a night off."

"I am having a night off—or, at least, I was," Cerdwin grumbled, more to himself than the male. But Eldwyn still heard him—he always did. *Godsdamned air magic.* The male tipped his head back and laughed. Cerdwin's breath caught. *He was beautiful when he did that.* Those silver eyes resettled on him.

"You sure about that?" The male leaned forward, stole his cup, and took a drink.

"Yes," Cerdwin said through clenched teeth. They'd had this circular conversation more times than Cerdwin could count. That night had been a mistake—one they wouldn't repeat.

One they *couldn't* repeat.

Eldwyn's face became the unreadable mask he wore when they played cards with Alanna. "We both know that's a lie."

"Lie it may be, but it changes nothing."

Eldwyn sat back. "You want to talk about it?"

It never ceased to amaze Cerdwin that, though he had dismissed—or, rather, denied—the attraction between them, the male remained. It was like having a friend.

"Trouble in the camp. Nothing I cannot handle."

"Trouble with them?" Now, it was Cerdwin's turn to assess the male—not that he would ever be able to break that blank expression. Neither of them needed to name the *them* the First Commander spoke of. Cerdwin nodded. "What do you intend to do about it?"

Cerdwin swiped his drink back—trying *not* to think about how pleasantly callused the male's hands were—and drained the rest of the ale. "I will give a warning, as is expected. Outside of that? Nothing." He willed some of the fire that ran through his blood into his eyes in challenge.

Eldwyn chuckled. "We'll make a rule breaker of you yet."

Chapter 13

Her body groaned with every movement—and it was only day two; it would only become more difficult from there. During one particularly challenging sparring session with Alaric, Elana wondered again how it would feel if she shifted, if she leaned into her stronger Elvish body. But she couldn't—not yet. Not when the shift or her magic might draw the Noir to the city. She wasn't ready to face them again.

Elana had caught her reflection in a polished shield as she and Cethin had walked to the training ring: a purplish-greenish mark ran from her temple to the lower edge of her ear on the right side of her face. It would've been much worse without Cethin's salve. She could almost feel his fingers trailing down her skin like a soothing, phantom touch. She'd also noticed the blue flowers he'd left next to her in his bed—the ones she'd loved in Ozul.

No, she wasn't ready to face that, either.

So Elana worked and pushed and trained—and avoided the hard looks Cerdwin leveled in her direction. Clearly, someone had said something.

"My tent, day's end," Cerdwin ordered her and Cethin before he left the ring at midday.

How long would it be before he told them to leave?

Cerdwin

Cerdwin waited for Elana and Cethin in his tent, pacing in front of his worktable. He stopped when he heard them enter and took in Elana—and the bruise that covered the right side of her face. Then he looked at Cethin, whose eyes were fixed on that mark as well. Cerdwin let out a short breath and leaned against his desk.

"Anything I should know?" he asked, crossing his arms. He already knew what had happened. He was also familiar with the other soldier's reputation—how impulsive the male was. He ran a hand through his curls. It was all a mess, and he had no doubt it was about to get a Hell of a lot messier. He watched Elana as she crossed her arms and stared right back at him. *Fearless.*

"You gave your males permission to do whatever they wanted. I disagreed."

Cerdwin's magic stirred beneath his bones, fighting the Healer's wards. "You *disagreed*." She nodded. "So you chose to ignore my warning about wandering the camp alone."

"I was not *wandering the camp*," she shot back at him. His temper flared. "I was *exploring* the city. This," she snapped, motioning to her face, "happened on my way back."

"What else happened?" Cerdwin asked as calmly as he could, willing the fire in his veins to subside.

"I put a stop to it, the same way any other soldier in this camp would have put a stop to something he did not like."

The beast inside of Cerdwin calmed a fraction. *Nothing else had happened.* But he wasn't finished—not yet. "Where were *you*, life-sworn, when this occurred?" he directed at Cethin, allowing his raging emotions to seep into his words. Elana had ignored him—that needed to be dealt with, even though she'd handled the situation correctly. But Cerdwin's frustration still needed an outlet, and Cethin was standing directly in his path.

"I was indisposed when she left," the half-Elf said. "I didn't realize she'd actually gone somewhere until supper." His words were spoken with a deadly softness Cerdwin supposed would've stopped a lesser male from saying anything more. That didn't stop his snort, though, or his next words.

"So I have one trainee who ignores a direct order, and another who cannot keep track of someone they are sworn to protect with their life." He caught the flicker of guilt that crossed Cethin's face.

"I didn't make it easy for him—or anyone else—to track me," Elana muttered. "You did teach me."

"That does not matter," Cerdwin snarled with frustration. "This is *not* Ozul, Elana. This is not a mortal town. The stakes are higher here." He ran a hand through his hair again. "I am constantly watched: everything I say, everything I do—I cannot show any weakness. This camp cannot show any weakness. And not being in control of two of my trainees—*especially* ones who are already an exception—is something that will be viewed as unacceptable. And you," he continued, pointing at Cethin, "need to keep a closer eye on the one you swore to protect with your life's blood. Unless—"

"That's enough." Eldwyn stepped into the space, just as Cethin looked like he might lose control.

Cerdwin stiffened. "And you—"

The First Commander held up a hand. "Enough, Cerdwin. As you said, there are eyes on you everywhere, and this conversation is becoming little more than another one of your displays." Cerdwin shut down at the male's words. He hated when Eldwyn pulled rank, hated when the male pointed out what little control he had over his magic—his emotions.

Eldwyn motioned toward Cethin. "Walk with me." The half-Elf glanced amongst the First Commander, Elana, and Cerdwin, then smirked and followed the male out of the pavilion. Cerdwin closed his eyes and exhaled deeply.

"What happened to you?"

Cerdwin opened his eyes and looked at Elana. "What do you—"

"The kind-hearted male I met in Ozul, my *friend*," she interrupted, putting an emphasis he didn't fail to notice on the word as she looked him up and down, "is not the same male who stands before me now."

Cerdwin met her stormy gaze. "It was different there. I was not bound by the rules and conventions I am now." Sensing she was about to offer a retort, he continued, "You have no idea, Elana, no idea of the pressure I am under here. To train these males so that we do not lose another battle. To be the son of a lord, *the* lord who is Head of the Council. To wield my magic..." He ran a hand through his hair again. "You have no idea the pressure I am under, the duties that bind me. Over fifty years in exile is a lot to live up to."

She let out a low laugh. "You think I do not understand pressure? That I am unfamiliar with duty?" She shook her head, hands clenching and unclenching at her sides. "You know nothing." Cerdwin stared into her eyes, falling into the dark gray look she leveled at him. Then, she turned on her heel and left him all alone.

Cethin

"I hope you'll forgive my brother-in-arms," Eldwyn said, sliding his hands into his pockets as they exited the Second Commander's tent. "The pressure he's under is enormous," the male admitted. "Unfortunately, it also tends to make him act like an ass." Cethin choked on a laugh. Eldwyn's eyebrows lifted in a bemused expression. "That being said, he isn't wrong—not about the warning he gave to Elana or his directive of you to keep a close eye on her." The male gave him an appraising look as they walked the narrow paths between the tents.

"Just because I'm life-sworn to her doesn't mean she can't take care of herself," Cethin ground out.

"Agreed," Eldwyn said to Cethin's surprise. "However, given what I know about the life-sworn, it must've been difficult for you to control your impulses."

Cethin cast a sidelong glance at the male, but Eldwyn's eyes were fixed on the tents ahead.

"It was," he admitted quietly. "But I trust her to handle things in her own way. It is her right."

He felt the male's gaze on him again. "I'm not saying I disagree with you," Eldwyn said, just as quietly. "Just that it's rare for a male to respect a female's wishes in sensitive matters like this. Typically, instinct would override any intention—good or otherwise." The male's gaze shifted forward again. "Perhaps," the First Commander mused, "the pull is muted, since you're a half-Elf, and she's still in her mortal form." He paused. "Yet...it seems to me that there might be something *more* there."

"I doubt that's any of *your* business," Cethin snapped. Eldwyn chuckled softly as he brought them to a halt in front of a small tent at the edge of the camp.

"There may be shields against magic in this camp," the male said, "but my gifts tend to be more fluid than most." A soft breeze ruffled Cethin's hair, as if in emphasis.

"The wind," the male continued, "is a friend, a spy, a lover, spilling all of her secrets—and those of everyone around us. So you will forgive us," he went on, and Cethin decided that by *us* he meant himself and the wind, "if we pick up on things others might not." Cethin opened his mouth, then closed it when Eldwyn took a step closer to him. "Your scent lingers on her." The male cocked his head to one side. "But not in the way anyone would expect it to." Cethin kept his expression neutral, and Eldwyn nodded. "I thought as much. You're better off keeping it that way."

"And why is that?"

"Because when she eventually shifts—noble lady or lower-born, powerful or barely gifted with Healing—she will be one of us. Any relationship outside of that..." Cethin's heart pounded wildly in his chest. A relationship with a half-Elf would pull her down.

But would that matter to her?

Did it matter to him?

"I tell you not to interfere or to judge," Eldwyn said. "But as a friend."

Cethin snorted. "A friend?"

Eldwyn shrugged. "Half-Elf or otherwise, you seem a decent male. You care greatly for my Cerdwin's friend. And you are not a terrible trainee, either."

"And what of your relationship?" Cethin questioned, raising a brow.

Eldwyn's smile disappeared. "I see I'm not the only observant one," the First Commander remarked, crossing his arms. "And you would do well to keep that particular observation to yourself." They stared at each other for several moments. Finally, Eldwyn sighed, lowered his arms, and motioned toward the tent.

"We are fools, both of us. Let's drink."

Elana

Cerdwin's words rang in her ears as she returned to the tent—his words about duty. Elana snorted as she scrubbed her face in the bathing chamber. *Duty.* He had no idea what that word meant to her.

Finishing washing up for the evening, she pulled on her soft sleeping clothes, then stopped and looked to her right and left. Where would she sleep? Where *should* she sleep? As if in answer, she heard the tent flap jostle and a thud as Cethin took off his boots in the adjoining section. She scurried from the washing room to her side of the tent and laid down, listening quietly while Cethin used the bathing supplies. When he finished, she could've sworn that a small sliver of her side opened quickly, then closed again.

Elana closed her eyes and willed sleep to come, but it didn't. After tossing and turning for what felt like hours—though it was probably minutes—she heard the seam to her quarters open again.

"Having trouble sleeping?" She glared up at Cethin, at that swagger—which, admittedly, she almost sagged with relief to hear again—in his voice.

"I'm fine."

"Really? Because I can hear you the whole way on the other side of our tent."

Elana sighed. She really wished she could throw him into the washroom on his ass. But there was something different, something softer in his eyes.

"May I join you?" His question was rough, barely audible, even in the silence of the camp. She swallowed. All of this talk about honor and duty—wasn't it part of hers to keep a boundary? Part of hers to withstand emotion, so that one day she might attain a relationship that would be praised, that would be the gain of the entire kingdom?

What could she possibly offer him then?

Nevertheless, she found herself saying, in a voice as quiet as his, "Yes."

Cethin gave her a soft smile that tugged at something in her heart as he made his way to the cot and lay facing toward her. They remained like that for some time in silence, though her heart was anything but quiet or calm as she stared into his amber eyes.

"I'm sorry," he eventually said. "I'm sorry I wasn't there for you." The guilt that laced his voice tugged at that piece of her heart even more.

"There's nothing to apologize for," she said, briefly closing her eyes. "You may be my life-sworn, but I'm still my own person."

"I know that," he said quickly. "But"—he swallowed—"what Cerdwin said tonight—"

"Cerdwin doesn't know a Godsdamned thing. About either of us." Surprise flickered in his eyes. Elana sighed. "He was different in Ozul, I mean. Not so—"

"Abrasive?" Cethin cut in. She grimaced but nodded. "You're disappointed," he said.

"What do you mean?"

"That he isn't the male you thought he was. That your feelings about him have...changed?" Cethin propped his head up on his elbow.

Elana stared straight into his eyes as she spoke. "There was never anything of that sort between us. He was like a brother to me." Something in Cethin's features relaxed. "But now..." She shook her head. "Now it doesn't even feel like that. His whole domineering male act...I worry. How will shifting affect things? How will that change—" She stopped when she felt his hand tangle in her hair.

"Nothing will change—not with us." There was a fierceness in Cethin's voice, though his tone was low. "Because you are simply *you*. No matter where you are, no matter what you do, you are yourself. Any shift—any change—will not change this." He traced his fingers down the side of her face, her neck, until they landed on her chest above her heart. Elana gazed down at his life oath–scarred hand over her scarred heart—ripped open and closed again by all she had and would endure.

"And about what Cerdwin was going to say, about my offering you the oath—"

"It doesn't matter." She covered his hand with her own. "Not anymore."

"El," he said, that softness returning to his voice and features.

"Yes?"

"I'm not proud of what I was sent to do," Cethin admitted. His hand shook under hers, and she held it more tightly. "But I'm glad it allowed our paths to cross. Even if only for this brief period in time."

The weight of his words tugged at her heart again, for—even if there were no duty waiting for her—she would outlive him by hundreds of years. He knew that, too—she saw it in his eyes before he tucked her into his chest.

"Sleep, El," he whispered into her hair.

So she did.

Eldwyn

Cethin hadn't been gone long when the wind alerted Eldwyn that someone else approached his tent. *Cerdwin*. Eldwyn wasn't sure if he was surprised or not—relieved or not. The male had visited his tent before, in addition to his family home; likewise, Eldwyn had visited Cerdwin's family chambers in the palace. But those instances usually included Alanna. In fact, the one night a week of revelry had started between Eldwyn and Cerdwin's sister while the Second Commander had been in Ozul.

Alanna had been assigned High Healer of the First Battalion, and she and Eldwyn had developed a camaraderie as overseers of the males in the camp. The two had started meeting weekly to drink and discuss the males—who was complaining too much, who would need to be released, whose injuries were improving, and to Eldwyn's surprise when Alanna had read him, who had caught their eye. Then, Alanna had mentioned a game of cards, and things had evolved from there. When Cerdwin had returned from Ozul, Alanna had invited her brother. The one night a week had turned into several nights a week with the three of them—the other nights used as time to help Cerdwin with his fire magic and shifting.

Eldwyn ran a hand down the side of his face, where that scar lingered, remembering.

Then, Alanna had been sent north with scouts, and things had become murky, at best. There was a natural connection between the First and Second Commanders—had been from the moment they'd met. But after that one night...

"Am I interrupting your thoughts on what my lecture will be, or did you drink too much with the half-Elf?" Cerdwin's sharp tone pulled Eldwyn from his mind. Cerdwin had made it clear that a night like that would never happen again—even though they both knew the words were a lie dressed up as duty.

Eldwyn quirked a smile, not bothering to get up. "Which would you prefer it to be?" He watched temper flare in the male's eyes. He was surprised Cerdwin hadn't already shattered the Healer's wards with how on edge he'd been since Elana and Cethin arrived.

Good thing Cerdwin didn't know who Elana really was. And Eldwyn wouldn't tell him. It wasn't his secret to share, nor his tale to tell.

"I need a drink," Cerdwin announced. He sat on the wooden chair in Eldwyn's common area. Eldwyn obliged, then filled a cup of his own.

"You didn't need to be so hard on them," he said, observing the Second Commander. "In fact, I recall you saying that you were going to give a warning and—"

"That *was* their warning," Cerdwin cut in, setting his now-empty glass on the low-lying table in between them. Eldwyn refilled it. "And they should both be grateful for it."

Eldwyn raised his brows. "It sounded like you were about to say something far worse before I intervened." He leaned forward and rested his elbows on his knees. "I would hate to see you lose your friend, Cerdwin." Emotion warred on the Second Commander's face. Then—

"I know," Cerdwin sighed, curls shifting as he bowed his head. "But I do not know how to do this."

"Do what?"

"This," Cerdwin said, tone picking up in anger. "How to be *everything*, to everyone, all of the time." He took another drink. "Every time I start feeling settled in my role here, something happens."

Anger twisted in Eldwyn's stomach. "You act like you have no choice in any of it."

"Because I do not!" Cerdwin shot to his feet.

"That was always your problem." Eldwyn didn't typically let his anger get the best of him when he spoke with his brother-in-arms, but since that night, since he'd brought Elana to the camp, since he'd seen the war raging inside the golden male, Eldwyn's emotions—particularly his patience—were short at best. "And it will always be your downfall. You act as though everything has been decided for you, when you could always just make a fucking choice for yourself!"

Cerdwin stared down at him, and Eldwyn saw the beast that'd scarred him. "And what would you decide?"

Eldwyn rose and closed the distance between them. "Even I cannot tell you what to choose."

Cerdwin leaned in, close enough that their lips almost touched. "And that will always be your downfall."

Chapter 14

ELANA

The days of training turned into weeks—passing by without further incident—blurring together in a haze of Avivan Light, sweat, and sore muscles. They'd moved from training with just their bodies to training with weapons. Elana noted the half smile Cerdwin couldn't hide when she worked with the blades he'd left for her in Ozul.

They hadn't spoken privately since that night in the Second Commander's tent, but Eldwyn's occasional presence in the ring seemed to have a positive effect on the male's mood. Elana mentioned as much to Cethin one night as they lay together. They'd taken to sleeping in his cot together every night—an unspoken agreement that they would share his side of the tent. But that was it: no flirting, no touching, and no kissing. She wasn't sure if she was disappointed or relieved. She *did* know the moment she said anything to Cethin...well, the images her imagination conjured were enough to entice her to spend extra time in the bath one evening and find her own release.

Regardless of their relationship, Cethin laughed when she mentioned Cerdwin and Eldwyn. "Well, now we know spying won't be a specialty of yours," he said smugly.

"You mean—"

He pulled her closer, and any additional assumptions she had about her friend's possible relationship with the First Commander vanished at the sudden, intense contact of Cethin's chest, torso, and legs against her body, his warm breath on her neck.

Her body wanted him, but it was more than that. There was something that felt so certain, so secure about falling asleep next to him. Something that felt like...home.

Cethin

Cerdwin's mood was lighter. His sister, Eldwyn told Cethin one evening while they shared a meal, was due to return from her mission within the week.

"Just what we need," Cethin muttered. "Another headstrong Satrara in the camp."

Eldwyn snorted into his wine. "Headstrong she may be, but in a different way. They are twins, yes, but there are still differences between them. Alanna, for one," he added, "is able to control her temper." Cethin smiled, but that smile faded when he thought about what Alanna's return meant for El.

When Cerdwin's sister returned, El would have no further excuse to not at least *attempt* to shift—although Cethin was convinced her lack of ability wasn't a magical issue or a mental block, but sheer will of her own making, for whatever reason. What happened from there remained the question. One, he decided, he was close to being done caring about. Sharing a cot every night with her warm, supple body between his arms was like being within both the Realm of Blessings and Hell at the same time: the sheer pleasure of her existence being so close to his, alongside the torture of keeping himself from touching her, tasting her.

While El kept her emotions to herself, he wasn't oblivious to the shift in her scent that'd driven her to take a longer bath one evening. He'd been aware of her eyes as she'd watched him and one of the other soldiers face off—shirtless—in the training ring, longswords flashing between them. He'd given her a roguish wink that had sent her cheeks flaming that perfect color before she'd turned back to spar with Alaric.

That same awareness had driven Cethin himself from their tent to walk off the pulsing need burning in his own blood. He'd run into Eldwyn, who'd taken one look at him and suggested they head into the city. They'd stayed out drinking late enough that El was already asleep when Cethin had returned and passed out beside her.

Sleeping next to her was the most comfortable thing he knew.

Cerdwin had an announcement: there would be a switch to the training rings.

And that wasn't all. Due to Eldwyn's extended stay in the camp—and with their first official scouting test coming up—Cerdwin wanted Cethin to train with the First Commander specifically. The orders ran congruent with the news that the magic wards would be lifted soon—most of the males would move on to train with their magic.

El would stay in their initial ring and train with new recruits being brought in. As Cerdwin delivered the news, Cethin sensed her frustration had less to do with them being separated and more to do with her being left behind, but he made sure to give her a smirk as he fell in line with the First Commander.

They were walking a fine line between a life-sworn and his charge; their friendship, their flirting, and the caring, intimate relationship that'd sprung up between them—and the desire Cethin knew wasn't his alone.

Elana

She luxuriated in the warmth of the water, groaning at the release in her aching muscles. Their training had been extra long, and while it would help her during their scouting mission, Elana could tell something was clawing at Cerdwin—something that had to do with his sister.

Alanna still hadn't returned, Cethin told her, having gotten the information from Eldwyn. Mention of his twin or lord father was difficult for Cerdwin—though it was his lord father he seemed to struggle with the most, only using one or two words when he spoke about the male before the flame of his temper caused an actual spark—which, according to Eldwyn, had happened once or twice.

Cerdwin had been having trouble controlling his power since returning to Aviva—as had countless others, on top of having trouble shifting back into their Elvish bodies, as Elana herself claimed. Cerdwin's sister had been helping him work through his issues. Alanna was one of the most trusted High Healers in the kingdom—and therefore the one who would be able to help Elana with her completely made-up shifting issue.

The soreness was also due in part to Elana pushing herself harder during training because of the scouting test. From what she'd overheard, it would take place in the Endurnal Mountains—a mission to see if any of the new recruits could recover information on the Dark King's army and its movements.

A small part of her hoped this first scouting mission would also be her last as a trainee, as Elana; that, from there, she would earn her people's trust, she would re-Bind the Balance, she would destroy the Dark King and his Night Queen, and she would reclaim her kingdom.

Elana sighed, reaching for the washing cloth and soap next to the tub, when she heard movement in the tent. It was enough to startle her out of the tub and reach for a towel—

But it was too late. Cethin strode into the space—shirtless—having just finished another one-on-one with Eldwyn. She thought the session wouldn't be over for at least another hour, if not longer. The two males had taken to eating together some nights and drinking on others.

She cursed when his head jerked up from where he'd been looking at his shoulder and rubbing at a spot on his neck. The wicked look that entered his amber eyes meant trouble. They'd never spoken about *them*—whatever they were. Not since that night in the barn, or when she'd fallen asleep on his shoulder on the boat to Aviva, or that second night she'd rested easily in his arms in the camp, or any of the nights after that. It'd been easier not to. And now...Elana swallowed, realizing this might be the moment she needed to make a choice.

"I didn't realize the camp provided such artful amenities," Cethin remarked, voice low as his eyes roved over every inch of her exposed skin.

Elana refused to balk under his gaze, even as she crossed her arms over her bare breasts. "I didn't expect you for another hour."

She was acutely aware of every movement Cethin took as he stalked around the room—of every breath he took—the space becoming unbearably small. He stopped behind her. "You must've lost track of time." He tucked her unbound hair over her shoulder to speak directly into her ear. The combination of the heat coming from his unclothed torso and his breath on her neck sent shivers through her, the waves all coming to concentrate as one thrumming spot between her legs. "Or I was just wrong about the time." His voice was barely more than a whisper.

It would always be like this between them, wouldn't it? This constant push and pull.

All it would take was for one of them to go too far.

"How was your training?" he asked. Such a simple, innocent question, even as they stood so closely, so intimately.

Elana closed her eyes and tried to think of a word—*any* word—that didn't sound sultry. "Harsh," was the word she landed on, before quickly adding, "someone must have done something to set Cerdwin off today."

"Mm," she heard Cethin murmur from behind her, the sound sending another wave of desire through her body.

If she denied how she felt, if she didn't give into this *need* for him…

It would be complicated—but they would figure it out. He was her life-sworn, after all. Elana made another note in her mind to ask Cerdwin for access to the Royal Archives—something she'd completely forgotten about—to read up on life-sworn bonds. Once upon a time, she would've had unlimited access to any book from the Annor. Now, she wasn't sure she'd even be allowed to request a book from one of the city's most well-guarded buildings. There had to be *something* there, though, about relationships between life-sworn.

But if she *did* give into the desire, it would become even more complicated. It would give Cerdwin a reason to kick her—or both of them—out of the camp. And, when she shifted, when she stepped into who she really was...what would Cethin think then? And what would he be to her? She'd have to marry a fully-blooded Elvish male, or a male or man from a distant kingdom to ensure the future of the kingdom.

Would Cethin resent her for it? For who she was? For not telling him?

"I imagine," Cethin whispered, "it must've been especially difficult for you, since you haven't shifted yet."

Or maybe he wouldn't care.

Elana turned to face him. He'd crossed his arms over his tanned chest, which had become an even deeper shade of brown from hours spent training outside under the summer sun they never saw because of the Light.

"I told you, I ca—"

"You can't," he finished for her, flashing that smirk that made her see red, even as those honeyed eyes threatened to devour her whole. "I sincerely doubt that. I think you're afraid to shift. Curious, for someone I called brave," he added, shrugging.

"I am not afraid," she announced. Cethin's eyes drifted to where her arms were crossed over her chest. Elana's mouth went dry when those eyes came to hold her stare once more. There was no more laughter or wickedness in his gaze, but something deeper. *His own longing?* The idea, combined with his mockery of her bravery, was enough that she lowered her hands to her sides. He was standing so close to her that her hands brushed against his bare skin as she did so, the warm, hard feel of his body threatening to undo her control. His eyes closed briefly at the quick contact.

"Like I said"—she heard the light flirtation he tried to work back into his voice, which had become rougher—"artful amenities."

"And if I were to shift into my Elvish body," she began, not sure where the question had come from—likely their whirlwind experience with Apolina, "would I be more *artful* to you then?"

Cethin's gaze locked on hers. "No." She blinked in surprise. "This attraction, El," he whispered, bending slightly to bring his mouth to hers, close enough their lips would touch if either of them faltered an inch, "it doesn't matter which body you wear, or what you call yourself. It doesn't matter if you are a barmaid, a soldier, or a spy—not to me. Some things are deeper than that." He lifted his scarred palm between them. "Maybe even deeper than this." Silence fell between them, until—

"I meant what I said on that boat. I would follow you anywhere. And I want you to know, you never need to hide anything from me. It will always be your choice, your decision, what to tell me, when to tell me. But know that I will not balk from whatever you throw my way."

Elana's heart raced at his unexpected honesty, at what he laid bare between them—as bare as her own skin—stripping himself before her with his words. She brought her hands to rest on his chest. He flinched, and she discerned they were cold from having been in the water, but she saw his smile as she closed her eyes and tentatively pressed her mouth to his.

He tasted of sweat and sun and sand, and she couldn't let go, couldn't pull her lips away from his. But she did, to open her eyes and look back into his. They were as bright as liquid gold. Cethin lifted the palm he'd raised between them higher and brought it to firmly hold her chin. Then, he hauled her mouth back to his and he kissed her—even more demanding than she'd kissed him, but she soon matched it.

Weeks of desire, weeks of need slipped the tight leash she'd kept on them. Her hands roved up his chest, over his shoulders, and down his back, settling around his waist. Her skin sang at the warm contact between their bare chests, the need for him doubling—tripling—as the hardness beneath his pants pressed against her nakedness. She gasped into his mouth when he released his grip on her chin and grasped her hair instead, his lips trailing soft kisses down her neck and across her collarbone.

"El." The word was like a prayer on his lips, and in that moment, Fate be damned, she wanted to claim this one thing—claim him—as her own. She reached for his pants, but Cethin grabbed her hand and twisted her, pulling her back against his chest again.

"If I remember correctly," he said in a low voice that sent a shiver of anticipation through her, "you were the one who had to endure the *harsh* training today." His free hand made soft, teasing strokes along her abdomen, then lower, lower. "And I'd hate for you to have to take care of yourself again." Her cheeks heated—so he *had* noticed that particularly long bath. "Allow me to give you release." He paused, waiting.

"Okay."

Elana's body tensed and loosened all at once as Cethin's fingers made those same circles at the apex of her thighs. She lifted her hands up and braced herself against his shoulders, feeling the strength and certainty that was her life-sworn, that was just *him—Cethin*.

She felt his kisses on the scar across her palm, until he dropped her hand and tilted her chin up, his kisses claiming her mouth once more, his scarred hand coming to rest over her heart, holding her close and keeping her upright. The feel of his calluses against her damp skin sent a tingling sensation through her breasts, one that connected with where his other hand pressed against her wet core. Then, all at once, his hand stilled and his kisses stopped. She groaned in protest, when—

"We should see," Cethin breathed into her ear, "if you can handle what I intend to throw at *you*."

And then one of his fingers was inside of her, then another, sliding easily with the wetness that'd begun pooling there the moment he'd looked her over when he'd entered the room. Her mouth opened in a gasp of surprise, but he was already there to catch it with his own. His tongue swept in, each flick and lick of it filling her, letting her know *that* was a tool he knew how to use elsewhere. She moved on his hand, and he slipped in a third finger, the full feeling sending her entire body tingling.

She met each thrust of his hand, her head falling against his shoulder, her eyes slightly open to see his golden ones burning with pure lust. Cethin stroked his thumb over the sensitive bundle of nerves at her center as he slid his fingers in and out, over and over again in a demanding rhythm, his other hand making its way back to her breasts. She let out a soft whimper from the pleasure, holding back the full volume of her moans.

"Good," he breathed against her neck. She hummed at his praise and allowed her eyes to close completely. The sweat from training she'd started to wash away broke out across her skin again from the heat they'd created between them. Gods, how long had it been since she'd been touched by someone like this? Desired by someone? She couldn't remember—could barely remember who she was, who she was pretending to be, where she was—as an intensity rose up from deep within her, coiling in her center, threatening to shatter every thought in her mind and dream in her heart.

Cethin swept his mouth over hers again, and the sudden contact of his lips on hers—and the spike of pain-laced pleasure that came from his pinching one of her nipples—unraveled Elana completely. He was the only thing keeping her upright, his fingers pumping and stroking as shudders of pleasure swept through her, in her, out from her, capturing her low moans with his mouth. He slowly withdrew his hand as her body stilled, the arm at her chest holding her upright.

Elana opened her eyes, suddenly aware that her vision had become clearer—brighter. Her hearing—she heard his heart beating rapidly. And that faint buzzing in her chest, that tingling in her hands—

Shit, shit, *shit*, she'd lost control, had let go not only of her body, but also—

Elana stifled her gasp: small, iridescent stars sparkled throughout the bathing chamber. She glanced up at Cethin, hoping the male hadn't picked up on the unexpected shift or magic use, and another tremor rocked her: he was sucking on his fingers—the same fingers that'd just been buried deep inside of her. His eyes were closed as he licked them clean, one by one.

Attempting to wipe further lust-filled thoughts from her mind, Elana willed her body, bones, muscles, skin, to shift back, carefully and agonizingly watching him as she did so, tucking her magic away deep, until it diminished.

She was in her human body again.

The stars were gone.

She exhaled a sigh of relief. Cethin opened his eyes, staring down at her. The lust and desire in his gaze threatened to send her to her knees.

"El—" he started.

"Noir!" came the shout from outside of their tent.

Chapter 15

Elana

C ethin's eyes instantly shifted to a different intensity. He released her, and Elana immediately went for the clean underclothes, tunic, and leggings she'd left next to the tub. He grabbed her arm.

"Wash up first." She gave him an appraising look as he washed his hands and face with the soap and washing cloth she'd discarded upon his arrival, then chugged a dark liquid from a flask he'd apparently hidden under a few towels.

"As much as I would love for every single soldier in this camp," Cethin said, tilting the flask toward her, "to know that I have touched you, tasted you, and given you release"—a low growl slipped from his lips and he tensed, seeming to will self-control back into his body—"and intend to do so many, many, more times over, I would assume this is something you'd like to keep private at the moment."

She stared at him.

"There are at least a hundred males out there, El, including Cerdwin and Eldwyn," he stated flatly. "You're the only female in this camp. Your scent"—liquid gold pierced his eyes, and he took another swig from the flask—"your scent is everywhere. If nothing else, I'm certain you'd like to keep *that* to yourself."

He had a point. Elana grabbed the flask, swished the hard alcohol, and handed it back to him. Cethin nodded once, grabbed a clean tunic from the pile of towels and clothes, then shoved the flask back under them.

She snatched up another washing cloth and the soap, quickly scrubbed her face, neck, and torso, washing gently where tenderness lingered between her thighs. *And that was just from his fingers...*

Cethin had finished buckling on his weapons. "See you out there," he said, turning to leave the tent as she tugged on undergarments, leggings, and a tunic of her own. She was just about to reach for her blades when he appeared back in front of her, gently grabbed the back of her head, and planted a soft kiss on her brow. Elana couldn't read the emotion in his eyes as he held her gaze. Then, he was gone. She couldn't stop thinking about what it might mean as she strapped and buckled her daggers to her thighs.

Cethin

The Noir had left as quickly as they'd arrived, Cerdwin was telling him, El, and Eldwyn in the Second Commander's tent not twenty minutes later. The creatures had made a sweep over the city and the castle, then wheeled back around, flying over the Endurnal Mountains and out of sight, back into the wretched land of Darkness. Though the Noir's appearance had been brief, it'd left the camp shaken—and, likely, the city.

Cerdwin was discussing strategy as the noises of a military camp roused to action sounded around them. Yet it was an effort for Cethin to keep his attention on the Second Commander when all he wanted to do was look at her. What they'd just shared in the bathing chamber...he was sure the image of El, stark naked, dark hair and pale skin dripping with water from the tub; the feel of her, her soft breasts against his chest, the slick wetness between her legs for him; the taste of her in his mouth, the feel of her tongue against his; her sounds, how he had to keep her from moaning loud enough for the entire camp to hear, was something he'd be replaying in his head until their next encounter. Cethin shook his head, clearing the images, the feelings, the taste—*her* taste—her scent from his mind. Gods, the last thing he needed was to stand at attention right there in the Second Commander's tent—and *not* in the way a soldier was typically requested to.

Besides, that wasn't the only thing on his mind: the Noir had come, just when she had. And while that didn't mean anything on its own, when El had lost control before—in fear or anger—she'd shifted without meaning to. Cethin could admit he hadn't been paying that much attention to the surrounding details while he'd sucked the taste of her from his fingers, savoring the sweet, familiar flavor of her—but *had* she shifted?

Cethin was pretty sure he would've noticed that. But was her piercing stare at Cerdwin—as the male recounted the Noir's aerial sweep for the third time—because she was having trouble focusing because of what had just happened between them, or because she was trying to avoid rousing his suspicion at what *might've* happened?

But what would the Noir want with her?

Not that it mattered to him—not anymore. He'd been more open with her in that tent than he'd ever been with anyone—ever. And he'd meant every word he'd spoken to her as he'd held her skin to skin: he would be by her side, no matter what happened next; no matter what her Elvish form was, though he could only imagine it would knock the breath from him; no matter how weak or strong her Healing gift was; no matter that, as a fully-blooded Elvish female, she would live hundreds of years past his lifespan.

Cethin had seen her bravery, her courage, her kindness, her compassion, her understanding, her cleverness, her skill. He would be there next to her, from that moment forward.

He would even wait for her through eternity.

Somewhere next to him, Eldwyn cleared his throat. "We are considering holding you two back from the scouting test," the male said, and Cethin watched El's head whip toward the First Commander.

"And why is that?" she snapped. Eldwyn let out the exasperated sound Cethin typically heard from the male when he spoke of Cerdwin's temper.

"Look," the First Commander said, pinching the bridge of his nose, "you—both of you—have made progress training here. But with the Noir back in Aviva, sending you into the Endurnal Mountains, especially to an area we have already had trouble with—"

"Would be a risk," Cethin finished for the male, and Eldwyn nodded.

"Neither of you possess the vision or other senses you would need in that Darkness. And without magic, against the Noir—"

"I saved his ass from the Noir already," El interrupted, and Cethin fought his chuckle as Cerdwin exploded.

"With no idea how it happened!" The Second Commander's anger was a sharp knife through the room. "And until you can learn to control your shifting, your emotions, *yourself,* it is far too risky to send you into the mountains."

From the set of El's jaw, Cethin knew she felt the male lecturing her about control was ironic and quietly agreed. She whirled back to Eldwyn. "And you two are in agreement on this?"

"For once," the male said, mouth twitching.

She turned to him next. Cethin saw the emotion swirling in her blue-gray eyes. He'd have to pick his next words very, *very* carefully. "They are the leaders in this camp, El," he finally said.

As she stormed out of the Second Commander's tent, he knew it hadn't been the right thing to say.

Elana

She stalked back to their tent alone, magic roiling in her veins, building, begging to be let out. She tamped down on the feeling, uncomfortable as it was.

They are the leaders in this camp, El. Cethin's words repeated in her mind.

She needed to push past them and prove herself valuable no matter who or what she was. Because she wasn't just El. Not just Elana, the female trapped in a mortal body.

She was their queen. The real leader in their camp.

Elana packed her bags. She wouldn't be left behind when the time for the scouting mission came—even if she had to go alone.

"I can't believe you sided with them about this," she hissed when Cethin entered the space.

"And I can't believe you're leaving because of it." She gave him a sharp look. "Ah," he murmured, "not leaving—sneaking out."

"I have just as much right to scout those mountains as anyone else in this camp," she challenged.

"And I'm not disagreeing with you." Elana threw her bag onto the table next to her cot as Cethin walked toward her. He put his hand on her arm, and she softened at the touch. "But you need to be smart about this, El. *We* need to be smart about this." She stiffened, feeling wary. "I'd prefer if you didn't go alone, when the time comes," he said gently, and she softened again.

"I could go alone," she grumbled.

"I know." He ran his hand up her arm and gripped her chin. "And whatever you decide, I'm at your disposal." He loosened his grip on her chin and left her space for the common area. Elana stood there, watching him walk away, emotions warring—

Only to follow him a moment later, turn him, press her mouth to his, and wrap her hands around his waist. His hands were immediately on either side of her face, then running through her still unbound hair. Even though it had been less than an hour since they'd touched, tasted, *felt* one another, she wanted more, *needed* more—and she could tell he did, too.

El. Her name was like a plea, or long-forgotten prayer, though she wasn't sure if he'd said it out loud or if she'd imagined it.

Cethin ran his hands down her spine, and she shivered against him in anticipation. He smiled against her lips and ran his hands back up her front, resting them just below her breasts. She tugged on his waist, pulling him over top of her on a low-lying table.

"This is dangerous, El," he whispered. She met his gaze. In that moment, she wasn't sure if he meant their—or rather, her—rogue scouting mission, or this *need* they shared. She bit her lower lip, watched his eyes track the movement.

"I know," she murmured. "We should start training—"

"I have an idea about that," he interjected with a wink. He reached into his pocket and withdrew a leather band—similar to the ones he, Cerdwin, and a few of the other males used to tie their hair back during training, only thicker.

"Do you trust me?"

She did—and not just because he was her life-sworn. What they shared had become far more than that to her, though she couldn't name it.

"Yes."

And maybe, just maybe, he trusted her, too.

Cethin kissed the outline of her mouth, up her cheek, to her ear, and stopped there. Heat blossomed in her core.

"It will be darker in the mountains," he said. "Far darker than it is here with that damn Light constantly shining down—even darker than it was in Ozul at midnight. My senses aren't as keen as a fully-blooded Elf's, but your sight—all of your senses—will be even more hindered in your mortal form." Her breath caught as he wrapped the band around her eyes, raising her head slightly as he tied it behind her hair. "Can you see anything?"

"No."

"Good," he whispered into her ear.

And then the presence of his body disappeared from above her.

Before Elana could move—or start yelling at him—a featherlight kiss brushed against her lips, the only part of their bodies touching. She reached out until her hands found his hair and held tight, her hips bucking off the table as she sought friction against wherever his hips had gone. Suddenly, his arms were pinning hers to the table as he whispered into her ear again. "Don't move." She stilled. "Engage your other senses while you can't see. Any taste." He released one of her hands, his fingers tracing down her face, a thumb sweeping across her lips. Instinct had her sucking on it. He removed it quickly, hissing when she gently nipped at it, moving his hand down her side.

"Any touch," he continued, swirling his fingers around the peaked nipple beneath her tunic and breast band.

"Any sound," he said, fingers continuing their lazy trail down, and down, until they dragged right down her center; she moaned at his touch. "Good," he whispered, as those fingers brushed the waistband of her pants.

"Anything you feel, lean into it," Cethin instructed as his fingers dug below that waistband, the movement causing her to hiss, her hips to twitch.

He slipped his fingers beneath her undergarments and Elana spread her legs wider, welcoming his touch. He slid two fingers inside of her, catching her sounds with his lips as he slid in a third. She felt him pull back slightly, a tug as her pants slid down. She moved forward to feel his fingers, riding his hand.

Gods. The feel of his hand, his scent, his presence—she trusted him, yes, but she needed to stay in control. Not just now, but on the scouting mission, too.

"Focus," Cethin growled, as if he could read her thoughts. "Concentrate. You are in control."

She inhaled deeply, mastering her breath, moving in perfect rhythm with his hand. Release built within her—

Then unleashed in slow, undulating waves. She felt Cethin withdraw his fingers from inside of her—and, from the sounds she heard next, he was licking each of them clean. Again. Then, her pants were back up around her hips, even as instinct screamed at her to beg him to bury his cock deep inside of her.

But she was in control—of her magic, her senses, herself. The band disappeared. Elana gazed up at him, the warmth of his eyes warming her heart—and the trust in them cooling it.

Cethin trusted Elana.

But would he trust Eleonora?

Cerdwin

"It was the right decision."

He looked up at Eldwyn. "Agreed."

They stared at each other until Cerdwin looked away, unable to bear the intensity of the male's gaze or the scar on his face. Cerdwin shuffled the maps on his desk. "If you will excuse me, I have—"

"A list of duties to fulfill so that our *lord father* can continue piling more work on you and claim it as his own stewardship of the city?"

Cerdwin almost dropped the parchment he was holding. "Sister."

"Brother. First Commander," Alanna said, breezing into the pavilion and dipping into a mock curtsy. Eldwyn let out a low chuckle at her pseudo-formality. Alanna lifted her chin and met Cerdwin's eyes.

"He hasn't become a total prick lordling since I've been gone, has he?" Her question was clearly directed at Eldwyn. Cerdwin threw the male a dirty look when the First Commander made a show of considering—accompanied by a low hum that sent his skin burning. "Are you not pleased to see me, brother?"

Cerdwin came around his desk and pulled his twin into an embrace. "Of course I am," he murmured, and she gave him an extra squeeze before he drew back. "Are you well?" He scanned her face and body for anything amiss, anything that had changed since she'd gone north, but Alanna was the same: golden skin, though slightly paler than his from her time in the darker, colder region of Aviva; golden curls, longer than his, flowing to her waist in an unkept fashion; purple eyes that carried a hint of the pale-blue light that was her extraordinary Healing gift.

She nodded, though her eyes narrowed as she assessed him in return. "And you? We just made it inside the city wall when the Noir left. Did you face them?"

Shit. He hadn't considered how her unit's return might have been compromised. He'd been so wrapped up in his frustration with Elana, Cethin, and...Eldwyn.

The idea to hold the pair back from the scouting trial had been the First Commander's. Cerdwin was actually surprised and annoyed he hadn't thought of it first. But it was the right decision. Elana wasn't prepared for something like that. Then, the Noir had come, and that had confirmed for Cerdwin that his friend needed to stay in the camp and away from any danger. He hadn't been able to protect her in Ozul. Hell, he hadn't even been able to protect her in his own camp. It stopped there.

Alanna, though—his sister could handle herself. He'd trained her, too, before he'd been sent to Ozul. She'd written that Eldwyn had seen to it that she'd kept up with it while he'd been gone. Still, the idea of the Dark King and Night Queen's creatures anywhere near his twin when she was his only family left besides their lord father...

"Did they give you any trouble on the road?"

"None." She shook her head, curls shifting against her white Healer's dress, the belt that cinched her waist the same color as the locks that brushed against it. "It was like they were tracking something, and then whatever it was vanished. So they left." Cerdwin clenched his jaw. He'd come to a similar conclusion.

But *what* were they tracking?

"I take it they didn't cause any trouble here?"

"None besides the disruption and excitement of the camp and disquiet in the city." Cerdwin sighed, motioning for her to sit in the chair next to Eldwyn's as he sat behind his desk. His sister's face pinched in concern—so much like their lady mother's.

"Did you find what you were looking for in the north, my lady?" Eldwyn asked. He was the only one who could call Alanna that without her causing a fuss.

"No," she said, forehead scrunching. "It's like there's nothing left there—or they don't want to be found." Eldwyn looked thoughtful, but Cerdwin fought his rising frustration. They'd been working to track a unit of the Dark King's soldiers since he'd returned to Aviva, with no success. This mission was supposed to have been a lead on whatever it was they were missing, and its failure—in his lord father's eyes—would rest entirely on him.

"I'm sorry." Alanna's voice drew him from his thoughts. She knew firsthand how cruel Lord Arel Satrara could be when he was displeased—not with his actions, but with his words. A true courtier.

"It is fine," Cerdwin said, running a hand through his hair.

"It's not," he heard Eldwyn mutter under his breath. The twins stared at the First Commander in unison. "If you would excuse me," the male said abruptly. "I have some matters to attend to."

"I hope said matters won't take too long," Alanna remarked. "It's been far too long since we've had a game of cards."

"I will always make time for you, my lady." The male gave her shoulder a squeeze as he exited the tent. Cerdwin listened as the entrance to the pavilion opened and closed.

"What in the Otherworld was that about?" Alanna demanded. Cerdwin tilted his head toward her. His sister's gaze was cool against his skin—a brush of her magic that sensed not only physical wounds, but mental and emotional ones, too.

"Nothing," he said, giving her a look. Her magic shoved against his skin. The camp Healer had set wards to impede the use of magic by males in his camp. *Semantics*—but they mattered when it came to magic. "Alanna," he growled in warning.

"I thought as much. A word of advice, brother," she said, expression softening. "You can't keep doing this."

"I am not doing anything!" he snapped, feeling his own magic—both the fire and the beast—warring deep within him, roaring to be released.

"Exactly." He stared at her. "You two have been off and on since you returned—"

"Alanna!" he hissed. "Not here. Not where anyone could overhe—"

"You think he didn't seal your tent with his gift?" she snapped, cutting him off. "No one can hear us." He closed his mouth. Eldwyn wasn't technically part of his camp, either—of course he'd used his magic. "Now," she continued, giving him a sharper look that reminded Cerdwin of their lord father, "I don't know what happened, but I know whatever is happening now cannot continue." Her expression softened again. "You are in pain, Cerdwin. And he"—she sighed—"he's hurt. More than he's willing to admit. But under his humor, there is sadness."

"Has anyone ever told you how exceptionally nosy you are?" Alanna glared at him. Cerdwin sighed. "There is nothing to be done. You know that as well as I do."

"There's always something to be done."

"I am not like you," he said, anger slipping again. "I cannot just throw away my life and our family's future for—"

"For what?" Cerdwin slammed his mouth shut again. "That's part of your problem, too," she said, leaning back in her chair with a nod. "You don't know what you want. You don't know how you feel."

"Don't you dare tell me how I do or do not feel," Cerdwin practically shouted, shooting to his feet and bracing his hands against the desk. His sister didn't even flinch. That wasn't surprising—she'd seen the best and worst of him.

"I don't have to tell you how you do or do not feel when I can feel it myself." She rose and came to stand in front of his desk. "I am sorry, Cerdwin," Alanna said, resting one of her hands on his. "I am sorry that all of this duty now firmly rests on you. But that doesn't mean there isn't another w—"

"There is no other way," Cerdwin interrupted in a tone that meant what he said was final. It was their lord father's voice, and he hated himself for it, hated the way Alanna removed her hand and retreated a step.

"Then you have to let him go."

Cerdwin bowed his head. Silence fell.

"I hear there is another female in the camp." Cerdwin lifted his head, watching as his sister's eyes searched his face, her own openly curious.

"Who is Elana?"

Chapter 16

As it turned out, the leather band had other, more practical—if less fun—uses. Each fake night after training, while the Light shone high above Aviva, Cethin wound the band around her eyes and handed her a wooden training sword. They sparred together in the obscurity of blindfolds, alone in their tent—along with subtle, seductive touches—but nothing more. He was giving her the time and space to figure things out for herself, and, even though Elana trusted him, she had made her decision: she would go into the Endurnal Mountains alone. She would scout. She would bring back any information she discovered about the movements of the Dark King's forces and present it to Eldwyn and Cerdwin. Then, she would shift for them—for Cethin—and they would take things from there.

Taking Cethin with her would be a risk—in more ways than one. She told him as much—at least, what she deemed relevant—the next evening as she lay in his arms.

"And you're sure about this? About going alone?" Cethin's body was tense around hers.

"Yes." Elana rolled over to gaze into his warm, honey-colored eyes, and shuddered when their foreheads almost touched—the meaning so precious to Elves, though not on the same level as a claiming or matehood. To be brow-to-brow with someone would mean...well, it would mean more than either of them could offer the other, she was certain of that. "I'm sure." She watched Cethin's jaw flex. "I'll be fine."

"El, please." She considered commenting on how rarely he must use that word but couldn't answer him—couldn't think about anything except the hardness of him that'd been pressing into her since their bodies had lined up. She wanted him—all of him—no matter what it might cost her later. She tugged on his pants, but he stopped her with one hand, then rolled her over so her back was flush with his chest.

"Not here," he murmured against her skin. "Not with the entire camp around us. Not now."

"When?" was her first question, followed closely by, "Where?" She pushed her hips against him, against the hard length that now pressed into her rear. Cethin snarled, nipping at her ear, sending her skin buzzing.

"When we return," he said, voice low and rough. The hand holding her to him left her middle and trailed down to *exactly* where she wanted a different part of him—and without clothes separating them.

"Are you trying to bribe me, Cethin?" Elana's voice came out weaker than she'd intended as his fingers circled lower, and lower, until she was trapped between them and the mass of his body behind her.

"Is it working?" Down and down his hand went, until he was cupping the sensitive area between her legs over her pants. She let out a strangled noise. He chuckled.

"When we return, you and I will go into the city for a week." His breath was hot against her neck as his hand moved up, then slipped under her clothing. "And we will be no one and know no one and have nothing to do." He slipped his fingers inside of her. "I will touch you. I will feast on you. And I will fuck you, El. Until you moan loudly enough to be heard above the sea—but it won't matter, because we won't be here, and no one will care." His thumb traced the sensitive spot between her thighs, sending her thoughts scattering like shooting stars. "And when my name is on your lips, when you are begging to the Gods, I will take that pretty mouth of yours."

A groan worked its way up Elana's throat, but she stopped it. She had to stay in control. She had been before—hadn't shifted, hadn't summoned the Noir back to the camp. Blissful release shivered through her body, sending her shaking, trembling, falling. But she was still in control.

"And when I have tasted you entirely, filled you completely, and fucked you so hard you can barely remember your own name," Cethin said, his voice little more than a rough growl as his fingers guided her through the aftershocks, "I will hold you, just like this"—he withdrew his hand, both of his arms resuming their hold around her middle—"for as long as you'll have me." Elana sighed contentedly.

"So," Cethin said, and she felt the smirk on his lips, "may I accompany you?" *Bribery indeed.* It might drive him mad not to, but she needed to do this—alone.

"No." He stiffened again. She sighed. "I don't know how to explain it, but I need to do this—alone."

She felt one hand leave her waist as his fingers came to tilt her lips back toward his. "Okay." Cethin sighed—then kissed her with more tenderness than she'd thought him capable of. "Just promise you'll come back to me."

Emotion swelled in her chest. She would come back to him—but she would come back as someone else: an Elf, the lost princess, heir to the throne of Aviva, the one who would re-Bind the Balance, the Queen of Aviva, and...

You will learn, child, that there are different ways to love, and to be loved. Different types of love to experience.

...a female in love.

Elana wasn't sure which type of love she felt for Cethin, but it was love.

And it was a love she wasn't prepared to lose—not yet.

"I promise."

Heart thundering in her chest, Elana grabbed the small bag she'd packed and strapped her daggers to her thighs. She quietly crept through the camp, though there weren't many people out. Cethin had shown her how to use a scattering of rocks and sticks to determine the time—Cerdwin, Eldwyn, and the other trainees deemed ready had departed not fifteen minutes earlier. Following the path she'd seen marked on a map when she'd last been in Cerdwin's tent, Elana made her way to the outskirts of the city and headed toward the wall. Reaching it, she embedded herself into a shadowy overhang.

A hand clamped over her mouth. Elana whirled, ready to fend off her attacker—

It was Cethin.

"What are you doing here?" she demanded. "I told you, I can handle this—"

"On your own." He looked amused. "But you won't make it to the mountains if you get caught leaving the city." She stared him down, and he stared back, not a single speck of gold in his eyes.

Different ways to love, and to be loved. Was this his way of expressing his own feelings? Or was it just the life oath between them?

"Fine," she sighed. As much as she wanted to go on her own, as much as she wanted to protect him from what was to come, this would give them the chance to talk. "But do *not* get in my way," she added, narrowing her eyes at him. He smiled—though it didn't quite reach his eyes—and motioned her forward.

They quietly made their way down the wall to where she'd seen one of Eldwyn's secret doors marked. It wouldn't open, but she'd anticipated that. Little did Cethin know, his lessons in *control* had paid off in more ways than one. Elana shifted—just her hand—and ran it down the door. A small risk—and a successful one: the door hissed and swung outward. She shifted her hand back, then paused, listening for the telltale sounds of the Noir. They did not come.

"Come on," she hissed, dragging Cethin through the door—easy enough, as he apparently hadn't brought a pack with him, just that wicked knife and a few well-placed daggers.

The door swung shut as soon as they emerged on the other side of the wall. Elana paused and scanned the skies again. Still no sign of the Noir. Perhaps the amount of magic she'd used had been so small and futile they hadn't marked it? Or they were preparing to swoop down and ruin Cerdwin's training exercise at any moment.

"Hurry," she said, tugging on Cethin's tunic. "First test is to cross the sands undetected."

"We've done that easily enough," he said, giving her another amused look.

"This is *not* funny," she snapped. "If you are just going to make jokes or belittle what we're doing, what I was going to do *by myself*—"

He raised his hands. "I'm sorry," he said, and she might've fallen over in shock that he even knew that word. "I didn't realize this was so important to you." Well, *that* would certainly be part of their conversation—but they were already lagging behind the group. Cerdwin and Eldwyn had probably already taken up their positions along the wall—or, if one or both were able, shifted into a birdlike form to track the unit's progress. She hadn't asked either of them what their animal forms were. "Let's move."

Sand was everywhere: in her boots, down her front, in her hair, clinging to the sweat pouring down her face as she and Cethin half jogged, half ran across the desert. Elana couldn't imagine how long it'd been when they finally hit the base of the Endurnal Mountains, her human form protesting the lack of water, food, and rest.

They'd arrived in a spot farther north than the official training, just like she'd wanted, hoping to get eyes and ears where Cerdwin wasn't able to. Never mind that she was deep in enemy territory. Maybe it was a good thing Cethin had completely disregarded her wishes and come along. They hadn't spoken since he'd apologized at the wall, but silence was even more important now that they'd left the Light mostly behind.

After a brief break for some of the cured meat, bread, and water she'd packed, they spent the next few hours climbing up, and up, the temperature dropping as they ascended the mountains. Elana earned her share of scrapes and bruises from the rocks, dead brush, twigs, and sticks that littered the Endurnal Mountains. But all of that became obsolete when they crested the peak and looked down on the smaller mountains and valleys below.

"It's something, isn't it," whispered Cethin.

Elana nodded, words failing as she added heights to her list of fears. It would be a deadly drop to fall down the mountainside—but where rock and dead wood had been the issue coming up, large, mighty evergreens would be the cause of death on the way down. The trees' thick trunks, long branches, and piercing needles blocked any space, fallen pieces blanketing the valley floor—at least, what she could see of it.

Because there was no Light of Aviva—not here. Here, there was only the murky gloom, the destitute dullness, the personification of the Breaking. It started with the gloom of the Endurnal Mountains, cascading downward, spilling toward the land beyond, covering it in true Darkness. Elana's human eyes couldn't see what lay beyond. For a moment, she tried to picture what it might have looked like before, when light—*real* sunlight—pierced the numerous branches, bathing the valley floor, and illuminating the river she could hear but barely make out in the gloom

"What are we looking for?" came Cethin's voice.

She blew out a breath, slowly pivoting in a small circle. "Anything," she murmured. "Any track, sight, or sound that could be connected with the Dark King's movements."

"We should go deeper then."

Elana swallowed. They held the higher ground, they could see more—especially with the Light at their backs. Down there...she hoped Cethin's lessons continued to pay off. "Agreed."

The ground was firmer on the other side of the mountains—covered with a grassy moss, and so, so many pine needles. Elana could barely hear their footsteps as they made their way to the valley floor. And the Darkness...it had stopped being a murky gloom—it pitched everything around her into blackness. It was a wonder neither of them had walked right into one of the evergreens, but she supposed Cethin's half-Elvish vision kept them tree-free.

They stopped briefly to share her canteen. She filled it from one of the streams that had appeared—*after* she'd accidentally stepped in one, cursing—and fed into the larger river she'd faintly seen and heard from above. She didn't remember seeing so many streams on Cerdwin's map—or from their initial scan of the area, but, then again, it was harder for her to see. Still, she felt in her gut that they needed to head farther north. She was about to say as much to Cethin when she heard him cry out in alarm.

"Cethin!" she hissed into the inky night that was thickening around her like a tangible entity. No response. Elana carefully made her way to where she guessed the origin of the sound was from—

Something hard collided with the side of her head, and blackness greeted her.

Chapter 17

She had no idea how long she'd been out for; it could have been minutes, hours—days. Elana groaned and pushed herself up from where she'd ended up face down on the ground, spitting out pine needles. Wincing, she put her hand to the back of her head—wetness. She sniffed. Blood. She fished around for her pack, found it a few feet to her right, pulled out the canteen, and poured the water against the wound.

What had happened? Where was—

Her hands went to her sides. Both daggers were gone.

"Shit," she muttered. What *had* happened?

"Elana?" The voice came from a few paces to her right.

"Cethin?" she whispered, crawling forward until her hands hit a body.

"Are you alright? Are you hurt?" came his voice again. Gods, it was so dark.

"A bump to the head, but other than that, I'm fine. What about you?"

"There were a few of them."

"A few of who?" Elana asked, although *what* also felt like a more appropriate question. She heard the shake of a head.

"I don't know. I pushed back the ones I could see. But then...I couldn't find you."

Emotion clogged her throat. "I'm okay," she told him again. And again, "I'm okay."

"Good," came his reply.

She smiled into the gloom, though that smile faded when she remembered. "They took my weapons." It was quiet for a few moments.

"We need to get out of here and find somewhere to regroup," he said. Elana nodded, sifting through the map in her mind again, trying to remember any safe spaces marked on Cerdwin's map. None came to mind, but she remembered some of the mountains in the center of the range housed small caves.

"I have a plan," she announced, moving to stand. She lowered her hand until she felt one of Cethin's clasp hers. She pulled him to stand. A light breeze passed through the pine trees around them, sending whatever birds that had paused there into flight, their wings the only sound. But there was no sound or sign of their attackers.

"I think we're in the clear," Cethin said. "Now, what's this plan of yours?"

Elana pushed them away from the stream she remembered passing, closer to the start of the mountainous barrier. Though her head throbbed painfully, her eyes started adjusting to the darkness—as well as mortal eyes could.

"There should be some caves at the base of the range," she said. "We can take shelter there." They moved in complete silence, with no indication as to how much time passed as they walked, listening, waiting for the enemy to attack again. Finally—

"There," he said, pointing toward a silver slash against a rock. "That looks like a cave." They crept forward with him leading the way. She kept pace behind him, one eye on his back, her hands ready to grab the twin blades at her sides should anyone—anything—approach them. Until she remembered the blades weren't there again. Elana exhaled in frustration. But they heard nothing else, save the sighing sound of the breeze. It might've been a relaxing place to travel, were they not being hunted and the land not consumed by night. He paused at the entrance to the cave.

"What is it?"

"We should make sure no one's home," he said quietly, drawing his blade. "Too bad we don't have any magic to help us see, instead of just poking around in the dark."

Elana opened her mouth, but any retort she had instantly died the moment she stepped into the cave behind him. She couldn't move, couldn't speak, couldn't think—couldn't *breathe*. It was like something out of a lost memory: in that cave were more *dianaflora* than she had ever seen.

"I am afraid there are few left, Your Grace," the young princess overheard the Healer tell her mother. The dianaflora. *After the battle—the battle that'd killed the young princess's father—the* dianaflora *had disappeared.*

The flowers were said to be a gift from the Goddess of Light, whose name, along with the other Gods, had been lost to time, as the Gods had been lost at the beginning of the Darkness.

"We will save what we can. For royal funerals only," the queen said.

"Yes, Your Grace," the Healer replied. "We will continue to try and propagate them as well, of course, but without the—"

"I understand," her mother cut in, then sighed. "I just wish we knew what happened to the others."

Not once—not even in the golden days of Aviva—had she seen so many of the bluish-white flowers in one place. She hadn't seen any since she'd returned.

How had they ended up there?

Elana's mouth dropped as she took them all in—as she took in what they were *doing*. She'd never seen them...*glow*?

Her mouth hung open as they walked through the space, Cethin's eyes wide now that she could see him clearly. *Dianaflora* lined the cave walls and floors, illuminating a path farther back that revealed stalactites, stalagmites, and a large chamber with several hot springs. The majority of the flowers were set back farther into the cave, almost so as not to be seen by passersby—only those brave enough to enter.

"Well," he murmured, seeming to overcome the shock of the cave as she continued to gawk, "I guess this place is magic in and of itself."

"Marked by the Gods," Elana whispered, slowly turning in the circular chamber. He couldn't understand what this meant to her—this inexplicable cave between the two kingdoms, one of Darkness, and one of Light. It was like the Gods were giving her a sign—what she needed to prove herself worthy as Queen of Aviva, and a sign she needed to figure out to come closer to re-Binding the Balance. She would think on that while they rested here. Then, it would be time to go home. She swallowed. Home. She could no longer be Elana; she needed to be Eleonora—Queen Eleonora at that. No longer just El. *His* El. And Cethin...what would his path be from there?

It had been a mistake to bring him into this.

"Elana?" The question drifted through the illuminated space as they continued walking through the open chamber. He never called her by her full—albeit fake—name. She turned toward him, his eyes a light brown in the glow of the *dianaflora*. "I'll take first watch," he said. "Get some rest.

"Or," he said, raising a brow, "you could wash some of that sand off." She wanted to roll her eyes at him then, but the layers of sweat and sand—now mixed with dirt and pine needles—clung to her arms and tunic, her feet inside her boots, her neck, face, and hair. Not to mention the blood from her cut. *Dianaflora* floated atop the hot springs and hung from above them, sending skittering rainbows across the stone walls. The effect was breathtaking.

"Fine," she sighed, but Cethin didn't look at her again as he moved toward the cave entrance to take his watch.

Elana shed her cloak and tunic, her pants and boots—the latter followed by a pile of sand and pine needles—and set them on the mossy grass around the pool she'd chosen. Without being able to tell how deep the pool actually was, Elana sat at the edge of the water. She dipped her feet in first, then her legs, sending the nearest *dianaflora* spinning away. They were truly exquisite in the water, the petals' light setting the surface ablaze like wild starlight. She sighed as she tilted her head back to stare at the cave's ceiling; more of the precious flower lined that, too, like so many stars scattered across a night sky. Constant, unfailing, and beautiful.

Like Cethin. She groaned and leaned forward to splash her face and hair with water. Was it completely foolish, this desire for him? This attachment they had—that she knew in her heart had to be outside of the life oath—wouldn't last. Couldn't last—for a million reasons. He had no idea who she really was. What would he say when he learned the truth? When he discovered that she'd been lying to him all of these months, these months when he'd become more than just her life-sworn? These months when he'd become her friend? Her trusted protector? Her lover?

Elana kicked at the water, sending *dianaflora* scattering. He would hate her or—at the very least—never trust her again. But who could she trust? *Really* trust with the secrets of her life?

She leaned forward and drew her hands through the water, catching a few *dianaflora*. She stared at them for a few minutes, hoping they had the answers—not just answers to her power, to the Darkness, to the re-Binding, but the answers to the questions of her heart.

They were silent. But she stayed by the water, waiting for her thoughts to settle. When she rose, re-dressed, and laid down on a mossy bank, sleep swiftly claimed her.

"Elana." Gentle hands shook her awake, and Cethin's face came into focus above hers.

"Oh," she said, pulling herself into a seated position. He watched her closely from where he crouched beside her.

"How's your head?"

She pressed her palm to the back of it. No blood, but she felt a bump and a scab forming. "I-I think I'm okay," she said. "Have I been sleeping long? I didn't mean to—"

"It's okay." He smiled and rested his right hand on her cheek. "You needed it. But we probably need to move now—and quickly." She nodded and rose, joints protesting as she did. It might've been a moss-covered cave floor, but it was still a cave floor she'd slept on.

"Did you hear anything while I was out?"

Cethin shook his head. "Nothing—and it's been hours. They must've moved on. But I don't know how long it'll be until they circle back. We shouldn't linger."

They exited the mouth of the cave, and it became nothing more than a sliver of silver in the night. "We should head north again," she said. "It's a risk, but I doubt they would expect us to try traveling that way twice."

"True," was Cethin's reply as he followed behind her. "But you don't have your weapons anymore. What exactly do you plan on doing if we come under attack again?" He had a point. But maybe, just maybe...

They were already here. She was going to tell him soon, anyway...

"Magic." She didn't give him time to reply as she marched toward the pine trees.

Darkness shuddered around them as if in answer to her statement. Elana turned. Outside of the cave, grounded, claws scraping against stone, wings out and sending waves of Darkness toward them, were four Noir.

The Darkness was everywhere. *They* were everywhere—the Noir—sucking up the air, leaching up not only sight, but sound, feeling, the space around them. Elana blinked her eyes once—twice. She couldn't differentiate the outside world from the backs of her eyelids—save for the darker figures, blacker than the blackest midnight, swirling about her, hissing in some strange, forgotten language. She felt drained in the Noir's presence. Trying to use that untamed light, that inner, moonlit magic, would be foolish.

Elana turned and fled through the forest, dragging Cethin along behind her, branches and pine needles whipping at her body, face, and hair. She should know more, should be able to *do* more than run. Most younglings were trained in their magic the moment it set in when they came of age. But she'd had no one, no one with her the day that light had burst forth from her, no one there to help her wield it—and then she'd been made to forget about it.

Now she needed it, and she was untrained—but not untried. Elana took a deep breath to squelch her rising panic. No one was coming to help them. No one knew she'd gone—except Cethin. No one was coming for her. No one was coming to help them. She was utterly alone in this. Cethin's blades would be no match against the Noir. It was up to her to find a way out. Unless it was already too late.

It was too late. A clawed hand—or foot?—gripped her leg and pulled her down. Elana tried to shift, tried to unleash her moonlight against them, struggling to rise. But everything felt slow: her body, her mind, and that well of power she'd just found within. She'd been able to draw from it in times of fear or need. Why couldn't she draw from it now? Was it the Noir's closeness? The Darkness of the mountains pressing in on her from all sides? Or something else entirely? She tried to focus, to find the connection to her moonlight—

She was scooped off the ground. Whispers of the Noir and trees whistled by in the dimness—

And then nothing.

A rattling hiss woke her. Elana trembled as something breathed in her scent, right next to her head—her blood. Her panic grew into an alarmed whimper: the Noir had caught her; she had somehow—in the midst of the chaos—shifted into her Elvish body; and now, they were going to drain her, gobble up every ounce of light she possessed as they had from this part of the world, until only Darkness remained. And she was all alone.

Cethin—*Gods, where was Cethin?* Had he somehow managed to escape? She hoped that he had, that he would be alright, regardless of what happened to her—

A new sound to her right. Elana twisted in the binds that held her hands and feet down on what she could only guess was a log. The Noir paused as well. Whatever—or whoever—was making the noise was unexpected. A slash of silver cut through the air and night. Hissing greeted it. Angry male snarls sounded in reply. Two glimmers of gold made their way toward her. Elana started: he'd somehow remained unharmed, untouched when they'd taken her. He'd tracked them across whatever distance they'd taken her, for however long it had taken.

Cethin had come for her.

Elana rolled to her left, cursing when her shoulder scraped rough bark. She leaned down as low as she could, hands scrambling for the blades he'd tossed in her direction. Fingers fumbling in the pitch-black, she managed to pick up one blade and set about using it to saw through the bindings around her legs. If they couldn't fight their way out, at least she'd be able to run when the time came. She heard the sounds of Cethin fighting interspersed with a few hisses of pain from the Noir. He was still alive—and, hopefully, still unharmed.

Something darker than night made its way toward her: one of the Noir had left the melee to guard their prize. She sawed faster, freeing her feet, right as the creature's presence towered over her. The Noir wrapped its taloned fingers around her throat, hauling her up and up. Elana's blade fell to the ground as the creature slammed her into one of the trees. She cried out in pain, eyes watering but still darting around for that silver slash that told her Cethin remained on his feet.

"Elana."

The first word she'd heard in ages.

"Elana." The word was weaker now and pained. There was no more silver flicker of a blade whipping through the air. There was nothing except for the rich depths of the night. Nothing but the bite of tree bark against her skin. Nothing but the searing pain of talons around her neck.

They were going to die here.

No. They wouldn't die—not here.

Not her—and not Cethin.

No. The thought settled deep into her bones.

No. They weren't going to die. They weren't going to fall in the Darkness. She was the Moonlight of Aviva, and she wouldn't allow it.

Elana closed her eyes and dove deep within herself, deep within the well of power that was rooted in her essence. The moonlight, the starlight, the reflection of the *dianaflora,* the legacy of the Goddess of Light, the legacy of *her* light, responded.

She could do this. She *must* do this.

So Elana did.

So El did.

So Eleonora did.

Chapter 18

She funneled her magic up like it was a wave building in the ocean, just as the tide would rise with the moon. She allowed that raw, undiluted moonlight and starlight to fill her chest, her heart, her mind; allowed it to flow down her arms, into her hands, her fingertips—to spark. She let that light break wild and free, wrapping her hands around the thing whose breath smelled of the darkness between stars—and she let go.

Light so bright she had to close her eyes exploded into the Noir, its screams almost more painful than its hunting hisses and sharp claws. Still, she kept her hands around it as it loosened its grip on her throat. She held on as it continued howling and thrashing—

Until she was holding nothing.

Silence filled the space. Then, the remaining Noir moved. The violent hissing sounded different—less angry and more desperate. It didn't matter how angry they were, how hungry they were, how determined they were, how frantic they were.

She would end them all.

Light, pure and white and silver, sang through the woods. It engulfed each Noir like a living flame, holding them, binding them as they shrieked and tried to scratch claws of shadow through their bright cages, until each spot of Darkness winked out—

Until they were nothing.

The light flickered, then faded. She sank to the base of the tree, downing air in greedy inhales. She'd done it. She'd controlled her magic. She'd banished the Noir. No, not banished—ended. Permanently.

A male groan was the only sound she heard then. *Cethin*. She moved to his side, each step heavier than the last, reminding her she wasn't used to using her magic like that.

"I'm here," she said, half walking, half crawling the last few feet to him. Her voice was a rasping whisper in the gloom, still choked from the stranglehold of the Noir and the emotion she felt for her life-sworn. "I'm here." His groans wavered as she took his right hand into her left where the scar of their life oath pulsed. "I'm here." The only words that ever mattered.

"We..." he panted. She tried to shush him, but he whimpered, "Can't. Must go." She stilled, muscles tensing. Her magic, though weakened, rallied within her, ready to strike like an asp should any of the Noir return. "Stars," he muttered, drawing her focus back. She looked up. Not stars, but...the *dianaflora* shining through the cave opening. How was it possible they were still there? Had the Noir not taken her elsewhere?

She helped him to his feet, her own body protesting with overexertion. Slowly, she dragged them both through the cave entrance. "We made it," she whispered, following the *dianaflora* to the springs. "We're safe."

Cethin groaned as she set him on the soft moss along the side of a pool. She looked at his wounds: two long, savage rips along his left leg through his pants; four along his bare arm; and two, deeper than the others, along his lower abdomen, cutting through his shirt and leathers. She took in a shaking breath and willed her heart and mind to calm. "You're going to be okay."

His eyes were half closed, breathing wet as he rasped, "Don't...don't lie to me."

Tears spilled from her eyes as she did. "I won't." *Never again.* She removed his shirt carefully, trying to not cause him more pain. As he lay against the moss, she dug into that raw magic made of the brightest stars and wove it into the Healing power that had to be buried somewhere beside it. She wouldn't accept anything less—didn't care that she'd never used it.

"When will she wake up." That was her mother's voice, and it wasn't a question—it was a demand.

"In time," a female voice replied.

"That is not good enough," her mother snapped. "She is your princess, she is heir to the throne—"

"And her body is susceptible to injury and illness, like anyone else's," was the firm reply. "But like all of us—especially with access to myself and the others—she will make a full recovery. She just needs time."

"That is what I have been telling her," came a tired male voice. Her father's. She heard her mother tut and a door open and close. "She will be fine, Serenity."

"This never should have happened in the first place," her mother hissed.

What had happened? She'd gone to one of the palace pools that morning to try and swim and—ah, yes, that's what had happened. She'd fallen under the water. That was the last thing the young princess remembered.

The sounds of her mother's and father's voices back and forth became a song, until she fell asleep again. When she awoke, her parents were gone, but a female wearing the white gown of the Healers was there.

"Welcome back, Princess," the female said. "How are you feeling?" The young princess sat up in her bed, wincing at the throbbing in her head. "You are in pain."

The young princess nodded. "My head."

The female came and sat on the side of her bed. "While we were able to effectively clear the water from your lungs and repair any damage there rather quickly, it was the head injury you sustained after you lost consciousness that we were more concerned about." The Healer—no doubt one of the High Healers—raised her hands to the young princess's head. Blue light flowed from the female's hands: her Healing magic.

"How do you do that?" the young princess whispered as the ache in her head receded.

The Healer smiled. "It takes time and practice," she replied, the blue light fading as she removed her hands. "You have to feel your gift here," she continued, moving her hands to her heart, "where your well of power resides. From there, you draw it up through everything that you are and loosen it through your fingertips." She shook her hands once, twice, and blue light softly flared.

"Is that it?" the young princess asked, puzzled. Shouldn't magic be more complicated than that?

The female chuckled. "Not quite. It will depend on what your elemental gift is, Princess. And Healing itself requires plenty of focus. We give our attention to one injury, one illness, at a time and pour our power over it like honey over tea. From there, we use our will to correct the issue."

The young princess wrinkled her nose. "That is all you have to do? Just think about it?"

Amusement sparkled in the Healer's eyes. "It is not always as easy as you might imagine. But yes, that is the basic idea."

She tugged at her magic, pulled it into her heart, then her hands. She moved her palms over the wounds on his legs, pushing that Healing energy into them, willing them to close. Slowly—more slowly than she ever could've imagined—they did. She loosed a breath then moved on to the wounds on his arms. Again, she dug into that well of light, allowed it to fill her—to fill him. He whimpered in pain. She sent her magic to calm him, to soothe him into a painless sleep. The wounds on his arms closed even more slowly than the ones on his legs.

She panicked. All magic had limits—and the wounds on his abdomen remained. She chewed on her bottom lip. She'd used so much of her magic—too much—to destroy the Noir. Was what she had left enough? It had to be. She pushed down the doubt and fatigue and threw herself into that life-giving Healing energy as Cethin's essence faltered.

She flung her power out, filling the space around them with it, drawing on the *dianaflora* to fuel her. The petals closest to them flared with light. She gasped as that light raced toward her—toward him. The light closed the wounds in his chest.

She let go of him as that light sealed his body, making him whole once more...

...and then her magic fizzled out, her consciousness along with it.

"Elana." The male's voice was so far away. "Elana!" The voice was closer now—panicked. She felt warmth against her face. Broad hands cupped her cheeks, and a familiar male face came into focus. Amber eyes stared into hers.

"Cethin." Gods, her voice was hoarse. She watched him sag with relief as his hands fell to her shoulders. She began to pull herself into a seated position—to pull herself back together.

"Are you alright?"

"I...I think so," she said, her hands going to her neck, to where the Noir had held her life. There was no pain. "I feel like I should be asking you that." She leaned forward and ran her hand down his arm where the Noir's scratches had wounded him.

They were gone.

He was looking at her with a wry smile. "My wounds seem to have miraculously healed themselves." His gaze shifted from her face to her hands—to her heart. "Unless, of course, there's something you'd like to tell me? It seems I was knocked out."

She stared into the eyes of her life-sworn, the male she had fallen for—

And then she told him. Told him *everything*: how she'd stopped the Noir—not just now, but in Ozul, too. How she'd Healed him. How the *dianaflora* had strengthened her magic. He didn't balk.

"The flowers," was the first thing he said, voice quiet in a way that made her uneasy. "That's why they were removed."

"Removed? From where?"

"Aviva. From the princess and her people."

"Who brought the *dianaflora* here?" *And how did he know they'd been moved?*

He was quiet again for a long time. "I'm not sure," he said, looking her over. "But I think I know who they were left here for." His gaze connected with hers again, and she remembered she was still in her Elvish form, still...*Eleonora*.

The lost princess returned.

The Queen of Aviva.

"You knew."

"I've known for some time now."

She raised a brow. "And you didn't feel the need to mention your revelation?"

He shrugged. "I figured you'd tell me—when the time was right, of course."

Of course. She rolled her eyes. He'd known but hadn't said anything, hadn't pushed her—until now. Now still didn't feel like the right time to tell him, not after everything they'd just been through. But time was never guaranteed.

She glanced back at the *dianaflora*. "All this time. All this time, I could have strengthened myself," she said, more to herself than to him.

"You still can." She looked at him again. There was nothing but conviction, determination, and something deeper in his eyes. "You can strengthen yourself. You can rally your people. You can re-Bind the Darkness and the Light. That's the legend of the lost princess, of course."

She was about to roll her eyes again, but Cethin released his grip on her, put his hands over his heart, and bowed his head as he knelt.

"Your Majesty. Queen Eleonora." The *dianaflora* brightened at his words. The cave became lighter, warmer, as if the flowers recognized whose power was in their presence. She glanced toward the pool of water next to them and caught sight of her reflection—her Elvish form. She closed her eyes, and—with half a thought—opened them to see herself as a mortal woman once more.

"Not El, anymore?" she said.

"I would've knelt before you either way." She raised a brow at him. "Yes, even though I was pissed as Hell at you for not telling me the truth about who you were. I would've knelt that very first day. I would've been yours to command in your royal guard. I would've been yours to command as your First Guard. Even if you were not Queen, I would still be yours. Yours to command." Her mouth ran dry as his eyes darkened and moved from her eyes to her mouth. "Yours to love."

"Queen or barmaid," he continued, cupping her cheek with his right hand. "Elf or human. Eleonora or Elana." Those darkened eyes met hers once more. "I will always be yours."

Moments passed—then she looked away. It was too much. It was all too much.

"Don't."

His hand tensed where it lingered on her cheek. "Don't...?"

She stood quickly. "Don't speak such words," she said, as though she could banish his speech to the furthest reaches of the Darkness and have the Noir devour them whole. "You shouldn't. We *can't*."

He was on his feet in an instant, reaching for her. "And why not?" he growled, pulling her back to him. "Why not speak the words that are etched into my heart, my essence? Eleonora, please," he said, voice and touch softening. "This doesn't have to change anything."

"This changes *everything*," she said, looking at her small, pale hands in his, both covered in calluses from long hours spent training. Training together. She looked back up at him. "My path has always been one way forward: to re-Bind the Balance. How that ends..." She shook her head as a tear rolled down her cheek. "How that ends could never end well. Not for me."

He lifted his hand and swept that tear away. She leaned into the touch. "Who says?" he murmured into her hair. "Who says that when you walk into the Darkness you won't return?" She pulled away and studied his face. "Who says that when you walk into the Darkness you must walk alone?" Something inside of her broke open. She'd been alone her whole life: had left Aviva alone, come into her magic alone—grown up alone. "Eleonora," he said softly. She didn't want to be alone anymore. But how could she pull him into this?

The world paused as she stared at him, until—one after another—*dianaflora* drifted from the cave ceiling and swirled around her, forming a crown atop her head. She shook her head in wonder as Cethin chuckled. "I told you it doesn't matter—I'm yours—always. No matter who you are."

"This is who I choose to be." She started at the voice that came out of her, once again in her Elvish body. It was different: not the voice of a human barmaid, not the voice of a princess in hiding. This was her true voice—the voice of the queen.

"I am Eleonora, the lost princess, heir to the throne of Aviva." She sucked in a sharp breath as she spoke the words aloud for the first time—before she said what she needed to say next. "You," she said, swallowing as he held her gaze. "I release you, Cethin, from your life oath." He flinched at her words—at the freedom she'd given him. The bond between them she wanted broken. In case it was the only way she could let him go. "I will ask nothing else of you."

His eyes became as smooth as honey as he stepped closer. "If that is your choice," he said, voice low and rough, "then allow me a new honor. Allow me the honor of being the first of your royal guard. Your First Guard."

Her heart thundered, threatening to beat right out of her chest. He would still choose her, even now. "You are not afraid of what awaits me?" *What awaits us?*

"No," he said firmly, wrapping his arms around her. And then he leaned forward and brushed his forehead against hers. She gasped at the contact, then let herself relax and sink into the familiar comfort of his body.

Except it didn't feel right—none of it did.

The earth shuddered. "We should go," he said. She nodded, reaching to pull a *dianaflora* from her hair, when the ground shuddered again, tossing her back.

"Cethin!" she cried out.

"Elana!" came the response.

But it wasn't Cethin's voice.

Chapter 19

The Lost Princess

She blinked once—twice. Bright light met her eyes. She groaned and lifted a hand to shield her eyes against the blinding light. Sunlight—

No, not sunlight. *The* Light. The Light of Aviva.

No more cave. No more Darkness. She wasn't in the mountains anymore. How long had she been out for?

She groaned again as she lifted her head, pops of light clanging through her vision. Pain scorched every movement, and the ground beneath her was moving. No, not the earth—a horse. She was sitting—or, at least, whatever an injured person atop a horse did. Its rider brought them to a halt and she swayed, the white mare tossing its mane as its golden rider dismounted.

"Cerdwin?" she choked. She made to dismount, and he was there in an instant, helping her down.

"Slow down," he said, lifting a hand. "Slow down and tell me something. Something only Elana would know." Not the voice of her friend, but an order from Aviva's Second Commander. She searched her mind, trying to think of something that only the two of them would know, but her head hurt.

And they weren't alone. A company of three other warriors—all Elvish males she didn't recognize—were also atop horses. They were all dressed for battle, surrounding them and staring. One had a dirty unconscious Elf sprawled across the back of his horse. The male's hands and feet were bound, and blood dripped from a wound to his head. She started—but it wasn't him.

It wasn't Cethin.

"We," she rasped, "we have to go back. Cethin." Something dark flashed across Cerdwin's face at the mention of the male's name. "What is it?" she asked, panic threatening to overcome her pain.

Cerdwin hesitated, then motioned for their companions to continue forward. "What all do you remember? From when you left the city?" he asked. *Even though you were under strict orders* not *to,* were the unspoken words burning in his eyes.

"I went to observe the Dark King's position along the mountains to the north. Cethin followed me..." She shook her head, pain reminding her that wasn't a good idea at the moment. "They captured me," she breathed. "And Cethin came, he rescued me, and..." She stopped when she noticed the shadow flicker over Cerdwin's face again, his pain—and his concern. "What is it?" she asked again, trying to pull herself together, to sound more queenlike than she felt. That was who she'd decided to be in the cave, after she'd told Cethin everything. And he'd accepted her for who she was.

"That was not Cethin," Cerdwin said quietly.

"No...what...what do you mean?!" she demanded, hands shaking. *That was not Cethin.*

"What happened?" she cried. "What happened?" Cerdwin stepped closer and she sagged against him. "Where is he? Where is Cethin?" she sobbed, not caring that the company ahead probably heard her, her weakness, her pain.

That was not Cethin.

"He was not there," Cerwdin said, the gentleness in his voice tinged with anger. "We do not know where he is."

That was not Cethin.

Cerdwin's words echoed in her ears as she collapsed to the ground.

There was a steady light shining through the window. Her vision swam as she rose to meet it. She was in a bed. She recognized the marble of the walls, the scent of the space—

She was inside the palace—the palace she was going to claim as her own upon her return. Claim as her own—

That was not Cethin.

"You are awake." The quiet statement came from the same voice. Cerdwin reclined in an armchair to her left, its elegant blue fabric and golden thread a stark contrast to his dirtied and bloodied clothing. Which meant he hadn't changed yet. How long had she been out this time? "Three hours," he answered, as if reading the question on her face.

She took a deep breath. "What happened?"

"As far as we can tell," he said, watching her warily, "you were taken by the Dark King's forces while you were scouting along a northern pass."

"I know that," she said impatiently, "but—"

"We did not find you wherever it was you imagined you were, Elana," he said gently. "It sounded like you imagined you were in a cave of some sort?" She nodded. Cerdwin exhaled and leaned forward, rubbing sweaty, dirty, bloody hands on his pants. He shook his head, curls shifting with the movement. "It was not real," he said as those piercing violet eyes met her gaze again. She took a shuddering breath.

That was not Cethin.

It was not real.

"When we found you," he continued, "you were in a makeshift dungeon—like they had constructed it for temporary use. Like they knew they would learn what they needed to from whomever they imprisoned there, and then move on."

That was not Cethin.

It was not real.

Tears filled her eyes and streamed down her face. She let them.

That was not Cethin.

It was not real.

They'd known. Whoever had taken her. They'd known what she was—*who* she was.

"What was on the horse," Cerdwin finished, "was a *mutatio*."

A *mutatio*—a changeling.

That was not Cethin.

It was not real.

Shock poured through her body, nausea rolling through her stomach in waves as her left palm tingled.

That was not Cethin.

It was not real.

When had the dark creature taken her life-sworn's place?

"Now, at least," Cerdwin said, "we have an idea of what we are up against. The Healers are already working on a salve that will help us see if there are any more like it in our ranks." He hesitated, then, "We have already used it on you, just to be sure." She glared at him. "We were able to get you out," he continued, switching from her friend to Aviva's Second Commander again, "but we need to know anything you told them, anything they might use against us."

Anything that would mean losing an edge in the war to come. And while she hadn't seen much, she had looked through the maps in Cerdwin's tent—had stayed in his camp. But what, exactly, had she told the changeling? Beyond who she was? She nodded again, moving slowly so as not to disturb the pain threatening to split her head open. Cerdwin inclined his head to her, then pushed out of the chair to stand. "Once you have had time to rest and recover, of course. One of the Healers has already been to see you. Her remedies will ease the pain and speed your healing."

"Thank you," she whispered. "When can I see him?"

Cerdwin paused, one hand on the doorframe. When he turned to face her again, that edge of anger and frustration had returned to his face, setting his eyes aflame. "I thought you understood," he said. "We cannot find him. He was not there, Elana. It was only the changeling."

"But," she said, throat tightening, "if it was only the changeling—"

"You were right. He did follow you, after you foolishly went out there on your own. But..." Cerdwin swallowed. "But it had already been a few hours. He told us something felt wrong with the bond between you." A nod toward her left hand. Her breath caught. At least everything they'd shared between them until then had been real. "But he did not return. For all we know, he is in another one of those makeshift dungeons, the enemy doing the Gods only know what to him, like they did to you." Cerdwin's mouth thinned into a tight line, burning eyes hardening into amethyst jewels. The torch on the wall flickered.

Would Cerdwin deem it worth it—deem Cethin worth it—if she asked him, or Eldwyn, or both of them, to send out a search party? It didn't seem likely, not when Cerdwin had shown so much contempt toward the half-Elf—something she had no doubt he'd learned from his lord father. She bowed her head and withdrew into herself. After a moment, she heard Cerdwin pass through the door, closing it behind him with a soft click.

That was not Cethin.

It was not real.

Hot shame flooded her body—shame at having failed her people once again. For getting caught and possibly revealing their army's secrets. Shame for not being ready to face what was beyond the mountains. Shame for not being enough. It was quickly built on by a cold and depthless fear that flooded her veins as she thought of where Cethin really was—what might be being done to him.

She was no queen to rally around, no queen to fight—or to fight for—and certainly no queen to love. She let her tears flow as she laid her head down, closed her eyes, and willed herself to sleep.

Light still illuminated the room when she awoke, but the castle had quieted, telling her its other inhabitants had gone to sleep. She forced herself to get up and walk across the room. It was simply—yet elegantly—decorated, as was the royal family's way for anyone who chose to reside within the palace walls. She went to the washing basin atop a wooden dresser and splashed water on her face. Then, with a steadying breath, she peered into the round mirror above the dresser. She was surprised that Cerdwin hadn't said anything about her shift, unsure if that was a relief or not. The aching in her head and bones had subsided, though the red gash above her brow was still healing. In a few hours, it would be a faint line that would leave no scar, no memory of the whole ordeal. No memory of what hadn't been real.

That was not Cethin.

It was not real.

She looked at her left hand, where the life oath continued to beat like a heart beneath her palm. She splashed at the water in anger, sending it rocking against the deep sides of the wooden basin. Her magic stirred at the emotion. She worked to squash it.

Gods, she'd used her magic in front of *it*. That part had been real. And whatever was happening to Cethin now was also real.

She looked into the mirror again. Her weariness and despair were replaced with something else—something new, yet something that had always been a part of her. Something queen-like. It was time to act like one. But she had something to do first.

She walked to the chair and picked up the cloak strewn over it—Cerdwin's, from the smokey cedar and amber scent clinging to it—and strode for the door, only to hear something clatter to the floor: her daggers. Despite herself—her grief, her anger, her disbelief—she smiled, sheathing and pocketing them in the cloak. It was time for a chat with the changeling, and there was only one place they'd keep a creature like that: the dungeons.

She ran her hand across the cool stone wall as she walked down the hall, making her way past other rooms, raising her hand so as not to bump the doors and disturb whomever dwelt within. Her head started throbbing again as she walked. She had some memory of this place and could hopefully make it to the dungeons without having to ask for directions—and without anyone raising questions about her wandering around the palace. Starbursts hit her vision. She sagged against the wall, resting her head against the cold stone for relief.

Hands, callused and sturdy, looped around her and under her arms, steadying her, then guided her to the ground. Footsteps retreated, then returned, and a glass of water appeared in her hands.

"Drink," came a firm female voice.

She drank gratefully from the cup, its contents settling her and her pounding head. "Thank you," she said, lifting her eyes from the cup to the female: she was striking in her plain white gown—which contrasted with her golden skin and hair to match—and sparkling purple eyes that watched her intently as she drank. She knew that face.

The female crossed her arms. "Who gave you authorization to leave your room?" Heat rose to her cheeks as she tried to think up some story to tell the Healer. "You could've collapsed walking so soon after a head injury like that. I told him to clear it with me first."

Head injury. Him. Cerdwin. There was no doubt as to who this was.

"You must be—"

"Alanna," the female interjected, uncrossing her arms to take the cup back. "I've been seeing to your care since he brought you back. My brother mentioned you went on an adventure against his wishes. I should've assumed your lack of regard for your own well-being wouldn't end there." Alanna arched a brow, then pulled her up from where she sat on the floor. She didn't have time to protest before the female linked their arms again and walked her to the closest room.

Her anger and frustration rose to the surface, the light in her chest surging. She needed to get to the dungeons. She needed to talk to the changeling.

That was not Cethin.

It was not real.

To find Cethin.

They entered a room similar to the one she'd just left, and Alanna pushed her into a chair. The female knelt in front of a low-lying table and pulled together what she assumed were Healer's supplies.

"Alanna thinks everyone lacks regard for their well-being when they do not follow her orders to the letter." Another voice—also feminine, but older—came from her left. She turned to the source of the voice as Alanna tutted.

The Healer made her way to a bed, to the female—no, the human woman—who rested there. "Oh hush," Alanna said, plying the woman with a cup. The Healer raised the pillows so the woman could sit up more easily and pulled the blankets around her. Fussing. She bit her lip against a smile.

"I have been under her care longer than most," the woman said as Alanna helped her rise to lean against the pillows. "I know her moods. When she feels she has encountered a, ah, *difficult* patient." The woman laughed then, the sound bright, young, and beautiful—a sound that tugged at the edges of her memory. "Oh, I am not saying that you are difficult, child," the woman continued. "Rather that Alanna's judgment might be a tad lacking." Alanna muttered something about the woman needing tea and strode from the room.

She suppressed a chuckle, slowly rising from the chair Cerdwin's sister had placed her in and walked over to the woman. She wasn't prepared for what she saw—*who* she saw.

Sonia, her former lady's maid—the woman responsible for her exile.

The autumn air was as crisp as the leaves on the ground as the young princess and the lady's maid walked the palace grounds to the stables, the wind whipping at the young female's braid and the human woman's long raven-black hair. They could've gone through the indoor entrance, but the lady's maid had insisted on going this way—the long way. It was almost like she was avoiding going—odd, considering the lady's maid had been the one who had demanded that the young princess learn how to ride.

The young princess had never been inside of the royal stables. They housed the best of the Elvish horses—the fastest horses. Her attention immediately caught and held on a mare with hair as white as the snow that would soon fall in Aviva as they entered the space; the steed was a beauty. The young princess walked up to the beast and reached out her hand. "She's beautiful."

"And far too big for someone so small to ride," a male voice answered, and the young princess looked up to see a stablehand approaching. "Good day, Princess Eleonora, Mistress Sonia," he added, eyeing the lady's maid.

Sonia inclined her head, but the young princess held her ground, retracting her hand to place both on her hips.

"What do you mean too little?" she challenged, drawing herself up to her full height and holding her chin high.

"Forgive me, Your Majesty," the male said, bowing, "you are well grown for your age." She was seven years of age. He wasn't wrong, but she really, really wanted to ride the white mare.

"Thank you," she said, dropping her hands and sighing. "Which horse is mine?" The male chuckled and led her to a small gray pony, already saddled, and helped her mount.

"And you, Mistress?" he inquired, somewhat hesitantly. Sonia remained by the white mare, her eyes fixed on the horse as though she'd seen a ghost. "It has been some time since she had a ride," he added quietly. When Sonia's gaze alighted on the male, her stunning blue eyes—which the young princess had always found uncanny for a human—were filled with an emotion so strong the young princess swore she could almost taste it: there was sadness there, sorrow, grief, and regret; also a fondness, a youthfulness, joy, and love. A weird mix of emotions to feel toward a horse, but what did she know? She was seven.

"I suppose it is time," the lady's maid said. The male nodded and turned to find a saddle for the mare as well. The young princess watched the lady's maid rub the spot above the horse's eyes, then reach around to scratch its ears. She murmured words the young princess couldn't quite hear—even with her Elvish hearing—and reached into one of her pockets for an apple, which the mare accepted quickly, causing the lady's maid to...giggle? The woman composed herself when the stablehand returned and secured a saddle onto the white horse. The lady's maid mounted with a grace the young princess envied.

"We will practice in the yard first," Sonia told her, any trace of emotion in her voice or eyes gone. She was once again the head lady's maid who was to be obeyed in all manner of royal training. The young princess nodded, watching as the woman gently kicked the sides of the horse, easing it into a slow walk.

She knew the woman: the raven black hair that was now entirely gray; the blue eyes that were now milky and unseeing; the body, once robust and strong, now weak-looking and bone-thin. Everything about her was wholly mortal.

How had she done it?

"Well, do not gawk, child," Sonia said. She blinked at that, and the woman laughed again. "I might look it, but I am not completely blind yet. Just another old woman. Sit, sit," Sonia pressed, waving a hand for her to sit on the cot, atop one of the soft blankets Alanna had put on the bed. She did. The old woman watched her.

"You are not one of the regular castle-dwellers."

"I am not." She wasn't sure what else to say—if her old lady's maid would recognize her.

The woman motioned for her to lean closer as she took her hand and whispered, "I hear they brought you back from the Darkness, child."

Her mouth went dry, all thoughts of lost memories fading to the background.

That was not Cethin.

It was not real.

"Yes," she whispered back.

Sonia released her hand, and she felt the weight of those milky eyes. "They forget that old as I may be, dwindling as my vision is, my ears still work just fine." She didn't know what to say to that, but her former lady's maid pushed the conversation forward. "He was most upset about it, you know." The old woman must've been able to see the confusion on her face. "Cerdwin," the lady's maid supplied. "It is good to have him back again. He was always such a good lad." Again, those eyes—unseeing yet seeing—roved over her. "You seem familiar, child." *Gods.* If the woman didn't remember her...would she remember what she'd done?

Alanna re-entered the room with a porcelain tray in her hands, a teapot steaming on top, and two small, painted teacups along with it. "She has been through enough for a few days, Sonia," Alanna said firmly—though not unkindly—to her older charge. "And my brother will want to ask her plenty of his own questions." A pointed look at her with that statement.

"It was nice to meet you," she said quietly to Sonia, angling her head toward her former lady's maid in farewell. The woman groaned as she lifted her hand, and Alanna immediately went to her side with a cup of tea. "Thank you for the water," she added to the Healer, and Alanna nodded.

"Go back to bed," Cerdwin's twin ordered.

She nodded back, withdrew from the room, and went back down the hall back to her room, hoping she would be able to return and ask the mortal woman the thousands of questions now swirling in her mind.

Cerdwin

Cerdwin stepped back from the changeling, its oily black blood dripping from the knife in his hand. It'd been hours of this—hours, yet he'd made little progress.

After delivering Elana to a room designated for Healing—and making sure his sister attended to her—he'd come directly to the dungeons. To challenge—torture, really—the creature who'd dared to capture and torture his friend, and now held her life-sworn somewhere.

It was folly to even consider sending a unit of his males to look for Cethin because his lord father would disapprove—but when he'd told Eldwyn what had happened and what he planned to do about it, the First Commander had *encouraged* it. It wasn't unusual for Eldwyn to encourage what some might consider slightly illicit or unnecessary activity, but still.

Cerdwin palmed the blade, refusing to let the thing see his frustration. Voice as calm as he could manage, he asked again, "Where are you keeping the half-Elf? The one you were impersonating?" The creature didn't answer. Cerdwin knelt and angled the blade toward its chest again. "I need a location. *Now.*"

The changeling peered up at him with depthless black eyes, nothing but cool defiance on its gray face now that it had shifted back into its body. Cerdwin made a cut down the creature's right side—taking care to ensure he didn't pierce anything vital. It hissed in pain but held his gaze. Then it laughed, a cruel and ancient sound that sent a shiver down Cerdwin's spine.

"It was by sheer happenstance that *you* were even able to find *her*," the creature said with a sneer. "You will not find him, not so easily. Perhaps not at all."

Cerdwin noted the emphasis it put on certain words—then stabbed the dagger down again, plunging the entire blade into the changeling's thigh, patience worn thin. He hadn't slept—not since Cethin, covered in a scent of terror Cerdwin had never tasted before, even on the battlefield, had rushed onto the wall saying Elana had disappeared, and that something felt *wrong* with the life oath that connected them. The changeling wasn't wrong: discovering the temporary dungeon, and the woman—female—chained inside of it had been pure happenstance. The wind had been beyond frigid there, the snow heavier than he'd ever seen, making the pass more treacherous than they'd typically risk—like it had known they were coming. But they'd made it—and then they'd found her, body likely only alive in the freezing temperatures because of her Elvish form. She'd been unconscious when they'd found her—after making quick work of the solitary guard stationed outside the space, like the enemy had assumed the Darkness and foul weather would be enough to keep them away. And the changeling...

Cerdwin would never forget its wrath the moment it realized they knew. He had seen what Elana had likely seen: Cethin, but not. None of it had been real—all of it had been a fantasy.

A fantasy where she'd been *happy*. Cerdwin exhaled through his nose and mastered himself again. It wasn't her fault. She wasn't trained for this, not really. Besides, the life oath could make people do strange things. Or was it *love* that could make people do strange things, as Eldwyn had said offhand one night? The notion was ludicrous. There was no way a half-Elvish mercenary loved anything beyond coin and whatever would save his own skin—that's who mercenaries were at their core. And the risk this particular mercenary could open them up to—their army, their spy network, the stability of his force, what was left of the kingdom...

It wasn't her fault. No, it was Eldwyn's, for allowing this. Cerdwin reached down, gripped the dagger, and slowly drew it out of the changeling's thigh. He met the creature's cruel expression with one of his own, willing dark amusement—and a little of the lion—into his eyes.

"If you cannot answer my questions, changeling," he said, in a cold voice that made him shudder because it belonged to his lord father, "you will find our uses for you grow...limited." He smiled a vicious smile that showed he had absolutely no issue with that—that he would be more than happy to show the dark demon just how useless it was if it continued resisting his interrogation.

The thing just smirked back at him. "I am giving you answers," it said with a sly smile—and then that smile changed and warped, until Cerdwin recognized that smile, the face that looked at him. It was his own. "Just not the answers you know how to hear." It cocked its head to the side then with an unholy smoothness no Elf possessed. Those little tells. Small, tiny tells. How hadn't she known? How much pain had they inflicted upon her that she'd been so oblivious? As if reading his mind, the creature added, "I could give you answers about her, you know."

"About your mistress, you mean?" Cerdwin said through his teeth.

His mirrored face crumpled, then shifted back into that twisted, gray face. "You know who I mean," it said.

Cerdwin shook his head and rose to his feet, casually brushing dirt and blood off his hands and tunic. He was dirty. He was tired. He hadn't had a moment to himself since he'd been back.

"We are done for today," he said casually, trying once again to keep the impatience in every pore of his body from spilling out and lighting the whole room on fire, that primal instinct that told him to sink his dagger into the thing's throat, belly, eye—wherever he could strike hard, fast, and be done with it—in check. Or better yet, his sharp lion's teeth. But they still needed it—at least for a little while longer.

The Lost Princess

She'd been resting in bed for a few hours when Alanna returned. "I'm here to make sure you haven't taken any more tempting walks," the female said by way of greeting. She rolled her eyes, stopping when they were pinpointed by the Healer's sharp gaze. "You're very lucky, you know," Alanna said.

"What do you mean?" She couldn't imagine her captors had done anything that would've caused an Elf to be in imminent physical danger—not with her body's natural Healing abilities.

Alanna sat in the blue chair next to her bed, where Cerdwin had sat. It was still shocking how alike they looked. Alanna even tossed her curls with the same impatience she'd seen Cerdwin shake his head with. *They both shared sensitive temperaments, too.*

"Your body," Alanna said pointedly.

"My body?" She looked down at herself: long, pale limbs, the strong muscle built underneath from training, made faster—or so she assumed—in her Elvish body; her slender hands, the left one reminding her that her life-sworn still needed her. She toyed with the end of her braid, with hair thicker and glossier than it had been in her mortal form.

Alanna pinched the bridge of her nose. Apparently the Healer also spent time with Eldwyn. "Your Elvish body."

"My injuries were that bad?"

"No…but, for our kind, they should've Healed quite readily on their own." It took her a few moments to wrap her head around *our kind.* "But not on you." Alanna continued. "Which tells me something."

"Which is?"

"That your essence isn't used to being in your Elvish form. You left shortly after the Breaking?"

She stilled, willing her heart and breathing to remain even. Did Alanna know? She nodded.

"One of the many puzzle pieces we're still learning about, even now," the Healer said. "Many who left, who dwelt in other places, who wanted to blend in as human…" The female looked to the window as she fell silent. "It takes a toll, and it takes time for the body to reintegrate itself. As far as we've been able to tell, the longer you're in your mortal form, the longer the adjustment period is."

"What does that mean?" she asked, relieved the conversation had stayed within the Healing space.

"It means," Alanna said, turning and leaning forward with Cerdwin's frankness, "don't go off fighting the monsters again for a little while, okay?" She made to protest, but Alanna interrupted. "Look, I don't know why you returned, I don't know why my brother is so interested in your well-being, and I certainly won't pretend to understand why you are so interested in training with him." Her mouth popped open and closed quickly at that. "But where he lacks giving a damn about his own safety, try to."

"Then why bother with me at all? Why does my safety matter so much to you?"

Alanna flipped her curls over her shoulder as she stood. "Because whoever matters to Cerdwin matters to me, too." With that, the female turned on her heel and walked out of the room; but her words hung in the air.

Would Alanna care for Cethin, when they found him?

If they found him?

Chapter 20

Leave it to Cerdwin to go all the way to Ozul, find someone just as stubborn as he was, and end up leading them the whole way back to Aviva. She snorted. Beyond Elana being *someone* to Cerdwin, Alanna hadn't been able to get a clear read on the female—on the true nature of her relationship with her brother.

Alanna and her twin had been young when their father had shipped his only son and heir—*his most prized possession*, Alanna recalled him saying, with no small amount of distaste—to the human continent, where he would remain safe, untouched, and unharmed. But they'd been old enough to have had their share of lovers. While Cerdwin managed to keep *most* of his liaisons secret, Alanna knew he invited both females and males to his bed. He hadn't written about any from the human continent, but it wasn't like she gave a shit about who her brother did or didn't fuck.

Alanna kept her affairs more private. It would've outraged her father to learn she'd lost her maidenhood before being dutifully wed. Not that it mattered once she'd taken the Healer's robes. Healers didn't marry and never bore children; their Healing magic was deemed their matrimony and maternity. But it didn't mean they didn't have lovers.

She'd missed her brother. Their initial reunion had been brief—and with their father part of it, not particularly merry. Especially when she'd told the lord about her assignment to the Endurnal Mountains. Sometimes she wondered why she bothered telling him at all. She rarely told the lord about her responsibilities anymore, as he deemed her becoming a Healer not an honor—as her mother would've seen it—but as shirking her responsibility to their house. Plus, he could always read about her work in the debriefs sent to the Lord's Council.

Guilt bit at her. That was why their father was so hard on Cerdwin now. His only heir. His only *real* child. But as soon as she'd mentioned traveling north, their father had called on his First Commander. Alanna liked Eldwyn. The male had a few decades on her and Cerdwin but hadn't become as distant as some of the other older warriors. He'd seen a lot but hadn't lost his touch of kindness: she'd seen him beside the beds of his injured males—or even in their homes, comforting their families. That kind of empathy was rare amongst the Elves anymore, and even more so in someone of the male's rank. Which was why she hadn't been at all surprised by the flush on her brother's cheeks when the First Commander had walked into their family's receiving room. She'd played enough card games with her twin to recognize the mask he wore and sent a prayer to the Gods their father hadn't noticed. *That* was a dangerous game. But with her ineligible to wed and unable to bear children—Cerdwin had a duty. One he didn't ask for. One she'd basically decided for him the day she'd chosen to claim her life as her own.

Shaking the tangle of thoughts from her head, Alanna kept a steady pace to where Eldwyn resided in the palace when he wasn't camped out with his soldiers. He'd never taken a First Commander's pavilion—something that grated on her father's nerves—but preferred to dwell in a smaller tent as one of them. He rarely stayed in the palace either, but with the scouting mission, he'd stayed to report to the Lord's Council. It was no real surprise her twin was already there.

"Drink?" Eldwyn asked her in greeting, rising swiftly to fill a cup when she nodded.

He kept his rooms in the palace almost as simple as he kept his tent in the camp: a small, two-chamber room that contained a small sitting area with a few chairs, a bed, fireplace, a small dresser, and the door to the attached bathing room. No whisper of his trappings as First Commander, or any of the numerous other honors he carried. He didn't even have night curtains against the Light. She'd asked him about that once, but he'd only shrugged. She supposed after having camped with his males in thinly lined tents, being submerged in darkness at fake night would be uncomfortable. She reveled in the darkness of her Healer's room—it was quiet there, a place for her to think. Not like the Darkness she'd seen during her trip to the north.

She must've shuddered because she heard her brother ask, "Cold?" A fire flickered to life in the hearth. Though it was summer in Aviva now, the nights still carried a faint chill with them.

"That female is impossible," she muttered under her breath, earning herself a chuckle from Eldwyn, who handed her a cup, and a grimace from her brother. She threw the latter a pointed look.

"Then you two should get along well," her twin snorted, eyes simmering. She downed the drink and handed the cup back to Eldwyn before taking a seat across from where he'd settled next to her twin.

"Remind me why *I* have to deal with her again?"

"Because we cannot have any of the other Healers tending to her."

"And why—"

"Because of our lord father," Cerdwin flatly cut her off. She met her brother's gaze once more, but he broke it and glanced at Eldwyn. "If he finds out we let her train, and not only that, but that she participated in the scouting trial..." He ran a hand through his hair, which was almost as long as hers now.

She surveyed him—not just with a Healer's eye, but a sister's. When was the last time he'd bathed? Had a haircut? A shave? Literally done anything but work? She shouldn't push him, but she couldn't help it. "Then why bother to let her do all that?"

Why was this female so damn important to him? And Eldwyn, apparently? And there it was: a quick, unreadable look swapped between Second Commander and First.

"Because she asked to. And she is my friend."

"You've had female friends before, brother." She heard Eldwyn shift in his seat. "What makes this one so special?"

Her twin held her stare now. "The last I remember," he spoke, voice dropping so low Alanna knew she'd hit a nerve, "I was a Commander, not you. I do not need to justify my reasons."

The fire in the hearth briefly blazed, then resumed its merry crackling. She nodded toward it. "At least you're learning to control your temper. Last time I questioned you like that, poor Eldwyn needed a new room."

They discussed recent events as the evening grew later, including the tonic the Healers—mainly Alanna—had developed to identify any more changelings in their midst. The conversation turned to the soldiers who'd gone through the scouting trial and completed it to Cerdwin's satisfaction—a higher standard than Eldwyn held, the male grumbled, receiving a mocking bow from her brother in return. Their findings aligned with what Alanna had learned in the north: the Dark King had stationed an army somewhere deep in the obscurity of the mountains. She told them about how she'd treated the wounded scouts there, and experimented with Healing practices on those whose minds had been torn asunder by some new, Dark magic. The latter, she admitted, had been an utter failure. What they could do—if they found a way to win the war to come—to help those whose minds were diluted with Darkness, she didn't know. Those lost to it on their mission had been executed and left behind.

Cerdwin gave her arm a reassuring squeeze. *It is not your fault,* the gesture said, and the warm breeze that wrapped itself around her echoed the sentiment. But it was. She couldn't fail again and still be worthy of her Healer's title. She couldn't fail her twin again and still be worthy of his love. Whether she was still worthy of their father's affection was unimportant.

Alanna lost herself in her thoughts as she wound her way back to her room—thoughts about the relationship between her brother and the First Commander. Eldwyn was blessed with the gifts of the wind and air, the animal form of the silver wolf; her brother, with fire, and the animal form of the golden lion. The Golden Lion of Aviva—their father had been so proud. But then Cerdwin had gone away to Ozul, and no one could've guessed how difficult things would be when he returned.

Alanna closed her eyes, remembering the first shift upon his return, and the chaos that had followed: claw marks, deep, long gouges in the marble of his room, the animalistic look in his eyes. Only she had been able to coax him back to himself. The servants having all fled his chambers—all fortunately unscathed. But the room itself...she'd held on to the line between them, the sense of self she felt in him—and he in her, as twins—and brought him back.

Eldwyn had been there for him, too, but the First Commander hadn't left that encounter unscathed. Neither male had, not really. Cerdwin had been devastated, and so much smoke had filled the room. That was when she'd promised her brother that she would work with him for as long as it took to get his magic back under control. It appeared he'd been practicing on his own, maybe with some help from Eldwyn.

Eldwyn. What did the wind whisper to him? What secrets did it reveal, beyond what Elvish ears could hear? What was he keeping to himself about this Elana? From the looks he exchanged with her brother, Alanna had a feeling that, whatever reasons Eldwyn had given him for keeping the female here, for training her, they weren't the whole story. But they were enough that her brother was willing to risk their father's wrath—and Eldwyn was willing to take the brunt of it. He was a good male, a good friend, and a good First Commander. Alanna didn't doubt his intentions—but she would find out the reasoning behind them.

As she drifted off to sleep, a whisper of wind ruffled her hair in response to the direction of her thoughts. Her room had no windows.

The Lost Princess

Her head injury was almost healed, and she was able to walk more than a few feet from her room without feeling dizzy. But the worry and anguish that flared in her heart every time she thought of Cethin—where he was, what was being done to him—the pressure in her palm steadily increased every minute—

That was not Cethin.

It was not real.

That was more painful than any physical injury she'd sustained. She made up her mind again to find the dungeons and see the changeling, no matter what Alanna said.

"Didn't she tell you to stay in bed?"

She glared up at Eldwyn, even as her head spun. His stance blocked her from going any farther down the hall. She put her hands on her hips. The smile on his face was nothing short of wolfish. "Has anyone ever told you that you toss yourself into other peoples' business far too often?" He raised his eyebrows at her. She sighed. "Yes, Alanna told me to stay in bed."

"I'm guessing you had to pause here because you got dizzy from your head wound." She stared at the First Commander. His bottom lip twitched.

"And I'm guessing everyone in the castle knows everything about me now, what with the three of you busybodies chattering." She mimicked a mouth opening and closing with her hand, and Eldwyn laughed, which warmed her mood. She'd forgotten how comforting his presence was.

He shook his head. "Not at all."

He took a step toward her. "Eleonora," he whispered.

She could've sworn her heart stopped when he spoke her true name. From the searching look he gave her, she knew that was all the confirmation he'd needed.

"Let's go back to your room," he said quietly. Not in warning or threat as she'd feared, and not in reverence, either. His tone was completely neutral, just like his expression. First Commander—and likely a fine cards player.

She swallowed, took a steadying breath, and nodded. "Let's." They walked in silence back to her room. He closed the door behind them and she sank onto the bed. He took the chair.

"How long have you known?" she asked, twirling the end of her braid around her fingers.

"When we met in Ozul." She flinched as she met his gaze. *Of course.* Of course, the First Commander, who'd been running that particular operation in Ozul, would run into her and Cethin. He raised his hands as though he sensed the direction of her thoughts. "It was by accident," he said, "but the wind..." He lowered his hands. "It likely pulled me there that morning."

"The wind likely pulled you there that morning?" she repeated.

"Yes."

"The wind...your magic..." She struggled to figure out what to say.

"It's not just filling sails, or pushing away unwanted storms," he said, silver eyes twinkling as he spoke. "It's also about listening, hearing, and expecting the unexpected. I knew when we collided you would be a force of nature of your own. Or, at least, my magic did. And when we departed for Aviva, it whispered to me—it told me to keep you safe."

He took a step closer, and she felt a breeze wrap around her in a soft caress. But, even as he drew that tangible breeze back, his magic remained. *How had she not noticed it?* "How long have you had your personal shield around me?"

"A while."

"How long is a while?"

His lips twitched. "Well, I put up the foundation when we left Ozul. But then I reinforced it when you and Cethin..."

Heat flooded her cheeks, and he winked at her. "You knew—you could—" she sputtered.

"It's nothing to be embarrassed about," he said with a shrug. "And while his idea to clean up once you'd finished—" Her cheeks were actually on fire now, and it wasn't the Dark King who would kill her, it was this conversation. "I thought I'd be thorough." She glared at him. "I know a thing or two when it comes to being discreet, Eleonora. You should be afforded that privacy, too, when it comes to who you love." *Who you love.*

She thought for a moment. "You let me pin you to that wall—before you knew I knew Cerdwin."

He shrugged. "The wind blew you in my direction. I simply propelled you forward. I heard about the Noir attacks," he continued, dipping his head toward her. "They were seen in Ozul a handful of times. Each time, a strange light was also seen. Like the light the day the lost princess disappeared from Aviva." Suddenly self-conscious, she folded her hands into her lap. "I was there that day, you know," he went on, eyes going distant. "The day you were supposed to ascend the throne. I was tasked with guarding the palace gates. I was one of the only guards who survived." Her stomach dropped. "But I remember seeing you." He gave her a half smile. "You looked different as a human. But now..." He shook his head, as if clearing the memories. "What's the plan?"

"What do you mean?" she asked, squirming where she sat.

"You left almost fifty years ago. Now, you've returned, but you've kept your identity a secret. What's the plan?"

She stared down at her hands and ran a finger over the scar on her left palm.

That was not Cethin.
It was not real.

"I don't know," she finally said. "I thought that if I could come back here, win the people's trust, reveal myself once I'd succeeded in *something*...then I would be worthy of...I don't know. My title. My throne. My crown."

She'd failed dismally in what she'd set out to do. She wasn't worthy to be queen of anything.

"You haven't failed," Eldwyn said softly—could the wind also read her mind? The male learned forward and placed a hand on her knee. "You haven't failed until the Darkness has consumed us all. And that hasn't happened—not yet."

She shook her head. "It's not just that. It's also—"

"Cethin." A statement—not a question. She nodded. Eldwyn sat silently for a few minutes. "The wind has whispered to me of him, too, Eleonora. Your paths crossed for a reason. Don't give up on him."

"I-I haven't given up on him!" she sputtered, and the male smiled.

"I know that," he said, squeezing her knee. "Why do you think I didn't immediately call Alanna down here to kick your ass back into bed?" She gave him a small smile.

"Take another day to heal," Eldwyn said, standing. "That's all your head should need. And when that's done, we'll pay Lord Arel a visit."

Chapter 21

CETHIN

There was only Darkness—unending Darkness, unlike anything he'd ever known.

Except for one light—one bright light within it—being smothered by it, buried by it...

"El!" he cried out, as he'd done so, so many times now. Nothing but Darkness and pain greeted him in answer.

Then the sounds of her screaming began again.

Chapter 22

Alanna

A difficult patient—and a demanding one. Alanna huffed as she brought the books the female had requested to the room—books about the life oath: where it had originated from, the effects on those who used it, and how the connection evolved over time. Alanna hadn't been able to find what she'd wanted in the Royal Archives, so Eldwyn had allowed her to raid his personal library.

Elana was connected to a half-Elf, Cethin—who was being held captive by the Dark King's forces—by this magic. *So stupid to swap the life oath with a mercenary.* But here they were. Alanna just hoped they didn't get her brother into trouble. None of Cerdwin or Eldwyn's males had been briefed on what had happened in the mountains, beyond the select few who'd assisted in rescuing Elana—all of whom Cerdwin trusted completely. She hoped he was right. If their father caught wind of *any* of this...

With their recent loss of the foothold in the north, the Lord's Council was putting increasing pressure on Cerdwin and Eldwyn to conserve their forces and wait for the enemy to come to them. *Like* that *strategy had worked well in fifty years*. She and Cerdwin had spent hours over what Lord Arel called *family dinners* trying to explain that, with no way to win, letting the enemy come to them could result in thousands more turning to the Darkness. So many could—and would—be lost in a war, the lord had argued. That was the cost of war. Too many had already been lost, they'd both shot back. But their father had become both proud and cowardly in his years of stewardship—not an ideal combination. Shaking her head, Alanna kicked the door of Elana's room. *Healer indeed*. Healer—and errand runner.

"Come in," came the female's soft voice. Alanna entered, smatterings of paper in tow, to see her halfway to the door. "Oh!" Elana exclaimed, immediately reaching for the bundle in her arms. "Thank you so much for bringing these."

"You're welcome," Alanna muttered. "I take it that this interest in reading means your head wound is improving."

The female nodded. "Yes, thank you. Your brother spoke highly of your abilities, though, so I had no doubt it would be a quick recovery."

Alanna's cheeks flushed at the compliment—not because the female had thanked her, but because her brother had spoken so highly of her Healing. "Anything for one of Cerdwin's friends." She waved a hand as she retreated through the door.

"Alanna?" The female's voice sounded quieter this time—hesitant. Alanna turned around and crossed her arms. "Thank you," Elana said again. Then, the female bowed her head. The movement shifted something in Alanna's heart.

The Lost Princess

She was grateful for the books Alanna had brought her—for anything that might help lead her to her life-sworn—but there was little she could use, even from the options Alanna had brought from Eldwyn's personal library. Those books that were more like journals, written by less-practiced hands, many of the entries almost illegible. She sighed, wondering when she would find something useful.

She skimmed a random passage about males and their ability to link their elemental magic to one another's to strengthen their power. The process seemed fairly straightforward, if not unhelpful to her situation: link hands, pull from the well of magic deep inside, then—

She sat up straight. When she'd first connected hands with Cethin after he'd sworn the life oath, her memories had come back. *What if...*

She closed the book, then her eyes, the idea flowing through her like a stream in the Riverlands.

Alanna

"You look like you've had a rough day," Eldwyn said that evening when she plopped down in her usual chair in his palace room.

"No Cerdwin tonight?" The male shook his head.

"Your lord father has him working on multiple renderings of our lines behind the wall." Her huff of frustration must've been audible, because Eldwyn murmured his agreement. "Frustrating, since he still doesn't seem inclined to actually use them. However…" He stopped, took a drink, then offered her one. "May I ask you about one of your patients?" His voice was neutral, gaze blank. *Damn, he was good.* Alanna sipped her drink.

"You know the Healer's rules," she said carefully.

"That I do," he said, eyes glinting with a bit of humor. "But when have you ever paid attention to things like rules or orders?"

She rolled her eyes, but nodded, leaning back in the chair. "Ask away."

"Cerdwin's friend, the one from Ozul." *What was it with these males and this random female from across their world?* "What did you feel from her, when you Healed her?"

"She had trauma to her head, but I'm sure Cerdwin told you that."

"I don't mean the physical," he said softly.

Alanna set her drink aside and closed her eyes. All Healers could probe their patient's physical injuries, but a few had been granted the ability to see deeper—to the emotional. Like she could.

Alanna felt her Healing gift flare at her palms as she positioned herself cross-legged on the chair. She sank into the soothing and calming energy of that power as she rooted through the emotional energy of the patients she'd recently worked on—Elana included.

From the female she could feel—see—Cethin, a cave she was all too familiar with, and, interestingly, Sonia. It was possible Elana had visited the older woman—they were practically neighbors in the ward. But there was also something else—a hazy memory. Alanna stumbled through the image until she locked on to Elana.

"Guilt," she said, sifting through the wounds that didn't leave a physical mark. "Anger. Sorrow. Despair." Eldwyn was silent as she pressed deeper into the inner catalog of the female's mind. "And...hope. Love. And...light. Not the light that comes with the Healing gift—not entirely. And not fire." *And thank the Gods for that.* One of the Fire Folk hadn't been seen in a very long time, and she hoped it stayed that way, for all their sakes. "But something else." She opened her eyes. Eldwyn's face remained impassable. "I'm starting to see how you continue to indebt our father when Cerdwin plays cards with you." Amusement flickered in the male's quicksilver eyes but quickly faded. "What is it?"

The male leaned forward and braced his elbows on his knees. "I need to know I can trust you," he said, voice low. She knew the First Commander walked a fine line when it came to compartmentalizing information—and who to share it with.

"Always," she said, leaning forward, too.

"Even outside of your brother."

"Eldwyn, I—"

"This is serious, Alanna."

They stared at each other as the minutes crept by.

"Okay."

The world went silent as she felt Eldwyn slip a wall of hard air around them. It would keep unwanted ears from listening to what he was about to tell her—one of the many perks of his gift, she supposed. *This was serious, then.*

"Elana is not who she says she is," he started. She leaned farther forward, knees brushing against his. "Her real name is Eleonora."

"You mean," she whispered, mind working to process what he was saying.

"Yes. The lost princess. The heir to the throne of Aviva."

The lost princess. The heir to the throne of Aviva. The one who would re-Bind the Balance, or so the people whispered. The only one who could save them all from the Darkness, they said. Their queen.

Alanna's mind whirled, connecting the information. This was why the female hadn't shifted into her Elvish body before—she likely couldn't control her magic. This was why Alanna had seen Sonia in her mind—the old woman had served Queen Serenity, had served Eleonora when she was a youngling. This was why the female was so important to Eldwyn—the wind liked to tell him things, and he'd likely used his gift to bind her scent so no one would mark her royal blood. But Cerdwin...

"Who else knows?"

"Me," Eldwyn said. "And now, you."

Eldwyn

Alanna ran a hand through her curls, the movement so similar to the gesture he'd witnessed Cerdwin do hundreds of times. He knew how it felt to run his hands through the male's hair.

It had started easily between the First and Second Commanders—the banter, the flirting. While Cerdwin clearly enjoyed his company, a wall went up as soon as his lord father came around. Eldwyn understood—to an extent. As the son and heir of a lord, there were expectations of the Second Commander. But Eldwyn had lost too many soldiers and too many loves over the decades to be bothered by what anyone—including a lord—thought. Unfortunately, it bothered Cerdwin. And after that one night...

Alanna cleared her throat. "And I would assume your other patient, Sonia," Eldwyn commented.

"She was a lady's maid to the royal family." He nodded, and Alanna pressed her palms into her eyes. "What a mess," she grumbled.

"I doubt the old lady is well enough to say anything. It's just as likely old age has barred her mind from remembering anything at all," he offered. Alanna reached for her drink.

"What of the half-Elf?"

"I don't think he knows." *Not yet, at least.*

"But why keep it a secret? Why wait, only to return now?"

He crossed his arms. "You were unable to see that?"

The female shook her head. "She didn't tell you?"

"No," he said firmly, deciding to keep the conversation between him and his queen to himself. "And, whatever her reasons are, they are her reasons. She is queen."

"It sounds like you've already decided to declare for her," Alanna remarked.

He met her gaze and held it. "You know I don't play in politics, Alanna—not as your father and brother do." Purple fire that wasn't entirely hers flashed in her eyes. He held up a hand. "Yes, they have—*we* have—all done our duty to protect this city. But war is coming. And war doesn't care about the games of lords and ladies and courts. The people need something, *someone*, to believe in, if I am to lead husbands, brothers, and sons into battle." Pain flicked across the Healer's face, likely imagining her twin fighting the Dark King's armies. "Eleonora is our best hope. Our *only* hope. I would ask that you consider aiding her, when the time comes."

"Why didn't she tell me this herself when I Healed her? Or today, when I went to deliver all of those stupid papers?"

Eldwyn suppressed a grin. He had no doubt Alanna had hated every second of playing messenger—but it had paid off. Eleonora had found a way to connect with the changeling to find her life-sworn—the next item on Eldwyn's long list of things to do. That, and get her into House Satrara, which would cross off alerting the Lord's Council—including one specific lord—to her real return, getting her to the dungeons to interrogate the changeling together, and, hopefully, keeping her safe, just as his wind had requested.

"If I had to guess, it's because she knows the strain it would put on your relationship with Cerdwin," he said and watched Alanna's brows rise in surprise. "She may not know you yet, Alanna, but Cerdwin is her friend. He was one of her only friends, all of those years she was in Ozul. She cares for him a great deal. She wouldn't see him hurt by all of this." The female chewed on her lip. "Keeping him in the dark, at least for right now, will leave him blameless in the eyes of the lord."

"They are betrothed," Alanna said after a moment. "Or were, before." He stayed quiet. He'd known that, but it wasn't something he was willing to voice aloud yet. Instead, he watched Alanna intently, like he did when they played cards. Finally, she rolled her shoulders back. He grinned at the tell. He'd won this round.

"Alright," the female sighed. "What do you need from me?"

The Lost Princess

She strode into House Satrara the next evening at mealtime, precisely when Eldwyn had instructed her to. The guards were on rotation, and Alanna was the only other person within—a family dinner, apparently. The First Commander had filled her in on his conversation with the Healer, his breeze bringing her the necessities of their conversation. Alanna knew who she was now. She only hoped she lived up to what she was sure were the Healer's very high expectations.

"What is the meaning of this?" Lord Arel demanded when she walked through the doors unannounced.

The young princess poked her head around the corner and watched her mother, accompanied by her First Guard, exit the Lord's Hall, then the lords. There were eight lords on the Council, including the head of the Lord's Council: Lord Arel. The young princess had never spoken to the lord directly, had only seen him with the other lords, or with her mother and father. He was what humans considered the epitome of Elvish beauty: statuesque, graceful, and handsome. But what the lord had in Elvish features he lacked in any sort of heart. No, though word was Lord Arel possessed the earth magic so few Elves now did, he may as well have wielded ice.

"I need to speak with you, Lord Arel," she said in her most commanding tone.

A motion to the left caught her attention. *Cerdwin*. He wasn't supposed to be there. She hadn't planned for her friend to find out like this—not here, not today. But the plan she and Eldwyn had set was already in motion. She couldn't back down. She took a deep breath.

"I am Eleonora. The one some call the lost princess. Heir to the throne of Aviva."

She saw Cerdwin's eyes flare and had to give Alanna a hand for the shocked look the Healer plastered on her face. The lord's face was cold. There was nothing of his children in him—their looks most likely from their mother's side, though she didn't remember the female. And the look Lord Arel gave her—she'd seen males quake in Cerdwin's presence for less.

Then the lord shook his head, thoroughly unimpressed. "We have heard that story many times over the decades, girl."

She stood her ground. "This is not a story. This is the truth, my lord."

The male sniffed. "What proof do you bring?" She opened her mouth, then closed it. She couldn't show him her power—not without risking bringing the Noir to the city. She wouldn't do that to her people. The lord sighed. "We will need all of your family history and documentation. Then—"

"My lord," came Eldwyn's voice from the doorway, drawing his attention away from her. "Shall I bring her down for a complete review?"

"Why yes, Commander," the lord replied in a bored tone. "That would be most helpful." She turned to meet Eldwyn at the door.

"Excuse me, Father." They halted on the threshold at Alanna's voice. "She is one of my patients. I would request visitation rights while she is being detained, as I was treating her for head trauma."

"That would explain a lot," Lord Arel muttered.

Moonlight sparked in her veins at his tone. How *dare* he—

Eldwyn escorted her from the room, before she could say or do what, she wasn't sure. But Cerdwin's stare singed her back as they walked away. To the dungeons.

Alanna

Another family dinner—Alanna snorted. He held them as a lord, the Head of the Lord's Council. She wasn't invited to attend as his daughter. She was invited to attend as a High Healer, the High Healer who tended to the First Commander's males. Cerdwin wasn't invited to attend as his son. No, he was invited to attend as Lord Arel's heir—and Second Commander. It was all a pretty show the lord put on every few months. And, while the dinners never held any of the familial attitude one would expect from an actual family dinner, they were held in the chambers dedicated to the noble House Satrara.

Alanna had mixed emotions every time she entered the stronghold of her noble family: anger was usually first, anger toward her father at being, well, him. The cold, arrogant, selfish prick he'd always been, the personality that'd only deepened after her lady mother had passed. Guilt, sorrow, and pain over her lady mother's death, how she should've been able to stop it, how she should've stopped it. Sadness for her brother, who still had to live there whenever he was called upon as the lord's son and heir. And underneath all of that, a sort of melancholy for the little lady who'd grown up there, who'd grown out of that environment and replanted herself, repurposed herself, elsewhere; whose rooms were always kept as they'd been when she'd left.

She also couldn't help peeking every time she was there: the golden bed with its emerald comforter was made, the night curtains were open, a fresh vase of flowers was on the sitting table, her old books were on her desk, new dresses in her current size were in the closet. She hoped no one checked the box she'd hidden above the hangers, but there was a rebellious sort of thrill that ran through her every time she imagined a lady's maid happening upon her...*collection*.

The dinner had started as usual, although she hadn't known her brother was invited. He and Eldwyn had been busy preparing their males for their next scouting exercise, and Cerwdin had been busy keeping things in his camp under control—to their lord father's standards. Eldwyn had also been busy—busy keeping secrets. Not unusual for the First Commander. He knew more about Alanna's secrets—and illicit affairs—than anyone. But this secret was bigger than all of them. Cerdwin had been betrothed to Eleonora. He deserved to know. So did the mercenary, who—after sifting through the female's emotions again—Alanna was fairly confident the female was in love with.

Alanna didn't remember much about the female prior to her disappearance from Aviva. After King Ewan had perished during the Battle of the Breaking, no one saw much of the young princess. Plus, Alanna had left court life before then to become a Healer. So she'd worked through the details she did know in her mind before dinner: How the female had returned to Ozul—through the interference of Eldwyn's magic, no less. *Busybody*. How the female had leaned on the kindness of the First Commander. How she'd challenged the ways of the camps to stay with the Second. The lost princess reminded Alanna of herself in many ways—but it was a dangerous game to play, especially with Lord Arel involved. And the stakes were much higher than a lady becoming a High Healer.

Beyond that, Alanna still didn't know much more than she had about the female her best friend was inclined to lay down his life for. To be fair, it was part of his responsibility as First Commander—Hell, Eldwyn had already fought for the female, had battled outside the palace gates the day she'd disappeared. The male didn't talk about that day often. But this was different—*he* was different about this. He'd kept this secret from her brother. Granted, that was an ever-changing dynamic, and Eldwyn had his reasons. But how would Cerdwin react when he found out his friend from Ozul was actually his queen? His betrothed?

Alanna sighed. How did *she* feel about it, based on what she knew? Irritation at the female for keeping her identity a secret, but also understanding. Respect for what the female was doing in garnering support and approval before she revealed her identity. Admiration for her strength and determination—even if they made her a pain in the ass.

Alanna sighed again. It was why she'd agreed to help free the damn mercenary. At the end of the fake day, she'd bet on the female, too.

Then everything happened at once: Cerdwin showed up for dinner, and Eldwyn and Eleonora revealed the female's identity to the lord—to Cerdwin.

Lord Arel wouldn't accept the female's identity—not without solid proof. Cerdwin though...

Alanna didn't have time to coddle her twin the way she normally would. This was bigger than him—than all of them. This was about the queen.

This was about their future.

The Lost Princess

"Told you that would work," Eldwyn said as he led her down the winding steps.

"I know," she hissed, "but Cerdwin was there. He wasn't supposed to be there."

The male's eyes dimmed as he looked at her. "I know. I'm sorry."

"I suppose it had to be done," she said after a moment of silence.

They passed the level Eldwyn noted as the one where they kept anyone claiming royal lineage—where Lord Arel *thought* the First Commander was taking her—and walked lower and lower still. Torches hung in brackets at various distances on the walls, the only light as they descended farther beneath the palace—into the rock itself.

Finally, Eldwyn halted in front of an iron door and pulled a key from his pocket. "Are you sure you're ready for this?" he asked in a gentle voice. She nodded. She was ready—ready to face the changeling. Eldwyn unlocked the door.

It was worse than she remembered: the spindly, gray-faced, almost skeletal creature of younglings' tales and nightmares, its body covered in tattered clothing. The changeling lifted its head—so much longer and more oval-like than any person's—its eyes wide chasms of Darkness itself, the slits for nostrils, its stumps of teeth showing as it smiled at her. She wanted nothing more than to turn and run in the other direction when it flicked a long tongue over its teeth and lips.

Lips that had been against hers. Shame and nausea turned in her gut. She felt Eldwyn place a steadying hand on her back. Drawing herself to her full height, she walked across the room and crouched in front of it.

"Hello, Eleonora," the *mutatio* hissed. "Hello, Queen of Moonlight."

She resisted the urge to shudder. "I have some questions for you."

"You have many questions," it said, "but not all of them are for me."

It would play mind games, Eldwyn had warned her—almost like it had in the mountains—had already done so with Cerdwin. At least here, with Healer's magic binding it, it couldn't transport her to another place or time. It could only change its appearance—and that was what she needed it to do.

"True," she acquiesced. "Some of my questions are for him."

"I do not know this *him* you speak of," it smirked. *Liar.* That was what these creatures did best: weave webs of truth and lies. The comment had her wondering how Cerdwin had questioned the thing and left it alive instead of burning the damn thing into a hole in the ground. She drew one of her daggers from inside of her cloak. The changeling laughed, a wheezing sound that sent a shiver down her spine.

"Steel and blades do not frighten me, Your Grace," it hissed. It seized, its long-limbed body surging until—

Until it was Cethin shackled there. "Do you miss me that much?" the Cethin who was not Cethin asked, giving her one of the wicked smiles she'd grown accustomed to. Then he—it—moved forward, as if to brush a strand of hair away from her face. She held herself perfectly still. The wickedness in that smile, in those eyes, grew—

She snatched the creature's hand away from her face and pressed her palm to his—its—sighing with relief when she felt it: the life-oath scar. She pressed her hand firmly to it, life-oath bond to fake life-oath bond—because a changeling would never be a perfect rendering: it had already forgotten that change, the change that should've happened when she released it from the life oath in the cave.

And then she hoped. The changeling hissed, writhing and twitching as it tried to shift back into itself—or another body—she wasn't sure. She didn't care. Not as those scars lined up to form a lifeline—a lifeline to find Cethin. To bring him home. Image after image tumbled through her mind—horrible, wicked images she'd soon rather forget—from an ancient, evil creature. Then, images seen through Cethin's eyes: looking at her, the mountains, the cave—and somewhere else. Somewhere farther north from the cave. A camp. A tent. Darkness.

"Eleonora." There was nothing but pure command in the male voice. Someone gripped her hand and tried to wrench it away. "Eleonora," the voice said again, and she dropped her hand from the changeling's. She opened her eyes. The changeling was back in its body, twitching and twisting, hissing with rage. Eldwyn knelt beside her.

"Northern range of the Endurnal Mountains," she rasped. "Near where they held me."

Eldwyn nodded, helping her to her feet.

"A word of advice, Daughter of Night," the changeling hissed at her. She didn't so much as pause to hear what it had to say.

She knew where Cethin was.

"We need to move—now," she panted at Eldwyn as she sagged against the cool marble wall outside of the changeling's cell. The First Commander's face was edged with concern as he locked the door. Being inside of that thing's mind...she could only imagine the horrors the Dark King and his Night Queen would unleash on their world if she didn't find a way—

"I'm fine," she said, brushing off his gentle touch to her shoulder. She pushed off the wall and began the ascent back to the castle proper. Eldwyn fell into step beside her. She rolled her wrist, rubbing at the ache in her hand that had intensified.

"But Cethin is not."

"No. And the longer we wait"—she paused, throat constricting at what she'd seen them doing to him inside of the changeling's mind—"the closer they get."

"To what?" Eldwyn's eyes swirled in calculation.

"To killing him," she said quietly, "and dumping his body on the border as a message—for me."

She didn't shake off Eldwyn's hand this time when he brought her to a halt. "Understand me now," the male said. "We will find him. We will bring him back. And we will bring Hell to those who took him." The First Commander motioned behind them. "To those who serve the Darkness." He looked at her, nothing but loyalty shining in his eyes now. "And to the Dark King." He squeezed her shoulder tightly, then turned forward.

"Come." He motioned for her to continue walking when she didn't immediately follow, but she was at a complete loss, emotions swirling at his words of loyalty to her—to Cethin. "We need to gear up."

Chapter 23

It would just be the three of them, Eldwyn had decided: himself, Eleonora, and Alanna. *Eleonora.* The name would take some getting used to saying again.

They all wore brown cloaks. Eleonora's hood was up, hair pulled back in a tight braid so that—hopefully—no one would recognize her. Like himself, both females were armed to the teeth under those cloaks. Alanna was trained as a Healer, but that didn't mean both he and Cerdwin hadn't seen to it that she knew how to defend herself.

Cerdwin. Eldwyn had seen the look on the male's face in the lord's chambers. He'd preemptively sent an order out for Cerdwin to return to the camp to continue training his battalion. He was not looking forward to having that argument later—hopefully in a place Cerdwin couldn't reduce entirely to cinders.

Eleonora wasn't sure what they would encounter in the camp where Cethin was being held. She'd seen the location, yes, but hadn't been able to give any indication as to what manner of Dark creature might be dwelling there, how many guards there might be, or even how large the camp was. Another reason Eldwyn had decided it would just be the three of them: they would be able to move about undetected more easily, and there would be less chance of loss of life on their side if things went badly. Which they wouldn't, he assured himself.

"Ready?" he asked. Alanna nodded.

"Only two horses?" Eleonora's brows rose. "I thought we were *all* going." Right—like he could really order her to stay behind.

"We are," he said with a wink. "But some of us won't need horses on the way back."

Alanna rolled her eyes. "No one likes a show-off, Eldwyn," the Healer said as she mounted her horse. Eldwyn gave her a bow and a smile as he mounted the other and reached a hand down for Eleonora. She took it, frowning as she slid into place behind him.

The trio remained silent as they left the stables. They wound through a back street to a door in the wall Eldwyn had used to sneak out of Aviva and work in Ozul many times. He smiled. The last time he'd snuck out, he'd ended up bringing back Cerdwin's friend. Now his friend—his queen.

"I switched the guard rotations," he murmured as they entered the plains and Alanna fell into pace beside them. "We have a few minutes before we need to clear the first few miles of desert. After that, they won't be able to see us." Alanna nodded, and their eyes locked. They'd spoken privately in the Healer's room that morning. It wasn't uncommon for the First Commander to make an appearance in the Healer's quarters, not when all of them—particularly Alanna—tended to his males. But what they'd discussed then hadn't been common at all: at the first sign of threat to Eleonora—true threat—Alanna was to take her and go. Leave him behind, no matter what—and not look back.

Eldwyn wasn't afraid of death, not really. He'd been a guard or a soldier for most of his life. He'd fought during the attack on Eleonora's first coronation. He'd seen what the Darkness could do. The best chance of breaking through that Darkness—should it take hold of him, of any of them—was sitting right behind him on his horse. And if he slipped into the Otherworld, only she would be able to reverse that, too.

In the end, the Healer had acquiesced, though she still didn't seem happy about it. But it was the right move, the smart move—a Commander's move. He only hoped Cerdwin would see it that way, too.

"Only a few more seconds," he said, dropping Alanna's gaze and looking at the brightly shining sands ahead. "Go."

At his word, they flew across the dunes, cloaks blending with the color. Eldwyn's magic pounded in his veins as he tossed a wind shield in front of them, blocking the gritty sand and stone that flew up to greet them.

"Handy," he heard Eleonora mutter from behind him, and he smiled. There was almost nothing he loved more than something like this—riding, running, he didn't care, didn't think about anything or anyone as he let the rest of the wind tear through him, setting his gift, his heart, free. Besides shifting into his animal form, nothing ever set his essence flying like this.

They cleared the first stretch within minutes, horses churning up the sand beneath them, hooves eating up mile after mile. He signaled to Alanna when they were out of the line of sight of the wall of Aviva, and they slowed their pace as they approached the mountains. He removed the wind shield and allowed the sounds and scents of what lay ahead flow toward him and sent his gift spearing forward to see what it could learn.

"When you said we wouldn't all need horses on the way back—"

"I will shift for the return trip, and Cethin will ride with one of you, depending." He swallowed, not wanting to say it out loud. "Depending on what state we find him in." Eleonora stilled, her hands tensing where she'd braced herself against his back.

"What is your animal form?" she finally asked over the wind. A distraction—to talk about anything other than how they might find Cethin. After how Cerdwin had found her...Eldwyn shook the images of the battered, half-frozen female body Alanna had administered her Healing gift to from his mind. Even in her Elvish form, the injuries Eleonora had sustained had been significant. The sight had infuriated him, even before he'd had confirmation she was his queen.

Cerdwin had been in an outrage like Eldwyn had never seen his fellow Commander in. The male had set several items in the room on fire before Alanna kicked him out. And now, he was steering Cerdwin's friend and sister toward danger to rescue a half-Elf both Cerdwin and his father wouldn't have deemed worth the risk.

"A wolf." He sometimes wondered why the Gods had given him a terrestrial form instead of an avian one—one born of air, as he felt he was. Cerdwin joked it was to keep him grounded, which always made Alanna laugh. Perhaps they weren't entirely wrong. If he'd been granted wings...

Eldwyn pushed their pace forward, Alanna's horse cantering beside them, the Healer's hood whipped free by the wind, her hair flying wildly around her. He was so close with her brother, and yet he'd still chosen her to come with them, had told her the truth about Eleonora—not Cerdwin. He let the cool rush of wind clear any guilt from his head. They all needed to be sharp for what lay ahead.

The Lost Princess

She scanned the rocks, looking for any sign of what she'd seen in the changeling's mind, anything that looked familiar or significant.

There was nothing.

"Farther north," she whispered to Eldwyn. The male nodded and motioned Alanna forward with them. They would stick to the base of the mountains until something triggered her memory, then move farther into enemy territory from there. Then unleash holy Hell on whoever—whatever—held Cethin.

She was surprised Eldwyn had asked Alanna to join them and not Cerdwin, but she'd seen the look on Cerdwin's face in his lord father's chambers: his surprise, his shock—his anger. She closed her eyes. If he spoke to the changeling, he'd have a pretty good idea of where they went—and that Alanna was with them. Yet, regardless of how Cerdwin reacted to that, she was glad for the female's presence. It was odd, really, to feel like she had people on her side. Not just as her friends—but as their queen.

She opened her eyes and scanned the mountainside again. "There." A memory tugged at her mind as her gaze landed on a fissure in the mountainside. "He—" Her voice trembled as sharp pain raced through her life-oath scar. "He is up there," she tried again. Eldwyn slowed their pace, then halted them in front of the crack in the rock. Alanna paced to face them.

"We all remember the plan, yes?" the male said, his voice that of the First Commander—the male who'd kept Aviva's army intact for fifty years. The male who'd seen soldiers suffer and die at the hands of the Darkness yet didn't let it consume him. Cerdwin's friend, who would protect her—protect all of them—and ensure Cethin made it out. Her friend. She made a note in her mind to ask Eldwyn to be part of her First Guard once she was crowned. Then, she nodded. Alanna, face grim, nodded as well.

They left their horses at the base of the mountains. It would make their escape more difficult, Eldwyn said, but not having the animals with them would make it easier to go undetected for as long as possible. If Cethin was too injured to travel down the rock with them, Eldwyn would shift and carry the half-Elf on his back. Her heart warmed at that.

"Alright, then," Eldwyn said. He reached out a hand to her, and she clasped it, allowing him to help her take her first step up the hill behind him, Alanna at their rear. The male maintained a calm composure, but she saw his other hand was ready for the blade at his side should danger cross their path. She felt the same awareness rippling behind her from Alanna. Cerdwin had trained his twin, Eldwyn told her, and he'd taken up practicing with her while the male had been in Ozul. The Second Commander had made a sword just for his sister—similar to her twin daggers. She wondered if her blades had meant more to him than just a way to keep her safe in Ozul—if they'd been born of his heart, a reminder of the sister he loved and had left behind.

They moved painstakingly slowly up the craggy slope, one of them cursing now and again when a rock slid and fell, or a foothold didn't, well, hold. But other than that it was quiet—eerily quiet. Darkness settled as they ascended. None of them dared to speak, lest they bring a Dark creature straight to them.

Then, she heard it: snarling, low, rumbling voices, and dark laughter that made her blood run cold. But she wouldn't run—not again—not without him. They reached a flat rock top with a few bushes and trees clustering in the center and halted. A tug on her arm from in front of her—Eldwyn. She turned behind her, doing the same to Alanna. They all sunk to the ground.

"That's the camp," Eldwyn said, voice so low even her Elvish hearing barely picked it up. She nodded. "You and Alanna stick together. Find him. I will create a distraction to draw them away. Whatever happens, *you get out.*"

With their feet quieted by more of the male's magic, she and Alanna made their way into the clearing. She wasn't sure she was ready for what she saw: all manner of Dark creature imaginable, all looking wicked, cunning, and deadly, illuminated or cast into shadow by campfires. Temper flared through her. Of course the Dark King and Night Queen's servants didn't fear lighting fires in these mountains. They didn't fear being discovered. They didn't fear the Elves.

It was time they learned to.

As pain blasted through the life-oath scar, she knew what she had to do.

"What are you doing?" Alanna hissed in a low voice, trying to draw her back. But she didn't care. Didn't care as she drew her blades—

And sent the first Dark creature back to the Otherworld.

Alanna

Her patient—the lost princess, Queen, Elana, Eleonora, or whatever the Hell she called herself now—was going to get them all killed. The female had dismantled Eldwyn's plan as soon as they'd stepped foot into the camp. Whether it was out of some need for vengeance for the male they were there to retrieve, or something else, Alanna didn't really care. The female had royally fucked up.

Loosening her own blade—one her twin made for her—from its scabbard, Alanna sucked in a breath and started cutting down all manner of creature in her path. Blocking one particularly nasty looking dark Elf from striking her down, she pivoted and ran his blade into the chest of another foe. Of course, *of course* she'd promised Eldwyn that she would keep the female safe—that no matter what happened Eleonora would make it out alive. Their only hope against the Darkness.

Alanna wasn't uncomfortable with death—it was a daily occurrence in the Healing arts, the twin to life. What bothered her was the female's sheer foolishness and direct violation of the plan they'd all agreed to that could lead to unnecessary death. If—when—Eleonora ascended the throne, she'd better learn it didn't mean she could just do whatever the Hell she wanted. Gods amongst them, Eldwyn was *the* First Commander. The fact that she would just completely disregard—

And there he was, joining the fray, throwing a *what the fuck* glance her way as he ran his sword across the throat of something that looked half human, half boar. Alanna shrugged at him, then struck down what appeared to be a half-horse, half-human creature in front of her.

Someone—or *something*—had sounded the alarm in the camp. More creatures made their way toward them, spreading out like mindless insects. The next one Alanna faced actually *looked* like an insect: large, beady eyes—which she assumed saw just fine in the darkness—and arms. Six of them. She stepped back, calculating which of the four blades the creature wielded to focus on first. She marked the first one correctly, parrying it to the side; then the next, sending that sword skittering from the creature's grasp, but the next one...*fuck*.

She miscalculated, and the creature's blade dug into her side, leaving a trail of blood and torn muscle in its wake. Alanna grunted, unable to make a louder sound than that, but somehow—likely the wind—Eldwyn heard her. The male sprinted from where he'd just decapitated what looked like it'd been an Elf, and the insect met the same fate. "Are you—"

"I'll be fine," she gritted out, mustering her Healing gift to work on herself. Eldwyn nodded, turning to kick away another insect-like creature—this one crawling along the ground—while she knitted her side back together. "Done," she said, and the male left her, diving back into the fray once more. Alanna sighed and ran in the direction the queen had gone.

The Lost Princess

She might've heard Eldwyn or the Healer shout something as she killed the fifth dark creature that got in her way, but she didn't care. Though darkness surrounded her, her objective was as clear as if the Light had illuminated it:

Get Cethin back. Make them pay.

So she continued, numb to any emotion or strike of an enemy blade, as she left a path of death in her wake, to where the scar along her palm told her they were holding her life-sworn.

Eldwyn

For fuck's sake. Eleonora had completely abandoned his carefully crafted plan. Yet, Eldwyn wasn't entirely surprised. The half-Elf meant more to his queen than she was willing to admit—and vice versa. *Still.*

Eldwyn loosed a shout—and was pretty sure Alanna did, too. Both went unanswered. So he drew his sword and stepped in front of the enemy that followed his queen, trusting that Alanna, at least, would heed his orders: to protect Eleonora, to make sure she made it out alive, no matter what. The Healer took off after the queen with a shrug.

The creatures that made up the camp's forces ranged from disturbing foes—like the half-human, half-horse thing he watched Alanna cut down in his periphery—to soldiers who looked just like any Avivan Elf. He'd just cut one of the latter down when the wind vibrated from Alanna's direction. *Shit.* She'd been jabbed in the side by a disgusting rendition of an insect wielding *four fucking blades.*

"What in the Otherworld," he muttered to himself, taking off in her direction and cutting the thing down. "Are you—"

"I'll be fine," Alanna snapped. Blue light flared around her hands, and he turned to kick away another fucking bug soldier as she Healed herself. This was partly why Eldwyn had chosen the Healer over her brother—but he knew he'd better make sure he got her back to her twin in one piece. "Done."

Eldwyn didn't hesitate. He turned back toward the mass of Dark creatures slithering his way. He rotated his sword, once, twice—allowed a bit of the wolf to show—and lunged forward.

Alanna

She cast her vision through the bodies and smoke. The female who would be queen strode toward an unremarkable tent to their right, cutting down more enemy soldiers as she went. Her brother had clearly trained the female, too. Alanna followed her down that trail of violence—leaving Eldwyn to handle the beasts as she knew he could—and into that tent.

The guards were dead when Alanna entered. The queen ran to the half-Elf chained to a central support beam, and Alanna went with her.

The Lost Princess

"Cethin," she half whispered, half sobbed. Blood dripped from her face, her hands, and her knives as she knelt. Her hands—the left one throbbing like it was being stabbed with a knife over, and over again—shook as she made to unchain him.

"No, no," he whispered, alarm flaring in his eyes. "Please—please don't hurt her," he whimpered. Something cracked in her chest—they were using her against him, just as they had used him against her.

"Move." Alanna's voice was quiet and terse. The Healer knelt next to her and surveyed him. There was blood. A lot of it. All his.

"Is...is he..." She couldn't bring herself to finish the question.

Soft blue light flowed from Alanna's hands as the Healer scanned Cethin's body. The female took extra time with her magic—and a vial she produced from her sack—on his head. *His mind*, she realized.

"It's him. He'll be alright," the female said shortly. "We need to get him up, and then we need to get out of here. You really pissed them off."

She winced but didn't feel guilty about the change she'd made to their plans as she looked at Cethin's tired, pained face again. His amber eyes, their golden hue so dull they looked plain brown; his tanned skin, so pale from blood loss and being in the Darkness and the cold; his lips, cracked and broken. She brushed a quick kiss against them as Alanna used her magic to undo his chains.

They held Cethin between them and headed for the tent's exit. Nothing but silence greeted them, and upon leaving the tent, she saw why. Eldwyn stood in the center of the camp next to one of the fires, his blade impaled through the chest of...*something*. Nothing was moving.

"Took you long enough," he said with a wink, but there was no humor in his eyes. The enemy soldiers had all been pissed, but they were also all now dead. Eldwyn was also pissed, but she'd deal with that later—without a fight. She wasn't sure she could say the same for the First Commander, whose eyes blazed with primal bloodlust as he said, "Time to go."

Eldwyn

Eldwyn was pissed—more pissed than he'd ever been in his life. They'd had a fucking plan, and Eleonora had immediately thrown it into chaos, drawing every Dark creature in the camp right to them. The queen had been lost enough in wrath that she'd taken out a good chunk of them herself, but—even with his military training—Eldwyn could've been overwhelmed. He'd given himself over to his own anger and frustration and unleashed himself on the rest of the enemy soldiers. Emotion and battle weren't a wise mix, but in a melee like that, being slightly out of control was the best weapon he had. Even with the fight over, he felt that violence twisting in his veins. He stayed in his Elvish body long enough to give his next orders—ones he hoped his queen would actually listen to—then shifted.

Eldwyn loved the wind, loved the wild freedom and reckless joy it brought him. But maybe Cerdwin was right: he needed his wolven form to ground himself. He'd shifted into that form during many a battle, had used that powerful body to rip out the throats of his enemies—to carry his wounded away from battlegrounds. But he'd also shifted into that form after so many long, never-ending days of fighting—either physically or mentally. It always gave him clarity and focus.

His blood had hummed in response to the bloodlust in Eleonora's eyes as she'd brought down enemy after enemy. His temper had flared, too, when he'd realized she'd blatantly ignored his plan. Eldwyn snarled at the memory. She might be his queen, but he was still...actually, Eldwyn wasn't sure who he was to her, if anyone at all. Did she view him as the Lord's First Commander of Aviva's army? Or did she view him as *her* First Commander—or something else entirely?

He cast a sidelong glance at the female who was holding up a very gray-looking Cethin on one side as they made their way back to their horses.

He'd need to shift back once they did—Cethin was in no shape to be carried across the plains by a wolf in his current state. Alanna would ride with the half-Elf on the return journey, in an attempt to hold his wounds at bay until they reached Aviva.

Eleonora would ride with him.

They needed to talk.

The Lost Princess

She felt Cethin's heaviness and exhaustion weighing on her with each step she took down the rocky hill—but he was breathing, and she could've wept tears for that alone. Breathing, as she and Alanna half helped him walk and half carried him down to the horses. Eldwyn had shifted into a wolf, which had alarmed her at first, even though he'd told her it was a possibility. A beautiful wolf, after she'd adjusted to the initial shock, with fur as silver as his eyes. *The silver wolf.*

This was all real she repeated to herself, over and over again. The half-Elf now half slumped on her shoulder—*he was real.* She'd found him. She'd gotten him back. She fought the burning in her eyes. He was going to be okay. He had to be okay.

Alanna hadn't said anything since they'd fled the camp, and she hoped that was out of their need for silence, and not because something was more wrong with Cethin and his injuries than the Healer had originally detected. She knew she'd be just as likely to receive a tongue-lashing from the Healer for wrecking their careful planning. She still didn't care. Part of her heart still pulsed from the thrill of slaughtering her enemies. It had taken more will than she'd thought to sheath her blades.

They reached the horses quickly, gravity helping their speed down the mountain, even with a wounded member in their party.

"Alanna, take Cethin with you," Eldwyn suddenly ground out in a voice that was more animal than male—he'd shifted back into his Elvish body. "You." He pointed a finger at her. "Come with me." She opened her mouth to protest, but one look into Eldwyn's eyes—ringed with a ferocity she'd never seen from the male—had her closing it and nodding. She swung up behind him, watching as the Healer expertly pulled Cethin into her saddle first, then mounted behind him, pale-blue light pulsing around his body.

They flew back across the dunes, the wind at their backs. She had no doubt Eldwyn had redirected some of it to help them. But even releasing some of that wild magic hadn't calmed the male—she could feel the tension in his body.

"What were you thinking," he snapped, turning his head when they were halfway across the sands. *So, it was to be now.* "We had a fucking *plan*."

"I know," she said quietly. "I'm sorry."

"You're *sorry*?" Eldwyn laughed bitterly. "That's all you have to say after going against orders and cutting down a dozen of the Dark King's creatures? You're fucking *sorry*?"

She stiffened at the bite in his words. "I was thinking," she snarled back at him, "that I didn't smell fear on any of them. I was thinking that they were able to light fires on the mountainside without dreading being caught. I was thinking that it was about time someone taught them a lesson in terror. I was thinking that they took something that is mine, and I was thinking that I would unleash every last bit of my power on them to get him back. Be grateful I at least didn't do *that*."

She could've sworn Eldwyn...smiled? But it was gone so quickly, she must've imagined it. "And while that was very *noble* of you"—she stiffened at the way he said the word *noble*—"it wasn't the fucking plan. And if you can't trust me, why should I trust you?" *Why should any of us trust you to be our queen?* His unasked question hung in the air between them. She fell silent, the pounding of their horse's hooves the only sound. Then, a low rumble of laughter.

"Good answer," he said.

"But I didn't say anything?"

"Exactly. If you were thinking of lording your title over all of us, you would've said, 'because I am your queen,'" he pointed out. "But you didn't. I know you're sorry." His voice softened. "And I can understand the feelings that led you to do what you did back there."

She wasn't entirely sure what to say to that, except, "Thank you." He squeezed her hand.

They made it back to Aviva undetected—almost. Eldwyn had specifically positioned the guards, timed their rotations, and given them extra duties. But there was still one soldier in the stable when they returned.

"Who—what—" the male sputtered as they skidded into the enclosure. She felt a wall of air go up around them to keep the male from scenting Cethin where he still lay wounded—and now unconscious—across Alanna's horse. "First Commander," the male finally got out, nodding to Eldwyn. "I didn't know we were expecting you from outside the wall today."

"Training exercise," Eldwyn smoothly lied as he dismounted. The male's eyes flickered over to where she and Alanna remained shielded and cloaked. Whether he recognized anything out of the ordinary, he didn't let on. "Back to your duties," the First Commander barked. The male nodded again and moved on.

"We need somewhere for Cethin to recover," she said, swinging down from the horse and running over to Alanna's. "Is there a room in the palace—"

"Not in the palace." Eldwyn gestured to his steed. "Get back on."

Chapter 24

The Lost Princess

They rode back out of the city, across the sands—but not to the mountains. No, this time they made their way to the shore—to where water connected Aviva and Ozul.

She scented the sea beyond the small village as they entered it, eyes taking in the small wooden cottages of the lower-born Elves, half-Elves, and humans cheerfully painted with all manner of waves, sea creatures, and suns. She shuddered at the depictions of some of the painted sea creatures on one home—creatures that, legend said, roamed the waters near The Islands, like the fearsome *cetuson*.

No one paid their group attention as they made their way between the homes—not even the First Commander. Eldwyn led them to a cottage bedecked in different paints that outlined plants growing beneath the sea: corals, reefs, and seaweeds. It was a simple two-story building, but the paint made it seem *alive* somehow. A chimney, painted blue, poked its head through the thatched roof. A small walkway led to the plain front door, with something that looked like it had once been a garden on either side. Three windows, two on the first floor, one on the second, stood stark against the Light, making it impossible to see inside.

Eldwyn swung the yellow, orange, and green-painted fence gate that surrounded the property open. "Welcome to my home."

His...*home*? She gaped as they passed the sad, overturned garden, and walked up the path. The male unlocked the front door with a pass of his hand. The inside of the house was painted similarly to the outside: bursts of yellows, oranges, greens, and some blues and purples, too. To their right was a small sitting room, which boasted the fireplace whose chimney she'd seen outside. Books lined the shelves to the left and right of it. There was a sofa and two cushioned chairs, all well-loved from how worn they looked. To their left, a staircase led to the second level. The kitchen beyond the stairs was small but with enough space for a dining table that held three chairs. Presumably, a bathing room and bed chambers were upstairs. Not an opulent room in the palace, which was his right as the First Commander. Not a Commander's pavilion in the camp. But here, this cottage. This was Eldwyn's home.

"It was my parent's," the male explained, obviously noting the expression on her face.

"Your parents," she murmured, voice trailing off as she and Alanna walked into the sitting room and carefully lowered Cethin onto the sofa.

Eldwyn nodded. "I wasn't born in a position to become First Commander," he said quietly as he surveyed the space. "My parents were lower-born. My mother barely possessed any Healing ability. And my father..." Eldwyn swallowed. "He possessed the Earth gift but..."

He didn't have to say anything more. Those blessed with gifts of the Earth had faced difficulties when the Darkness had come. She reflected on the mountains they'd just come from, the sands beyond the wall—and the sad garden outside.

"What happened to them?"

"My mother died in childbirth, the babe as well," he replied, sorrow lining his eyes. "My father's life slowly drained away after that. It was hard for him, I think, having me around, with my mother gone." Misery and pain flickered across his face. "I look like her. And they truly loved each other. Not mates, but enough that he would follow her into the Realm of Blessings." Despair rose in her body—sadness for the male she'd come to consider her friend. "One of the Healers had a theory that my mother had such a difficult delivery because the babe's gifts were too strong, especially compared to her own, and her body couldn't handle it." She glanced at Alanna, whose pale-blue Healing light bled into Cethin. Whether the Healer heard Eldwyn, or understood more about his mother, she didn't let on. "I channeled all of my emotions into learning about my own magic," Eldwyn said, waving a hand to the books that lined the shelves. "And, when I came of age, I had more control over my gift than most. I enlisted and moved through the ranks quickly for the same reason. Keeping my mind occupied, my body focused, helps me not to dwell on the past."

"And he's *so* humble about it," she heard Alanna mutter under her breath.

When she looked up at Eldwyn again, there was a faint twinkle of humor back in his eyes. "I may be First Commander, but this is still a part of me," he said, eyes meeting hers. "All parts of our stories make us who we are. Not just one. And certainly not just a title," he remarked, giving her a small smile. She offered him one of her own in return.

"How is our patient?" he said after a moment, and she understood that this part of the conversation was now closed. Eldwyn hung his cloak on one of the pegs next to the door and chucked his boots underneath the stairwell. She looked down at her own clothes, covered in blood and filth like his were. The mess didn't seem to bother him one bit. A good thing, since all of the grime and blood coating Cethin was now on his couch.

"*Our* patient?" Alanna asked, face twisted in concentration as she continued funneling her magic through Cethin's body. Eldwyn winked at her. "His physical wounds," the Healer stated with a sigh, "won't be a problem once I clear out any potential infection." Alanna sighed again and tossed her curls over her shoulder. "But the deeper injuries..." The female fell silent, then turned to face her. "I'm not sure if it's a good idea for you to be here when he wakes up."

She started. "What—why?" she sputtered, her temper flaring, raw moonlight creeping through her veins.

Alanna's expression softened a fraction. "What he thinks they put you through are scenarios that any decent male would rip someone to shreds for even thinking of," the Healer said gently. "If he wakes up and sees you here, he might very well think he's still there. It could put all of us—and I don't mean just the three of us, but this entire village—in danger. Just as everyone was in danger when you gave in to your emotions at that camp and fed your need for personal vengeance," the Healer finished, a familiar purple spark gleaming in her eyes.

She took a deep breath and closed her eyes.

"My brother was beside himself when they pulled you from the changeling's camp," Alanna said. "But that will be nothing compared to how Cethin feels when he awakens."

She opened her eyes, suddenly exhausted. From the way the female held her gaze, she knew the Healer understood she didn't need to say anything more. She and Cerdwin—they were friends, yes. He wouldn't want her in danger if he could help it. But she and Cethin, the life oath between, the feelings that lurked beneath it...

"Please. Please help him."

Alanna nodded, and Eldwyn retrieved his boots and cloak with a sigh. "Looks like it's back to the palace for us, then."

Her body threatened to collapse as they walked away from Eldwyn's home. Leaving Cethin behind when she'd just come so close to losing him...

Fortunately, Eldwyn excelled at distraction. He pointed out the window in the side of a neighboring home—and restaurant, apparently—that he'd accidentally broken whilst practicing with his wind one day as a youngling, as well as some of his favorite local shops and trading posts as they departed for the city proper. It was there the conversation changed, and she knew he'd put his shield of air around them.

"When we return to the castle," Eldwyn said, voice low, "we need to put you back where Lord Arel thinks you are."

"How long have we been gone for?"

"Almost a full day," he said, face grim. She knew that being gone that long—or any longer—would lead to questions for him. Eldwyn shook his head, as if following her thoughts, and rested a hand on her shoulder.

"It was worth it," he said. Her heart clenched at his words—at someone thinking she wasn't only worthy of help, but that the half-Elf she cared for was, too.

"I'll be your official interrogator, so there's nothing to worry about there. But what will the results of my interrogation be?" he asked, stopping them before they entered a door from outside the wall.

She knew that question was a long time coming—it had been on her mind on their way back from the mountains. Since she'd abandoned the First Commander's plan and killed—not in defense, but in rage, for her city, for her people—for *him*. Since she'd taken matters into her own hands—and had almost cost Alanna her life, something she hadn't realized until she'd seen the female's torn clothing on the return journey. Since she'd felt the rage and the fury, but also unconditional support, of the male still by her side—his forgiveness and understanding. Somewhere, in the midst of all that had happened, she knew she could see this through.

"I think," she said, holding her head high as she looked at the First Commander, "I think they will be the truth." He stared and stared at her, and while his expression didn't change, she noted the flicker of approval that flared in his eyes, setting the silver in them swirling.

"Very well." He inclined his head to her. She made to move down the narrow street but stopped at his hand on her shoulder. "A word of advice, if I may, Y—" He stopped, voice dropping again. "Be careful. There are some who might not exactly celebrate your return. Especially the Council."

She'd thought as much—especially Lord Arel. But what would Cerdwin make of all of this? And Cethin, once he awoke?

"I will be your eyes and ears and do my best to smooth things over where and when I can," Eldwyn promised her. "But I will feel far more comfortable once he is awake and by your side."

"What if he doesn't accept everything?"

What if he doesn't accept me?

Eldwyn's face softened. "He will. Of that I have no doubt."

Eldwyn

"How is he?" Eldwyn asked as he stepped back into his home. He watched Alanna's hands pause over the half-Elf's body.

"I drew out the infection that settled in," she answered as he observed her handiwork. Most of Cethin's injuries were already knitting muscle and skin back together. As a half-Elf, they would leave scars, but the male already had quite a few of those. Eldwyn dropped into his favorite chair. "There were no major physical injuries beyond that. He should be able to walk on his own as early as tomorrow."

"And his...other injuries?" Eldwyn asked, drawing the sentence out long enough that Alanna stopped her work, sat back on her heels, and turned to face him, eyes dull.

"He suffered extreme trauma, Eldwyn," she said, voice tired. "Greater than hers—and for longer. From what I saw, the changeling took over the morning she left. He was going to go after her, but they intercepted him and took him to that camp. And what he endured there....it will take some time."

Eldwyn frowned, then sighed. "I can't explain it, but I'll feel more comfortable when he's in the castle with her. Closer to her." He felt guilty for taking Eleonora back to the dungeons and locking her in a room. She was the fucking queen—even if the Lord's Council didn't want to hear it. Alanna's swallow was audible.

"What is it? What did you see in his mind?"

Alanna looked back at Cethin. "There's something *different* about him. Something that seems unrelated to his injuries." She shook her head. "Strange, too, for a half-Elf."

Eldwyn made the long-suffering sound he knew always provoked her twin. "Out with it."

"Well, for starters, his heart—it's protected."

"Like if I stabbed him in the chest he wouldn't be injured, protected?"

"No," Alanna murmured, placing her hands over the male's chest and running her magic around the location of his heart. "More like a shield—a guard. To keep it...pure."

Eldwyn sat up so fast his head spun. "Pure? You're telling me that this half-Elf, a *mercenary*, no less—"

"Has a one-way ticket to the Realm of Blessings," Alanna finished for him. "*If* the Balance is re-Bound."

When someone passed, their deeds, acts, works, their very hearts and essence were balanced on a scale by the Goddess of Love. Light and Dark. Love and hate. Depending on the outcome, they would then either pass into the Realm of Blessings or Hell. Except now, no one could access the Realm of Blessings. Those who would normally go there were stuck in the Otherworld.

Eldwyn shuddered. Although Alanna couldn't bring anyone back from the dead, not without giving up her essence, she'd been with enough soldiers as they'd passed to have touched the Otherworld—and not liked what she'd felt.

"Shit," he said. "But why? *How?*"

Alanna shook her head. "I'm not sure," she said, and he watched her magic make another round of the male's heart. "The magic, it's"—she tilted her head to one side—"different."

"Wonderfully vague," he said dryly. "What else?"

"His mind." Eldwyn's body went cold. The Healer didn't often speak of the work she did within her patient's minds—not even when she tended to his males. Hell, Eldwyn was fairly confident Alanna's father and brother didn't even understand the full extent of what she *could* do if she wanted to. He'd only been able to guess at it, with all the magic he'd studied as a child, and what the wind whispered. He'd figured out that, with the strength of her power, she could work her way into a person's mind and bend and shape it to her will, make her thoughts their thoughts, make her will their actions. When he'd asked her about it, she'd told him she never touched that part of her power. It reminded her too much of the way the Dark King held the minds of their people. But Alanna did use that magic, to a lesser degree, when the patient suffered an emotional or mental wound—a trauma—to see it, to experience it with them, and pull them out of it.

"It will take time to sort through the trauma he experienced in that camp," she continued, "but there's also"—she frowned, hands moving from Cethin's chest to his forehead—"a block."

"Something they did—"

"No. Something older—a memory. And the magic binding it..." She removed her magic and hands, sank back onto her heels again, and wrapped her arms around herself. "It feels familiar but foreign. I know I've seen it before, but it's like it doesn't want *me* to remember it, either."

"That can't be good," Eldwyn muttered. He sent a warm breeze to wrap itself around Alanna like a blanket. She was always cold after an intensive Healing.

She shot him a grateful look, then asked, "What do you think it is?"

"I'm not sure," he admitted. The wind—usually *so* chatty—had been quiet the past few days. "Again, I'll feel better once he's back with her.

Taking her to the dungeons..." He blew out a breath, then said quietly, "She is our queen."

"All the more reason for you to head back." He opened his mouth to reply—

The door shuddered, groaned, then blew open, ash sputtering in its wake. He'd recognize that scent anywhere. Eldwyn set a hard shield of air around Alanna and Cethin. The same shield that *had* been around the house.

The one that Cerdwin had broken through.

"*What*," the male growled from the blasted doorway, "were the two of you thinking?"

Chapter 25

CERDWIN

He wasn't sure he'd ever been more furious. Elana had lied to him. Eldwyn had lied to him. Alanna had lied to him. All to retrieve a *half-Elf*. A mercenary. As if he were more important than the rest of them.

"Do *not* start," he said, holding a finger up when his twin rose next to Cethin's unconscious body. "You," he snarled at Eldwyn, fire roiling in his veins, body torn between whether to give into it or shift into the ferocious beast that threatened to claw its way out of his skin. "You put *all* of them at risk." *You put* yourself *at risk.*

Eldwyn took a step toward him. Cerdwin felt a cool breeze around him, preparing to soothe his fire; he saw the glow in the male's churning silver eyes, letting him know the male was also prepared to shift should they need to settle this with claws and teeth. That's what hurt more than anything. His brother-in-arms, who knew him that damn well, hadn't given him the same trust he'd given his friend and twin.

"We had a plan." Eldwyn took another step closer. "They were all safe."

"There was no way for you to guarantee that," Cerdwin snapped. "If you would have just *told* me, I could have—"

"You could have what?" Alanna's voice came from his left. "You could have told our father? If you had, he would've ordered everyone to stand down, and he"—she motioned toward the body on the couch—"would've died."

"So?" Cerdwin ground out, and from the anger swirling Eldwyn's eyes, he knew it had been the wrong thing to say.

"You would put your friend through that, the death of her life-sworn?" the male asked softly.

"That is not what I meant, and you know it." Cerdwin lowered his head and ran a hand through his hair. *Gods, he needed a haircut.*

"I know what you meant," Eldwyn said, voice cold.

"It does not matter what any of you *meant*, either," he snapped back, crossing his arms. "Your guard was not as discreet as you had hoped." Eldwyn's mouth became a hard line, so at odds with the curving smile Cerdwin had seen grace it when they were alone. He shook those thoughts away. "You," he pointed at the First Commander, "are to bring the half-Elf to the palace immediately for Healing and interrogation, then return to your camp. I will be taking over Elana's interrogation—that is *if* she is still where she is supposed to be."

"And you"—he turned to his sister—"are to return from your sojourn to the Healer's quarters." He pivoted and made his way to the door—or what was left of it. He'd conveniently left his twin out of as much of his report as possible when he'd spoken with their lord father about what the guard had witnessed in the stables. Eldwyn, on the other hand—Cerdwin couldn't help it. He was pissed off and wanted to show it the only way he knew how, and using his lord father to pull rank had felt like a good idea at the time. But he saw the way the muscles in Eldwyn's jaw flexed. Maybe he'd made a mistake. But it was too late. As for Elana...

He paused on the threshold. "Is it really her? Is she the reason you were both so willing to toss everything else aside?"

Neither of them answered.

The Lost Princess

She stood the moment she heard the door open, rising from the uncomfortable chair she'd been half sleeping, half dozing in for the past few hours, expecting Eldwyn. But it wasn't him.

It was Cerdwin. She froze, unsure of what to say or how to act. His smooth courtier's mask was entirely unhelpful in that matter as he sat in the chair across the table. Sorrow rose in her chest. He hadn't come as her friend.

"That was an interesting proclamation you made to the Head of the Lord's Council," he said. She stayed quiet, considering. She'd told Eldwyn that when they concluded her interrogation, when she left the cell, she would be Eleonora. But that was when Eldwyn was to be the one with her. Now that it was Cerdwin...

The fact that he was there, and not Eldwyn, told her enough about what her old friend suspected, if he didn't already know. So she held her chin high and spoke.

"It was the truth."

Cerdwin tilted his head to the side, hair spilling over his shoulder in ringlets. "How is that possible? We would have scented it on you after you shifted. Royal blood does not lie."

She'd wondered about that, too, and come to the only realistic conclusion. "You might want to ask your friend who controls the air about that one."

An emotion passed across Cerdwin's face, shifting too quickly for her to read. Then she felt it, a crack in the space around her, a small sliver of Eldwyn's shield opening. Knew what was happening from the way Cerdwin stiffened, the way his jaw flexed, the way his fist opened and closed on the table.

"So. It is true, then." Flat, unfeeling words.

She nodded. And then, because she couldn't stand another moment of her friend—if he was still her friend—looking at her that way, she told Cerdwin everything: how she'd lived on the mortal continent, how her memories had come flooding back when she'd met Cethin, how they'd traveled back with Eldwyn, how she'd wanted to prove herself. The only thing she left out was Sonia—she would protect her former lady's maid, even if she didn't understand how the woman had done what she'd done.

"I never meant to keep any of this from you to hurt you," she whispered. "I only wanted to protect you—and to be worthy of being your queen."

Cerdwin sat with that unwavering look of control on his face. Then, he stood and walked toward the door. "I will have to speak with the Lord's Council about your return," he said. Each step he took away from her was another weight on her heart. "Eleonora," he added, as if he were saying her name for the first time.

"Cerdwin—"

"Welcome home," he said. But there was nothing welcoming about his tone.

Cerdwin

He paused outside of the interrogation room, gripping the door's handle until it began to burn and steam beneath his hand. Cerdwin let go and took a deep breath, trying to ground himself the way Alanna taught him. It wasn't easy. The only time he remembered feeling at peace with his gift was at the forge. That was partly why he'd been assigned to the blacksmith in Ozul. But now that he'd returned—as his lord father had ordered—his magic kept dormant for so long, not even that completely helped. Nothing did. Nothing but the patience and encouragement of his twin...and the First Commander.

Cerdwin leaned against the wall opposite her door and allowed the coolness of the marble to seep into his skin, breathing deeply. It was *her*. Elana was the lost princess. Elana was Eleonora. *Their queen*. The female his lord father had intended for him to marry.

It hadn't been so much a discussion—or even a conversation—as it'd been an order. His lord father had walked into their family chambers one day and announced that he'd spoken to Queen Serenity and that Her Grace had offered her daughter's hand in marriage. Cerdwin hadn't thought much about it at the time—it would've been ages before they'd actually wed, anyway, and he was still a youngling who was living and experiencing. And living and experiencing what he had, he wasn't sure if marriage to a queen was in the cards for him, if he'd be content as a monogamous married male, siring heirs.

And now...Cerdwin had seen the way she looked at her life-sworn. Not that the half-Elf would ever be King Consort—the Lord's Council would never allow it. But the golden lion and the moonlight of Aviva? Could they ever be happy as husband and wife? Then again, what was their happiness compared to the future of a kingdom? And, right now, that future was directed by the Head of the Lord's Council.

Cethin

Where is she where is she where is she—

The question circled around in his mind, over and over again, an endless cycle, a constant loop. The pain was gone. The Darkness was gone. But so was she.

Where is she where is she where is she—

She is safe, came a gentle—yet commanding—female voice that wasn't hers. *She is safe.* You *are safe. You have not broken your oath to her.*

His eyes fluttered open, and he found himself staring up at a ceiling made of swirling white-and-cream marble. No Darkness.

He sat up, wincing as pain lanced his side. Warm female hands that were not hers braced him. "Easy," came that same voice.

He looked to his left, forcing his eyes to focus. "You look like a female," he said to the Elf who looked so much like Cerdwin yet...wasn't?

The female's mouth twisted. "I should certainly hope so." Cethin blinked. The hair, the eyes—they were almost identical to Cerdwin's.

But she was female, and she was wearing the dress of the Healers. "I'm Alanna," she said. "You know my twin, Cerdwin." He nodded in response and cringed when his back twinged. "Sorry about that," the Healer commented, noticing his grimace. He felt it then: soothing, warm magic flowing into his body. He looked down, watching as blue light flowed from her hands and up around him to his back. "I told them not to move you yet," she muttered.

"Move me..." His thoughts were murky, but he pushed through them, trying to remember what had happened to him—to her.

Alanna sat back in her chair and gave him a long, hard look—the same assessing stare he'd seen Cerdwin give hundreds of times. "I assume you remember some of what happened to you. It's alright—and not unexpected—if you don't remember everything right now." When he didn't immediately reply, she spoke again. "You were taken by the Dark King's creatures and held captive for almost three weeks. You were rescued by a small group of soldiers from Aviva. I've been working on Healing your body for almost three days, since they didn't listen to me." She tossed her curls over her shoulder. "Though you are Healing more quickly than I would've guessed for a half-Elf," she said, so quietly, he almost didn't hear her.

"Where is she?" He fumbled with the linens around him, looking for a fresh tunic. "Where is El?"

Pale-blue light wove around him, holding him in place. He cut the female a look most of his foes bowed to—but she didn't. *Fuck Satraras and their stubbornness.*

"She's here in the palace. She's safe."

He stilled. "What are you not telling me? Is she hurt? Is she—"

"She is Healing, and well cared for."

"Healing? What happened to her? And why can't I—"

"Cethin." It was the first time she'd used his name, even in the conversations they'd had mind-to-mind. Intense emotions and memories trickled through him. He looked up at the Healer, and she held his gaze. "Do you know why they took you?" He ran through what he remembered: He'd known that El planned to go scouting, to learn what she could in order to help the city. Asked him to stay behind. But something had gone wrong. The bond of the life oath had stretched, strained, and then gone quiet. He'd been like a rabid animal on the wall, raging at Cerdwin and Eldwyn to do *something*, to let him go—and then he'd gone on his own, following any trace of her he could find. And then they'd found him, brought him to that Dark place, where they'd also held her. At least, that's what he'd thought, but what if he was wrong, what if—

"That wasn't real." Alanna's voice broke through the Darkness again, purple eyes lined with palest blue. "She wasn't there. She was already back here. But..." The Healer hesitated, as if she were about to tell him something she shouldn't. "She was taken by a changeling. She thought she was with you."

Agony, sharper than any pain he'd ever felt, shot through his chest. And dampness, in his eyes, on his face...he was *crying*? Cethin couldn't remember the last time he'd cried—if he'd ever cried.

Misreading his emotion, the Healer spoke again. "Cerdwin brought her back, Cethin, and she's fine. She's here. She actually helped rescue you." He closed his eyes, willed the tears to stop, the pain flowing through him to stop. "And"—*How could there possibly be more?*—"she isn't who you think she is." He opened his eyes, tears slowing to a stop.

Her name isn't Elana, Cethin, he heard Alanna say in his mind. *It's Eleonora. She is the lost princess. And now, she will take her rightful place as queen. They took you because you mean something to her.*

He opened his mouth to speak, to deny it, even though it *felt* true—all of it—but the door to the room opened, and Cerdwin entered. "Good, you are awake." The male stood next to where his sister sat. "First, I hope you recognize that leaving the city alone was incredibly foolish."

Alanna sighed. "Brother—" But Cerdwin held up a hand, and she fell silent.

"However, that in and of itself is not a crime. My sister looked into your mind and deemed you free from the Dark King's control. She also confirmed that you did not divulge anything of importance to his creatures while you were in their camp." Cethin stared at the male. "Additionally, she reported that your Healing is almost complete. So, when you are ready, you are free to do as you wish."

What he wished.

What did he wish? Thoughts swirled through Cethin's mind faster than sand being tossed by a wave. *What did he wish?*

"I'd like to go back to the camp." The words surprised him as much as they seemed to surprise the twins, two sets of golden brows lifting. "Train and contribute in any way I can." He nodded at Cerdwin. He needed *something*—something to busy his hands and quiet his mind.

The male leveled him with that assessing gaze. "Fine." The word was edged, but not entirely unfriendly. And then Cerdwin left the room.

"Are you certain you don't wish to stay here in the palace?" Alanna asked quietly. *To be close to her.*

But right now he needed space. Time. Distraction. *Something.*

El had lied to him. From the very beginning, she'd *lied* to him. His mind raced, thoughts spiraling like a whirlpool.

He needed distance from her. The female he'd been sent to take. His life-sworn. His friend he'd traveled so many miles with, who he'd fought alongside for their lives.

The female he'd killed his only friend for.

The female who'd really seen him. Cethin had thought he was beginning to see her. The one he lov—

And now, after the changeling...

She should've known. The thoughts stopped, hanging above a vortex he felt himself being pulled under by.

"She should've known," he said, then laid back down and closed his eyes. Emotions kicked back up like an undercurrent through his body, his heart, his essence. He heard Alanna leave the room a moment later, leaving him to drown in them.

Chapter 26

She found her twin at the forge, fire flaring around him as he hammered what looked like a new sword. "Cerdwin." He didn't respond. "Cerdwin!" she yelled more loudly. He stopped, and the fire around him winked out. "I didn't know you still came here."

"When I need to." He wiped sweat from his face, smearing ash on his cheeks in the process.

Alanna crossed her arms. "And you needed to today because…?"

Fire rekindled in her brother's amethyst eyes. "You lied to me. You *all* lied to me. And now—" Cerdwin paused and ran a hand through his hair. "She is back," he finished with a whisper.

"That she is," Alanna said as her brother sat on an old barrel. She wondered if any of his males had ever seen him like this—messy. If Eldwyn had ever—nope, she shut that thought down. Today probably wasn't the day to push that point. "You're worried about Father?" she said instead.

Her twin sighed. "Partly."

"And the other part?"

Eyes twin to her own met hers. "We were betrothed, Alanna," he said in a hoarse whisper.

"I remember."

"She is in love with that half-Elf."

"So? You are in love with—" A sharp glare and flicker of flame kept her from finishing that sentence. Nope, *definitely* not the day to push that point. Silence followed, then—

"Everything is going to change now," her brother said, eyes distant in a way she knew hers sometimes were when she was thinking—that's what Eldwyn told her.

"Probably." Cerdwin let out a hollow laugh. "What did Father say?"

"He has yet to summon me," he said. Now *that* was concerning. "Have you received word?"

"Is it time for another family dinner already?" The response didn't create the lightness she'd intended it to.

Cerdwin leaned forward, looking at his soot-covered hands, then back up at her again. "Do you believe in her?"

Alanna shook her head. "I don't think that's the question you should be asking."

The Lost Princess

She sighed and stretched her neck from right to left, sifting through the papers Eldwyn had smuggled into her cell, papers that showed the latest maneuverings of what was rightfully her army—and the Dark King's. The First Commander had been her only visitor since Cerdwin, and they hadn't spoken about the Second. Or Cethin. The former, she supposed, was likely still angry with her. The latter…her heart squeezed painfully every time she thought about him. But she trusted Alanna. He needed to heal, so she wouldn't push. Hell, she was still recovering herself, still seeing the changeling's mask when she closed her eyes. She was exhausted but knew sleep wouldn't come easily that fake night, if at all. Not that it mattered—she had work to do.

The next scouting mission listed—and signed off on by Lord Arel—was a mess. It didn't seem to matter to Eldwyn that she was still being detained after her confession in the lord's chambers or her conversation with Cerdwin. The First Commander had fully accepted her as his queen and would ensure her involvement in such matters. They still held a foothold in the south. But the north…she chewed on her bottom lip. There had to be a reason why they'd had such difficulty gaining access to the north—beyond the weather.

Then there was the lord himself to consider. Since revealing herself to him, to Cerdwin, there'd been no summons from the Lord's Council. She wasn't sure if she was relieved or if she should be worried. Eldwyn's warning still rang in her ears. *Be careful. There are some who might not exactly celebrate your return. Especially the Council.*

She moved to where a pitcher of water and several unused cups sat on an oak tray when a motion to her right caught her eye—

Cethin. His wounds had healed, and his color had returned. But there was a shadow to his face, and his golden eyes were dull. It was him—but he wasn't himself.

"How?" he demanded, the anger in his voice coating her skin like the dirt and grime of the mountainside had. "How didn't you realize it wasn't me?"

She trembled as she held his empty gaze—not from fear, but from guilt. Regret. They'd told him about the changeling, then—either those who'd taken him, or someone in the palace; likely Cerdwin, as a way to get back to her. The idea stung.

Voice shaking, she told him: How she'd gone to scout the mountains. How he'd come with her, even though she'd asked him not to. How she'd been captured. How she'd thought he'd come to save her. And...her voice trembled when she told him what had happened in the cave.

"And what promises did it make to you, as it knelt before you?" His voice was low and laced with wrath.

Her mouth was dry, voice hoarse, as she spoke. "He—it," she stumbled over the words, "it promised me to be mine—my royal guard, my First Guard, mine to command." She swallowed. "Mine to-to love. He—it—promised to always be mine. With or without the life oath. Even into the Darkness."

He stood there, filled with rumbling rage and a fury that would've rivaled Cerdwin's magic if he'd been a fully-blooded Elf. She crossed her arms like they could protect her from his reply and bowed her head. Suddenly, he was standing directly in front of her, hand tilting her chin up so she couldn't avoid meeting his gaze again.

"You should've known," he said quietly—too quietly. "You should've known that I never would've accepted your breaking the life oath between us—no matter that you'd decided I'd fulfilled it." He raised his other hand, still bearing that scar, that scar that united them. "You should've known that I never would've accepted your offer to make me your First Guard so lightly," he continued, lowering the scarred hand to his side. "You should've known that I wouldn't have vowed to protect you in that capacity. That I would've stopped there."

Tears filled her eyes at his words. The *real* Cethin's words. Her mouth quivered, but he held her chin firm, refusing to concede a single inch as he stared into her eyes, his own harsh and unforgiving as he said, "I would've sworn to protect you until the mountains turned to dust and ash, until all of the kingdoms in this world crumbled and became forgotten songs." She closed her eyes, feeling the truth of his words reverberate through her essence. "And even then," Cethin continued, "I would've loved you, waited for you, until you crossed into the Realm of Blessings. I would've guarded its gates and loved you from afar, until the Gods themselves cast me aside." She opened her eyes, opened her mouth to speak—

"And even then," he snarled, the snap in his voice rippling through her, "I would've crossed through every realm, faced any challenge, taken on every one of the Gods themselves to see you, to watch over you, and to love you, until the end of time. For eternity, and even an hour after."

She shuddered, his fingers still firm against her chin. "You should've known that I wouldn't have disobeyed your wishes to go alone. Because I loved you, trusted you, and believed in you." He released his grip on her chin. She looked away, unable to keep her tears from falling to the floor.

"Please, Cethin...please." She swallowed. "Please..." She sounded pathetic—she *knew* she sounded pathetic. "I'm sorry," she whispered. Because what else could she say when love had become loved, trust had become trusted, and believe had become believed.

He stalked to the door, reaching to open it again, when he paused and turned back to her. "I am not who you need me to be," he said quietly. And then he was gone.

Cethin

It had been a mistake to see her again. Just like it had been a mistake to ask Apolina for help. He'd cared for both females—cared even more for the one he'd just walked away from. They'd both lied to him. Now, one of them was dead. He'd killed her. And the other had come for him, had been willing to risk death for him...

As he marched from her cell to the Healing room to retrieve what little clothing and supplies had been left there for him—along with his weapons—Cethin couldn't shake the feeling that what he'd said to her had been a bigger mistake. He shook the thoughts from his head, but the thoughts bounced right back—thoughts that told him he should forgive her, that she wasn't Apolina—would never be like Apolina—that he should apologize for his spiteful words and be done with it.

But he just couldn't.

He walked past tent after tent in the camp where they'd trained together, where he'd...Cethin shook those memories from his head, too: memories of her taste, her touch—the *feel* of her—as he wove his way toward Cerdwin's pavilion. The sentries immediately allowed him entrance. It was mostly dark inside, and he assumed the male's magic lit the small brazier in the center of the space. The Second Commander sat next to a drinking cart. The male reached for it, handing him one of the bottles that lined it. Cethin opened it and drank deeply from the dark ale inside. Then, the male opened another bottle, took a drink of his own, and said, "Talk."

He didn't—*couldn't*. Cerdwin let out a long breath and a low whistle. "So, that is it," the male said, setting his drink on his desk and leaning back in his seat. "You will step away because of her title," he continued at the same time Cethin growled.

"She should've known." He blinked. Apparently, they were both upset with her for different reasons.

"But she did not," Cerdwin supplied, leaning forward on his elbows.

"She should have," he growled. Cerdwin shook his head.

"Cethin," he said, more softly than Cethin had anticipated, a look of pity—no, a look of sorrow—on his face. "You do not know what they did to her in that place. Physically. Emotionally." The male exhaled sharply through his nose as if imagining it. Perhaps he was. "She was in poor shape when we reached her. She had been there for weeks. *Weeks*, Cethin."

"So was I." Shame flickered through him at the distaste that streaked across Cerdwin's face.

"And yet she still went back. For *you*." *A half-Elf* were the words the male didn't say—someone unworthy of an Elvish female, one of royal blood at that. The lost princess. Their queen. That was what really mattered to the lords of Aviva: titles, families—heirs. But Cerdwin's eyes were distant as he then murmured, "When it comes to love, Cethin, you do not know what you would give, take, steal, or destroy for it. And she thought you had come for her, that she had saved you, that she could give you both a life you only ever dreamed of sharing." The male shook his head. "What she must have endured to believe it was true, that it was finally over, that the two of you..." His eyes shifted to the entrance of his tent. Eldwyn entered a second later. "What are you doing here?" A sharp question from Second Commander to First. "You were sent back to your camp."

Eldwyn threw him a small smile, then gave Cerdwin a cool gaze. "And I went back," he said, tone flat. "My camp is running smoothly. They have no need of me at the moment." Cerdwin's face remained neutral. Eldwyn glanced between them—and their bottles. "I take it you've been discussing how *displeased* you both are with her." Careful words spoken to a male who could burn the entire camp to the ground now that the Healer's wards were removed. Cethin wasn't entirely sure what Cerdwin would do if pushed right now. Even though Cethin just dismissed her being held captive, just as he'd been, he had fantasized about what he would do if—

She'd come back for him, seen where he'd been held. Pain flickered through Cethin as he grasped that she likely hadn't left any of the Dark creatures alive when she'd come for him—same as he would've done, and still wanted to do, damn it, for her. Eldwyn sat down next to him, across from Cerdwin.

"No one is angry with anyone," Cerdwin said, sinking back into his seat. Cethin opened his mouth to disagree. "It is a simple matter of trust. Of loyalty." Cethin closed his mouth and nodded in agreement.

Eldwyn threw his head back and laughed. Actually *laughed*.

"And why should she trust either of *you*?" he finally asked once his laughter subsided. "*You*," he said, eyes on Cerdwin, "who acted like you didn't even want her here, who refused to help her retrieve her life-sworn, who visited her in an interrogation room—only to be upset when she finally revealed the truth, which has always and only ever been hers to tell when she was ready?"

Cethin watched the shadows cast by the brazier flicker and hoped Eldwyn wouldn't rile the male further. "And *you*," the First Commander rounded on him, "a half-Elvish mercenary who I'm pretty damn sure was *not* in Ozul to do anything or take her anywhere particularly pleasant—until the Noir showed up, of course, and you found your way out by swearing the life oath."

"A life oath *she* apparently wanted to rescind—tried to the moment she revealed who she was to that creature. It was nothing more to her than a debt to be paid," Cethin snarled.

"Was it?" the silver male asked, lip curling. "Was it that debt alone that kept you by her side when you traveled across Ozul together, across the sea to Aviva? Decided to stay here with her, to train with her?"

"It's my duty."

"Did it feel like duty when you came to us half out of your mind because she was gone and you felt like something was wrong with your bond?" Cethin didn't respond. "Did it feel like duty when your hand was between her legs?"

Cethin snarled; Cerdwin was doing the same. Eldwyn's eyes glittered. "The wind whispers everything. You may have been able to wash away what the two of you did, but the truth always comes out eventually."

The male looked at Cerdwin again. "Would you still marry her, knowing she took a half-Elf to her bed?"

"Technically, we weren't *in* a bed," Cethin muttered, turning to look at Cerdwin. The male had gone incredibly still, his usually golden skin pale.

Eldwyn shrugged and leaned back in his chair. "That doesn't matter. Why do you think neither of you"—his words were now directed at the Second Commander—"have been called before the Lord's Council? They're trying to figure out how to use her return to their advantage."

Cethin's chest sank, even though he'd known something like this was bound to happen. It was why he'd tossed those parting words at her: no matter what he felt—before she'd given her heart to that *thing,* that thing that wasn't him—there was still this.

"One of their proposals was to marry the two of you," Eldwyn was saying to Cerdwin. Blood roared in Cethin's ears. "Therefore giving you—and, by extension, your lord father and the Council—partial control of the kingdom. Their reasoning is that, with your lineage, and between your fire gift and whatever magic she possesses, you could bring the Darkness to its knees. And, of course, breed that power into a new bloodline that would secure Aviva's future for centuries to come. And, apparently, this was *not* the first time this was discussed." Cethin wasn't sure he was breathing. Eldwyn and Cerdwin were staring at each other.

"If that is what the Lord's Council decides," Cerdwin finally said, voice steady but tight, "I know what my duty is."

"Do you?" Eldwyn asked, tone harsh. "Do you remember the vows you swore to the kingdom, to the royal family, when you became a Commander?"

"Yes," Cerdwin hissed through his teeth. "Do you?"

"I do," Eldwyn said, tone turning into something deeper, deadlier. "And you," the First Commander shot at Cethin. "You know there's far more between you than the life oath, so stop pretending there isn't."

It was Cethin's turn to laugh, though it was devoid of any real humor. "And what does that matter? A Queen of Aviva could never be with a half-Elf. The Lord's Council would never allow it, any more than they would allow any other marriage they don't deem advantageous." Emotion flickered across Eldwyn's face, and Cerdwin's hand tightened on his bottle. Cethin smirked in satisfaction. "I guess I'm not the only one who won't get what they want in the end." The brazier roared.

"Do not," Eldwyn said, too quietly. "Do not speak of what you do not understand." Cethin shrugged and reached for his own bottle. A beat of silence passed.

"So, you're not going to fight for her?" Eldwyn's voice was still raw, but with a different emotion now, and Cethin knew the First Commander had already made his choice—had sworn his allegiance to her. From the torn look on Cerdwin's face, he knew the Second Commander had worked that out, too. But, when it came to his friend—his betrothed—or his father, where would Cerdwin's loyalties lie?

"I'm here, aren't I?" Cethin said, taking a drink and waving a hand to the camp that lay outside the Second Commander's tent.

"That's not what I meant and you know it."

Cethin let out another dark laugh. "There's nothing to fight for." *Not anymore.* Draining the last of the liquid from the bottle, he stood, the alcohol burning in his throat. He almost wished Cerdwin would burn him for saying those words.

"You think it was mere coincidence you were tasked with taking her from Ozul?" Eldwyn's voice was barely a whisper, and Cerdwin was watching the male carefully. "That you swore the life oath to her? That you are here, now, together?"

"If you know something, speak it now," Cerdwin murmured, and Cethin stilled.

"I don't believe it was a coincidence," the First Commander announced. "I believe it was Fate."

"If Fate had a point to make, she needed to be clearer about it, for she knows I don't believe in such things." Eldwyn opened his mouth to speak again, but Cethin had had enough. He left the Commanders and returned to his tent—their old tent. It smelled of her, of her—and of him. Together. He gritted his teeth. "Fuck Fate."

Cerdwin

"So that's it." Piercing silver eyes met his, sharp as the blade Cerdwin had been forging to avoid his new reality.

"What do you mean?" He averted his gaze, but it didn't matter; Eldwyn's presence encompassed him like he was in the eye of a twister.

"You will do your duty." Not a question.

"Yes." What else could he say? *You could say plenty* he heard Alanna say as if she were right there next to him. But he couldn't. "I will."

Eldwyn

He left the Second Commander's tent without another word or whisper of wind—though the silver wolf was clawing its way through his skin. He needed a fight, and the male exiting the tent ahead of him was a prime target.

"Sparring ring. *Now*," he growled at Cethin. The half-Elf opened his mouth in what Eldwyn assumed was an argument, then shut it when the tents around them shuddered in a sudden breeze.

"Fine." Honey-colored eyes flared with a similar frustration as they met his. Good—it would be a fair fight, or as fair as a fight could be between an Elf and a half-Elf. The male was talented enough. Angry enough.

Eldwyn snagged a sword and quickly weighed it as they entered the empty sparring ring, watching as Cethin pulled a twisted hunting blade from his side. They circled each other silently for a few moments. Eldwyn kept his face neutral as he observed the male. He was patient—but he knew the half-Elf would eventually give in.

Cethin did, snapping forward fast for someone not of fully-blooded Elvish heritage. But Eldwyn heard the blade on the wind first and stepped aside faster. Cethin snarled in frustration.

"Not angry indeed," Eldwyn commented, smoothly dodging another maneuver.

"She lied to me."

"And if she'd told you the truth? Would you not still have been bound by the life oath? Would you not still be here? Would you not have *pleasu—*"

"I would stop right there if I were you." The male's voice was low in warning.

Eldwyn grinned and let a little bit of the wolf show. "How does it feel, knowing that pleasure won't be yours much longer?" He threw up a wind shield and *tsk*ed as Cethin threw a dagger directly at his head.

"Probably the same way it feels knowing your *friend's* cock will—" Cethin stopped speaking when his dagger fell to the ground and the air in the ring went eerily quiet and still. Edwyn walked until he stood eye to eye with the male.

"I told you to not speak of what you do not understand."

"I think I understand *perfectly*," the half-Elf said with a half smile. "You will support her—in everything but this."

"And you," Eldwyn said quietly, "will not support her in anything. Because of this." Silence fell again as the males stared at each other, then Cethin averted his gaze.

"I'm not who she needs." Cethin's voice was barely more than a whisper.

I think you are more of who she needs than you realize, he replied just as quietly on the wind.

The half-Elf glanced back at him. "What's it like being so certain all of the time?"

Eldwyn grimaced. "Even with my magic, I can't be certain of everything all of the time. Some things require hope."

"And do you have it? Hope, I mean?"

"For her? Yes," Eldwyn said without an ounce of uncertainty in his bones.

"And for you and—"

"I—" Eldwyn started but couldn't bring himself to finish his thought. He hadn't tried to read the wind on his and Cerdwin's relationship—ever. Hadn't wanted to know.

Not knowing left room for a desperate kind of hope.

A hand on his shoulder had him meeting honey-colored eyes once more. "I suppose we're both still fools," Cethin said, lips quirking to one side. "I think we need to trade our blades for drinks tonight." Eldwyn nodded, even as his wind picked up the undercurrent of sadness in the male's words. Whether for himself—or both of them—he wasn't sure.

Chapter 27

THE LOST PRINCESS

T he door opened. She lifted her head and wiped away the tears that lingered on her face. She hadn't stopped crying, hadn't been able to move, breathe, or speak. She had no idea how long it'd been since he'd left, since she'd hoped he'd return. But it wasn't Cethin.

"I heard you had a headache," Alanna said, stepping into the space. The Healer scanned her face in that frank, assessing way of hers.

"Looks more like heartache to me," the female muttered and flopped into one of the chairs. "Sit." She couldn't help the smile that tugged at her lips. No matter what was changing around her, some people remained the same—no matter what her title was. It reminded her of Sonia. She hadn't been to visit the woman since everything had changed—she needed to.

She sat in the chair across from the female.

"Talk."

"He hates me," she said quietly.

Alanna huffed. "Which one?"

She almost laughed. "Both of them, I suppose."

"My brother does *not* hate you," Alanna declared, as if it were fact. "He just doesn't take well to being lied to."

"I never lied," she interjected. She hadn't—technically.

The Healer tilted her head to one side. "But you didn't tell him the entire truth, either."

"Do any of us ever really present all parts of ourselves to others?"

The female smirked. "You're catching on to a courtier's ways, I see. But this truth...this was a big one. And it affects him in more ways than you could possibly imagine."

She swallowed, unsure of what to say. She knew the lord was likely displeased. But he also hadn't summoned her. And then there was the matter of their past betrothal...

"As for Cethin." She dropped the female's gaze. "He might not be ready to forgive you—yet," Alanna amended. "But he doesn't—could never—hate you. It doesn't matter to him that you are who you are. He may be upset about what happened with the changeling, but he doesn't hate you. It isn't in his nature."

She snorted. "His nature?"

"Yes," Alanna said simply. "His nature."

"What the Hell does that even mean?" She was out of energy, out of emotions, and slowly running out of patience, too.

"I oversaw his recovery. You saw what I was able to do for him, physically," the Healer said. "But Healing goes deeper than what you see marked on the flesh. He might be a half-Elf, but he's also..." Alanna's voice trailed off for a moment, as if she were trying to find the right words. "He's also something else. Something *more.*" The Healer shook her head, as if frustrated that even with her depthless knowledge of both human and Elvish physiology, she hadn't been able to crack Cethin's true nature.

"And his heart," the female went on, "it's pure. Pure light. I've never seen anything like it, not in any of my patients."

"Pure light?" She repeated. "I don't understand."

Alanna let out a frustrated noise. "Neither do I. A pure heart in a half-Elf's body. Beyond entrance to the Realm of Blessings upon death *after* the re-Binding, I don't know what it means." The Healer ran her hands through her hair. "But I'm reading whatever is in Eldwyn's library, and whatever we have in the Royal Archives to try and find out. If I had access to The Islands' Libraries..." The female chewed on her bottom lip, wringing her hands in her lap. She'd never seen the female...*nervous?*

"It doesn't matter." Alanna leaned forward and squeezed her hand. "What matters is that he does *not* hate you. Give him time. Give my brother time. They will come around." The Healer sent a flicker of blue Healing light toward her as she spoke, soothing her aching body, her aching head—and her broken heart.

"I hope so," she whispered.

"I know so," Alanna said with certainty.

They sat together in contemplative silence for a long while. Finally, she asked, "Can you teach me? Like how you taught Cerdwin?"

"About magic?" The female's brows knitted together. She couldn't blame the female. She hadn't spoken about her power with anyone. That surprise morphed into uncertainty on Alanna's face. "I'm not sure. I've never worked with a female on elemental magic before, for obvious reasons. And I would hate to summon anything here."

"Oh." The female wasn't wrong. Any use of her moonlit magic prompted the Noir to follow. But she knew she needed to start working with it if she had any hope of learning how to re-Bind the Balance.

"We'll start with some readings," Alanna said, leaning back in her chair and blowing a curl out of her eyes. "From Eldwyn's collection."

"Anything I can do to start, I'm open to it," she said, giving the Healer a smile.

The female returned it. "Alright then."

Cerdwin

The Lord's Council summoned him the next day. As he stood in front of the doors of the room he hated so much, Cerdwin wondered if anyone had been summoned with him, if their fates had been decided for them. The two guards who stood outside of the carved wooden doors were his father's, he noticed, in green and gold—not from Aviva's forces. Neither gave him a second look.

"Enter," came a cool voice from within. His lord father's voice. The doors to the council room opened. Cerdwin entered the space, barely registering the room. He'd sat in so many of these meetings since he'd returned that any grandeur the hall was supposed to convey had lost all influence. But he still scanned it.

It was just the two of them. None of the other council members were present.

She wasn't present.

"I was told to meet with the Lord's Council," he said to the lord. As Second Commander, he might not easily dismiss the influence or rule of the council, but he didn't feel warmly toward his father outside of familial loyalty. He still remembered the male's reaction to their lady mother passing, to Alanna announcing she was leaving their family's line of succession. Lord Arel never reacted to anything, decided anything, conveyed any expression, out of love. It was the family and kingdom first. It was *their* family and *their* role within the kingdom first. That's how it was—especially after their lady mother passed. Cerdwin didn't remember much about her. They'd been young, and he hadn't come into his power yet—but Alanna had. He remembered his sister screaming, screaming to be let into their lady mother's room, to work with her, to try to Heal her. The lord had said no, though he'd summoned the best Healer in Aviva to save his ailing lady wife—to no avail. Cerdwin knew how often his twin still thought about that day from the long silences that followed her any time they passed by those doors in their family's quarters.

Fire pounded in his veins. The lord's lip curled. "Still working on controlling your power, I see, boy." *Boy*—like he was still some youngling with no concept of the way the world worked. Like he hadn't lived on another continent, become invaluable to the people of the oceanside town, made a life for himself there; like he hadn't returned when his lord father had summoned him and taken up the mantle of a Commander in Aviva's army and trained his own unit—all while respecting the lord's politics and playing the part of courtier when needed. No, Cerdwin doubted his lord father would ever see any of that, just as he refused to see the worth of his daughter. He only saw the merits he wished. How his children might be *useful* to him.

Cerdwin willed the roaring fire in his veins to bank, until it became nothing more than a hollow echo in his chest. He knew it would be followed by a swelling sensation in his muscles and bones to shift. Cutting off one source of his power from emotion always led to the building of the other. He focused on his breathing, as Eldwyn and Alanna had taught him, and willed his body to remain his own. The lord's smirk grew, as if he could see the internal battle unfolding within his son.

"As far as meeting with the Lord's Council, you will remember that I am the Head of that Council, and I speak for all of us," the male remarked.

This was true. While the Lord's Council was historically a democratic body, his lord father had increased his control over it the past few decades—the decades they hadn't had a true member of the royal bloodline to oversee them, no king or queen to lead them. But that would—*should*—change, now that she'd returned. At least, in theory. Cerdwin knew his lord father had learned to love the authority and status presiding over the Lord's Council had given him and their family, knew the proud male would not give it up easily. Since the passing of his beloved lady wife—and the perceived slight of his daughter—it was all Lord Arel really had left besides Cerdwin himself. His only son. His only heir. And Cerdwin despised him for it.

"Meaning no disrespect, Lord Father," Cerdwin said, bowing his head toward the male. The words tasted like ash on his tongue. Had the male not been his lord father, Cerdwin wasn't entirely sure where his loyalty would lie.

The male gave him a knowing smile, like he could feel Cerdwin didn't quite mean the words he spoke. "It seems you have brought us quite a boon."

Cerdwin lifted his eyes to meet the male's. Nothing but cunning and shrewdness in those otherwise cold and empty green eyes. He refused to let any emotion show as he asked, "You have confirmed her heritage then?"

The lord waved a hand in dismissal. "I suspected it was only a matter of time before she returned." And there it was—the start of a plan Cerdwin had no doubt the lord had been working on since Eleonora set foot back on Aviva's shores. Perhaps even longer than that. "And now she has." No flicker of the lord's emotion or power shone in his eyes as he spoke. The collapse of the land beyond the Endurnal Mountains had been particularly difficult for his lord father, Cerdwin knew. As one of the Elves gifted with the power of land, earth, and the growth of new life, the loss of those beautiful lands—their forests, streams, hills, and valleys—had been particularly devastating.

"And now that she has?" Cerdwin asked, trying to keep his tone neutral. A casual question, from the Second Commander to the Head of the Lord's Council. The lord's eyes gleamed as if he knew. As if the bastard knew he would marry Eleonora if instructed to—even if he wasn't sure he'd be happy, if either of them would be happy. Even as King Consort. Even with his children as heirs to the throne. He would do his duty. But his fire would die along with it. His loving friendship for her was not the same as his passionate love for—

"There have been many discussions regarding what to do with the lost princess," the lord hedged, and Cerdwin stiffened, shaken from his thoughts. His lord father would toy with him, he knew, try to get a rise out of him. He had to know by now that Cerdwin had known her in Ozul, that they had been friends. Or perhaps the lord was more concerned Cerdwin would swear fealty to her as a First Guard, leaving the male with no true power. Cerdwin would be lying if he said the notion hadn't crossed his mind as one of the potential outcomes of her return. If he were certain of his loyalty to her, he would swear the oath in a heartbeat if she asked him to.

But she'd *lied* to him, kept secrets and vital information from him. He could've helped her—with all of it. Now, he wasn't sure he was ready to look past any of it, let alone forgive her. For now, he would wait. Hear all of his options and weigh them—unlike Eldwyn, who was ready to lay down his life for the female. Even Alanna had encouraged forgiveness. Cethin was a wild card, but one the people would likely admire her having in her hand—which she would, in the end. A half-Elf, life-sworn to the Elvish Queen who was promised to save their kingdom, their world. Any half-Elf or mortal who dwelled in Aviva would celebrate Cethin's connection to their Queen—certainly more than they celebrated anything his lord father did. The nobility—his lord father included—would turn their noses up at the bond Cethin and Eleonora shared, but Cerdwin had an inkling that some of them would see Cethin's offering the life oath as proof of his strong Elvish heritage and accept him. Bitterness left a sour taste in his mouth. Was he becoming as calculated as the male in front of him?

"And what has been the outcome of those discussions, my lord?" Cerdwin asked. The lord motioned to the papers on the table, and Cerdwin finally closed the distance between them. The papers were outlines of military formations—ones in the north. The bitterness morphed into dread.

"We have decided that the best way to properly announce the return of the Queen of Moonlight is to allow her to display her power against the Dark King, to show the people her strength." Cerdwin couldn't help the way his mouth dropped open. "You disagree?"

He had to choose his words carefully—a Commander speaking, not someone who, loath as he was to admit it, still cared for her in some way. "She hasn't shown a drop of her power since her return," Cerdwin said.

"But she has in the past," his lord father said, steepling his fingers. "Here, when she left the kingdom. And in Ozul." *How had he learned that?* "One would assume that radical power has not simply disappeared."

"Agreed, but—"

"But what?" the lord asked, arching a pale blond brow.

"She did not use it when she retrieved...him." Cerdwin was unsure which would irk his lord father more—using the half-Elf's name in connection to Eleonora or not using it at all.

"And how would you know that?" A small, unkind smile danced on the lord's lips. "You were not there. In fact, the First Commander orchestrated things so that you would most certainly *not* be there. In fact, I heard"—Cerwdin's jaw tensed as his lord father spoke—"that you were not even aware of what was happening." The fire in the hearth behind the lord rose as a crackling monster of flame. "Oh, settle down, boy," the lord said, waving a hand. "I do not hold it against you." Cerdwin doubted that.

"Since you had eyes on the situation, I am sure that you would know better than I, then." Cerdwin gritted his teeth, willing the roiling flame and ash in his blood to calm.

"Indeed." The lord pursed his lips. "And you are correct, she did not use her magic there. Likely because use of her magic seems to attract the Night Queen's greatest creation." *The Noir.* That was why his lord father had chosen the north as the scene for this folly. It was far enough away from the city that should anything go wrong...

But then why had they come to the city a few weeks ago? Had she shown her power to him? That wasn't possible. Cethin hadn't known the truth, either.

"You would put my males at risk, and for what, to see if she can put on a show?" The lord cocked his head to one side, a predator assessing his prey. "And if she cannot?"

"The way I see it, son, it works in our favor either way." Cerdwin's blood ran cold at his lord father's words—at him using the word *son*, something the lord rarely did. "Either she is able to muster her power and blasts them away, and we have a symbol we can use, or we protect this kingdom. As we have done for the past fifty years."

"You mean to use her. In life, or in death," Cerdwin said quietly.

The lord laughed. "What else do you think the monarchy is for? Even Queen Serenity was no more than a figurehead in the end." It was jarring hearing the former queen's name from his lord father's lips. The male didn't often speak of the royal family he had long ago served. "Even in Ozul, where they think they are *so* progressive"—the lord waved a hand in dismissal—"the true power always lies with the nobility. The true ruling families. And that is us." He fixed his cold gaze on Cerdwin. "If the first scenario is indeed the outcome, you will marry her, just as we'd planned all those years ago." Even though Eldwyn had warned him, even though he'd suspected it himself...

"And the second scenario?"

The lord gave him a harsh look. "Then we do as I said. We continue to protect this kingdom."

Realization slammed into Cerdwin. *We.* "You do not mean for me to go north with her?"

"You will be here, overseeing training. It is the First Commander's right, duty, and honor to escort any member of the royal family, and to lead their forces into battle."

It felt like the floor was slipping away from beneath him. "And Alanna? As a High Healer, would it not also be her *honor* to—"

"Your sister will find herself occupied here," the lord cut in sternly with a look Cerdwin knew meant the male was done with questions. "The half-breed this apparent *queen* has been taking to her bed will be amongst the ranks."

His friend, Elana. Eleonora.

Her lover.

And his brother-in-arms, his...

Cerdwin ran both hands through his curls. His lord father would put them all at risk for the sake of his own power. For their family. For the kingdom he'd dutifully run for almost fifty years.

But to this end...was it right? Could he support this?

"Suddenly so quiet." The lord gave him a sly look. "Are you fighting your conscience or the animal inside?" Cerdwin reined in a snarl at the fact that his lord father knew he would rather shift into his animal form than sort through this mess of a plan.

"This is the plan the Lord's Council agreed upon?" he finally asked. "This is our best and only option to garner continued support, to protect our home?"

"Yes," the lord replied, voice smooth yet flat. "This is the decision." The male's eyes flickered. "And I would urge you to adhere to it."

Cerdwin swallowed. How many other decisions like this had been made? That he was utterly unaware of or too indifferent to have cared to hear? But what else could he do? He bowed his head.

"Yes, my lord," he acquiesced. Fire crackled along his bones, as if in protest.

Chapter 28

THE LOST PRINCESS

She pored over the books Alanna had left for her, sorting through what may or may not apply to her power. There were countless records of how to use the basic elemental gifts: water, wind, fire, and earth; but so few records on how to use the more ancient gifts—gifts of the moon, the sun, of night itself; of lightning, ice, and even death. The only more extensive records pertained to the Healing arts, learnings that the Healers had trained in and perfected over the centuries.

The records also touched on the gifts of the Dark King: documents theorized he'd been gifted the magic of the earth but had wanted more, and twisted an old, ancient magic to harness the gifts of the sun and moon to bind them to his will.

And the Night Queen. Some theorized the same about her, others guessed that her gift wasn't attached to the solar powers at all but rather to death itself. She shuddered reading those passages. How Eldwyn had gotten ahold of these texts outside of the Royal Archives...

A sound at the door scattered those thoughts, and she shoved the books under her cot—but it was the First Commander himself who entered the space. Eldwyn's normally jovial face was grave.

"What is it?" she said, shooting to her feet, hoping that something hadn't happened to Cethin. He'd returned to Cerdwin's camp, she'd learned from Alanna, and had been staying there, continuing training with the Second Commander. She hadn't been able to bring herself to ask if either male had mentioned her to the Healer, and the female hadn't brought it up—something that surprised her, considering how close Alanna was with her twin. Or had been.

Guilt embedded itself into her gut every time she thought about it: the forgiveness—or something akin to it—the Healer had granted her; the way that Eldwyn had regarded her the last time they'd spoken, as though he were prepared to declare for her. Two people she'd only just begun to know, compared to those she'd known longer and assumed she knew well: Cerdwin, who hadn't spoken to her since she'd confessed her truth, and Cethin, whom she'd had no word of, let alone spoken with, since he'd stormed out of her cell.

I am not who you need me to be. His words had echoed in her mind over, and over again while she waited to be called by the Lord's Council—yet another reason she'd asked for Alanna to bring her the books. She needed a distraction to be free of her personal troubles.

I am not who you need me to be. If only he knew she did not need him to be anyone other than who he already was.

"We're being sent to the north." Everything eddied from her mind as the First Commander spoke and a solid wall of air encompassed the room.

"We?" She sat up straighter from where she'd sunk to the floor to shove the books under her bed—the bed Eldwyn now sunk onto. He nodded, lips pursed.

"The Lord's Council has decided that the best way to show the people that you have returned is to send you there to display your power against the Dark King's forces." She started. She'd already spent sleepless nights sifting through the potential outcomes of announcing her return to Lord Arel—and to Cerdwin. This hadn't been one of them. Panic seized her. Hell, she didn't even know *how* to use her power, not really.

"But I—why?" Eldwyn tilted his head to face her, and she saw dark patches underlined the male's eyes.

"Because he knows there are only two potential outcomes." Goose bumps rose on her arms. "Either you return victorious, a formidable weapon on the battlefield and a powerful ally for his house in marriage to his son"—she couldn't help her sharp intake of breath at his words—"or..."

"Or I don't return at all."

Grief and sorrow swirled in Eldwyn's eyes—but also challenge. "I will do everything in my power to ensure that is *not* the outcome," he said fiercely, and she could have hugged him for it. But the reality of the situation had her folding herself into a ball on the floor. The reality of either situation.

"I wouldn't put you at risk like that," she said.

"It isn't up to you. The lord has decreed it shall be me, my males—plus Cethin—and you, who travel north." Her mouth dropped open in protest, but Eldwyn shook his head. "Of course, his children have been tasked with other duties while we're away."

She reached out a hand and placed it on his knee. "That he would place Cethin in this position—" she started.

"Would lead one to interpret that he doesn't expect us to return." They sat in silence for a few moments. Eldwyn placed his hand over hers.

"But to what end?" she whispered. "Doesn't he understand that he needs me alive?" But even as she spoke the words, she questioned their validity.

"The lord believes he needs no one but himself," Eldwyn said coolly. "From my own reports, the meeting that decided this wasn't even really a meeting—and it certainly wasn't a discussion. And these plans and orders were given to Cerdwin, and Cerdwin alone." Ire flickered across his face.

"But, he has to understand, the Noir came to Ozul, and the Darkness—"

"The lord believes he has been able to deflect the Dark King on his own for fifty years and will be able to continue to do so. With or without you."

"That's likely not possible," she said slowly, shaking her head. "To re-Bind—"

"His lordship may no longer be interested in re-Binding anything," Eldwyn said, tone sharp. "As long as his people are safe—and his status is intact—there is no telling what he is capable of."

"But the people—" she started, and Eldwyn let out a cool laugh that sent a shudder down her spine.

"Let me assure you, Eleonora, the lord has cared less and less about the people in this city as the years have gone by. He puts on a show of caring for them."

"This isn't right," she whispered. "Any of it. I should be allowed to meet with the Lord's Council. I should be the one ordering Aviva's armies. I should be able to use my magic, somehow, to re-Bind the Balance. I should be able to create a new life for the people of this kingdom—one built on trust and compassion, not fear and selfishness."

Eldwyn squeezed her hand. "Then, to start, we'd better make sure you return." A ghost of a smile appeared on his lips, and her heart squeezed at his loyalty.

"We'd better make sure *all* of us return," she said.

Alanna

She paced in her room in the Healer's quarters, restless and anxious despite the scents of lavender, eucalyptus, and other herbs that wafted under her door and mingled in the air. There were no windows in her bedchamber, just as there were none in any of the other Healer's rooms. Total darkness for the deepest sleep.

But sleep had evaded Alanna since she'd learned Eldwyn and Eleonora were to go north with his males and Cethin while Cerdwin remained in the city. She hadn't received word on whether she'd be going or not, and that left her even more uneasy. Her oldest charge—both in age and length of stay in the Healing wing—was in failing health.

Sonia had been in and out of a lucid state, and Alanna wasn't sure how much time the old woman had left. She wanted—needed—to be by the mortal's side at the end. But, given her position as a High Healer, Alanna knew she could be called up in service to the First Commander at any time. So why hadn't she received word yet? Why hadn't her father summoned her when he'd summoned Cerdwin? And, worse still, why hadn't he summoned Eleonora to meet with the Council?

Something wasn't right. Alanna sighed and brushed her curls away from her face. Her father hadn't always been so cunning, so closed-off—so cold.

The death of their lady mother had changed him. Then, there was her utter failure in saving her lady mother; leaving her father and her brother behind to study the Healing arts. She supposed she knew the lord now as well as she did any of the other nobility in the palace; they'd all become the same, stagnant, power-hungry creatures. But Cerdwin...

Did she still know her own brother? Her twin? That gnawed inside Alanna's mind most of all. She didn't want to believe that it was possible for her brother to be part of some ill-conceived plan to rid the lord of what he had to know was the only way to save their kingdom—and, potentially, their world—but instead viewed only as a threat to his power. Could her father—in addition to his penchant for scheming and manipulation—have become cruel and...and dark himself? Not in the way the Dark King had become—but there was a darkness besides what coated the lands beyond the Endurnal Mountains. A darkness of the heart. Cerdwin would never—could never—be a part of something like that, she told herself. Whether or not he was angry with Eleonora, her brother had to understand what her return meant for the people, for the kingdom. And he couldn't hold so much disdain for half-Elves that he would allow anything to purposely happen to Cethin. Alanna hoped Eldwyn, at least, would speak with him, Commander to Commander.

Her brother had cut off communication with her since he'd learned the truth about Eleonora—always busy training, planning, or speaking with the Lord's Council; at least, that's what Alanna was told when she approached the guards outside his tent to speak with him. She hadn't worked up the nerve to return to their family's chambers, and she certainly didn't expect to run into him in the Healing ward. That had always been Eldwyn's prerogative: visiting the sick, wounded, injured, or dying guards, soldiers, and scouts. He was a good male, and she'd seen the way he and her brother looked at one another. The longing for something Lord Arel would never allow. Perhaps that was why her brother had put the First Commander at a distance lately, too. *A shame.* She could think of no better partner for her twin.

Alanna had never felt that way about anyone—that longing to share a life with someone. She'd had a number of male lovers over the years, but as someone who'd given her life to the Healing arts, she'd never allowed herself to feel too deeply for any of them. They always walked away, anyway.

She hoped a different future awaited Cerdwin—but now there was a good chance he would end up betrothed to Eleonora; that the two of them would both end up stuck in a marriage that wasn't right for either of them. Alanna knew they would never be able to bridge their way to each other's hearts, no matter their history and friendship.

A slight breeze in the garden outside of the Healer's quarters, sent by Eldwyn, had delivered the news she was processing. That troubled her even more—knowing the First Commander wasn't close enough or able to deliver the news himself.

And what of Eleonora and her magic? Alanna hoped the books she'd brought from Eldwyn's family home were a help to her. Whereas males of Aviva trained with their power from the moment they reached maturity, most females were only taught the basics about their Healing gift, unless they—or their families—wished to become Healers.

Alanna knew enough about the History of the day the princess was lost to know she hadn't matured into her power until then—and it was awake again now. Alanna had felt it: a beautiful, cool, pale moonlight, like something out of a dream—a dream to banish the nightmare of the Darkness; and starlight, beautiful and pure—it had felt like love. But it didn't mean anything if the queen didn't know how to use it.

Alanna paced the length of her room. One of the books she'd found had spoken about how Queen Serenity had been able to bind her power to a male's—to magnify hers. Historians had reasoned that this was why the kingdom remained protected after the Breaking. It hadn't been her husband's—King Ewan's—power, as far as Alanna could tell. But if Eleonora could do something similar with Eldwyn or Cerdwin, perhaps they could help her manage her power, control it, turn it into something concrete and effective. But, she supposed, that would put the males at risk as well, draining their energy, which they would need as Commanders.

Alanna stopped pacing and sighed. She hadn't minded being alone for a very long time—but then she'd met Eldwyn, her brother had returned, and Eleonora and Cethin had come from across the sea. She'd gotten used to their particular brand of chaos. She hoped she wasn't about to lose it—lose them. Her brother. Her friends. The beginning of something new in the court.

A knock sounded, startling her from her musings. Alanna opened it to find a flustered Healer-in-training there. "What's wrong?"

"I-it is your charge, my lady," the apprentice said. Alanna tried not to roll her eyes at the title she no longer cared about. "The older woman, Sonia?"

"What's happened," she demanded.

"I-I am not sure. I just went in to bring the books she requested"—*Goodness, were all the Healers little more than Annor aides now?*—"and she was in pain," the apprentice whispered, eyes widening. "So much pain. I tried, my lady, but I could not help her."

"I will go there now," Alanna said, brushing past the younger Healer. She paused and laid a hand on the trembling female's shoulder. "Go get a drink. Take a breath. Digging into someone else's pain, physical or otherwise, can be a difficult experience." The young female nodded, murmured her thanks, and walked in the direction of the common area. Only then did Alanna allow her panic to rise.

Sonia's pain—while consistent—had never been overwhelming.

Alanna kept her pace steady as she headed down the hall and through the common area. But as soon as she hit the stairs, she ran. The old woman's room wasn't far from the Healer's Quarter's.

Her door was ajar, likely left open by the fleeing trainee. No sounds came from the room—no moans or screams of pain. Could the young female have been mistaken? Alanna took a breath, steadied herself, and walked into the room. Sonia lay flat on her back in the bed, eyes wide as she stared at the ceiling.

"Sonia?" Alanna spoke the woman's name gently. The woman didn't move, didn't turn to look at her or greet her with her normal hubris. Alanna approached the bed, spooled her magic up from the well deep inside of her, and allowed the pale-blue power to flow from her to the woman. Before her magic even touched Sonia, Alanna felt it: pulsing pain, radiating all over the woman's body, echoing in every muscle, every ligament, every bone. Alanna doused it with her Healing gift, as she knew Eldwyn had done so many times to Cerdwin when her twin's fire became a raging, living thing.

That was what this pain was—alive, like a burning flame. It bucked under her power, refusing to be extinguished. Alanna pushed, drawing deeper from that spring of magic, sending wave after wave of cerulean light into every space the pain occupied.

Sweat poured from her brow. It could've been minutes or hours. Alanna wasn't quite sure, but the pain finally receded. She panted as she drew her gift back into herself, her power nearly at its limit. No wonder the novice had been so shaken. She sank onto the edge of the bed.

"Sonia?"

This time, the woman responded, eyelids fluttering with awareness. "Alanna?" came the voice, familiar, but hoarse—like she'd been silently screaming for hours. Alanna shuddered. Perhaps she had been.

"Yes, I'm here. I'm going to get you some water—"

"Please," the old woman said. "My son, my boy…" Alanna stared down at her. Sonia rarely spoke about her personal life. Most of her stories were about the palace, living there, serving there, what Aviva had been like before the Darkness. She didn't remember the old woman ever mentioning any children. A thrum of sorrow passed through Alanna. *If she even had any.* Perhaps this was just a hallucination, brought on by whatever pain the woman had just experienced.

"It's just us, Sonia," Alanna told her, bringing a pale, clammy hand into her still shaking one and giving it a squeeze. "I'll get you that glass of water now." She stood and walked toward the dresser that held a pitcher and a glass, and beside it, what she assumed was the stack of books Sonia had requested. Books on Histories of the Gods. A strange request. She willed her shaking hands to still as she poured the water and handed it to the woman.

"Where is El?" Sonia suddenly asked, and Alanna froze. She'd never heard anyone call Eleonora by that nickname—except Cethin. Before Alanna could answer, Sonia sighed a long exhale through her nose and closed her eyes.

Chapter 29

THE LOST PRINCESS

She joined Eldwyn's camp at the end of the week. The First Commander's sprawling base was more orderly and organized than Cerdwin's was, though she couldn't help but wonder if it was because they were packing up to head north. Maps and papers for their mission had been passed down by Cerdwin, though she hadn't seen her friend, if she could still call him that; as far as she could tell, neither had Eldwyn.

The peak where they would set up camp had been selected—one that overlooked what was now supposedly the Dark King's main northern encampment. From there, they would take up position and begin a direct assault on the creatures and soldiers that dwelled there. Her stomach knotted. It had been different, to fend off the Noir, to kill the men who'd attacked her in the clearing in Ozul, to slaughter those creatures of Darkness to find Cethin. But marching into battle to purposely engage and destroy...she knew that it was foolish, that these people and creatures were her enemies, but something about trapping them just felt wrong.

She'd said as much to Eldwyn, though she wasn't sure the First Commander understood: this was his job—he'd probably done something similar hundreds of times. But he'd sat there, patiently listening to her. In the end, he'd conceded that she had great empathy for those who'd fallen into the clutches of the Darkness, but that, unfortunately, this was the result of it. The plan of action came directly from the Lord's Council—from Lord Arel. They had to follow it. She reined in the urge to retort that the Council was not the queen. Thoughts like those were becoming more difficult to suppress: what she would do differently, if given the opportunity. She supposed it wouldn't matter if they didn't return from this. But if they did...

They had to. She'd already decided that. Even if she didn't, Eldwyn and Cethin *had* to survive this.

She hadn't seen Cethin since she'd joined Eldwyn's camp, but she also hadn't looked very hard, even though she knew he'd been moved there from Cerdwin's as part of the lord's orders. She wasn't entirely sure if she wanted to see the male before they faced the Darkness.

I am not who you need me to be. His words continued to fill her head anytime her mind wasn't otherwise occupied. And that was why she had made sure to keep it occupied—whether with Eldwyn's accounts of strategy, the books on magic, practicing fighting techniques, or preparing with the rest of the camp to move out. As long as she kept moving, kept her mind and her hands occupied, she didn't think of him or the words that had hit her heart like a dagger—until she came across a book about legends of the life-sworn and their relationships. Many became lovers, although the Histories pointed toward this being more out of convenience, friendship, and proximity, than anything else.

Was that what it had been to Cethin? Had she simply been a convenience, until she'd become who she was, and from there become *inconvenient*? But what he'd said before that parting blow...it ran deeper than convenience. Deeper than proximity. Deeper than friendship. And she'd felt the same way. But it didn't matter now. She could never be who he needed *her* to be. Maybe Cethin had known she would never be able to say those words, so he had, had ended it—ended whatever it was between them—before it ever really started. She couldn't be his El, not when she was destined to be Eleonora—destined to be queen.

She shivered, even though it wasn't cold in the camp. At least, not yet. A fur-lined cloak had been supplied for her for when they reached the northern ridge of the mountains. It was colder there, Eldwyn had told her, colder than it had been in the middle of the mountains where they'd found Cethin; farther north than where Cerdwin had found her. Before everything had well and truly gone to Hell. A sound behind her startled her, and she turned to see Alaric.

"Elana?" the male asked, taking her in with his startling green eyes, and she remembered that he hadn't seen her in her Elvish form—hadn't seen her at all since she'd been taken by the changeling. She shivered again but forced her lips to form a smile.

"Looks like you did so well in the Second Commander's camp, they had to move you here," she said. Second Commander. She couldn't get herself to use his name right now. Whether or not Alaric noticed her careful selection of words, he didn't let on.

"You look different," he said, ignoring the compliment, then sniffed. "You smell different, too."

"I'll try to take that as a compliment," she said dryly, and he laughed, clapping her on the shoulder.

"I would hope so, considering it looks like we'll be traveling together. And training together again, too."

She gave him a real smile this time. "I bet I'll pummel you like this."

The soldier raised a blond brow. "You can try. Although it sounds like we will be moving out soon, to pummel the real enemy." Her heart strained. He had no idea what they were about to walk into, this elaborate ploy set up by Lord Arel. She made a pledge to herself right then and there—Alaric would walk away, too.

Alaric. Eldwyn. Cethin. They would all walk out of this, even if she didn't.

"So I hear," she said.

"Meaning no offense, but I'm surprised the First Commander had you join us." His eyes scanned her face. "But I suppose, given this"—he gestured to her Elvish body—"you're likely full of surprises." He must've read some emotion on her face, because his expression softened. "I'm not mad that you didn't shift with us. But if you're going to best all of us males on the field in this form..." He winked, and from there, the two of them fell into casual conversation. Alaric told her about his training since they'd last seen each other. She didn't have much to offer in return—not ready to tell him the truth—but Alaric didn't seem to mind, carrying the conversation forward effortlessly.

It'd been comfortable between them in the Second Commander's camp: working together, training together; something about the male put her at ease. She didn't worry about who she was or what was to come when they spoke. It was just about their training, their companionship—nothing more.

He would walk away, she repeated to herself. The world needed more males like Alaric.

Eldwyn

The order came in the middle of the fake night: they were to head out immediately. Scowling, Eldwyn ran a hand over his face. He'd been awake, anyway, looking over maps and plans again and again, trying to find some way—any way—to keep Eleonora as safe as possible. It was proving an impossible task.

Between the lord's own carefully crafted plans and the supposed position of the Dark King's forces in the valley, there were no easy ways out, no easily accessible escape routes if things went wrong. The safest Avivan military outpost was miles south—easy enough for someone on horseback to get to, or someone used to running long distances, or a male Elf in their animal form, depending on the animal. Not only was the First Commander certain that horses would be of little use once they summited the peak, he also knew that, despite her training, Eleonora wouldn't be used to running such distances. He also wasn't sure he'd be able to convince her to leave if and when the time came.

Cerdwin—or rather, Lord Arel—had put Cethin on their front lines, and Alaric being moved had been another unwelcome surprise, although the male's promotion was well-earned. At least the young soldier wouldn't be directly in the line of fire. He also wasn't Eleonora's life-sworn. Eldwyn knew the connection was established so that Cethin would protect the queen with his life, but he also knew Eleonora wouldn't hesitate to protect the half-Elf with hers.

Eldwyn shook his head, gathered the papers into a small satchel, and exited his tent. One word to his sentries had them in motion, running to rouse the rest of the sleeping camp into action. Most of the tents and supplies were already packed. His males would share space three or four at a time. Except for Eleonora. Part of him had almost ordered her and Cethin to share a space, but, given what was ahead of them, that particular situation would have to wait for another time—if they made it out of this mess.

He exhaled and pulled his own tent down. He didn't have to. As First Commander, he could've just as easily ordered some of his males to do it. But he liked these tasks—tasks he knew Cerdwin deemed beneath him. They helped ground Eldwyn. Plus, he knew it was helpful for his males to see him doing the exact same tasks they were ordered to do. It was also why he helped cook meals, sat around the fires to drink with them, openly sparred with them, visited their families, and went into the city to unwind with them. Pride flickered through Eldwyn: He hadn't just built a unit of soldiers. He'd built a family, a brotherhood, willing to defend not only their city, but also each other, until their last breaths.

And if he had anything to say about it, their last breaths would not come in those mountains.

The Lost Princess

"You want me to *what*?" she asked, gaping at Eldwyn. The male's jaw twitched with restrained laughter.

"I want you to ride me," he said again, lips quirking up slightly.

"In your wolf form."

"Yes," he said. "I'm not sure what you're not understanding about this."

"What about the horses?"

"The horses were already divided up amongst the males. We can only take so many, given the nature of our task, and we don't have time to retrieve yours from the royal stables. So, you riding me is the obvious solution."

She stared at him. She had a feeling a lack of equine wasn't exactly the issue—knew that some of the males in the camp could shift into other animals she could ride. No, this was likely about her—her safety—when all she cared about was his and Alaric's and Cethin's.

She raised a brow at him. "Will that be comfortable for you?"

He took a step closer, and a breeze tightened around her like a hug.

"It'll feel a bit like that," he said.

She shook her head. "What will the others think about me *riding* you?"

"They'll think that you are the Healer assigned to our unit for this particular mission," he replied, any warmth that had been there leaving his face. It made sense: besides him, Alaric, and Cethin, no one in the First Commander's camp really knew her, especially in her Elvish form.

"No Alanna?"

Eldwyn shook his head. "You haven't heard?" It was her turn to shake her head. "One of her charges took a turn for the worse. An older, mortal woman. She's been preoccupied."

Dread curled in her stomach. It had to be Sonia.

"What happened?"

Eldwyn shrugged. "It's hard to say. Mortal bodies," he mused, "they're different. Complex. Even the most skilled Healers sometimes have difficulty understanding them. And she is of an older age for a mortal, yet..." Her dread grew.

"You don't believe it's a coincidence."

He met her gaze. "No. I don't."

She sucked in a sharp breath, at once both outraged and saddened for her former lady's maid. She had so many questions for the woman, knew that she would likely not be present at the end, an end brought about by...

"Him?" she whispered. The First Commander's eyes burned a bright silver.

"No," he said, intensity lacing his words. "He isn't capable of something like this."

"And his father...I mean, he knows who I am now. He gave us these orders..."

"Of that," Eldwyn said slowly, "I'm not sure." She closed her eyes. She would have words with the lord when they returned. If she returned. A strong, callused hand gripped hers. "You will come back. And when you do, you will be able to pursue whatever retribution you seek and deem just."

She opened her eyes. "I'm not sure what is right or fair. I'm not sure I don't deserve to be held responsible for some of what has happened here. I'm"—she swallowed hard—"I'm not even sure who I am anymore." Eldwyn held her hand, waiting. "I was so sure of what I would do when I returned to these shores. But then I saw the divides amongst...the people." *My* people, she'd almost said, yet something about it still didn't feel real. "I was so sure of who I was when I used my power against the Noir, when I thought...when I thought I was with him." She squeezed her eyes closed again.

"But it wasn't real. He wasn't real. What happened wasn't real. How could who I felt I was ready to be have been real?" She opened her eyes and found Eldwyn studying her. "And now that so much has fallen apart..." She shook her head. "I'm not sure I'm worthy of this power, this title. The people. I know what I need to do, but do I do it as Elana, or...?"

Eldwyn lifted her hand in his and pressed both of their hands over her heart. "It's not my place to say." She opened her mouth to argue, but he shook his head. "Not as a Commander or a low-born citizen or even your friend. However, I believe you will make that choice, and it will be your choice. The best choice for you—for the love, courage, and Light you hold in your heart for the people, the kingdom—when the time comes. And that, Eleonora"—she smiled at his use of her true name—"is what will make it the right choice."

Chapter 30

THE LOST PRINCESS

Their party moved as a stealthy mass of animals—a bizarre sight, she imagined, if one had an aerial view—with a few Elves riding the horses that carried their supplies behind them. They didn't all travel together at once; in fact, there were three departure times, she learned. She and Eldwyn were part of the second. The first zigged and zagged in front of them at a dizzying speed. Alaric was above them in his hawk form, something new she'd learned about the male that fake early morning.

Where was Cethin? She still hadn't seen him, hadn't asked Eldwyn about him, and the male hadn't brought him up again. She assumed he was in the third party, since, as a half-Elf, he wouldn't have the ability to shift, and he clearly wasn't in the second push. She would've felt him.

By the time they reached the base of the northern reaches of the Endurnal Mountains, she was covered in a rough mixture of sweat and the sand that had kicked up around them. Eldwyn had been focused on maintaining his strength for the shift and whatever lay ahead, so the frigid air of the snow-capped peaks that came into view slammed into her like a punch. He had her dismount then—it was a bigger risk for her to fall off his back while he climbed than for her to just make the climb beside him. She immediately missed his body heat. Suddenly, the air around her became warmer, as if he sensed her discomfort. She threw the wolf a look. He still needed to save his strength. He ignored her.

The journey to the top was an endless climb of rocks, sticks, and, in some places as they went higher, ice that got into her boots. It scraped her feet and legs, and, in spots where the climb became a complete upward slant, her hands, arms, and face. She envied the males who transformed into animals made for the terrain, watching Alaric gracefully move from rock to rock until he joined the other airborne males at the top.

She shivered as she approached the summit. Eldwyn's shield was still in place, but the warmth was barely more than a whisper as the weather shifted from the early summer of Aviva to the year-round cold that was the northern part of the continent, especially in the mountains. But she kept going, one step and handhold at a time, her fur-lined cloak pulled tightly around her, reminding herself of the warm tent and blanket she'd set up once she reached the top—along with whatever else awaited her.

Cethin

It was absurd for him to be a part of this mission—even more absurd for him to be part of the first scouting group since he couldn't shift. But Cethin heeded the orders that came through all the same, not willing to discuss or debate with Eldwyn. He knew this wasn't the First Commander's idea. It was likely the Second's.

Though they'd reached a tentative peace in the pavilion, Cethin had a feeling this was still some sort of punishment—for knowing her, for being her life-sworn, for loving her, for being *with* her, for being a half-Elf, he wasn't quite sure. It didn't matter; he wasn't about to give Cerdwin or Eldwyn the satisfaction of requesting to be placed in the third line with the males whose shifting wasn't suited for the mountains, along with the horses and supplies.

He also knew from reading the orders that Eldwyn would be in the second line, which told him enough about where she would be. That had been the biggest jolt in reviewing the plans: she was coming with them under the name Elana, listed as their Healer. An unpleasant feeling had settled in Cethin's gut reading that. She hadn't shown any Healing gift as far as he'd seen. And with her listed, and Alanna absent...

It had bothered Cethin as he'd packed up their tent, that he was still so concerned—not for himself, though he'd gleaned from the orders that he was either being tested or disposed of—but for her.

Still for her.

Always for her.

He looked down at his left hand where it held his horse's rein and internally cursed himself for how hasty he'd been in swearing the life oath. *If he'd just done his Godsdamned job and brought her*...the thought drifted away like the sands beneath the horses' hooves. But he hadn't. He'd sworn his life to her.

He'd been close to swearing his heart to her, too.

He still felt it, that deep, aching pain in his chest that had started when he'd said those last words to her. If he made it back from this reckless assignment, maybe she would release him from his oath. She'd said as much when she'd told him about the changeling.

The ache in his chest deepened, and Cethin cursed under his breath at the possibility that the oath would even let him consider breaking it. But if she did, where would he go? He'd seriously fucked up a job and killed a fellow mercenary—he wouldn't be welcomed back into that life. So, if not Ozul, then where? He glanced northeast to where the Endurnal Mountains became the mountain range at the northern reaches of the continent, creating massive sea cliffs. Maybe The Islands, where so many half-Elves already dwelled—so many outcasts and rejects, he thought with a snort. He'd be one of many.

And if she didn't release him from the life oath? It was likely she wouldn't. But what would his role be, if they came back having achieved whatever it was Cerdwin's lord father and the Lord's Council expected? They wouldn't be able to dismiss her or her wishes then. He would still be her life-sworn. But she would be his queen.

If she survived this journey. That feeling in Cethin's chest tightened again. Was that why she'd been sent out, too? Had the Lord's Council dismissed her and her claim entirely? Were they *that* angry that she'd been gone for so long? Yes, he was still angry with her, but, life oath or not, he certainly didn't wish to see her harmed. Anger replaced that uneasy feeling, fresh and hot. If that was the reason she'd been sent along, whether harm came to her or not, he'd find Lord Arel Satrara and the others who sat on the Council and take his time ripping each of them apart. Slowly.

He growled at that feeling, that part of him that still cared for her in a way that felt deeper than the life oath. That feeling that, no matter how angry, frustrated, or annoyed he was with her, refused to go away. Perhaps they'd sent her for another reason entirely. Was she there to unleash her power against the Darkness? Had she figured out how to wield it? Or some other plan he wasn't privy to? Cethin inhaled deeply and let the brisk, cold air from the mountains clear his head.

Eldwyn

They hadn't run into anything on their way across the sands, or anything while they'd climbed the mountain. That unsettled Eldwyn, though he refused to let it show as his soldiers settled in for a true night. His males warmed themselves in the frigid snowcapped peak by fires from those who had that power; others, like him, with the gift of wind, shielded those fires from sight and smell—something he pointed out to Eleonora once he was back in his Elvish form, since she was ready to protest the use of fire. Once he'd told her no one would be able to see or scent them, she'd slumped right in front of one and accepted a warm drink from Alaric. He left Eleonora with the male while he made his rounds, set sentries around the camp, and sent a few of his particularly stealthy—and less exhausted—males down the mountainside to see what might be waiting in the snow-covered valley below.

He stayed awake long enough to see that his orders were carried out—and to watch Cethin disappear into his tent, and Eleonora into another right next to Alaric's—before he closed his eyes and let the bitter wind know he'd like to wake up in two hours.

It did just that, the crisp, frozen breeze biting into his temples. Odd hours had stopped bothering the First Commander long ago. Between the work he did with Aviva's forces—and the work he did on his own time in bringing Elves back to Aviva from Ozul—he could go much longer without sleep, likely a good three days. But it was different with her here. He'd seen the sorrow and distress in her eyes when she'd pieced together the real reason the Lord's Council was sending them north; and knew her well enough, he presumed, that it wasn't from any concern for her own life or safety, but rather his, Cethin's, Alaric's—and Sonia's, with the woman being used as a pawn to keep Alanna in the city.

Eleonora claimed she didn't know who she was anymore, and perhaps Eldwyn had overstepped by telling her his opinion. But he felt as though he *did* know her: she was brave; she was kind, empathetic, and compassionate; she was bold and cunning when needed. Eldwyn knew in his heart that she was his queen. But he couldn't tell her who she was. Only she could decide that. Her fate—all of their fates—was tied to that decision. He only hoped she would overcome her doubt before it was too late.

Sighing, Eldwyn rose and took a quick drink of water from his canteen, chucking some of it over his head. Traveling in his wolven form always left him in dire need of a bath, but there would be no taking one anytime soon.

Eldwyn made his rounds and checked in with his sentries. They informed him that the scouts had returned. What those scouts told him came as a shock: all of the previous reports were wrong. There was nothing in the valley below—no sign of Darkness beyond what was typical for the

Endurnal Mountains. No sign of the Dark King's forces. Nothing. That disturbed Eldwyn even more.

Something was wrong—perhaps even more wrong than Lord Arel had hoped.

Cerdwin

"I need a drink." While the sound of his sister's voice wasn't unwelcome or unsurprising, her words were. For starters, the last thing Cerdwin needed was a drink. It was the first time he'd ever thought that, but after the conversation with his lord father, after the order had gone out—after *he'd* sent the order out—Cerdwin felt even less in control of his magic than usual. And it wasn't usually Alanna who initiated the trio's nights of drinking and cards. It was usually—

Cerdwin shut the emotion down as Alanna stalked through his tent and went straight to the liquor. "What is wrong?" he asked from where he sat behind his desk. Because that's all he ever did anymore outside of training: sit at his desk, take orders from his lord father, issue orders from his lord father, review plans from the Lord's Council—which was actually his lord father—put people he cared about in danger. His heart burned and twisted.

"I lost someone today." Cerdwin immediately focused all of his attention on his twin. She never spoke about her patients. She would tell him what was happening with any of his or Eldwyn's males if they'd been injured, wounded, or worse, but this was different. This was personal.

He scanned his sister. She seemed diminished, sad in a way he hadn't seen since their lady mother had died. He waited for her to continue.

Alanna took a drink and sat. "And it wasn't..." She shook her head, curls swaying. He leaned forward, really concerned now. Alanna never ran out of words. "It wasn't just that she died, Cer," she finally continued, using the nickname only she ever did. "She was human, and—Gods, had to be well into her ninetieth year, if not older. But she'd been fine under my care all of these years." His sister chewed on her bottom lip the way she did when she was trying to figure out if he or Eldwyn were cheating at cards. "It was *how* she died. It was so sudden, and I just..."

The fire that'd banked out of concern for his twin restarted as she told him what had happened to the mortal woman named Sonia, a previous royal lady's maid who'd stayed in the palace under the care of the High Healers—per Queen Serenity's orders, even posthumously. Alanna's voice shook as she described how the trainee had come to her, how she'd found the older woman screaming in silent pain. Blue light flared at his twin's fingertips as she described the woman's passing.

Your sister will find herself occupied here. The lord's words rang in Cerdwin's mind as she finished.

"What is it?"

"Nothing." He shook his head, waving a hand in dismissal.

"I don't need to use my magic to know something is weighing on you." And she could, Cerdwin knew. She could use her Healing gift to pry into his feelings. But this? This was pure twin intuition, from the time they'd shared in their lady mother's womb, years growing up together, though Fate had grown them apart. She still knew him better than anyone else. "I might not have been able to save Sonia, but, Cer, let me help you."

"I had to issue an order," he finally conceded.

"An order from the illustrious Lord Arel?"

Cerdwin sighed. "You should not speak of him like that," he warned.

"Like what?" There was the non-magic fire in her eyes.

"Like he is not your lord father, too." Alanna huffed and fiddled with her dress.

"Your loyalty to our family, while admirable, will likely be the death of you." Concern pinched his twin's features. "What did he ask of you?"

By the time he finished, Alanna was on her feet. "You're a fucking idiot," she announced, and Cerdwin bit back a grin, despite how angry she looked. She was the only one who ever called him *that*, too. "This was the reason Sonia died. And you know he doesn't intend for them to survive—for *any* of them to survive—either." Her eyes met his. "Lord Arel may be your father"—she never used *our* or *lord* anymore, hadn't in years—"but family isn't always blood. You care for our people, yes?" He nodded. "You care for Eleonora, yes?" He nodded again, even though shock rippled through him to hear her true name from his sister's lips. "Then you should care about what happens on that mountain, Cer. You should care about whether or not she succeeds." He turned away, remembering what the outcome would be if she did. "You still care for him?"

"That does not matter," Cerdwin replied through gritted teeth. "We know that situation could never—"

"That doesn't matter," Alanna interrupted. When Cerdwin looked back, she was standing right in front of him. "There will come a day, brother, when you will have to make a significant choice. This may not be it." She tilted her head to one side, and Cerdwin could've sworn he saw something older staring back out at him through her eyes. "He may not be it. But every choice you make will lead to that moment. And when that moment comes, you'd better be prepared to make your choice. Because blood, loyalty, honor—none of those will matter more than that choice."

Whatever was in her eyes faltered, then faded. He gripped her shoulders as she shook her head.

"What I'm trying to say is, whether you're sure you love him or not, whether you're sure she'd be a good queen or not, none of that matters. What matters is that these people, your friends, are the future of this kingdom. I know you know that." She stepped out of his hold. "What are you going to do about it?"

Chapter 31

THE LOST PRINCESS

She lay awake in her Healer's tent—stomach clenching, thinking of the Healer who *should* be there—listening for Eldwyn's voice. It was quieter in the camp than she'd anticipated. The First Commander's males moved silently and spoke in hushed voices as they went about their duties. Perhaps it was true night that had them so quiet.

It wasn't until Eldwyn's scouts returned that she heard him. His males had found nothing—absolutely nothing in the valley below.

As if the Darkness were waiting for something—someone.

She made up her mind and let her eyes drift closed.

She awoke to sound. The soldiers were more restless now. She hoped they'd been able to get some sleep, or at the very least, some rest. They would need it.

She made her way to the tent clearly marked with the First Commander's sigil. A scent hit her as she walked through the flaps, one she hadn't fully recognized before—not Eldwyn's, but another male's.

His. She closed her eyes and inhaled deeply, as deeply as she had water the day she'd almost drowned.

"Eleonora." She opened her eyes and scanned the space. She wasn't ready for this reunion yet. But he wasn't there. It was just Eldwyn, sitting on the edge of his cot, poring over endless piles of paper. He looked up as she sat on the ground in front of him. "I hope Alaric isn't giving you any trouble," he said, but she could feel his exhaustion under his humor.

"Not at all." She paused for a beat, then, "You need to use me."

Eldwyn's eyes flew from the page he'd been reading to hers. His jaw locked in place. "What do you mean?" he asked, eyes narrowing.

"I'm what—*who*—they're waiting for. That's why there's nothing down there. Either they're gone, but close, or they're shielded. But they are waiting for me. Use me—use me to draw them out."

The First Commander shook his head. "Absolutely not."

"Then what is our purpose here?!" she exclaimed. "I know why we were sent here, Eldwyn. Why *I* was sent here. So do you. If I don't display some show of power against the Dark King, his soldiers, his creatures, no one will have any reason to trust me. To...follow me." The words tasted strange in her mouth. "You might not like his ways—neither do I—but Lord Arel isn't entirely wrong about this."

"That may very well be the case, but surely there's another way about this. Surely this is a sign that—"

"This is the way," she cut him off. "You told me I would know. And if..."

"You will survive," he promised, clasping her hands. She looked back up at him. There was something smoldering in his eyes. She held his gaze. It was what she'd decided, waiting in the Darkness, thinking of the soldiers, the Healer, her friends—*him*. What she'd decided before she'd rested, preparing her body, her mind, her essence for what was to come. Eldwyn sighed.

"Alright," he said. "Let's get this fucking show started."

Eldwyn

He didn't like it—not one bit. But what could he do? They'd been on the plateau for almost a full true night and nothing had happened. There was no sign, no scent—nothing to indicate where the Dark King's forces were. They needed to do *something*.

He also knew Eleonora was bound to do whatever she set her mind to, whether he approved of it or not. And beyond that, she was right that she was technically the reason they were there. She knew that. He knew that. She would do everything she could to give them a chance—but he'd be damned if he let her do it alone. She would survive this. Whether or not he did...well, that didn't matter.

Eldwyn decided not to warn Cethin about her plan—he wasn't about to jump into the middle of their relationship; at least, not at the moment. He had things beyond either of their egos to worry about. He had Eleonora to worry about as his queen—the future of the kingdom, the people—as his first priority. Making sure as many of his males as possible—Cethin included—walked away from whatever was about to happen was a close second. Taking down as many of the Dark King's soldiers as possible was a close third. Besides, he told himself, Cethin would know immediately if she were in danger.

Taking a deep breath, Eldwyn released the order throughout the camp: all soldiers were told to dress for battle, arm themselves, and be ready for the signal.

Cethin

Something wasn't right—he felt it in his bones.

Something lurked in the Darkness of the valley—even though the scouts hadn't seen it. Cethin couldn't explain how, but he knew something was there.

Could she feel it, too?

The Lost Princess

She felt it, even though she couldn't see or scent it: somewhere in the valley below, in that vast Darkness, was the Dark King's host. She'd felt it as she'd dressed for battle, only half listening as Alaric muttered his disbelief that they were walking into nothing.

There was nothing special about her armor—at least, not as there had been for her mother. Queen Serenity had always stepped into battle wearing armor of the most brilliant gold and a helmet bedecked with sapphires and swirling suns, the rays of the largest sun cresting its peak.

Serenity's sword, Nar, had a pommel that matched the helmet. She wondered if both were still in the castle somewhere, or perhaps with the Annor. Maybe Nar had been lost in the sands during the Battle of the Breaking. The armor she wore wasn't as famous as her mother's, but in her mind, it was equally important: the opalescent uniform of Aviva's military. It was a special design, made to reflect the Light of Aviva when they were in their own territory and blind their enemies, and to absorb the Darkness, making them nigh invisible in the mountains, as their enemies were to them. She'd wondered what it would look like in the moonlight, under starlight, as she'd strapped her blades to her thighs.

She'd felt it as she'd lied to Alaric, telling the male she needed a walk before whatever was to come. Concern had flickered in his eyes, but he'd merely nodded.

She'd felt it as she'd walked at a brisk pace to meet Eldwyn where they'd chosen to descend the other side of the mountain together. The First Commander's armor was identical to the rest of the Avivan soldiers'—except for his helm. Where the soldiers had nothing to denote rank or role, his had a floral design on the side—a *dianaflora*.

She felt it as she recognized the flower and sent a quick prayer to the Goddess it represented to protect her First Commander, her friend, if the divine could still hear her.

It was almost time.

Eldwyn

The world was eerily still as Eldwyn walked down the mountainside with his queen.

They stopped halfway, and he unsheathed his sword, the sound loud in the sinister silence. He looked at Eleonora. Her blue-gray eyes swirled with the light of the cosmos.

"Ready?" he asked, gripping his sword tightly.

"Ready," she said, chin held high.

Eldwyn grinned. She really was.

Eleonora

Ready didn't feel like the right answer to Eldwyn's question. It wasn't the truth—but also not entirely a lie. She could—would—find the light she needed within her. She just wasn't sure she would be able to control it.

Squeezing her eyes shut, she sank into her body and mind; her blood, muscles, bones, and heart; her essence.

I am Eleonora, the Moonlight of Aviva. I am the Queen who was promised. I am here to re-Bind the Balance.

She repeated the words to herself over and over again until they filled every pore of her body, detailing who she was, who she had been, and who she would be.

She sank into the depths of her essence, and bit by bit, drew that power up. She let every moment of her life, every experience she'd had, everything—everyone—she'd ever lost—or found—flow; she let that power know who she was, had been, and would be once more. It thrummed inside of her, begging for release. *Soon*, she told it. *Soon.*

The First Commander raised his sword, ready to defend her from whatever came their way.

It was time.

Like an unleashing of the cosmos, Eleonora released her moonlight and watched it race into the night sky.

Cethin

Wait for the signal. You'll know it when you see it.

That was the word that had gone out with their orders—their orders to dress and arm themselves for battle and wait. Now, Cethin knew why—knew what *it* was. Knew *who* it was.

Pale yet brilliant light raced into the night sky above them. The males around him shielded their eyes. It was as if that light contained the essence of the moon within it, illuminating everything around them in a silvery glow. But Cethin didn't cover his eyes.

He stood there and watched—watched as her magic filled the air, the power in it raising the hairs on his arms beneath his armor, raising emotions he'd buried deep, deep down.

Then, anger rose from those emotional depths—anger that they would use her like this. Anger that she'd been sent here with them. Anger that had Cethin raising his blade and loosing a cry that shook the mountain range as he set off in a sprint down the hill.

Eldwyn

The light Eleonora had released was so bright that Eldwyn took a step in front of her—both to shield his eyes from it, and to see what lay in the valley below. Only sixty odd years of training kept him in place.

The valley was full. Hundreds upon hundreds of the Dark King's forces waited, creatures created or consumed by the Dark power he wielded. Some of them, Eldwyn noted with a twinge of pain in his heart, were humans or half-Elves. A few were fully-blooded Elves—or, at least, they had been. The rumors of their missing people were true: they'd been taken and twisted by the Dark King and his Night Queen. Those former Elves would be the ones to look out for, Eldwyn knew, if they still possessed their magic underneath their corruption. Yet there was no sign of some of the Dark King's other evil beasts—his trolls or changelings. And no sign of the Night Queen's Noir—a small mercy. It was almost as if they'd known how small the First Commander's force would be, that his males could easily be overrun by sheer numbers.

Eldwyn looked up as Eleonora's moonlight receded. Her power left behind a crescent moon that remained constant, illuminating the area around them—and the oncoming enemy below as the Dark King's soldiers charged for the base of the mountain.

Eldwyn faced the female he would defend with his life to see on the throne of Aviva—even if he only caught a glimpse of it from the Otherworld. Then, he lifted his wind shield so the enemy could see and feel *all* of her. As his receded, he saw her own shield of silver light flare to life around her, fitting the armor she wore like a second skin.

A cry sounded behind them—and then the air shifted as his males descended. Eleonora's eyes met his. *Go,* they urged him. Eldwyn nodded, one male already having pushed past him, and ran down the side of the mountain to fight the Darkness for his queen.

Cethin

He allowed himself one look at her—just one—as he ran past her down the mountain. She was dressed in Avivan armor—an idea created by some female whose name had long since been forgotten—just as he was. But moonlight and starlight filled every fiber of her essence. It made his breath catch.

But Cethin didn't stop as he continued his path to the army that had started its ascent.

Eleonora

She'd done it. She didn't know how, exactly, but she'd done her part. Her first of many.

Avivan soldiers rushed past her. She knew Eldwyn needed to be with them. She encased herself in her own shield, a vibrant silver glow of her magic layered around her armor. She'd read about it in one of the books Alanna had left—likely from Eldwyn's personal stash.

There were so many Dark beings below. She'd felt them before, but seeing them now, outlined in the pale moonlight from the crescent that lingered in the blackness of the sky...it was an entirely different reality. She saw some Dark, twisted versions of fully-blooded Elves who used to be just like the males with her. That was something she wasn't prepared to defend herself against—to kill.

Then, she heard it: the booming of their wings. Their hisses and whispers.

The Noir were coming.

No one knew exactly how many of the Night Queen's creatures existed in their world, but there were three of them headed for the mountain. She took a deep breath and willed that moonlight, that starlight, into her body, her lungs, her blood, her whole being. At the very least, she could send them far away. And, if she could find Eldwyn and bind their magics together like she'd read about, she could destroy them, like she had in the changeling's fantasy. The Noir came closer and closer. She waited, counting down the seconds until they'd be in range—

And then she let go, blasting her power into them—a raw force she didn't feel entirely in control of. The two on either side banked hard and wheeled back into the palely lit sky around them—but not the one in the middle. She sucked down a breath as she rallied her power again, but it was more difficult now. She'd used too much of it already, unable to control her energy. But she had to try—if not for herself, then for her soldiers, her friends, her...

She let her power loose once more—but it was different this time. Her silvery light raced toward the creature, but it was now woven through with strands of gold. Emotion clogged her throat.

"Mom?" she whispered, watching as the cold lick of her magic and the searing heat of golden flame barreled into the Noir. The creature shrieked in pain and frustration. She pressed harder with her magic, and the flame matched her will. Only when a rippling wound appeared in the Noir's side—only when the creature was screaming in terror—did she dare to drag her eyes from it to look around, desperate for a glimpse of her mother somehow peering into their world from the Otherworld, helping her, guiding her—

But it wasn't her mother.

It was him.

Cerdwin had come.

Chapter 32

ELEONORA

Shock and relief swept through her as she looked at the male, and he at her. His normally blazing purple eyes were now nothing but bright, burning golden flames—twin, she knew, to the silver moonlight she felt in her own.

Neither of them said anything as they turned back to the Noir screaming above them. She felt the push in Cerdwin's power at the same time she pushed hers. Together, they set the creature ablaze in a wash of silver and golden flames. The Noir twisted in on itself, its shrieks like nothing she'd ever heard, until it was nothing but a whisper of black smoke drifting away on a phantom breeze.

She spooled silver light back into herself, her power dragging, Cerdwin's bolstering it so she didn't burn out. It was just like what she'd read about in Eldwyn's books. *Had he read them, too?*

"You came." Her voice sounded ragged in her own ears, her breath coming in pants. She needed more practice—a lot more practice—before she faced the Noir, or something more powerful, again.

"Alanna said it was the right thing to do."

She would unpack that sentence later—if later came. "She's here?"

Cerdwin nodded. "In your tent."

"Good," she said, watching as he reached for his blade. She flinched. He must've caught the motion, because something flickered in his eyes as the flames receded.

"My blade is not for you. It will never be for you," Cerdwin said.

Then he sprinted down the hill and into the fray. Reaching for the twin blades he'd gifted her, Eleonora followed.

Eldwyn

Where he slayed one Dark creature, another one took its place. Again and again, like some sort of magical battle simulation. But Eldwyn kept going—his males kept going—kept breaking through one after another, after another.

Magic was reserved as a last resort in battle—a rule that'd been instituted after the Battle of the Breaking—yet he couldn't help but use his on the enemy soldiers that had once been men, half-Elves, or fully-blooded Elves, couldn't stand the idea of his blade ripping away their essence. They'd already been stripped of their being. So Eldwyn used his magic, cutting off their breath at the source. A quick, less painful end. It still wounded his own essence. Eldwyn blocked and parried, his shifting magic pressing against his bones, the silver wolf begging to be released. Eldwyn gritted his teeth and lifted his sword again. He needed to stay in control.

Three Noir came. The booming of their wings created a frantic sound over the noises of the battle. Two of the winged beasts disappeared back toward the direction they'd come from. Eleonora's light flared against the third that remained—but her magic felt different as it tore the Dark being apart against the wind.

Eldwyn didn't need to look to know whose magic bound itself to hers, whose magic kept the untrained queen from burning out. He knew the signature of that power as well as he knew his own: Cerdwin had come.

That spurred Eldwyn forward. He knew what the Second Commander's presence would mean for their soldiers—what it meant for himself. And, if Cerdwin was there, Alanna likely was as well, which meant they had a real Healer available. Relief briefly blossomed under his exhaustion. He had a feeling they would need her before this was over.

Cethin

He wasn't sure how long he'd been killing for. It could've been minutes—it could've been hours. But he was starting to feel the weight of the repetitive motions, of striking with his knife over and over again, the strain of remaining balanced on the ground that, in addition to being littered with rocks, snow, and ice, was now also littered with bodies.

Sweat beaded on his brow, and Cethin lifted a dirty, bloodied hand to wipe it away. He couldn't stop—wouldn't stop. He wouldn't lose her. And in the heat of battle he knew it wasn't just because of the life oath.

It was because of *her*.

The moonlight—her moonlight—that flared overhead had subsided, and the Noir that had been engulfed in it had become nothing but ash on the wind. He hoped the damn thing burned in Hell. But it hadn't been just her light, he realized in a brief break from the slaughter, but a combination of hers and Cerdwin's.

The Second Commander had joined him and the other males on the front lines—lines that quickly blurred and faded. But Cethin didn't need to look around to know he now stood in the thick of it, enemies coming at his front, his side, his back. He kept a swift, endless, pacing circle, cutting down each enemy soldier he sensed.

It was all he could do, all he could think about—except for their bond, which remained steady and alive.

Eleonora

She set into a half walk, half run down the hill—not nearly as nimble as Cerdwin. There were bodies every few paces she took, and they weren't all wearing the uniform of those who served the Dark King. A few wore the same armor she did. She took a deep breath, almost tumbling over one of those bodies, and swore, knives slicing through the neck of an enemy soldier still moving the next step.

The enemy soldiers were doing their best to reach the top of the mountain. She'd assumed it was just for her, but now, she wasn't so sure. What if this was a first push into the north of Aviva? Unless—without the Noir—they really didn't know where she was.

She struck the next wicked looking creature—one that reminded her of a deformed winter bear—right in the eye and yanked her blade free, blood spraying from its skull. There were still too many. In front of her, some Avivan soldiers had started using their magic: most throwing fire at the enemy, some drowning them on dry land, others pulling the air from their lungs, and—she could've sworn she saw an enemy soldier turn to ice, then shatter.

Magic is to be used as a last resort, Eldwyn had told her. But she wasn't just anyone. She could use her magic whenever she damn well pleased—was certain Cerdwin had ensured that. So Eleonora reached into her essence and searched for that well of power, pleased that it had already replenished.

She looked at the enemy soldiers surrounding them at the foot of the mountain and smiled as she rallied her moonlight. She might be undisciplined and unpracticed, but when there was that much Darkness, it didn't really matter.

Eldwyn

Where Eleonora struck, Darkness recoiled. He would've been impressed if he hadn't been busy using his own power to keep as many of their own soldiers alive as possible, sending walls of hard air to drive enemy soldiers back, too drained to rip the air from their lungs.

Cerdwin binding his magic to hers had had the intended effect, though: Eleonora's magic was stronger than theirs now. Still, enemy soldiers burned to ash in the Second Commander's path, his golden flames sending them to Hell—or so Eldwyn hoped.

During a brief reprieve, Eldwyn swung around to look for Cethin. The half-Elf would be more physically drained than the rest of them and had no magic to fall back on.

What Eldwyn saw sent his heart lurching for his queen.

Eleonora

The crack of pain—sharp and deep—echoed in her body, in her essence.

Cethin.

She wasn't sure if she'd thought his name or screamed it. She flung her power out, silver light erupting through the dark, rocky foothills and tall pines, casting long shadows over the struggle. She glanced around wildly, carving down soldier after soldier with her blades as she whirled.

Where is he where is he where is he—

She spotted him at the base of the foothills. Cethin was on his knees before what had to be one of the Dark King's Commanders: Darkness leaked from the creature in an oily sheen. She'd never seen one of them, had only heard about them from Eldwyn. Now, she was sure she wanted to kill one. Gritting her teeth, she pushed and pushed, rocks and icy mud and bodies slipping beneath her boots as she made her way toward them.

The Dark Commander's eyes met hers. *Almost there.* She was almost there.

Then, the creature smiled—and struck Cethin across the chest.

She screamed as Cethin's body fell to the rocky earth, his head colliding with a nearby rock. The Dark Commander beckoned to her. Eleonora snarled as she barrelled into it and struck the creature hard and fast, over and over again—

Until the servant of Darkness was nothing more than a dark clump of flesh on the earth.

She dropped to her knees beside Cethin. Blood leaked from the wound the Dark enemy had slashed over his heart—and black. Something black and oily was leaking in.

Poison. She screamed again, screamed in a voice she didn't recognize as her own. "HELP! SOMEBODY HELP!" she bellowed as moonlight exploded around them.

Alanna

She heard a scream—a cry for help. The voice shook her.

Eleonora.

Alanna grabbed her Healer's satchel and ran down the hill in the shadows, the light from the crescent moon above waxing and waning without warning. She grabbed a discarded spear from the ground in one hand—one of the Dark King's soldiers, or theirs, she didn't know or care—and hefted it to her side, her satchel of salves and bandages on the other. Faster, faster Alanna flew, Avivan soldiers paying her no heed as she ran. She crested a smaller hillside, and—

There was a glowing, pulsating orb of pure light turning anyone who touched it into black dust. The shield cast the entire valley into long shadows. Alanna saw golden hair and a golden sword flash—her brother, fighting three enemy soldiers at once, his fire singeing any who got too close. But his fire wasn't so bright. He was burning out.

There were too many enemy soldiers in the valley—too many for their small unit to defeat, even with both Commanders and the queen. Still, Alanna kept her pace, making herself as small and quiet as possible as she edged toward that silver light—to where Eleonora and Cethin were ensconced inside. She sent a whisper of magic toward it. It didn't evaporate like the soldiers had. The pulsating sphere paused—hesitated, as if it were a living thing. Alanna didn't allow herself to give in to fear as she pushed a hand through—

She was inside. One look at the half-Elf, a thread of her Healing power winding toward him, set her head spinning. Cethin was unconscious. Blood streamed from a wound on his head, coating the rocky earth around them, mixing with the snow. And his chest—so many slashes there, but the one above his heart...

Alanna gritted her teeth at the oily poison that poured into his body from it. "We need to move him." Eleonora stared at her as if she didn't recognize her. "We need to move him somewhere quiet," Alanna said, gesturing to the melee around them. "So I can properly Heal him." Eleonora opened her mouth, as though she were going to say no, or ask how, but no words came from the queen's lips.

"There's a quiet place nearby, south, blessed by those with Earthen gifts," Alanna said to the queen. She hoped the female wouldn't be too shocked by it when they arrived. She'd seen it before—Alanna had seen it when she'd Healed her. "We'll go there. We won't make it up the mountain and back to the city in time."

The queen's body shook, as if she knew it, too: the half-Elf's essence was draining, his life, dimming. But then, Eleonora lifted her head and looked around. "We can't just leave them," she said, voice raw.

Alanna seized the female's hand and squeezed it. "If we don't go now, he will die," she said firmly. "And whether we stay or go, this is a fight that cannot be won—not here. Not now."

Eleonora took a deep, shaking breath. "Eldwyn can lead them back," she said in a quivering voice.

"Yes," Alanna said softly. "He can." A snap came from their left. Alanna turned to see a lion prowling outside of the light, watching them with fear in his eyes—fear for her, and fear for the male they needed to leave behind. Her twin snarled, but Alanna held up a hand. This wasn't up for discussion.

This might be their battleground—but *she* was their Healer.

Eldwyn

Eldwyn lunged—cutting down the enemy who'd just tried to impale his left side—moving as swiftly as the wind would carry him, trampling the enemy soldiers who dared to cross his path as he went, pushing himself harder, and harder, until he approached what looked like the moon itself on the ground. Seconds passed as he took it all in: Cerdwin, in his lion's form, outside of that light, pouncing on approaching enemy soldiers and ripping their throats out; Alanna, inside that pale light, helping Eleonora bring a pale male to lean between them; Cethin, that was Cethin, unconscious, pale, and bleeding between them.

Eleonora looked up at him, as if she'd sensed his presence. *Fall back.* She didn't need to say the words out loud—they were written on every inch of her face.

"Fall back," Eldwyn roared, power rippling through the clearing, amplifying his voice to their remaining males. There were so few of them left now. "Fall back!" he yelled again. He looked again at the group inside the shield as the light faded. Once it was gone, Alanna pulled herself onto her brother. Eldwyn rallied his power, preparing to shift, but Eleonora spoke.

"Be careful," she whispered. He knew what she meant—that Cethin wouldn't survive the return journey without stopping somewhere to Heal—but he wouldn't do it. He wouldn't leave them—leave her—not when they needed help the most. Not unless she ordered him.

"Let me help you," he said. The queen paused, then, to his surprise, nodded. Maybe she'd finally realized he could be as stubborn as she was.

"Alaric," he whispered on the wind, searching for the male in the sea of shadows and death. He felt the soldier's ears twitch at his words. "Take them back." The air rippled as the male nodded in confirmation.

Eldwyn shifted into his wolven form. Eleonora pulled Cethin up first, then settled in behind the half-Elf. His queen looked to the Healer on the golden lion next to them. "Lead the way."

Chapter 33

ELEONORA

The First Commander's power was a harsh blast as they fled the battle—towering pine trees were coming down behind them, slamming into the enemy soldiers pursuing them—but it was starting to falter. None of them would hold out with their magic much longer. But Alanna's was all she cared about.

From what Eleonora could see over the fallen pines, their soldiers were retreating to the foothills and making their way back to the camp at the summit. She sent a flare of moonlight to the base of the mountain to help guide them.

Cethin moaned in front of her, his breath nothing more than a ragged, choking noise. She'd stopped screaming some time ago, but she could feel the silent tears falling down her face as they rode, hard and fast, following the golden lion with the golden rider in front of them. The forest became darker and quieter as snow-free evergreens rose all around them. It was familiar for a reason she couldn't place. Not until—

"There," Alanna called back to them. There—a sliver of light cutting out of the mountain, like the edge of a knife in the darkness.

A cave.

The cave? The cave she'd mistaken the changeling for Cethin in? The cave where she'd been tortured? The cave where the changeling had baited her, tempted her, and she'd fallen for it, almost given him—given *it*—everything?

"No." Alanna turned back to look at her.

"We must—" the Healer started.

"Not. Here." Never here—no matter that it hadn't been real. Alanna halted. Eleonora pulled up beside her, watching as the Healer's mouth pressed into a hard line.

"I know," the female said in that tone that was gentle, yet brokered no room for argument. "I know what you went through. I know what they put you through. In there." Alanna angled her head toward the cave as she spoke, curls like live flames in the dark. "It wasn't real, Eleonora." The female motioned to Cethin. "But this is. This is real. He is fading—and fast. If I am to do my work, it must be now. In there."

Eleonora's body shook. She clenched her fists, willing the trembling to stop. *She could do this.* She could go back there, to that place, for him. *For him.*

Alanna

"Stay toward the entrance," Alanna ordered Eldwyn, and the wolf bobbed its head in submission. With Eleonora's assistance, they carried

Cethin farther into the cave. Cerdwin walked back with them until she ordered him to stay as well—two layers of protection if the enemy picked their trail.

Alanna lay Cethin's body next to one of the cave's pools. She'd been there before—had transplanted most of the *dianaflora* that now called this space home. Just as her father had ordered. Just in case.

"What can I do?" Eleonora asked. Alanna considered: the queen was still trembling, though she'd stopped crying. Alanna pulled a clean cloth from her Healer's satchel, dipped it into the pool, and handed it to the female.

"Clean the wound at his temple, but don't push too hard," she ordered. Eleonora nodded, her hands steadying as she gently pressed the damp cloth to the male's head. Alanna pulled out a second cloth and began doing the same for the wounds across his chest. *Thank the Gods she'd come, and thank the Gods Cerdwin had agreed to come with her.* Cethin had so many cuts, scrapes, bumps, and bruises that needing tending to ensure they didn't fester and become infected. But the life-threatening injuries he'd sustained, those deep in his chest, and the one drenched in poison...

Alanna pulled away and sank onto her heels, white Healer's war uniform covered in mud, blood, and that black, seeping poison. Eleonora did the same, the queen covered in blood as well—and, from the smell of it, not her own. The female splayed her hands, holding the now blood-soaked cloth back out to her.

"What now?" she asked. Alanna looked at the wound on Cethin's head. The bleeding had stopped flowing freely, and the injury was now clean, thanks to the queen's ministrations. Looked at the wounds on his chest, now also clean.

But the one above his heart...

"Now," Alanna said, sinking into the Healing calm she hadn't needed to draw upon in so many decades, "I will work." She let her Healing energy flow from her heart, her essence, through her very being, drawing it through her like the first breath of life into the world; let it drift into her hands, guided it over organ, muscle, tendon, and skin; willed the wounds on his chest, the ones on his head, to Heal. Even if Cethin had been a fully-blooded Elf, his wounds still would've required some degree of assistance. And that poisoned one...

Alanna forced herself to focus on the task at hand: one problem at a time. That's what her teachers always told her: focus on one ailment at a time and allow each to give you the confidence to Heal the next. Eleonora sat quietly on Cethin's other side, her once again trembling hand now tightly holding one of his.

"Can I help?" Her voice was a whisper through Alanna's trance.

Alanna continued working, the wound to his temple now merely a scar. Focusing on the ones on his chest as she asked, "Have you used your Healing gift at all?" From the way Eleonora hesitated, Alanna knew the answer was likely no or not much.

The queen swallowed. "Please."

Something in Alanna softened at her voice. "Take my hand," she said, extending hers to the queen. She guided their joined hands over Cethin's torso. "When you pull up your moonlight, what does it feel like?"

"Like..." Eleonora paused. "Like I am pulling from some great galaxy inside of my essence. It's a part of me. I bring it through my heart and allow it to fill me up, and then push it out into the world."

"It's similar to my Healing gift, then," Alanna said, continuing to move their hands. "Instead of a galaxy, though, it's life itself." Respect shone in the queen's eyes. "Search for it, now," Alanna continued. "Find that space inside yourself that's connected to life itself." Her own blue light flowed into the horrible gashes, sealing one, moving on to the next. "Then draw it through yourself, your heart, and push it—not out into the world, but into him." The queen closed her eyes, a look of determination on her face as she drew in a sharp breath. Slowly, so very slowly, a faint, blue light flowed from her center to her hands. Not as vivid as Alanna's own, but it was something. Eleonora opened her eyes.

"Good," Alanna said, offering her a half smile. "Now pour it into here." She moved their hands over a wound in Cethin's chest, watching as it pulled together. As they worked, Alanna allowed her Healing magic to reach out and touch Eleonora's. It wasn't a Healing gift like the High Healers had, but it was better than nothing, given what the queen was likely to face before the end of the Darkness. Eleonora's breathing evened out as a scar appeared, then picked up again as they both looked to his final wound: the poisoned one. Alanna dropped the female's hand. Eleonora looked like she was ready to argue, but Alanna held up her hand and gave the queen what Sonia called her "look."

"Let me explore it," she said, and Eleonora settled back onto her heels. Alanna probed the Dark wound with her magic, blue light faltering in the presence of whatever nasty poison tried to seep into his heart. His pure heart. The Darkness of the poison swirled, reveling in destroying that pure heart of love.

Alanna had never seen a wound like it—but she trusted her Healing intuition, as she'd always done. She hadn't been able to save her lady mother when she'd passed. Now, she felt in her heart, in her essence, that she was being called to give the half-Elf the same precious gift she'd tried to give the female she'd loved so dearly.

This time, the love was for Eleonora and Cethin.

This time, the gift wasn't for herself. It was for Aviva.

Alanna would never be able to explain how she knew it; Eldwyn had often joked she'd been gifted with the foresight Elves in millennia past had had. But she knew. She knew what she had to do.

Alanna stood and began picking the *dianaflora* around them.

"What is it?" Eleonora demanded, jumping to her feet. "Can I help?"

Alanna shook her head at the queen, the hope of their people and kingdom. "No," she murmured softly. "You can't." Alanna walked to one of the nearby pools and dropped the *dianaflora* she'd picked into it. The water sparkled as the flowers touched its surface, every petal charged with her Healing power.

"Alanna," the queen said, voice raw with emotion. Alanna turned toward her, the headstrong female who'd become her friend—and her queen—in such a short period of time, and smiled.

"This is all that can be done," she said, feeling resolute in her choice as she stepped into the shimmering water. "This is the only way."

Eleonora

She watched in horror and sorrow and honor as Alanna, her friend, Cerdwin's twin, backed into the pool. The Healer's power set the entire surface glowing with blue light, *dianaflora* like blue sparks of flame. The female would do it. She would yield her Healing—yield her essence—for Cethin. Eleonora reached out a hand, stumbling toward the Healer, but Alanna stood feet deep within the pool now.

And then she went under.

Blue light, blinding and brilliant, flashed through the cave, and Eleonora threw up a hand to cover her eyes.

"Eleonora," came a female voice—Alanna's voice. "This is the way it must be. This is the only way. When I'm gone, when the light fades, give him a drink from this pool. It will drive the poison from his heart and restore him completely." Eleonora let out a strangled sob. *This couldn't be happening.*

"It's okay." That soothing voice sounded again, from nowhere and everywhere. "He is pure of heart. There's a reason for it, Eleonora. There's a reason we were all brought together. This is only a part of it. You must save him. You must continue forward. You must find a way to re-Bind the Balance. Promise me," Alanna's voice intoned, "promise me that you will see it through."

"I promise," she choked out as tears she didn't know she had left fell. "I promise." She could've sworn she felt Alanna's smile, the warmth of the golden, gifted Healer—

The light vanished. Eleonora blinked, willing her vision to settle and herself to focus on the task at hand. The promise she'd sworn.

She remembered the pool first—the water Cethin needed to drink from. She fumbled with the Healer's satchel, found a small cup, and dashed to the pool where the female had stood only moments ago. She filled the cup to its brim, sloshing pale, blue-gold water around in it, crash-landing on her knees beside Cethin. He was still unconscious. She pulled his head into her lap and brought the male into a half-upright position. She opened his mouth and tilted the cup, urging shimmering liquid past his lips. Then, she waited, eyes fixed on that black, rotting flesh above his heart. And then she went back to the pool.

Again and again, hoping she wouldn't have to drain the entire pool dry, hoping her friend's sacrifice hadn't been in vain, Eleonora retrieved water and gave it to him. Until the Darkness of his wound recoiled, then faded. Until color flowed back into his body, and a healthy pink tinted his cheeks.

Cethin's breathing eased, and his chest began rising and falling in a normal rhythm. The poisonous Dark wound above his heart turned a regular, fleshy color, then sealed. He remained unconscious, but he was alive.

He was alive. He would live on. Eleonora let out a sob of joy—

And then she heard it.

Cerdwin

Something was wrong. There was a familiar tug—a pull to his twin. Cerdwin had only sensed it one other time: when Alanna had pushed herself to the brink of burnout trying to Heal their lady mother one night when she thought everyone else was asleep. He still remembered that feeling, that panic, like his twin was slipping away, along with—or instead of—their lady mother.

Post be damned. The lion turned and bolted down the path she'd taken—

And stopped dead in his tracks. That bond, that tether that had always been his and Alanna's alone—nothing as powerful as a mating bond, but one that linked them together in the world as one essence—was gone.

As if it had never existed.

Cerdwin let out a sound—not a roar, but a howl—as that absence, that silence, barrelled through him, threatening to shred his heart, his essence, his very existence.

There was a presence next to him. He let out a low growl. Eldwyn stood there in his Elvish body, hands raised. "Cerdwin," he said. Cerdwin growled at him. "Cerdwin," Eldwyn said again, in that inherently dominating tone of the First Commander.

He allowed his name to ground him. Shifting back into his Elvish body, Cerdwin fell to his knees, stone biting into his legs and palms, but everything was numb. He didn't move, didn't flinch, as Eldwyn hauled him upright and pulled him down the corridor.

Cethin

He'd seen Darkness before. Darkness blacker than blackest night. Darkness that made it impossible for him to see his own hand in front of his half-Elvish eyes. Darkness so unbelievably striking that there was no beginning and no end. A void.

He'd seen Light before. Pure, undimming Light. Light so bright it could blind you but was so beautiful, so clear, so pure, it chose not to. Light that was the light of essence. The light of the stars. The light of the moon.

This gloom, this gray and shadowy gloom, was a dreadful, life-sucking mixture: the threat of the Darkness, and the tantalizing promise of the Light, swirled together into looming shadows and swirling mists—a gray that drained one from the other. The opposite of the Balance. The Balance she needed to re-Bind. She. Her.

El.

He had a vague memory of her shouting his name before he'd come to this place. He couldn't see her now—couldn't see anything or anyone.

He heard something, something other—something not of their world. Not the terrifying creatures of the Darkness—not the Noir. But something, somehow, worse. Much, much worse.

He didn't know how long he'd been there. Didn't know what he was supposed to do. The gray gloom stretched around him on all sides, as vast as the ocean he remembered seeing as a child, standing on a dock with two people he imagined were his parents. But this depthless space, gloomier than clouds on a stormy day, didn't fill him with the spark of joy the sea had. No—it was draining something from him: his life, his essence, he wasn't sure. But each step he took in that gloom became slower, weaker—less alive.

Suddenly, pain lanced through him, and he fell to his knees. Any cry he let out vanished immediately, swallowed up by the gloom. He put a hand to his chest, then pulled it away. Blood—blood, and something black. *Poison.*

He was dying.

The shock was enough to set Cethin on his feet again, to run blindly through that mist. To find a way back. To them. To her. Another wave of pain took him to his knees again. He trembled, shaking with pain and agony and rage. This wasn't how things were supposed to end.

Tears streamed down his face, falling into his wounds, saltwater mixing with blood and Darkness. He looked around wildly, hoping against hope he wouldn't see anyone else with him, anyone else dying from their battle.

He was alone. Totally and completely alone—except for the voices. Those ancient, menacing voices, pressing closer, speaking in a language he didn't know, or couldn't understand. Whatever dwelled in this place was coming for him, and he would meet his end.

No. Cethin staggered to his feet and pushed forward, one hand at the wound on his chest, the other in front of him, as though he were playing hide me and find me as he had as a child. The memory startled him.

Keep going. Another voice joined those in the pale gray mist, but this one was different from the others: it was young, joyful, and female. He knew without understanding that it was a lifeline for him.

And then it appeared: a bridge of blue light. Cethin staggered toward it, took a hold of its railing, and followed it, letting it take him up, and up. A second bridge appeared then, not alongside but binding itself to the first, as though it were a support. A beautiful, strong silver line closed around him like a net and helped pull him forward. He clung to them, followed them.

Those ancient voices were angry now, angry that he was getting farther and farther away from them. The bridge of blue trembled as he continued, and those voices drew closer. He tried to hold on to the blue support, but it faltered, then faded. He took a stronger grip around the silver support, that silver line, and willed them to hold on to him, to stay, stay. The ancient voices in the gloom slowly took form—whispers of hands and cloaks and faces from his own nightmares. Something—or someone—grabbed ahold of his leg. Cethin cried out, willing all of the strength to his arms to hold on to that silver promise.

Suddenly, the blue bridge was there again—no, not a bridge, but a pathway, threaded with pink and gold, gold as pure and undiluted as the Light of Aviva. Those ancient voices hissed at it, as though they couldn't endure its presence. The pathway expanded, grew brighter, illuminating the gray mists, so bright he had to shield his eyes. It flared...

...and was gone.

Eldwyn

Half running, half dragging Cerdwin, Eldwyn made his way down the passage. He wasn't sure what, exactly, Cerdwin had felt, but the First Commander knew that one more growl from the male would damn them all—more than they already were. It was only a matter of time before the enemy tracked them there, and, while Eldwyn had conceded to stopping to Heal Cethin, they'd already lingered longer than was wise.

They entered an open space filled with *dianaflora* and warm springs. Eldwyn allowed himself to feel shock at the sight only briefly before he scanned the space until he found Eleonora. The queen was kneeling before her life-sworn. Cethin didn't look as gaunt as he had—that part had gone well, at least. Eldwyn scanned the rest of the area. Alanna was nowhere. Sparks from Cerdwin hit his skin, the male's red-hot anger leaking like liquid metal running at a forge.

"What happened?" Eldwyn asked as he made his way to his queen. She shook her head, her hands over Cethin's heart. He left Cerdwin to lean against a nearby stalagmite and kneeled beside her. "Eleonora, we must go—and soon," Eldwyn said, keeping his voice even and calm, even though Cerdwin's emotion threatened to break his training. "Tell me what happened."

Eleonora looked up at him then, as if just realizing he was really there. "She's gone," his queen whispered. "She..." Eleonora swallowed, as if she needed a moment to gather herself. "She gave up her essence."

Hot air vibrated around them. For an Elf to give up their essence, their immortality, their very existence...Cethin would've had to have been on the edge of the Otherworld for Alanna to have made that choice—as noble, as brave, as heroic a choice as any Elf could make. Eldwyn placed a hand over his heart, closed his eyes, and briefly murmured the Hero's rite in ancient Elvish for the fallen female.

"She saved him," his queen choked out. "She said—she said there was a reason for it."

Eldwyn rested a hand on her shoulder. "There will be time for mourning later," he murmured, fixing his gaze on Cerdwin. The way heat was rising in the chamber, he was certain the male had overhead every word. "Right now, we need to focus on getting out. They're coming."

He lifted Cethin—alive, but still unconscious—onto his back, as Eleonora strode toward Cerdwin, hands outstretched. "Cerdwin..." Eldwyn heard her voice shake. The Second Commander put out a hand to stop her, embers flying forward. The female didn't seem to notice where they made contact with her skin.

"Cerdwin," Eldwyn repeated, not as a friend, not as a lover, not as anyone or anything but the First Commander. Cerdwin looked at him, and Eldwyn saw the anger, pain, rage, grief, fire, and flame in his eyes. But Eldywn didn't back down until Cerdwin averted his gaze.

"We move out. Now."

Chapter 34

ELDWYN

The four of them—Cethin across his shoulders—made their way to the cave's entrance. Eldwyn set the half-Elf down. "We go quickly and we go quietly," he told them, exhaustion and sadness wearing on him, even as he set their path. He took a deep breath. "Their scouts are close now, the Noir not far behind." He heard Eleonora suck in a sharp breath, but Cerdwin just stood there, arms hanging at his sides.

Eldwyn considered: he could toss Cethin across his back again in his wolven form. But what about Cerdwin? The male could get left behind in their mad dash if he allowed his grief to consume him—could end up wounded in a fight or dead himself. Eldwyn had seen death and loss make even the most disciplined soldiers sloppy. The male needed to let some of his emotions out. "Eleonora, you'll ride Cerdwin. If—when—they find us, I want you to keep going."

Eleonora's mouth tightened, but she nodded. Eldwyn watched the grief in her eyes turn into fierce determination—determination to not waste what Alanna had given them, given her—given Cethin. "Okay," she exhaled.

"Cerdwin," he continued, eyes locking on the male's. Only a slight flicker of recognition passed over the Second Commander's face, but he nodded. Eldwyn looked back to Cethin.

But Cethin wasn't there.

Cethin

He opened his eyes.

Not to that gray place where Light and Darkness mixed together in a way that threatened to suck the essence from him, but to what looked like a cave. The cave looked different from the caves he remembered.

A male's voice sounded from behind him. *Eldwyn.* That was Eldwyn's voice. But it sounded deeper, richer—like smooth velvet. And he could *smell* the male—vividly. The First Commander smelled like winter—winter and pine. It was different from the snow-covered mountains and trees he vaguely recalled being in. No, this scent belonged to the male alone.

He heard a female voice. It was barely more than a murmur, but it was a sound he would've known if it were a faint whisper in a crowd or a shout across the continents. A female voice he'd heard a thousand times. A female voice that was lined with the same silver light the bridge in that ancient place had been.

A rushing, roaring noise as loud as the seas filled his ears, his head, his heart, his essence, as her voice and her scent flooded his senses—her scent that was sweet and familiar and smelled like vanilla and jasmine and *dianaflora* and *her*.

Another voice—not hers, not Eldwyn's, not one from that otherworldly place, but one from deep within his own essence—spoke: *Protect her.* He slipped away from them and out of the cave. Exiting the rock led him into a dark forest—

He felt them, saw their shapes in the trees: the eternal beings of Night that had hunted her for her whole life. He smelled their rotting flesh and tasted their stinking breath. He grinned. Their hunt would end today. He would end them.

"You know," Cethin drawled, flipping the sword he'd taken from the First Commander back and forth in his hand, "you bastards don't have to hide your ugly faces." His grin grew as one of the Noir stepped out from behind a tree, its full, winged body darkness against darkness—but he could see it. "I'm about to make them a lot uglier."

Eldwyn

He dashed out of the cave, Eleonora a step behind him, Cerdwin bringing up the rear. Eldwyn half gasped, half barked an order for the queen to get down—

Water.

Mountains upon mountains of water towered in front of Cethin. The half-Elf held one hand outstretched, forming and shaping the masses as his other clutched a sword—one of Eldwyn's swords. *Damnit, how had he done that?* Then Cethin angled his head toward their group. Wrath blazed in his golden eyes, unflinching death written on his face as that water drowned the Noir.

Those aren't the eyes of a half-Elf, Eldwyn thought.

That isn't the wrath of one, either, the wind whispered.

"You. Shift. Now!" Eldwyn barked at Cerdwin. "You, ride him back to the camp," he commanded Eleonora. She opened her mouth, but Eldwyn ignored her as he took up a spot next to Cethin and bound his wind to the water.

Eleonora

She blinked once—twice, not sure what to make of what she saw.

Cethin. It was Cethin, but he looked...*different*.

And where had that water come from?

She barely heard Eldwyn's shouted directions as the male went to stand beside her life-sworn and spun his wind into those towering waves—literally. The water churned, and then Eldwyn and Cethin flung their arms outward, sending a tsunami crashing into the Noir.

She turned to Cerdwin as the creatures shrieked and howled. The male stood with a hollowness she felt in her heart. "We have to go."

They wove in and out of the trees, the screeches of the Noir following them. She looked back, just once, to see the water and wind funnel together again, taller than the Endurnal Mountains behind them.

She had no idea how much time had passed before they reached a clearing in the forest. No, not a clearing—the scene of the ambush, the trees taken down by Eldwyn's magic to give them a chance. Like he and Cethin were doing now. And amongst the fallen trees...bodies. So many bodies. Soldiers from both armies were strewn all over the forest floor at the base of the mountain and up the steep slope, the rocks slick with blood and melting snow.

They traveled forward and upward, no sign of life, no sign of the enemy lurking, and, she noticed with no small amount of dread as they reached the summit, no sign of their army. She leaned forward to catch Cerdwin's eye. He shook his mane, and she took that as her cue to get off. In an instant, the Second Commander appeared in his Elvish body.

"There is another base a few peaks over," he said, voice steady, if not flat and lifeless, as he pointed back south. "It was a backup, in case anything ever happened here." She nodded, and he shifted back into the golden beast.

Eldwyn

He couldn't believe the power flowing from the staggering presence beside him. From a male—not a man. Not half-Elf, not half-breed. Not anymore.

Where Cethin had been tall, the male next to him stood a foot taller. Where the mercenary turned soldier had been strong, this male was muscled all over, holding the sword in his hand as if it were a piece of parchment. His features, once ruggedly handsome, were now striking and bold. His ears, no longer the smaller, rounded ears of the half-Elves but as tall and pointed as all Elves' were. And the magic. Wave after wave of raw power sang from Cethin as he pushed the Noir back. The creatures screamed, for they were beings of the sky, not the sea. And that smell of the ocean wasn't just from the male's magic—it radiated from Cethin himself, as powerful as any sea-God of legend. *Incredible.* Eldwyn forced himself to focus on the task at hand: mix his air with the male's water, send gusts of it to rally the strength of that water further, and crush the Noir beneath their storm. Cethin's teeth were bared in a wicked grin as they took them down, one by one by one.

"Cethin," he finally called over the roar and whoosh of the tsunami they'd created. "They're finished. Pull back." The pressure of magic built in the air again. "Pull back!" Eldwyn roared. "We have to catch up to the others." Still, that power rallied. "We have to catch up to her." The water calmed, flowing, trickling, and seeping into the earth as the male closed his fists and eyes. As the last of the droplets vanished, Cethin fell to his knees in the mud, gulping down air.

Eldwyn knelt beside him. "That was something," he remarked, and offered the male a hand. Cethin clasped it—more firmly than Eldwyn remembered—and they both stood. "I need to know what happened," Eldwyn said. "But right now, we need to get back to the camp."

Cethin tilted his head to one side. "Is she back at the camp?" he asked, voice hoarse. Then, "Is El back at the camp?" the male practically roared.

"She should be. I sent her there with Cerdwin while you put on your fancy little water show," Eldwyn said, gesturing to the muddy clearing around them.

"Then let's go."

Eldwyn nodded and shifted into his wolven form, inclining his head for Cethin to mount. The male swung himself up, and Eldwyn grunted beneath his weight. Elvish Cethin was definitely heavier, especially since his strength and magic were depleted. He was surprised that Cethin hadn't—

Nope. The male had drained himself and fallen into unconsciousness on his back.

Cethin

Darkness surrounded him, but it was different. It wasn't true Darkness. It wasn't the gray space of the Otherworld. No, this was a comfortable darkness, a peaceful one, like he was underwater, and everything was calm and quiet—tranquil. And there was a line there, a silver one. It was leading him somewhere, somewhere he would feel whole, completed, loved—

Cethin opened his eyes. Trees raced past in a blur of green and brown and silver. Silver that was the color of the wolf beneath him. The wolf he was...riding? He yelped, startled, and the wolf halted. Cethin dismounted, but there wasn't a wolf there anymore. *Eldwyn.*

"Morning," the First Commander said, crossing his arms with a smirk. "I was wondering how long you'd be out for."

"Is it really morning?"

The male chuckled. "Figure of speech. You've been unconscious since you burnt out. I'd say probably half of an hour." Cethin blinked at him. Eldwyn sighed, then spoke as though he were trying his patience with a youngling. "Magic isn't infinite, Cethin. It's part of your essence, your energy. Deplete too much too fast and you'll burn out. Most of us sleep for a day or more when that happens," he added, raising a brow. "But you came to rather quickly. Anything you'd like to share?"

"I know as much as you do." Cethin shook his head. "Where is she?"

The corners of Eldywn's mouth tugged up again. "Where is who?"

"You know who," Cethin growled. "Where. Is. El."

"Out of everything that just happened," the First Commander said, waving a hand in Cethin's general direction, "*that* is what you're most concerned about?" He sounded amused. Exasperated, but amused. Something Cethin most definitely was not.

"Where. Is—"

"Your mate?"

Cethin started. "My-my—"

"Your mate." Eldwyn nodded, and Cethin closed his eyes.

His *mate*. El was his *mate*. Not just his life-sworn. Not just his friend. Not just the Queen of Aviva. But his *mate*.

The silver thread he'd seen in sleep danced behind his eyelids. It vanished the moment he opened them, but Cethin knew where it would lead him: it would lead him in the same direction Eldwyn had been taking them—to her.

"It's a lot to take in." Eldwyn's voice was softer now. The male placed a hand on his shoulder, and Cethin met his eyes. "And it's incredibly *uncommon* in this time. Nevertheless, it's the truth."

"You knew, didn't you?"

The male nodded again. "Yes." A playful breeze lifted the hair around Cethin's shoulders. "I told you. The wind whispers."

Cethin glared at him. "And you didn't think to tell one of us?"

Eldwyn glared right back. "She wanted to do this her way. To come home and reclaim her throne *her way.* I wasn't about to interfere with that. And, if I recall correctly, *you* were the one who walked away from her the moment there was the slightest hint of uncertainty."

Cethin opened his mouth, then closed it again. He really couldn't argue with that. The male squeezed his shoulder once, then stepped back, rolling his. "I won't tell either of you what to do," Eldwyn said. "But you need to make this right." Then, he was gone in a flash, in his wolven form once more. Silver eyes landed on Cethin, eyes that said *get on*. So Cethin did.

As they sped through the forest again, Cethin didn't sleep. No, this time, he thought. He hadn't seen his life in stories behind his eyes as he'd faded into the Otherworld—he'd only seen his regrets. And his biggest regret was walking away from her.

His biggest regret was not telling her that he loved her. Not *had* loved, like he'd said before he'd walked away.

Loved. Here and now, he loved her.

And he always would.

She was his mate.

She was his El.

Chapter 35

The flatness in Cerdwin's voice and the pain in his eyes when he'd shifted into his Elvish body made Eleonora grateful they traveled with him in his lion's form. She had no words—no words that would make up for the depths of such an unspeakable loss, no words that would bring comfort to the male who'd just lost his twin.

Cerdwin let out a low growl as they crested the summit he'd indicated. She heard it then: the silent footsteps, the quiet retraction of bowstrings. Five scouts.

"Hold," came a male voice from her left—and not just any male voice. Alaric's. She sagged in relief, sliding off Cerdwin as the male approached them.

"Commander," he said to Cerdwin with a sharp incline of his head. She hadn't realized Cerdwin had already shifted back into his Elvish body. "The Dark King's forces have disappeared, but I thought it was best to move the camp," he continued, motioning to the thin pines and robust bushes that flowed upward to their right. "We hoped you would find us, after…" The male's green gaze came to rest on her.

"Your Grace," Alaric declared, and dropped into a low bow.

She shook her head. "There is no need to—" she started, but Alaric's face was solemn as he looked up at her.

"After the courage you displayed on the mountainside, where this unit is concerned, Your Grace, our loyalty is yours. The throne and the kingdom are yours. Not only by birth and by right, but by your bravery in fighting for and protecting them."

Then, Alaric dropped to his knees, gesturing around him as more Avivan soldiers appeared from the rocks and brush. They, too, dropped to their knees. Alaric placed a hand over his heart, and the rest of the company did the same. Eleonora rotated, taking in each of them in turn.

She should be elated, should feel a sense of victory in knowing that—even if the lords didn't trust her—her people trusted her. They saw her, acknowledged her, understood the light that fueled her forward. Instead, there was only a weight—an understanding that this was only a small start in the direction she'd been heading in since she and Cethin had set foot on Avivan soil.

"This bravery and strength you speak of are not mine alone," she said, bringing Alaric to his feet and motioning for the others to stand. "They belong to all of us," she proclaimed. "You all saw what Darkness will bring, what the Darkness will take," she added, glancing in Cerdwin's direction. "You did not falter. You stood your ground until the final signal. And now," she finished, looking at each soldier in turn, "we will regroup. We will rest. And then we will bring forth a force of Light that will drive the Darkness from this world." No cheers erupted around her, for fear the enemy might still be too close, but each soldier who heard Eleonora's words softly beat his hand over his heart.

Alaric bowed deeply to her again, then led her and Cerdwin into their new camp. "Should we expect the rest of your company to rejoin us soon?" he asked as they walked up the steep incline. She glanced at Cerdwin, the pained look on his face.

"Eldwyn and Cethin bought us time to escape from the Noir," she said carefully to the soldier, whose face tightened at the mention of the Noir. "But I would expect them back in the next hour or so."

Alaric nodded. "And the Healer?" he asked, eyes again darting between her and Cerdwin.

Eleonora shook her head. "No."

Alaric's eyes widened, but he quickly steadied his composure and clasped Cerdwin's arm. "I'm so sorry."

"And she wasn't just a Healer," Eleonora found herself saying. "She was a loyal sister, a good friend, and a lady—a lady of my court." She wasn't sure Cerdwin was breathing as the male stared at her. "She will be observed and honored as befitting her status. She will be mourned and celebrated as those who faded in her care were—as she would have seen done for them." Tears took over the flames in her friend's eyes. Cerdwin inclined his head to her, a silent thank you.

"It will be done, Commander," Alaric promised as he released Cerdwin's arm. "We're on the Avivan side of the Endurnal Mountains now," the soldier continued, motioning to the Light on the other side of the tents that'd sprung up around them as they'd walked and talked. "We'll move out after a fake night, and when we return to the city, we will begin preparations for the lady Alanna, along with our fallen."

"We've prepared tents for both of you and will begin setting up additional ones for the First Commander and Cethin," he went on, motioning to their right. "We have scouts around the perimeter. Even though we are on the Light-designated side of the demarcation line"—his eyes went from solemn to serious as he scanned the sky—"we need to be on our guard." Eleonora's hands went to the daggers at her sides, her familiar friends. She nodded, and Cerdwin did the same before he shifted back into his lion's form and stalked off to one of the tents Alaric had indicated. She made to turn to the one next to it, but Alaric's "Your Grace" gave her pause.

"I would ask your leave to post someone outside of your tent," the soldier said.

She smiled and patted her daggers. "I appreciate your concern, but I have what I need. And you all deserve rest before we go back, especially after..." She swallowed, but Alaric swiftly picked up where she left off.

"Yes, Your Grace," he said with a bow.

She took in the droop of Alaric's shoulders, the sword sheathed and crusted in blood across his back. "Alaric," she said softly, and the male's eyes rose to meet her gaze in query. "I want to honor all of them. Each and every fallen soldier who fought so tirelessly and fearlessly for our home here."

Wonder and gratitude shone on Alaric's face, but he didn't speak; only placed his hand over his heart once more, then backed away, leaving Eleonora to enter her tent alone.

Cerdwin

Rage. Exhaustion. Despair. Sorrow. Cerdwin saw each emotion as a flame in the small fire he'd conjured in his tent as he paced. Each flame flared, then slowly died with every step he took back and forth. Finally, he shifted back into his lion's form and curled his body around himself. Golden, as he was. As his sister, his twin, was.

Had been.

What she'd done, what she'd given for Cethin, was the greatest gift any Elf could give another. And he knew, deep beneath his pain and grief, that for her to have given her essence, Cethin must've been fading.

But to lose her, his twin flame, the only person who'd ever really understood him, *seen* him...hollowness tugged at Cerdwin, threatening to pull him under. His claws slipped free. He took a breath and willed himself to regain control. He'd never been able to command his elemental power or his shifting the way she had her Healing gift. His raging flames and violent shifting happened at emotional highs or lows. She'd known that, had been teaching him more, working with him and Eldwyn. And now that was gone. She was gone. Not to the Realm of Blessings, but to the Otherworld. Not a place of Light, as the Realm of Blessings was, but an endless gray space, full of unknown. A place where no Elf or mortal would ever be at peace. Not until there was Balance.

He whimpered, but the noise turned into a growl at the sound of his tent opening. "Easy," a female voice said. Elana. No. Her name was Eleonora now. No, it always had been. She knelt next to him. He lifted his eyes to her, the female who'd been with his sister during her last moments. Who'd...

No. He lowered his head. The female who sat with him, who would defend their kingdom no matter what the lords said about her, whom the soldiers in the camp acknowledged as their queen—the true Queen of Aviva, of Light—wouldn't have asked anything of her. No matter how much misery and darkness tugged at his heart and mind, Cerdwin knew: the decision his twin had made to save Cethin and yield her essence for his had been hers and hers alone. She had always been the bolder of the two of them. He would miss that, too.

He felt the female who was with him press a soft kiss to his lion's mane. When she pulled away, her tears and heartache mingled with his own. Something patched itself over a small part of the hollow space in his chest.

But Cerdwin knew that he would never be whole again.

Eleonora

Eleonora stumbled into her tent, energy low, grief tugging at her heart. She'd sat with Cerdwin until he'd fallen asleep, his head resting in her lap. She knew that rest would be short-lived, knew that the weight of Alanna's choice would push and pull at both of them for a long time. Giving Cerdwin rest—at least for a short while—was the least she could do for her friend. Just as his twin had been her friend—her friend, Healer, and lady. The first lady of her court. She smiled sadly to herself at the idea: at what could have been, at what they might have done for Aviva together; then laughed—Alanna would've hated being called a lady.

Eleonora sat quietly through the fake night as she sifted through the last moments she'd shared with the female—and the future moments they would never have, heart aching. And next to that pain...something else. Something that was growing stronger with each pound of her heart, with every breath she took—a force she'd felt before, but never truly seen. It was cresting like a wave over a peaceful shore, washing away sorrow and doubt, leaving nothing but love and peace in its wake. She allowed that feeling to flow around her, to engulf her, as she drifted off to sleep.

A rustle at the tent flap had her on her feet. Eleonora's hands went to her weapons as she crouched behind a support beam holding the makeshift structure in place. She paused, listening for sounds of a fight in the camp, scenting for wounds, looking for—

Cethin. She loosed a breath and straightened, hands drifting away from her daggers, but—

Her breath caught. It was Cethin—but it wasn't the Cethin she'd known. This Cethin was something *more*. This was the Cethin she'd watched unleash pure power outside of the cave—and more than that still.

In his half-Elf body, Cethin had been attractive, but now, he looked like a fully-blooded Elf, which enhanced, well, *everything*: he was devastatingly handsome, bigger, somehow—taller; his muscles rippled beneath his clothing as he entered the space; his ears, pointed at their tips, curved upward into his dark hair—which was now almost as dark and brilliant as her own; his eyes, still golden, were somehow even more striking, luminous; and his mouth...

Eleonora swallowed as his eyes met hers. Cethin took slow steps toward her, a predator stalking its prey, and she suddenly found herself trapped between the support beam and him. "H-how are you feeling?" she asked, willing herself to stand tall, her hands to stop trembling.

"How am I feeling?" Cethin's voice was low and rough, like it had been in the barn a lifetime ago. He was so close they shared breath, so close she could hear the steady beat of his heart—and was certain he could hear the wild pounding of her own. His scent engulfed her: the smell of sea and storm and beach and something she couldn't quite place, but nevertheless caused heat to burn low in her belly. He leaned forward slightly—*Gods, he was so tall now*—and breathed in deeply, as if taking in hers.

"I'm feeling like my whole world has shifted on its axis," he whispered in her ear, his low tone sending a shiver down her spine—a shiver that wasn't only because of his proximity, but because her world had shifted, too.

The wave of emotion Eleonora had felt cresting in her heart crashed into her fully as he stood before her, threatening to send her to her knees. And a queen didn't kneel for anyone. Anyone, except...

"I'm feeling," Cethin continued as he brushed his nose down her neck and rested a hand on her shoulder, a single finger drawing its way down her arm, "like I woke up, and my world became you." That finger worked its way back up her arm. Eleonora wasn't sure she was still breathing. "I'm feeling," he pressed closer into the nape of her neck, and she reined in a low whimper as his lips brushed her skin as he spoke, "like my first and only instinct the moment I awoke was to protect you, to defend you." His finger reached her shoulder, and his hand made its way into the dark curls she'd unbraided for sleep. "I'm feeling," he went on, voice near guttural, hand twirling one of those curls around, and around, "as though after I'd killed them all, my only priority was *you*. And I'm feeling"—he tugged on her hair, and she felt the scrape of his teeth against her neck, the hardness of him pressing into her core, sending her entire body aflame—"like you are mine. And when I say mine, El, I don't mean as your life-sworn. I mean as *my mate*."

He withdrew from her neck, and his golden gaze slowly raked over every inch of her. Her mouth went dry when he met her eyes again, his own heavy with desire. "You're mine."

The truth surged through her, that wave breaking, rumbling through her bones, her heart, her essence—even as a small, independent part of her protested against his possessive words—her magic, some deep, ancient, primal part of her coming to life. Heat, luxurious and rich, surged through her again, pooling in her core. Eleonora willed herself to take a breath, the scent of him, of his arousal, nearly overwhelming.

"Yes," she whispered. "I am yours. And you are mine."

Cethin

He was starving for her, desperate as he pressed his lips to hers and wrapped an arm around her waist, sealing every last inch of space between them. He tugged on her lower lip and she opened for him, letting him slide his tongue in as she moaned. He liked hearing that sound from her. *His mate.*

He reached down and pulled her hips closer still as she lifted his battle-tunic over his head. They paused then, mouths the only parts of them apart, both of them panting. Starlight lined his mate's eyes—silver, white, bright light—as she looked up at him, and he could *feel* her wonder, her desire—her love. She was the most beautiful thing Cethin had ever and would ever see in his life—a life that would be even longer, even more meaningful now. Now that she was his. She placed her hand over his heart, sorrow briefly clouding her brilliant eyes. Then, she removed her hand

and kissed that spot on his chest—that scar that could've ended their lives together before they'd truly begun; the scar that would never fully heal; the scar that even Alanna's magic—and his rebirth—hadn't erased.

"El." He caught her hand, lifted it to his lips, and pressed a kiss to her knuckles. She melted into him, her other arm wrapping around him, pulling herself closer still. His breath caught as the hand he'd held slipped up into his hair. He allowed her to search, to explore, to own every inch of him, to feel her way across his body. He was hers, as much as she was his. Cethin reached for the weapons he knew she kept strapped to her sides, unbuckling the belt and tossing it to the ground.

"Are you sure I won't need to protect myself?" El's eyes flickered with mischief as her hands wended their way to his front. He groaned as she grabbed at his cock through his britches.

"Not at all." He grinned as he moved his hand up and up, until he had access to the soft breast band beneath her battle-tunic. He raked his teeth down the side of her neck again, and she tilted her head back, giving him greater access to the spot.

She wasn't afraid. She would let him mark her—claim her.

So he ripped the battle-tunic and breast band from her body and used his teeth to break the sensitive skin by her pulse. The sounds of her pleasure and pain-filled ecstasy at being claimed rippled through the world as he bit her throat, grinding into her just as desperately as she moved against him. He used his mouth, his tongue, his teeth, working his way down to her now-exposed breasts. He worshiped each of those peaks with his mouth, watching as she turned her head to the side, attempting to stifle her gasps with her shoulder as he nipped the creamy skin above one. Then, losing himself to the primal need inside of him, he marked her there, too. He grinned against her skin as her gasps turned into screams.

Fuck taking her somewhere in the city. He didn't care that they were in a war camp. Didn't care that they were still technically in the Endurnal Mountains where their enemy dwelt. Didn't care that the whole world would know, would scent, would *feel* that he had claimed his mate.

Eleonora

Gods, she wanted him—wanted him more than anything she'd ever wanted in her life. *Her mate.* Cethin's hands worked into her pants, easing them so slowly, so carefully down her legs. Her boots came off. Her pants followed, then her undergarments. She stood there, bare. She'd been naked in front of him before, but now, she was a queen, and she was completely exposed. But Eleonora didn't feel any embarrassment, any shame, as her mate studied her, his eyes glazed golden as they grazed over every inch of her bare skin.

"Beautiful, El," he whispered when his eyes met hers again. There was something deeper than desire there, something that looked into her mind, her heart, her essence. Something that connected them past their world, past the Realm of Blessings—past eternity. *Eternity, and even an hour after.* That was what he'd once meant to promise her. So Eleonora looked at her mate and repeated his words.

"For eternity, and even an hour after." Cethin smiled, pure joy shining in his expression. A soft, golden light radiated from him at her words; no, not just from him, but from her, too—not the silver moonlight or brilliant starlight of the power she bore; not a brilliant, high noon sun, as her mother's light had been, but quieter, softer light, like the first rays of dawn breaking over the ocean's horizon.

Cethin

El was beautiful. Not just in her appearance, but in her heart—in her essence. And she was *his*. She wrapped her arms and legs around him as he picked her up and carried her to the cot. He laid her across it, then slid off his pants, chucking them unceremoniously onto the floor next to hers. He climbed over her and took in every feature that was his mate's, every inch of her that was his: her unruly dark curls; those eyes that looked like the ocean after a storm; pale cheeks that were currently flushed his favorite shade of pink; a mouth that beckoned to him once again; his bruising bite mark on her neck, and above her left breast—over her beautiful heart; the porcelain plains of her body, the toned muscles she'd built with him but were her strength alone; hands with the power of a universe.

Every part of the primal nature that'd come alive when Cethin had awoken bellowed at him to take her quickly and aggressively, to leave his declaration of their matehood everywhere for everyone to see. Maybe she did need protection from him, Cethin thought, though he doubted she would stop him—not if the feral sound she'd loosed when he'd claimed her was any indication of her need for him, too. But this very first joining...he would take his time. Well, as much time as a male who'd claimed a female could—especially a mated one.

Cethin settled himself between her legs as slowly as instinct would allow. The heat and scent and wetness of her taunted him, and he couldn't help his moan as he luxuriated in it. Her back arched at his gentle nudge and sound. He pushed his hands into hers on the cot, leaned forward, and brushed another kiss to her lips.

"How shall it be, Your Grace?" he murmured against her skin, sliding one hand away from hers to make lazy circles at the apex of her thighs. The low, primal sound she'd been making turned into—a laugh? *Ah.* It was the first time he'd addressed her as anything other than El. Cethin grinned. "Oh, this is no laughing matter, Your Grace." He kissed her again and moved his fingers farther and farther down, over her center, brushing her seam. "I take your pleasure very, *very* seriously." He heard the breath she sucked in as he worked his fingers inside of her. "Whether it be with my hands..." He pumped his fingers in and out of her, thumb circling her center. He pulled his mouth from hers and trailed a kiss and nip across both of her breasts, then lower still.

"Or with my mouth." He replaced his thumb with his lips as he worked his way down her body. Her low moan and the sounds of her hands grappling for anything she could find to ground her only encouraged him to nip lightly at the top of her core, too. She gasped, and then her hands found their way to his hair, pressing him harder against her as he braced her hip with his other hand. "So very demanding, Your Grace," he said, running his teeth along the edge of her. He replaced his hand with his tongue and swept through her center, then plunged inside of her. Her panting gasps, low moans, the honeyed taste of her, were a catalyst to his own desire.

"You make that title sound so filthy," she gasped. Cethin slowed his ministrations, even when she reached to pull his face back down. He chuckled and brushed another kiss between her thighs.

"Not at all," he said, moving over her again. His own body shuddered at the slickness between them. He needed to be inside of her. *Immediately.*

"I'm calling you that now, Your Grace, because I worship you—because I intend to revere every inch of your body." El cupped his face in her hands, her stormy eyes lined with silver, and his heart squeezed. "Because you are not only the Queen of Aviva, but the queen of my heart, the queen of my life, the queen of my essence. My mate. And from this point forward, *Your Grace*"—Cethin thrust inside of her then, gritting his teeth as every one of his senses threatened to be undone by the feel of her—"anytime anyone calls you by your title"—he held her gaze as he pulled out a few inches—"I want you to remember that my hands"—he pushed back in, lingering, pulled out a few inches again as he looped one hand behind her head, using the other to bring her to him—"my tongue"—another push and pull—"and my cock have been inside of you." Her eyes sparkled as he thrust into her again.

"And I want you to remember that you might be their queen, that you might have a duty and an honor to your people"—he leaned forward and licked up the column of her throat, over his claiming mark, groaning as she shook with pleasure beneath him—"but you are *mine.* And I am yours." Another thrust. "And we are bound to one another first."

Eleonora

"Cethin." She gazed up at her mate, lust fogging anything that might've been functioning in her brain when she'd returned to the camp. Her mate. *Hers.*

"Your Grace," he whispered, kissing her lips, her cheeks, her mouth. "My El." The sound of the only name he'd ever called her was her undoing as he thrust in deeply again and again, kissing her neck, her breasts. She wove her fingers through his hair, hauling all of him—everything he was—into her; merging with everything she was so deeply she could've sworn true day unfolded in the darkness around them—

And then she shattered completely. "Cethin," she moaned, as he rode her through her pleasure. She felt him find his, spilling deep inside of her, bellowing loudly enough the mountains around them shook.

Time ceased to exist as they lay there together, breathing heavily, bodies intertwined. She didn't know how long they'd been joined together, bodies warm despite the crisp air of the mountains. All she knew was Cethin: the scent, the taste, the *feel* of him—like a part of her that had always been missing—that had always been just out of reach—was now woven into her forever.

He pressed a kiss to her brow and she smiled, curving her body closer into his. He snarled as his mouth passed her ear, and every one of her senses tightened, her body homing in on his. *Gods save her.* She felt his satisfied male smirk against her neck as she pressed against him, warm and wet and needing *more*, felt his body's response as he sunk into her and—

He claimed her again, adding another mark to her skin, this one on her right breast—a twin to match the one on her left—head buried between them as they matched each other's rhythm. She felt her release build once more, beautiful and joyous as it broke through her; felt Cethin's release as he held himself deep inside of her, as if he would own every last inch of their pleasure, pour every last ounce of himself into her; felt the sweat on her brow, on her skin as he nuzzled her neck. "My beautiful, powerful mate," Cethin murmured, sending another thread of heat through her.

But she forced herself to focus—there was so much they needed to talk about. As Cethin eased from her, Eleonora placed her hand on his chest—over the scar that would linger for the rest of his immortal life. "How?"

"I'm not sure," he said after a moment, folding her other hand into his. Surprise rippled through her: his life-oath scar also remained. "I was in a place full of shadow, with ancient beings speaking ancient words. But then"—he moved her hand, rubbing at the scar above his heart—"there was a bridge. A pale-blue bridge guiding me. And then"—he sighed, twining their fingers together—"and then it faded. But in its place"—his eyes met hers—"there was a silver bridge—and a line—as strong and sturdy as I've ever seen. It held me"—he swallowed—"and I made my way back here. To you.

"I think," Cethin went on as she blinked back tears, "I think Alanna's power faded when she..." His voice turned hoarse, and she nodded, encouraging him to continue. "I think Alanna's essence passed to me. I think her essence reshaped me, stripped me of any mortality, and made me..." He closed his eyes. "Made me this."

"And—" She hesitated. "Your magic?"

His shoulders caved inward as he opened his eyes. "Whether I am more my father or my mother now..."

She squeezed his hand. "We'll figure it out," she promised. "Together."

He smiled. "I think..." She stared. "I think I knew you were my mate when my power manifested in Ozul. I hadn't used it since the day I left, but to protect you..." She shook her head. "I didn't know what it meant then. But I had only ever used it once before. To protect what I love most—my home."

"I think that innate sense to protect is part of who we are to each other—permanently." His eyes flicked to hers as he spoke. "And I know, El, the force you unleashed to protect me during that fight." She lowered her head, but one of his hands left hers and lifted her chin. "You used your power at great risk to yourself." She blushed and watched his eyes blaze, the scent of a warm sea breeze wrapping around them. "I will forever be grateful for it," he said, bringing their hands to rest upon her own heart. "I will forever be grateful for you."

"And I'm sorry," she began. "I'm sorry I didn't tell you earlier—"

He silenced her with a kiss. "There is nothing to be sorry for. Not when it has led us here."

She arched a brow. "Are you certain?"

Cethin rolled her onto her side and parted her legs, pushing his cock toward her entrance. "Do I feel certain to you, Your Grace?"

Chapter 36

CETHIN

A noise echoed from outside. Cethin quickly dressed and tugged on his boots, pulling out a dagger he'd hidden in one. Teeth bared and knife in hand, he whipped the tent open to the frigid air—and Eldwyn, standing there in a thick, green wool cloak. *The male's elemental magic was still drained, then.*

"It's time to move out," the First Commander said, raising his eyebrows.

"Of course." El—*dressed, thank the Gods*—stepped up behind the protective position Cethin had taken in front of their tent.

"Your Grace," the First Commander said with a bow, then, "Cethin." He grinned with a wink. *Bastard*, Cethin thought, as the male walked away.

Alaric approached them next. "Your Grace," he said, with a nod to Cethin and a bow to her. "We'll be pushing directly down the side of the Endurnal Mountains from here." The male pointed, indicating the steep, sloping land back toward the sands. "It will be a rough journey, but we expect to be back within the city walls before the next fake night. The supply party has already brought horses for us."

"Thank you, Alaric," she said.

"Forgive me, Your Grace," the soldier remarked, "but will you be riding back separately or together?" Cethin stepped closer to his mate and snaked an arm around her waist.

"Together," she said, as if it were the most natural thing in the world. Alaric nodded and bowed again, then moved forward with orders for the remaining soldiers.

Cethin sensed it then—the twisting emotions of his mate. It would be tricky to navigate everything once they returned: her title; the tale of her power that was sure to spread the moment they set foot back in the city—along with the account of the battle beneath the mountain; Alanna's death; his rebirth; their matehood.

He moved his arm from her waist and joined their hands between where they stood. "Together, El," he whispered, just as she'd promised him. "We'll figure it out together."

Cerdwin

He'd slept. It had been a dark and dreamless—but not unpleasant—sleep, after Eleonora had left the tent. The two females—Elana, or rather, Eleonora, and his twin—so different, yet so similar in so many ways, had that in common: the gift to calm, to comfort. Something Cerdwin needed in his life, something he desperately craved—something his lady mother was no longer there to give, and, now, something Alanna was no longer there to give, either.

He came around to the sound of the camp stirring, awake and alert, but still with that endless ache in his chest—one he was certain even centuries of existence through time couldn't Heal. They would leave the mountains soon and return to the city. To the castle. To his lord father. Cerdwin leaned his head against the bedroll and yawned, the heavy sound alarming him: he was still in his lion's body. *Shit.* He closed his eyes and willed himself to settle, to find that thread inside of him that would lead him back to his Elvish one, the form of the Second Commander who needed to guide his soldiers back home. The body of the son who needed to tell his lord father what had happened.

But the shift didn't happen. Cerdwin snarled in frustration, restraining the full roar that threatened to rip from him. Another animal's scent wafted into the tent. He stilled as a wolf sauntered in, dominating the space. It held the lion's gaze. But the wolf was only there for a moment. Light flashed—

And Eldwyn was there. The male let out a low whistle. "Nice form," he said, eyes sparkling, and Cerdwin grunted in reply. Jokes wouldn't bring him back from the edge—not this time.

"It's okay," Eldwyn said softly, kneeling and reaching out to touch his front paws. "It's okay if you can't or don't want to be a person right now." Cerdwin lowered his head to his outstretched paws and allowed the male to ruffle his mane, purring at the affectionate touch. It'd been so long since he'd allowed the First Commander to touch him like that.

"It's not her fault," the male said, gently running his fingers through his mane. Cerdwin let out a chuffing sound, and Eldwyn nodded his head. "I know, friend," he murmured. "I know." They both paused and cocked their heads toward the sound of Alaric's voice giving the official order to finish packing up and head out.

"I would travel with you, lion," Eldwyn said, "but one of us needs to lead our soldiers home." Cerdwin flopped onto his side, and Eldwyn laughed, though it sounded melancholy. "Once we're back in Aviva," the First Commander promised, "we'll go on a proper hunt. We'll drink. We'll talk. We'll remember her," he finished quietly. A different venture for the two of them, compared to their last.

Cerdwin pulled himself onto all fours and watched Eldwyn pick up the spare clothes and weapons in the tent. He wouldn't need them in this form. "I'll be up front, with Alaric at the rear. Stay with the queen," the First Commander said in parting. Cerdwin flicked his ears and tail in acknowledgment, even as he let Eldwyn's choice of words sink in: the queen—for that was who Eleonora was to the First Commander now, to the soldiers. To him, as her word would now overrule his, her station outrank his.

But she might also be his bride.

Cerdwin left his tent, leaving the tearing down to the other soldiers. He padded over to the tent Alaric had designated as Eleonora's before sleep had pulled him under. The other male stood watch while Eleonora worked to pull down the canvas—with *him*. Cerdwin took a beat to absorb all that he saw, felt, scented, and read on Cethin: the male's fully pointed ears and taller posture, the stormy power rumbling deep within him. He sent a whisper of his flame the male's way. It was immediately doused without the former half-Elf so much as flinching. Then, there was the defensive and possessive stance he presented around Eleonora, and their scents—

Their scents mingled like the sky above the ocean on a starry night. And something more ancient than that—

Cerdwin's nostrils flared as his lion's senses—even greater than even his Elvish ones—picked up a primeval scent. They were fucking *mated*—a bond stronger and more binding than the life oath that had first brought them together; honored above an Elvish betrothal or marriage; created, or so History was written, by the Gods themselves—specifically, the Goddess of Love.

Cerdwin blinked, and the scent dissipated; he was back in his Elvish body. Alaric had moved on, and the mated couple was mounting a horse. Together. He made his way over to them, unsure of what to say, unsure of what he wanted to say before he escorted them back to Aviva, to where their lives were about to become infinitely more complicated, whether the pair knew it or not. But the joy and grief mingling in Eleonora's eyes as he approached spoke what Cerdwin couldn't find the words to voice.

So he inclined his head to her and said, "Your Grace."

Eleonora

Every pair of Elvish ears was alert for remnants of the Dark King's army as they made their way back to Aviva. That was a challenge in itself, to remain as silent as possible themselves, as horses, riders, and Elves in their animal forms made their way down the rocky mountainside. Eldwyn led their company from the front. She and Cethin rode close to the rear. Cerdwin trotted beside them in his lion form, paws padding more silently than any horse along the rough terrain. Alaric led from the rear, and the remaining sixteen soldiers who'd survived the skirmish traveled in between.

Sixteen. Sixteen out of the seventy-five who had gone with them.

They hadn't been able to go back and recover the bodies of their fallen—or what was left of their bodies after whatever Dark creatures in addition to the Noir feasted on them. Of the sixteen who remained, four were injured—fortunately, not with poison as Cethin had been, but enough that Eldwyn increased their pace. They needed Healers.

The Light of Aviva shone brightly as they descended, illuminating the city across the sands. Even though the soldiers spoke in quiet voices, she picked up on their words—words about her, the lost princess of Aviva, the Queen of Moonlight who'd returned to save them in what had quickly turned into their darkest hour. She wasn't sure how true that was, but any soldier who passed her and hadn't been part of the party she'd seen with Alaric gave their oath, one hand over their heart as they went by. Something twisted in her gut at those pledges, a weight settling heavily on her shoulders. This was why she'd come back the way she had—as an unknown, as someone who just wanted to help the people and earn their trust and faith without any grandiose displays of magic.

But that time had ended.

Eleonora knew that one of the males in their company—one who'd remained uninjured, and had shifted into a bird, a falcon, she believed—had gone ahead to the city to prepare the Healers. She had no doubt that wouldn't be his only stop. Word would spread about her, about her magic, about Alanna—and about Cethin. Her heart pounded faster. So much had changed in such a short time: the loss of a blossoming friendship with the female, the amplification of her relationship with Cethin—her *mate*—and his magic, her oldest friend's grief; the loss of so many soldiers in the First Commander's unit, the release of her power into their world once more. The return of the lost princess.

The return of the queen.

She felt Cethin wrap his arm around her waist and grasp her hand. He squeezed it, and she turned toward him, tears stinging her eyes. A reflection of those tears shone in his, and she knew he was feeling everything she was. So much had been lost, so much had been destroyed, so much had gone wrong; yet so much could now be made anew—could be made stronger—together.

Cerdwin

He kept pace beside the queen and her consort—for now, he supposed. The lion snorted. *What would his lord father make of it?* His lord father, who'd wanted to see them wed. His lord father who'd so easily dismissed her. His lord father who'd kept the city—the people—together for fifty odd years, something Cerdwin knew had been no small feat. But with the Darkness coming closer, the people needed her. *He* needed her. Almost as much as he needed—

He reined in a wince. Almost as much as he needed Alanna. His sister. His twin. He felt like he had just reunited with her, only to lose her all over again—permanently.

Something warm and wet matted his fur. A single tear had slid into his mane—and there was something atop his head. Eleonora's hand rested there. He leaned into her touch, feeling her sorrow—and a small glimmer of hope. A whisper of shimmering calm settled into Cerdwin, easing his pain. He looked up at the blood-splattered, exhausted female who rode alongside him, who'd been like a sister to him when they'd been in Ozul, the daggers he'd fashioned hanging at her sides even now. Her magic had to be drained to the dregs, and yet she shrugged as the lick of Healing magic went through him, as if to say "it's the least I can do." Cerdwin knew that feeling. It was why he'd come to the mountains. It was the least he could do. But now...

There was nothing he could do to bring his sister back. There was nothing he could do to ease the pain of telling their lord father what had happened. There was nothing he could do that would temper his lord father's anger and rage over the loss of his blessed daughter after his beloved lady wife. There was nothing he could do to restore the lives of the males they'd lost on the mountainside. There was nothing he could do to ease the grief and burden it would put on whatever families they'd left behind.

That was all Cerdwin thought as they crossed the last of the sands and approached the wall. There was nothing he could do now.

Chapter 37

Unease spread under her skin as they reentered the city. There was already a small host of Elves lingering directly inside the wall: some were soldiers—but more than were necessary to maintain the boundary.

"Word spreads fast," Cethin murmured, and she nodded. It seemed her suspicion about the falcon had been correct. There would be no hiding, no standing in the shadows—not anymore.

But these soldiers also pressed their fists to their chests in homage before they helped their brothers-in-arms move the injured members of their returning party to a Healer's tent. The three Healers she saw repeated the motion, followed by a kiss to their palms and an uplifting of their hands: a release to the Gods of their fellow Healer who'd been lost.

Alaric remained there with the injured soldiers. Eldwyn joined her, Cethin, and Cerdwin—who remained in his lion's form—as they made their way to the First Commander's camp, although she suspected Cerdwin would part ways and return to the palace, to recount what had happened to his lord father. Alanna's father.

Eleonora's chest tightened. She'd never had a sibling, or a child for that matter, and Cerdwin and Eldwyn were the closest thing she had to brothers. She'd lost her mother and father. But Cerdwin had lost his mother; Lord Arel had lost his wife. Now, they'd both lost Alanna.

She closed her eyes and willed her thundering heart to steady—but it picked up again when a male—a messenger, she noted, with his brown jacket—ran up to them. "Lord Arel summons you to the palace," he said, voice steady considering the pace he must've kept to meet them there, but she heard the undertone of fear.

Cerdwin shifted back into his human form. The messenger jumped. "You may tell his lordship that his son is on his way," Cerdwin told the male, voice even.

The messenger's wide blue eyes bounced from the Second Commander, to her—and then to Cethin. "Begging your pardon, Second Commander," the male said, an edge of panic underlining his words as his attention snapped back to Cerdwin, "but you are not the only one my lord wishes to speak to. He also requests the presence of"—the male's gaze flicked back to her and Cethin—"the so-called queen and her paramour."

Eleonora hissed at the word, and the messenger stumbled back a step. A cool sea breeze kissed her cheeks, soothing the temper simmering under her skin. A breeze not from Eldwyn, she realized—but from her mate.

"Hi-his words, please," the messenger added, trembling.

"Tell my lord father," Cerdwin said, voice cool, eyes pinning the messenger to the spot, "that his son, his Commanders in Aviva's Army, his Queen, and her Consort, will see him shortly. Those exact words."

The messenger nodded and bowed, then sprinted back up the path. Cerdwin, drawn to the height and presence of his Commander's title, turned back to her and Cethin. "I will handle my lord father," he said.

"You will not have to handle him alone," she promised.

A hush followed them as they proceeded through the streets, past Elves, half-Elves, and humans alike. A few Elves pressed their fists to their chests. Some turned away, leaning toward one another, voices so many and so hushed her Elvish ears couldn't pick up their words. Eleonora pulled herself up taller, drew her shoulders back, and held her chin high. Cerdwin and Eldwyn made it look so easy, the former walking in front of her and Cethin's mount, the latter keeping pace behind them. Cethin straightened his posture as well, and she reined in a grimace. Her mate certainly hadn't been born for any of this.

I am not who you need me to be, he'd said. Was that still what he thought, even now that they were mated? Because Eleonora felt in her essence that Cethin was exactly who she needed.

Royal guards met them outside of the keep and guided them to the stables. Eleonora closed her eyes, remembering the sounds and smells of the day a kind male stablehand had helped her flee the city through those very same stables. It had been so long since she'd really been home, been in the palace as Eleonora, as royalty.

But was the palace still her home?

An older male dressed in the same uniform as the rest of the royal guard, but with golden medals and other regalia attached to his dress, met them where the stables connected to the palace. Likely the head of the royal guard, she supposed, though she didn't recognize him. He inclined his head—only to Cerdwin, she noted. "Lord Arel waits in the Lord's Hall."

A shiver went through Eleonora as they followed the male into the palace. *Home.* Yes, this was still her home: the high ceilings, the smooth and cool interior, the scent of bread and something sweet but familiar wafting through the halls. It was an effort not to turn her head this way and that, to peer into doors and out of windows, to not glance at the servants bustling through the corridors they marched down, to not see what else—who else—she might remember from her life in the palace. Her life before.

The male brought them to a halt in front of an ornately carved wooden door with images of Elvish males with books, maps, and elemental magic crafted into it. The entrance to the Lord's Hall. *That* Eleonora remembered—remembered her parents entering the space and leaving her behind for so many meetings. She hadn't been ready, they'd told her, to be a part of those gatherings. Although, it hadn't always been her parents...

"She is too young. She is not ready." She peered out of her room to see Sonia quietly arguing with her mother.

"She is heir to the throne. With Ewan gone—"

"That does not matter," Sonia snapped, and the young princess physically recoiled at the lady's maid's tone. "She is not ready to learn the reality of the situation."

"She is my *daughter," her mother said in the tone of the queen.*

"And she is his *child." Her mother's body tensed.*

"This will be her rule one day."

"Yes, and you would put the substantiality of that on her shoulders now? She is but a youngling."

"You of all people should not be one to lecture me on parenting, Mistress Sonia." Her mother's voice was cold and flat. What would Sonia know about parenting? She was a maid, both in position and in station. The young princess often thought of herself as the older woman's daughter, in a way.

"I did what was best. You forget, Your Grace—"

"I do not forget, Mistress," her mother said, voice holding a tone that brokered no room for argument.

The young princess watched the lady's maid's shoulders fall. "But you did forgive. Will you feel the same, saddling her with all of this?"

The queen sighed, then, "Eleonora?" she called out. The young princess stepped into the space, taking her time, so as not to be caught eavesdropping. Her mother knelt so they were eye level. Their eyes were so similar, though her mother's shone as if the sun were behind the blue-gray color, like the real sun behind a cloud on a gloomy day. Queen Serenity gave her a soft smile.

"I know we discussed you coming to the Lord's Council meeting today. But I do not feel you are ready yet." The young princess nodded and forced a complacent smile on her face, even as she eyed Sonia standing by the window where the Light of Aviva shone through. For, even though she'd overheard their conversation, she hadn't heard that she wasn't ready.

She'd heard she wasn't worthy.

Eleonora closed her eyes and took a deep breath. She lifted her head and chin and threw her shoulders back. She heard the doors open at three thunderous knocks. She opened her eyes.

She was worthy of being there today.

"Enter," came a male voice from within—a courtier's voice. The voice of a lord.

Lord Arel. Eleonora hadn't gotten a good look at him when she'd stormed into his chambers, armed with what had barely been the semblance of a plan. She took his full measure now, comparing it to when she'd last seen him on her coronation day: there were sharp lines across his face, and his expression and posture were cold and calculated. The years had hardened the male's appearance. And his eyes...his eyes were so different from his children's—both in color and in warmth.

She stared at him: the father of her beloved friend, the father of the Second Commander—*her* Second Commander now, she supposed. The lord didn't even give her a cursory glance. "Report," he said, leaning back in his chair—one of an expensive, decorative make—more like a throne, she noted with disgust. With his green robes—a shimmering silken material—pooling around him, his pale blond hair that touched the garment at his shoulders, and the golden circlet with a knot at the center that touched his brow, he looked every inch a lordling playing king.

Eleonora was suddenly very aware of her appearance—of Cethin's, of their whole party's—though she supposed the lord was used to seeing his son and First Commander in various states of battle-worn grime. But appearing before him covered in blood, dirt, black poison, and her mate's *scent*...

To ask the lord for her proper seat, after the death of his daughter, like this...

Eleonora felt small, like the unworthy young princess years ago.

The sound of a throat clearing caught her attention. Her eyes slipped from Lord Arel to the male seated to his right. While his fine pale-blue robes and sliver of silver marked him as a lord as well, Eleonora knew on instinct there was more to him than a courtier's life—perhaps he'd once been a warrior. This lord's eyes did find hers. A brush of familiarity crept toward her—the lord's power, reaching out to brush up against hers. It was curious. Eleonora held perfectly still—

It left as quickly as it had come, and the lord who wielded it gave her a measured look, something like approval and sorrow mingling in his eyes. She knew him, somehow—

"The northern outposts have fallen." Cerdwin was speaking. "An unfortunate but inevitable situation for us."

She wasn't sure how he didn't flinch from Lord Arel's cold stare, his empty yet vicious voice as the lord asked, "And how many were lost?"

Cethin shifted uncomfortably beside her. Candles flickered throughout the space, and the fire roaring in the hearth guttered behind the lords and their infamous table. The table was a map of their world—or what the lords recognized as their world: Aviva, and the Darkness. She heard Cerdwin's jaw tighten, his teeth grind, as he wrestled for control of his magic.

"We lost fifty-nine males and one female," Eldwyn said for him. Lord Arel drummed his fingers on the table, the clang of each like a coin dropping to the bottom of a wishing pool. It was the only noise in the room for several moments.

"I suppose that information is correct," the lord said, voice echoing in the empty space, angling his head from Commander to Commander, "if not a bit lacking in context." A shiver ran up her spine. He already knew what had happened on the mountainside.

"Would you like us to supply further context, my lord?" came Eldwyn's strong, assured voice.

Lord Arel gave Eldwyn a dark smile, but the lord seated beside him remained still, face unreadable. "I believe I have been given all the context

I need, First Commander," Lord Arel said in a silky—yet deadly—voice as he leaned forward in that beautiful chair. "But, please, enlighten us." He waved a hand toward Eldwyn.

"We were ambushed on that mountainside, my lord," the First Commander said, voice clear and even. "The enemy knew we would be there, knew our position. It would have been further slaughter, my lord, had it not been for Her Grace." Lord Arel raised an eyebrow. "Her magic drove them back, held them off, and gave us a chance to regroup and retreat. She saved the life of one of our most skilled warriors and gave our surviving wounded soldiers a chance to make the return trip."

Eleonora felt the unnamed lord's eyes on her, but didn't move her eyes from where Lord Arel sat. His countenance remained unchanged, but she felt the energy simmering beneath his courtier's mask.

"Interesting," Lord Arel said through his teeth. He stood and walked toward them—toward his son. "*I* heard that it was a sloppy, chaotic order that lost us those males." He halted right in front of Cerdwin. She wasn't sure her friend was breathing as his lord father continued. "I heard that it was an unintended, uncontrolled bit of magic that attracted more Darkness and caused us to lose our foothold in the Endurnal Mountains. That *my daughter* was *required* to give up her essence for a half-Elf." Eleonora's temper sparked at the sheer dismissal of Cerdwin's own loss in his father's words "Would you say this *context* is *accurate*, Commander?" She tensed as Cerdwin stared down his lord father. This would be the worst possible time for Cerdwin to lose control of his elemental magic or shifting. Tension, magic, anger—it was all palpable between father and son. The room became a vacuum for it.

"I would not." The words burst from her, but they had the effect she'd had been looking for: the tension simmering between the two males broke.

The lord finally turned his full attention to her. He paced down to where she stood. She heard Cethin's breathing turn steady and even—just as it did prior to a fight. *Stand down*, she willed her mate, her life-sworn, with every fiber of her being. *Wait.*

Lord Arel was taller than she was, a lord of the time before the Breaking, older, ancient. But she wouldn't diminish in his presence, no matter how small his physical presence made her feel—no matter how small he tried to make her feel. She glared up at him, trying to summon the defiance Sonia had repeatedly told her was unbecoming of a princess. She didn't care. She wasn't some wild princess to be tamed. She'd lived countless lives over the decades. She was a fighter, a warrior, and a survivor. She was the mate of the powerful and steadfast male by her side. She was the daughter of Queen Serenity, born to re-Bind the Balance. She was heir to the throne. She was Queen of Aviva.

"And you are?" Lord Arel asked, arching a brow. Her blood boiled at his tone, his arrogance, like they'd never met, like she hadn't stormed into his chambers and revealed herself as the lost princess, like he hadn't orchestrated a betrothal between her and his son, like he hadn't been there on her coronation day.

Like he hadn't sent them to die on the mountainside.

"Eleonora."

"Eleonora. Our lost princess." Eyes as sharp as emeralds—but without their sparkle—drilled into her.

"I am lost no longer. I am Eleonora, heir to Serenity's throne and Queen of Aviva."

Lord Arel's position, expression, and temperament didn't change. "The Lord's Council does not recognize your claim."

"Not at the moment," she said, holding her head high. "But I believe that both the Council *and* the people have a right to vote on the matter of any claim."

The lord's eyes narrowed. "Be that as it may, this is a time of war. The Lord's Council has every right to hold this city while a claim remains unresolved. And your claim, child, remains unresolved."

"Then resolve it," she said through her teeth, crossing her arms and shifting her weight to her left hip.

"Spoken like someone who is still nothing more than an untrained princess at best and an impressive imposter at worst," Lord Arel said, turning his back on her and stalking toward his chair again. Cethin hissed through his teeth. "In times of war it is important to keep the people united."

"It is. But it is also important to give them something to unite around," she shot back.

"The Lord's Council is enough," the male stated, leaning back in his chair. "It has been enough for fifty years. It will be enough now."

"Lord Father." Cerdwin's interjection gained both her and his lord father's attention. "I understand your hesitation," the Second Commander said, walking toward the table. "I understand your grief," he continued, splaying his hands open. "I understand change during times of war can be challenging." He looked toward the other lord, then back to his father. "But word of what happened—what *really* happened—in those mountains will spread. You will not be able to control that narrative, not entirely." Lord Arel's mouth tightened.

"Your son is right," Eldwyn agreed, and the lord stiffened. "The people need a beacon of hope. They need their queen. They need her," he said, motioning toward Eleonora. "By law, this Council is required to put her claim to a vote—whether it has had the opportunity to research her lineage or not."

Rage, unruly and wild, wove through the room like a weed. "A queen, lineage or no, is still no one and nothing without a court, regardless of her claim," Lord Arel snarled. "How do you expect to rule without one, *Your Grace*? Alone?"

Eleonora smiled. "I am not alone, *my lord*," she said, the title dripping from her lips like a Southern snake's venom. She watched his eyes widen as his former First Commander and the half-Elf his daughter had given her essence for turned away from him—toward her. As one, the two males knelt. As one, they bowed their heads to her. As one, they placed their fists over their hearts.

She motioned to them as she walked to where the lord sat—though it pained her to see Cerdwin still standing. *Would he always be torn between his loyalty to the crown and his loyalty to his family?*

"I present to you Cethin, my life-sworn and *my mate*." Lord Arel's nostrils flared, and she knew Eldwyn had pushed a breeze of her and Cethin's scents—now eternally tangled together as one—toward him. "My Consort and one of my First Guard," she finished, giving her mate a loving smile as she bestowed the new titles upon him. Unconditional love and pride sparkled in Cethin's golden eyes, and any doubts she'd had about his being there for her vanished. She turned toward Eldwyn.

"The silver wolf, my First Commander, and another member of my First Guard," she continued, "Eldwyn." She dipped her head to where he knelt on the cool stone floor, and the male returned the gesture with a smile.

"It is with great sorrow that the first member of my court, the Lady Alanna"—she watched Lord Arel's eyes flicker at the mention of his dead daughter's name—"could not be here with us. But I believe, *my lord*"—he flinched—"that this is more than a start."

"It is enough to put her claim to a vote," the other lord said, his voice one of courtly demeanor—but not cold like Lord Arel's. He inclined his head to her, and Eleonora returned the gesture. There was something so familiar about the male's face, his blue eyes, his presence—but she still couldn't place him.

"Then let us vote after this war against the Darkness is over," Lord Arel said. The other lord shook his head.

"As the law is written," he said to Lord Arel, though his focus remained on Eleonora, "any claim declared before the Council must be put to a vote—both here and with the people—and resolved, within three true days' time, unless the claimant defers."

"I do not defer my claim." *I will not defer my claim*, she glared at Lord Arel.

"Then we must move forward," the unnamed lord said. "For, as I understand it, Lord Arel, it has been far more than three days since she made her initial claim."

"You would dishonor the mourning period for those who have passed on because of this chaos? The soldiers who gave their lives for this kingdom? My daughter, who gave her essence for *that*," Lord Arel said angrily, jerking his head to where Cethin still knelt. The smell of smoke and ash filled the room, and the candles shuddered.

"I would not seek to dishonor the fallen," Eleonora snarled. "Not my soldiers, and not my lady. But I will ensure that their sacrifice for this kingdom—*my* kingdom—was not in vain." Silence fell.

"It is decided, then," the other lord said, breaking the silence. "One day and a half shall be observed for mourning, one day and a half shall be observed for the vote regarding her claim."

"So be it," Lord Arel spat, waving a hand in dismissal toward Eleonora and her court.

The other lord stood. "Until that time, they will be housed inside the palace as our honored guests—*not* in the dungeons."

Eleonora inclined her head to him again, preparing to ask his name—but a warning flashed in the lord's eyes. *Later, then.*

"Captain," the lord said, directing his attention to the male who'd remained at the closed chamber doors. The male stood at attention. "Please show Her Grace and her court to the third level."

Eleonora reached a hand down to Cethin. Her mate grasped it as he came to stand, the pride and warmth radiating from him intoxicating. Then, he and Eldwyn flanked her as they followed the captain out of the Lord's Hall and back into the winding marble corridors of the palace.

The queen was home.

Chapter 38

CERDWIN

Cerdwin had never felt more prey than predator standing between the Queen of Aviva and the Head of the Lord's Council—his friend and his lord father.

Now one was gone and had taken her court with her. And he was still standing there, alone, with his lord father—and Lord Evailel. The male had taken upon himself what Cerdwin had not been able to and openly defied Lord Arel to ensure Eleonora's claim was put to a vote. He had no doubt the male would also ensure that the vote would end in her favor, if the rumors surrounding the lord about his involvement with the royal family were true.

"I expect to see you at the mourning ceremony tomorrow." His lord father's voice jolted him from his ruminations. The mourning ceremony for the soldiers—and for his sister. Cerdwin hadn't been to a mourning ceremony since his lady mother's. He likely would've attended Queen Serenity's, had Lord Arel not sent him to Ozul years prior. He would've had more time with Eleonora if he'd been allowed to stay, gotten to know her better—not just as his friend, but as his princess. As his betrothed.

"I will be there," he confirmed, nodding at the lords. He looked at his lord father. "And what of the lady's maid? Will she also be mourned tomorrow?"

Lord Arel's expression remained unchanged. "She had no family, no close friends to speak of. She will go to the common ground."

"She was head lady's maid to the royal family," Cerdwin reminded his lord father. "Eleonora would know who she was, and your daughter tended to her through the end of her natural life. Although, between us, I am not sure how *natural* her death was." Something shifted in Lord Arel's expression, and Cerdwin reined in a combination of fury and satisfaction at the confirmation it gave him: his lord father had killed Mistress Sonia in order to hold Alanna in the city and keep her from joining the battle on the mountainside. He'd failed. But...

If Alanna had remained, would she still be alive?

Was it possible his lord father had been right to—

No. Cerdwin took a deep breath. *No.* It'd been right to go to Eleonora's aid.

"Until then, I expect you to stay close to her," Lord Arel commented, reclining in his Godsdamned chair and scheming like his child hadn't just died.

Cerdwin's lip curled. "What, exactly, would be the point of that, now that she is mated and claimed?"

Lord Arel met his gaze and waved a hand. "Just because she is claimed or mated does not mean he owns her. She is bound to her title, her crown, and her throne, first."

Cerdwin couldn't breathe—the room had gone still, as though all of the air had been sucked from it; then, just as quickly, it came alive again.

"I would caution against that," Lord Evailel commented, tone light, posture anything but. Cerdwin watched his lord father's head swivel in the male's direction. The two held one another's gazes. To Cerdwin's surprise, Lord Arel looked away first. The other lord clucked his tongue. Cerdwin wanted to toast him with a drink.

"Fine," Lord Arel said in an irritated tone. His dead green eyes returned to his son. "Stay close to her. Monitor the situation. We will revisit this conversation." Cerdwin inclined his head to both males, intending to depart, when his lord father spoke again. "Do not think for a moment, boy, that this relieves you of the duty you have to your house."

Cerdwin ground his teeth together as he straightened. "I wouldn't dare dream of it, Lord Father."

Cethin

The captain showed them several moderately sized rooms on the third level of the palace, then pointed the way to the washing rooms—much to Cethin's relief. While he'd done his fair share of reports to males and men of different status while in different states of cleanliness, he'd never felt the blood, poison, dirt, and grime of battle and death on him like he had standing in Lord Arel's presence.

The male's presence—his power—was stifling, so different from the brilliant flame of his son. It was like being held underground. Cethin had barely been able to breathe in the Lord's Hall. The tension and power had been so thick it had made the hair on his neck, the skin on his arms, raise. He'd barely been able to contain the deep, primal instinct that made him want to lunge across the table and rip out the lord's throat for the disrespect the male had shown his mate. He'd come close—too close—to losing control. He'd also known it wouldn't have served his mate's purpose at the moment. But Gods, it would've eased the tension that tightened every muscle in his body.

Cethin watched her as she walked beside him, Eldwyn on her other side as they finished their brief tour: the captain showed them where the third level led to the stairs to the passages above and below, should they wish to access the stables, dining hall, or gardens. Then, the male left them at the doors to their rooms, each right next to the other. El turned to him and then Eldwyn in silent question. They all entered the first room together.

It had simple furniture: a bed, dresser, washing basin, small table, and chair. Light curtains waved in a faint summer breeze. There were several candles, but no fireplace. The other lord in the hall may have accepted El's claim to the throne and agreed to put it to a vote, but the room wasn't one befitting a princess—and certainly not a queen. Cethin gritted his teeth and tried to shake the insults Lord Arel had thrown at her—at him—at both of them. *Insolent little man.* The curtains fluttered faster, riled by his rising temper.

"Sit." His mate's gray-blue eyes tracked him as she motioned for him to sit on the bed. She perched there beside him as Eldwyn leaned on the wall closest to the window. His mate and queen. His brother-in-arms. His court. Cethin's breathing eased, though the coiling tension in his body remained. Sitting on the bed next to her, breathing in her star-kissed scent...he could think of a few ways to work that tension out of his system. He heard her breath hitch. El knew *exactly* what he was thinking. But before he could say something indecent in front of the First Commander, the Second Commander entered the room.

Cerdwin ran a hand through his curls as he plopped into the chair across from them. "So," the lord's son said, breaking the silence that had followed, "that is my lord father."

"He's—" El started.

"A prick?" Cerdwin cut in. She laughed as Cethin took in the Second Commander's appearance: the male's usual fire seemed dim after the conversation in the hall. Still, while he might be there now, he hadn't kneeled before her in front of his lord father. He hadn't sworn his loyalty to her—not entirely.

"That's one way to put it," Eldwyn muttered under his breath.

El's laughter quieted, and Cethin turned to look at her. "I suppose now we wait," she said softly.

"Just because we're waiting doesn't mean we can't strategize," Eldwyn declared. El lifted a brow at the First Commander. "If you win this vote," the male continued, "you'll have the support and resources of Aviva to help win this war, and to find a way to re-Bind the Balance."

"And if I do not?"

"And if you do not, as unlikely as that may be"—a glare from her at that—"you won't have all of the people, or all of the resources. But there are some who will remain loyal. And you will have us," he finished.

Cethin took his mate's hand in his, but she shook her head. "If I do not," she said, voice barely more than a whisper, "all is lost." She waved her other hand at Eldwyn as the male opened his mouth to speak again. "I don't know how to explain it," she said, swallowing, "but I can feel it." Silence dominated the small space.

"I will speak with my lord father," Cerdwin said. "He may be a hard old bastard, but he must be open to reason." Cethin considered the male again as El gazed up at the Second Commander, some light returning to her eyes. *Could they trust him?*

"Thank you," she said. Clearly, she did.

"There's nothing more you can do right now," Cethin told her, squeezing her hand.

Eldwyn grunted in agreement. "There's always a break in the battle, Your Grace," the First Commander said. "The quiet before the rest of the storm."

El swallowed again, then nodded. "Then we prepare the best we can," she finally said, looking at each of them in turn.

Cethin saw it, the hope in her eyes. The hope of a people, a kingdom—a world. The hope he'd sworn with his life to protect; the hope the soldiers had sworn themselves to; the hope that had brought him and Eldwyn—their court—together. The hope of Aviva. His queen.

Eldwyn sniffed then. "May I suggest we all start with a bath?" Light flooded El's face again as she tipped her head back and laughed. It would always be the most beautiful sound Cethin had ever heard.

Eleonora

She walked into the female's main bathing area, where a long—but mercifully shallow—pool was set into the floor, and took a deep breath. A warm, heavy fog with scents of rose and sandalwood wafted in the air. The whole room was carved of the marble the castle was built into, but the coolness of the stone couldn't stop the warmth that seeped from the steaming water.

The bath, the entire suite, was empty—a small luck she was grateful for, though it was an odd time of day. Eleonora peeled off her dirty and bloodied clothing, wrinkling her nose at just how filthy her garments were—how filthy *she* was. And she had met with Lord Arel and his counterpart that way. She placed her daggers next to her clothes—they would need to be cleaned, too, she knew. Then, she descended a step into the bathing water.

Gods. It was warm and calming, its soothing scents immediately immersing her senses. She focused on that, squelching that panic that rose at the feel of water rising over her body. She took another breath and went down the next step. The bath was shallow—she wouldn't drown in it. She took a few steps to her right, to a small, rounded out space at the edge of the tub. She reached behind her and ripped the strap that held her loose braid—currently in an extreme state of disarray—at the bottom, unwove her hair, and tilted her head back, letting her curls drift in the water.

Though she hadn't sensed anyone else in the chamber, a cloth for washing and another for drying appeared beside her head, in addition to soap. Eleonora reached for the washing cloth and soap immediately. Even her hands were filthy: covered in blood—Cethin's, she recognized from the scent—and that foul, Dark poison from his wound. She scrubbed and scrubbed her hands, until they were a light shade of pink from her ministrations, then moved on to her face, arms, and legs, all covered in the same grime. She grimaced at the few small cuts along her arms, willing them closed. Her legs hadn't sustained as much injury, though they were peppered with small bruises she knew would heal quickly. And then there were the *other* areas.

She blushed at the faint ache as she washed between her legs, the memories of the pleasure, the roughness with which her mate had taken her that first time in the tent. Heat flooded her body from more than just the water, spreading up to her breasts, tingling at the mark he'd left above her left breast, above her heart. She pulled her Healing magic from those marks, willing it to work on her arms and legs instead, allowing those other marks—Cethin's claiming marks—to remain.

Eleonora took a shaky breath as she ran her hands through her hair, fingers working on the knots that had formed, wishing the Elves had what the humans in Ozul did—a substance called conditioner that helped soften and loosen tangles. She and Cethin still had so much to talk about, so much to make clear between them. Would he be her consort? Her husband? She exhaled deeply and closed her eyes, her heart beating steadily under his mark.

They would figure it out—together.

Cethin

Much to Cethin's surprise, Cerdwin joined him and Eldwyn on their way to the male's bathing chamber. Eldwyn inclined his head, allowing Cethin to enter first. A sign of respect, Cethin realized, recognizing his new status as mate to the queen. There were many things he'd have to get used to now.

He'd told her once that he was not who she needed him to be. Now, Cethin knew that was a lie. He would be everything she needed and more.

The three males stripped themselves of their gear, weapons, and clothing, and entered the pool, its warm water rising to greet them. Cethin let out a sigh as the pine-scented steam met his nose and the comfort of the bath melted some of his tension. He'd seen bathing pools like this before but had never had access to them. They'd been for his *employers*. He was used to dunking himself in a river or a water barrel when the opportunity presented itself.

"Is the bath suitable, your princeliness?" came Eldwyn's voice from across the pool. Cethin opened his eyes and used his magic to send a wave of water toward the male. Eldwyn laughed and threw his hands over his face as it sprayed him.

"It is a good thing you gained control of your magic so quickly. I thought my lord father was going to unleash his on all of us when she staked her claim," Cerdwin said quietly from where he'd re-emerged from under the water next to Cethin.

"It's a good thing he didn't," Cethin grunted as the tension that had eased upon entering the water returned.

"Ah, the primal instincts of mates," Eldwyn snorted. The male rolled his eyes and sent a splash of water back at him. "Although it is impressive how quickly you've gained control over your new abilities." Cethin sent a rushing spiral of water upward—only to watch it evaporate. He whipped his head toward Cerdwin. The male gave him a lazy smile and tilted his head back into the water. Cethin did the same, allowing the crisp smell and warmth of the water to ease that tension once more—or, as much as the pool could do for him.

"I fear my lord father's mood has only worsened and will remain that way since..." Cerdwin's voice quieted.

"I'm sorry for what she had to give," Cethin said—and meant it—as he turned toward the male.

The Second Commander inhaled sharply. "It was her choice." Cethin felt Eldwyn observing them closely from where he lounged, giving them the space they needed to speak candidly.

"I swear to you," Cethin said, looking directly into the Cerdwin's eyes, "I will not waste the gift your sister has given to me."

The male hadn't knelt before El, nor was he a member of her court. But Cerdwin deserved his respect for being there.

Alanna's essence had Healed all of his wounds—including the persistent ache in his back. Cethin started at his reflection in the water—the scar along his face was gone. Only the scar on his chest and the scar of the life oath remained—along with his mate's claiming marks. But there were cuts along Cerdwin's arms and chest, he saw, and a large bruise making its presence known on Eldwyn's neck and—no, that was a tattoo spanning the length of the First Commander's upper back; a map of sorts, but not a map of any of their known lands.

Eldwyn caught Cethin's attention. "A map of the story of the Realm of Blessings," he answered, awkwardly twisting to gesture toward the tattoo. "Many of the soldiers in our army bear the same one, though not to this scale. It's for when we pass on, so we are able to find our way back and answer the call, should our loved ones ever summon us for protection."

Cethin's eyes slid to Cerdwin, but the male shook his head. "I have never bought into that, nor had the desire to have anything inked upon my skin for eternity." The Second Commander smirked. "Plus, those lines would not blend in nearly as well with my golden fur as they do with his shaggy wolf's coat. Why ruin a perfect mane?"

Eldwyn rolled his eyes again, then began to laugh, and Cethin couldn't help but join. Though he still felt Cerdwin's raw pain—still felt his own guilt, and likely would for a long while—Gods, it felt good to laugh about something.

The three males returned to the hallway, wrapped in their drying towels. Eldwyn and Cerdwin entered their individual rooms. Cethin raised an eyebrow at the latter, which went unanswered. Then, he turned toward the remaining doors. One, to what was supposed to be his room; the other, to where they'd gathered earlier. *Her* room.

Her door wasn't locked. He slipped quietly inside, following the gentle floral aroma that mixed with the star-frosted vanilla and jasmine scent of his mate. El stood wholly naked in front of the washing basin and mirror, drying her hair. The sight of her bare, pale skin—now clean—kissed with pink patches from the bath was enough to refocus any remaining tension in Cethin's body to one spot.

He moved for her—faster than he was used to—and tossed her onto the bed, pinning her legs open wide beneath him with his knee. She gasped as Cethin spread his body over hers and pinned her wrists to the mattress.

"You would do well to lock your door, Your Grace," he purred. "You wouldn't want just *anyone* entering your room, now would you?" El tilted her head back to look up at him and bit her lip. He knew her—knew all of her tells as well as if they were his own—and kept her from pushing upward and out of his grip, his knee nudging higher, the scent of her arousal unmistakable. He noticed her smile then. "What?"

"You don't remember?" she said, voice low and teasing. Cethin shook his head, and her mouth quirked to one side. "I believe you had me in a similar position in Ozul." He frowned. "I believe you were trying to kill me—or, at the very least, take me hostage," El added, sighing heavily. "But now you can't get enough of me."

Cethin grinned and released one of her arms, trailing his hand down and down, before pressing three fingers into her wet heat, listening to her moan. He raised his now slicked fingers between them—letting her see them—and put each into his mouth, one at a time, relishing the taste of her. He felt her whole body tremble beneath his as he reached his hand back up to take hold of her wrist again. Still grinning, Cethin bent his mouth to her ear and whispered, "I believe it's *you* who can't get enough of *me*."

Willing restraint into every fiber of his being, Cethin pushed off the bed and stalked for the door. He turned his head back to watch his mate push herself up onto her elbows, her dark hair falling to one side, covering her left breast; her legs curling to her chest, hiding her sex from him.

"Yes?" he said, willing his face to remain neutral as El stared at him, her eyes shining with desire, those soft red lips parted, the scent of her teasing him, heard her breathing. She was fighting to control herself as much as he was.

It had been necessary, that first mating of theirs—that uncontrollable, raging desire they both felt for each other given life with his rebirth. Even now he felt it, throbbing inside of him. But—right now at least—it would be a game, a distraction from the outside world, the two of them trying to master their control around each other. And Cethin had no intention of losing. He turned to face her again and allowed his drying towel to slip to the floor, revealing the rest of his new body, and his...malehood. *Male.* He was a male now. That would take some getting used to. El's swallow was audible in the silence between them, but he knew it had nothing to do with the changes rebirth had brought to his body. She'd always wanted him.

"Shouldn't we discuss..." Her voice was soft and low, running its hands down his chest, his back—*Gods*, he felt it in his bones. That would take some getting used to, too—this new hold she had on him. *As though she hadn't always.*

"Yes?" he asked again, refusing to give up a step between them.

"Shouldn't we discuss our room situation?" she blurted, rising from the bed and taking one step toward him. Cethin tried to keep from smiling as she took another, then another. She finally halted, scowling up at him. She was losing, and she knew it. He would have to lay out his next moves carefully.

"I believe that should be left to the discretion of the queen," he said, matching her low tone in a way he knew would send her blood ablaze. He smirked as he watched her thighs clench together. "Don't you, Your Grace?" he added, widening his stance and giving her a slight bow. She took another step forward as he straightened, then another, bringing her directly in front of him. She tossed her already drying hair from where it clung to her skin, and her scent hit him like an unblocked blow to the face as she exposed both of her breasts to him. Cethin cocked his head to one side. She wore his mark so beautifully—and she could fight just as unfairly.

"I suppose there will be many things left up to my discretion for the rest of my life," she said, a slight heaviness to her words—but also an edge—as she ran one hand down the plane of his chest, halting at his lower abdomen.

Definitely not fair. Cethin conceded a step, closing the space between them. He took her hand and guided it to wrap around his cock.

"And what is it that you want now, El," he breathed into her ear, shaking with restraint. Her hand moved exactly how he liked it, and he was fairly sure this meant he was about to lose this round.

Then she whispered her reply. "You."

Damnit. He'd lost—but he also didn't give a fuck.

Eleonora

She wanted him—that was Eleonora's only thought as Cethin lifted her onto him and buried himself inside of her. She moaned, her hands roaming through his hair as his settled on her waist, locking her in place, his mouth already moving between her breasts, kissing, licking, teasing her above his mark. He carried her to the bed and pinned her again, seating himself inside of her to the hilt. Eleonora cried out when his teeth grazed her left nipple at that exact moment—

—and then his mouth was on hers, claiming her sounds of pleasure. And thank the Gods, because she doubted the walls were particularly soundproof. Cethin groaned loudly as his mouth broke from hers. She wove her hands around him, pulling him, needing him, deeper and deeper, wrapping her legs around him until there was no space left between them.

"Gods, El," he panted, giving her exactly what she wanted. She felt his entire self, his entire essence, deep within her, pulsing, and alive. She was panting now, too, eyes closing as a pillar of starlight swelled within her and built and built—control. She needed to control her magic, because—

"Cethin." His name and her building release were all Eleonora knew as she pulled him deeper, feeling like she might be pulled under by the very waves that dwelt within him as he crashed against her, as she found her pleasure, ripple after ripple of light ripping through her body, her senses, her essence—

She molded it, willed it to stay, to not break out into the world. She felt him then, the tidal wave of his own pleasure breaking as his name left her lips again. Her mouth found his, quieting the roar she knew would shake the foundations of the palace as her mate spilled inside of her.

Eleonora opened her eyes and stared up at the peace and joy that filled Cethin's, the love and wonder that was always in them when he looked at her. "You," she whispered again, releasing her hands and legs from where they wrapped around him as he tenderly lifted a hand and stroked her hair. "I just want you." He smiled and kissed her softly.

It was building again, that need, that unending desire that would always exist between them—

So Eleonora deepened the kiss and pulled him closer, growling, "You're mine," as she flipped her mate onto his back and took her rightful place on top of him.

Chapter 39

He supposed he'd drawn the shortest straw: he was staying in the room closest to where the mated couple slept. Well, *slept* wasn't exactly the right word for it. Eldwyn threw a wall of hard air around his room—and then, for the benefit of the entire castle, one around his queen's room as well.

There hadn't been a mated couple in centuries—at least, not as far as he could recall from the hours he'd spent poring over books as a youngling. He supposed that was because most of the books he'd read had been about magic. But what was a love that deep, if not magic itself?

The late king and queen, Eleonora's parents, hadn't been mates, but they'd still borne her as the result of their union. Royal babes were precious. Typically, only one or two were born as the promise of the future of a kingdom—unlike in mortal cities, where queens sired multiple heirs. In those cities, queens even rode into battle pregnant—something that would never happen in Aviva. Royal Elvish babes were too valuable—protected at all costs. But even non-mated love seemed more like a blessing than a curse to Eldwyn.

Cerdwin had put a smile on his face and openly defied his father earlier, but Eldwyn knew the male was in deep pain—pain over the loss of his mother, now amplified by the loss of his sister, and the situation he was in: between his father's plan and what Alanna had known was right.

But if Alanna hadn't encouraged Cerdwin to go with her, would the male still have come? What was done was done—it didn't matter.

But how would Cerdwin cope? Eldwyn sighed and brushed back the curtains. He rarely stayed in the palace, preferred to be out in the camp with his males. That would be Alaric's responsibility now. His was to remain with his queen—but he missed it. Something about the palace was stifling. *Was that how Cerdwin had felt growing up? Why he'd made the choices he had?* Not that it excused the male, but, on some level, Eldwyn understood.

And he understood—not just understood but knew—that Cerdwin would need time to process. To grieve.

To heal.

Cerdwin

He was alone—and not just alone in his room. Cerdwin was utterly and entirely alone. His sister, his twin whom he'd shared a womb—significant part of his life—with, was gone. That connection, that bond between them, severed forever. And knowing she wasn't in the Realm of Blessings, that she was stuck in the Otherworld—also alone—was a whole new level of pain and grief. Pain and grief that rubbed at the old wound of the loss of his lady mother.

Alanna had convinced him to come with her, had convinced him that—family loyalty be damned—this was wrong. That some things were more important. That Eleonora was more important. And he'd listened.

Cerdwin had always listened to Alanna. Sometimes, he'd *only* listened to Alanna. This time, listening to her, allowing himself to combine his magic to support Eleonora's, all so she could save *him*, so his sister could give away her life for *him*...

In that moment—and the hours that had followed—there hadn't been time to truly think about it. But now—alone—in a room that was his—alone—Cerdwin had nothing to do but think about it. Alone.

She saved him...She said—said there was a reason for it. The garbled words Eleonora had spoken to him floated around in his mind. *But why save Cethin?* He was—or at least, had been—a half-Elf. One life-sworn to Eleonora, of course, but that oath only went one way. Had Alanna known? Had she known that they were mates?

Cerdwin closed the curtains and sank down on a chair near the bed. That seemed impossible for many reasons—including the fact that there hadn't been mates in a very, very long time. He looked back in his mind over the Histories of Aviva he'd studied as a child. As far as he knew, the last mated couple had been around five hundred years before their time. Most knowledge surrounding the mating bond had been lost. Alanna had spent a lot of time Healing both of them, though. *Had she seen something in their minds or hearts that indicated their status as mates?*

Cerdwin sighed and tipped his head back, turning it to the side. His hair stood out against the royal blue fabric that covered the furniture—the blue of the royal house. Not his own house, which he would be solely responsible for now that his sister was well and truly gone. The heaviness of that responsibility weighed on his shoulders—it always had.

Cerdwin closed his eyes and allowed his thoughts to drift to the time he'd spent in Ozul—the first time he'd really felt free. Away from the palace. Away from his lord father. Away from a future he hadn't asked for. It had taken time for Cerdwin to acclimate to the mortal world, but despite the differences between their cultures, he'd come to respect the way they lived. It was liberating—it was free. They chose where they lived; they chose how they made a living; they chose who they loved.

That thought sent the rest of Cerdwin's memories scattering—replaced by memories of quiet words exchanged, kisses and touches given in secret. With *him*. That future, that love that had never really been a possibility, was also truly well and gone now.

Tears fell. It was an odd sensation for someone who'd been born with fire in their veins. But they fell nonetheless. His lady mother was gone. His sister was gone. His future—the future he would've chosen for himself—was gone.

Court or no court, lord father or no lord father, Cerdwin was alone.

Eleonora

She couldn't recall the last time she'd slept so well. Maybe in Ozul, where there was true night—or on the ship, on her way back to Aviva with Cethin. But even then Eleonora didn't remember having slept so soundly or waking up and feeling luxurious contentment through her entire body. She had no doubt it was a combination of the breezy curtains that faced her from across the room, the cool air from the marble space, the firm yet comfortable bedding and pillows, the soft blankets—and, of course, the male she shared that bed with. Cethin was still asleep, his arms wound around her chest and stomach, his legs tangled with hers.

She used the Light of Aviva peeking through the curtains to study the planes of her mate's face, so peaceful in sleep: eyes softly closed, mouth slightly parted, hair resting against his cheek. A different face than she'd come to know during their time together until...until he'd died. Even thinking about it shot fear and panic through her heart like a fiery arrow. But Alanna had saved him. And now, the ears that had once been rounded were pointed—she could see one poking up through his dark hair; the skin that had been warm practically glowed. But the only thing that mattered to Eleonora was that Cethin was there—he was alive.

She traced her fingers down her mate's cheek, until her hand rested on his partially concealed chest—on the scar over his heart. Golden eyes fluttered open, as though her touch had been a call to wake. "Hi," she said quietly, and Cethin smiled—a real smile.

"Hi," he said, and every pore of her body was thrilled at that one word, that one smile. He placed his hand over hers and brushed a soft kiss against her lips. One soft kiss was all it took for heat to pour into her body, for any space they weren't touching to become cold and unbearable. She felt his wicked smile against her lips as he rolled her onto her back, claiming his place on top of her. "So very demanding, Your Grace," Cethin whispered as he began a sweep of kisses from her temple to her collarbone.

She reached for him, but Cethin pulled back and began a trail of kisses across her breasts, tugging on the left one with his teeth where his claiming mark remained. She sucked in a sharp breath, feeling heat and wetness pool in her core, rubbing her legs together for any friction. Cethin stopped her with his knee as he continued trailing kisses down her stomach—then lower, pausing at the apex of her thighs. He held her gaze as he pressed a kiss there. She grasped the soft sheets of their bedding, toes curling with anticipation—

A knock sounded at the door. "Eleonora, are you awake?"

Eldwyn. Cethin held her gaze as he licked straight up her center. She shuddered and tried to rein in her very loud moan that was *not* a queenly response to the First Commander's question.

"She's awake," Cethin said, voice rough and heady with desire. "But she's currently occupied." His tongue made a second pass between her legs, and she bowed off the bed, wanting more, needing more.

"Be that as it may," came the First Commander's amused voice, "this can't wait."

Cethin's mouth closed around the sensitive bundle of nerves at her center, and Eleonora gasped. "I think Her Grace would disagree," her mate said as he pulled away.

Eldwyn made a noise that sounded like a pointed cough, and Eleonora closed her eyes. She was going to murder him for this. "One moment, Eldwyn," she said, voice unsteady as Cethin's teeth scraped the spot again. She eased herself up the bed and away from her mate, then patted the space next to her. Cethin let out a low growl—that she silenced with a look—then mercifully pulled himself up into a seated position. She grabbed the robe that had appeared next to the bed and quickly tied the satin sash around her waist. Cethin didn't dress, simply pulled the bedding over his lower half, reclining with a gleam in his eyes that told her that this wasn't over. "Come in," she called to Eldwyn. Cethin licked his lips, and her body thrummed. *No, this* definitely *wasn't over.*

The First Commander entered their room carrying what looked like three body bags over one shoulder and a small box in his hands. He wore a simple white tunic and brown breeches—not what he would be wearing to the mourning services, when all of Aviva would be dressed in black. "Sorry to disturb your morning activities," he said by way of greeting with a wink, earning himself a dark look and low snarl from Cethin.

She raised an eyebrow. "With all of your reading and Histories, I would assume you'd know better than to bait a male in front of his mate." Even with her limited knowledge of mates she knew that much.

Eldwyn rolled his eyes but inclined his head in Cethin's direction. "He knows, as should you, that I am no threat to your bond—or your relationship, for that matter." She softened at his words: they had nothing to do with Eldwyn's personal preferences, but the love he bore in his heart for another.

"Cethin," she murmured. She heard him relax—ever so slightly—on the bed. "What did you need to discuss with me?" she asked Eldwyn, eyeing the bags and box he'd brought.

"With both of you, actually," Eldwyn replied as he tossed the bags onto the chair. "But we'll start with you." He handed her the box. It was a simple wooden box, one she might have mistaken for holding herbs or spices. But that wasn't what lay within—no, within the box was an elegant circlet crafted from silver, with diamonds scattered around the band. Diamonds that...

"They look like tiny hearts," she mused, moving the jewelry in the Light.

Eldwyn nodded. "My males found it"—he cleared his throat—"when we did a sweep of the Royal Archives this morning, to see what remained of your effects as heir to the throne." She grinned, knowing he meant himself and Alaric, and that—*technically*—they'd stolen them. But was it really stealing when they were heirlooms of *her* royal house? "They belong to you," the First Commander said softly, as if he could read her thoughts.

Eleonora had never seen the circlet, but her mother had owned so many pieces it was impossible for her to remember all of them. "It's beautiful," she whispered, meeting his gaze. "Thank you."

"I want you to wear it today. It's time the people saw their queen wearing a crown."

Tears spilled down her cheeks as she reached up and hugged the First Commander. "Thank you," she said again, pulling away and wiping the tears from her face. She knew that Cethin monitored every movement she made, every emotion that swept through her, though he remained still. She threw her mate a grateful smile as she placed the circlet atop the bedside table.

"Now this," Eldwyn continued, grabbing one of the bags, "is for Cethin."

She opened the bag to find nothing but white and gold material inside. "Is this..."

Eldwyn nodded. "The uniform of the First Guard." He tilted his head, studying Cethin. "It's rare for a consort to also step into this role. So rare, in fact, it's the first time I've heard of it—even with all of my reading." He gave her a wink. She rolled her eyes at him.

"And what role am I to play today?" she heard her mate ask quietly. It was a fair question. What role would he play at the mourning service? Would he be her consort? Her First Guard? Both?

"That's up to you," Eldwyn said. Eleonora watched the males. Cethin nodded once, and Eldwyn inclined his head again. Whether it was due to their combined magical defense in the mountains or because Cethin now acknowledged everything Eldwyn had done to protect her or because they'd both sworn themselves to her, some bond, some friendship had taken root there, and she was grateful for it.

Cethin's eyes shifted to hers. "It's up to you," she said. She wouldn't allow the words he'd spoken once in anger—that he could never be what she needed—ring true. His eyes softened, and an ocean breeze tousled her unbound hair in affection.

"What are you wearing today?" her mate asked the First Commander, though his gaze remained on her, his earlier promises blazing in his golden eyes.

"The complete uniform of the First Guard," the male instantly replied. "Even though she hasn't been voted in by the Council and the people yet, she is queen by birth and right. The people should see that she already has a court around her."

"And what about..." Cethin didn't finish his sentence, and Eleonora sensed the distrust her mate still had toward Cerdwin for not coming to their aid sooner.

"That will be his choice, too," Eldwyn said smoothly. Cethin's mouth became a thin, hard line.

"As it should be," Eleonora said, reaching out a hand to her mate. Cethin's features softened once more, and he began to brush idle, lazy strokes over her palm. Strokes that she knew he would repeat elsewhere, not only with his hand, but also with his mouth, and—

"I guess it's time to make myself scarce," came Eldwyn's chuckle, pulling her back to the current moment and what they'd been talking about: clothes.

"What will I wear?" she asked.

Eldwyn grinned. "We found something for you, too." The First Commander brushed an invisible speck of dust off his shoulder. "That is, if you'll both be present later this morning." Another grumble from Cethin.

"We will be," she said, firmly gripping Cethin's hand. "Thank you," she told Eldwyn again. The male gave her another wink, hefted the other two bags over his shoulder, and was gone.

She felt Cethin rise up behind her. He pulled her into his lap as she studied the circlet on her bedside table. "A rare gift for a rare female," he said against her skin, picking it up and placing it atop her brow. "Beautiful El," he breathed, and she twisted to face him, heat rising to her cheeks. Her mate's gaze dropped to her mouth—then her robe. He tugged the sash free, and the cool material fell away from her. "Always beautiful," he said, planting a kiss to his claiming mark over her breast. Her skin hummed at the contact, every warm and lustful thought rushing back in an instant. She made to reach for the circlet and remove it, but he lifted a hand, stopping her. "Leave it on," he said, mouth moving from her breast to just below her ear. She sucked in a tight breath.

"Remember," Cethin whispered, that hand beginning those same lazy, idle strokes up and down her thigh, "you are their queen out there, Your Grace. But in here..."

He moved so suddenly she barely registered the motion. She looked down to see him on his knees at the side of the bed, spreading her legs open.

"In here, you are *mine*."

Eldwyn

Eldwyn chuckled as he walked down the hall, putting the wind shield he'd momentarily taken down back up around Eleonora's room. He'd known *exactly* what he was interrupting and had been more than ready to take the brunt of Cethin's wrath and frustration. That was something the male would have to learn to cope with now that he wasn't just a full-blooded Elf in love—one who'd claimed a female and been claimed in return—but a mated one.

Eldwyn had noted that there wasn't any new information on mated pairings while he'd scoured the Royal Archives with Alaric that morning, but he recalled some of what he'd overheard the older Elves—those who did remember—speak of: the intensity of the bond, especially when it was new, often led the male—or either partner—to be intensely protective and defensive of their mate, and both sides of the partnership would be insatiable when it came to, well, *morning activities*. Except they would be morning, noon, *and* night activities. For most mates, those feelings would linger at their highest intensity for a few weeks, and then the couple would learn to better control themselves. But for a newly mated pair, where one was of royal blood? The Gods only knew how long that would take. Eldwyn just hoped they both left themselves enough time to wash and dress before the mourning ceremony.

He paused outside Cerdwin's door with the intention of offering the male the other First Guard uniform. He listened intently but could neither hear nor scent any sign of the male's presence. Knocking softly, Eldwyn entered the space. Cerdwin wasn't there—and his bed was made, as though he hadn't slept there. Eldwyn set the uniform on the chair, then left the room and headed down the stairs and out to the yard. The only other place he could imagine Cerdwin sleeping or going to so early was the camp—*certainly he hadn't gone back to House Satrara for the fake night?*

Eldwyn made his way quickly through the city in the early fake morning, as most of its citizens hadn't risen yet; though some had evidently been awake during the fake night: black banners hung from the homes of those who'd lost someone during the battle on the mountainside. He knew them—had been the one to deliver the news. As First Commander, Eldwyn had plenty of experience delivering difficult news to families, friends, and lovers. But there'd been something different about it this time, due to word of Eleonora spreading throughout the city. He was no longer just the First Commander—someone their loved ones had been under the orders of—but someone who knew their queen.

Eldwyn quickened his pace as he made his way through the Second Commander's camp. Most of the soldiers had already been up for some time working on their early morning duties. They paused as he walked by to either offer him a salute or a fist over their heart. It was the latter he marked—the latter who acknowledged loyalty not only to him, but to her.

When he arrived at Cerdwin's pavilion, it, too, was empty. Eldwyn sighed, frustrated, and sat down on the ornate—yet comfortable—chair behind Cerdwin's map table. Where in the Otherworld was he?

Cerdwin

Cerdwin hadn't slept. He supposed that was normal—he hadn't slept after his lady mother had died, either. Alanna had been there for him then.

Now, he was alone. The thought repeated itself in his head, over and over again. He was alone. So he'd gone somewhere he knew he wouldn't be alone—and, at the same time, somewhere no one would think to look for him.

He didn't visit the Healer's quarter's often—the mystique of the place had always unnerved him, so many smells weaving together from the various plants and herbs the Healers grew and the ingredients they prepared. Far too many of them reminded him of tending to himself or his males.

The day their lady mother had died.

The place opened old wounds—but Cerdwin had gone there for a different kind of healing.

The Healers who were already awake—either to work in the complex garden on the terrace that jutted out from the palace, or to tend to their patients in the wing below—didn't acknowledge him, his rank, or his noble status. There was no rank there—not amongst those the Healers considered outsiders. There were only people, and anyone could fall victim to an injury or illness.

Cerdwin made his way down the long, dark hall that ran toward the heart of the palace. More than anyone else in Aviva, the Healers needed sleep, so they dwelled in that space, where none of the Light that shone so brightly over the city made its way inside—another piece of the quarters that unnerved him. Yes, his family's quarters had night curtains, and his Second Commander's pavilion was well insulated, but nothing compared to the blackness of being so deep inside of the mountain. Alanna was so talented, her Healing gift so strong, that she'd been offered the final room at the very end of the hall: the most restful of all. Cerdwin remembered she hadn't been very happy about it because it made for a longer walk to the gardens and her patients. But it was a high honor to be given that room. He'd urged her to accept it.

He took a deep breath and placed his hand on the door, gently pushing it open. The soft eucalyptus fragrance that often mingled with his twin's natural scent filled the space, soothing him and scattering his preoccupations.

He wasn't alone here. He was with his sister.

Eleonora

She managed to get ready—barely. Cethin ordered a private bath to their adjoining bathing chamber, and she'd enjoyed about five minutes in the warm water alone before he'd joined her. They'd washed together, and she'd forever remember the way his fingers worked soap and water through her hair, rinsing it clean, pulling the tangles apart. Her mate.

Cethin worked with his magic as they bathed, learning that he could heat and cool the water with a thought. He also sent droplets of it flying through the air like rain and created small waves in the tub. His control over his magic was astounding, and she had to admit to herself that she was slightly jealous. But it wasn't what was most important—what was most important was that he was alive.

He's alive, she told herself, over and over again. Cethin was alive, immortal, and blessed with magic. Her mate.

It made what they were about to do feel that much more difficult.

She dressed while Cethin contemplated what to wear to the mourning service from the additional selection Eldwyn had brought. In the end, he decided on a plain black pair of pants with polished black boots and a black tunic with silver thread that matched the silver woven into the mourning gown Eldwyn had left her. While Cethin would wear no crown—as she was not yet fully recognized by the Lord's Council, and he had not yet formally asked her to be his wife—there would be no mistaking him for anything besides her other half.

Her mate also elected to wear the white cloak of the First Guard. It contrasted starkly against the black mourning clothing, making his golden skin glow. When he'd asked her what she thought of the pairing, she'd merely said what Eldwyn had: that this was a first—his occupation as both future consort and First Guard. It would be up to them to create the rules. And, while wearing a color other than black—or at the very least a dark color—to a mourning ceremony typically wasn't done, this was an important exception, as it would be for any First Guard.

Memories of the day she'd walked with the First Guard to bury her mother threatened to spill into her thoughts. It was an effort to keep them and her tears at bay as she dressed, pulling the locket she'd carried through Aviva and Ozul around her neck. But she knew her mate read her every emotion as he tugged her into a tight embrace. His warmth, his ocean-kissed scent, the feel of his body around hers, was the greatest comfort, the greatest blessing she could've ever dreamed to know. When he released her and tilted her head back to brush a soft kiss against her lips, she began crying in earnest. Alanna had given her a gift beyond measure. Now, she would have to say her final goodbye to the brave and talented Healer. They all would.

Cerdwin would.

Cethin finished helping her dress. The fingers he brushed against her back as he buttoned the black fabric together were a soft promise of how he would comfort her later, the thought sending a tingle of warmth down her spine. He gently placed the circlet of diamond hearts on her brow—the diadem holding her mourning veil in place—then spun her around. Her silk skirts swished, her breasts swaying in the low-cut gown as she moved. She saw the appreciative gleam in his eyes. But she also felt the trepidation and uncertainty that flowed from him, about where they were about to go, who they would see, what would happen.

So Eleonora brought her mate's hand to her heart, and whispered in his ear what they would do.

Cethin

He sighed in relief—Eldwyn was wearing the full, all-white uniform of the First Guard. He felt less out of place in his cape. *Gods, how ridiculous was it to feel concerned about fashion?* But that would be one of the many, *many* things he would be judged on today.

Cethin shifted in his boots—which were a tad uncomfortable compared to the travel-worn boots he'd worn for fifty some years—and tried to ground himself in the confidence that had always been an instinctive part of his essence. But that had been before. A cool breeze that almost reminded him of his own sea breeze brushed his shoulders. He glanced up at the male whom he trusted with his mate most after himself. Eldwyn gave him a small bow and the flash of a grin.

Princeliness, the wind whispered in his ear. Cethin opened his mouth to retort, but the door to their bedchamber opened and El joined them. "Your Grace," Eldwyn said—out loud, this time—offering her a bow and his arm, which she took. The male threw a cheeky wink in Cethin's direction, but was solemn as he turned back to El. "I've seen to it that an additional member of your court is honored at today's service—Sonia."

Her former lady's maid, Eldwyn's voice said into his ear. *From when she was the princess.* Cethin didn't take his eyes off his mate as her expression shifted. Then, El let out an anguished sob that pierced his heart as she slid to the floor.

Eleonora

She wasn't sure what noise she made—if she made any sound at all. But she found herself on the floor, her mate's arms wrapped around her, supporting her.

Sonia. Her former lady's maid, the mortal women who'd somehow taken her memories—who was the only one who could explain her fifty-odd years in exile—was gone.

"I want to wear it," she argued with the lady's maid.

"It is simply not proper," the female told her sternly, if not a bit apprehensively. "The traditional mourning dress—"

"My mother—who we are mourning today—was the one who gave it to me," the young princess said, hating how her voice shook with anger and sadness, tears stinging her eyes. She fought to hold them back. She couldn't show weakness. She was going to be queen. Queens didn't cry.

"I understand, Your Highness, but protocol—"

"What seems to be the issue?" A mixture of relief and tension flooded the young princess as her mother's head lady's maid—now her head lady's maid, she supposed—Sonia, stepped up to the dressing platform.

"She wants to wear jewelry," the other lady's maid sighed, as though the situation were one of her life's greatest disappointments.

Sonia eyed her, the silver locket in her hand, and arched a dark brow at the female. "And?"

"I—" The other lady's maid swallowed. "It is not typically part of the traditional mourning dress."

"I am aware of the traditional mourning dress, Lyona." Silence stretched between the two.

"Perhaps it would be alright, since it was given to Her Highness by the one passed?" the female said, lowering her eyes.

"Why, perhaps it would," Sonia replied in a tone that suggested the female had just discovered something as simple as the ceiling above them. The young princess almost smiled, even on the day of her mother's—her last living relative's—funeral.

Time warped and steadied around her, until her tears slowed. Holding on to her mate, Eleonora rose to her feet. "We should go."

"We only go when you're ready," Cethin told her firmly, wiping those tears away and pressing a kiss to her brow.

She shook her head. "Today isn't just for me and who I've lost."

It was for all of them.

Chapter 40

Cethin

They walked to the burial grounds—The Meadows—in silence. Most of the friends and family of the deceased were already there, or on their way.

And the nobility obligated to Lord Arel.

Nerves filled Cethin. What would it be like to see the lord who'd so easily dismissed his children—one of whom had given all of herself so that he might live? The lord who'd dismissed El—her claim to the crown and the throne?

Frustration crept through Cethin's veins like the calm before a storm as he walked in pace with her, shouldering her sorrow and grief—her own anticipation of what would come next. She hadn't faltered in the lord's presence in the hall—she wouldn't falter in front of her people today.

"Perfect," he'd murmured when El had told him her plan for the end of the mourning service. A flush had colored her cheeks when he'd reached up a hand to brush her locket and the secret it held. That blush wasn't just from his words of praise or touch, he knew—it was from his presence. He was alive, and she was his—and he was hers—for eternity, and even an hour after.

But the heaviness of the day made his chest tighten. He was partly to blame for the pain they were all feeling. Guilt had given him restless sleep, though he didn't think El had noticed—he'd left her sated enough to ensure she'd slept soundly. His lips curved upward at that, and he could've sworn he heard a sharp intake of breath from where she walked at his left—and an exasperated sigh from Eldwyn at her right. But even the very thorough worship of his mate's body hadn't been enough to drive out memories of the Otherworld, the final words Alanna had spoken to him, or the grief of those around him.

Cethin had no doubt that facing Cerdwin would be difficult. No matter how much he despised the male for going along with his lord father's idiot plan—one that would've gotten them all killed had Alanna not convinced her twin to come—he did feel sympathy for the Second Commander, for his loss. Blood was blood.

It was why Cethin still wished for his mother, even though he barely remembered anything about her, and his father, whom he'd never met, as far as he remembered. He wasn't sure how much his *blood was blood* sentiment would extend if he ever met either of them—the parents who'd abandoned him. If either were still alive.

He also didn't hold Cerdwin responsible for his wounds—or for the choice Alanna had made to save him. He only blamed himself.

Seeing El, breathing in her scent, hearing her laugh, seeing her smile, and joining his body together with hers was the only cure for his guilt. Cethin looked at her again. The Light of Aviva set the diamonds sparkling around her dark hair, which she'd left unbound and flowing down her back with her mourning veil; like true day and true night itself. Then, he looked to the male farther to his left. The one who made him feel less uncomfortable wearing the First Guard uniform.

The dress was striking on Eldwyn's figure, making his presence that much more unmistakable. The male offered Cethin a small, sad smile and a nod, which Cethin returned, knowing full well what Eldwyn was saying: Cethin was El's life-sworn, her mate, her consort-to-be, and her First Guard. He would protect her until his last breath. But Eldwyn would be there to ensure that that never happened—that Cethin would have a partner in protecting her. The male wasn't her life-sworn, mate, or future king, but he was her First Guard, her First Commander, and her friend. Eldwyn would guard El with his life, and by extension, Cethin's.

Absorbing Eldwyn's presence with Elvish senses was...interesting. Although Cethin couldn't read the male like he could read his mate, he could note the details, the tells, and the shifts that he hadn't been able to read before—even as a highly skilled mercenary. But as Eldwyn looked to the unpaved path ahead, to the others making their way toward the burial grounds, Cethin didn't need any heightened senses to recognize the tension in the First Commander's body.

Cerdwin

He was wearing a black mourning suit threaded with the green and gold of his house—no trace of the Second Commander's uniform, although it would've been acceptable, considering the males who'd died on the mountain were also technically his.

Cerdwin had selected his clothing after he'd visited Alanna's room. He might support Eleonora—as his sister would've wanted—but today wasn't about her. It was about his family.

He watched as the court approached the burial grounds: Eleonora in a silk black gown and matching veil secured by a small band of diamonds around her brow—*that* would certainly send a message to his lord father—to all of the Lord's Council present; Cethin, the silver thread of his tunic a match to that woven through the bodice of her gown. The male wore no crown and looked slightly absurd with the white cloak of the First Guard flowing behind him, but there was no mistaking him for who he was to Eleonora, nor she to him—not as he took her hand in his and pressed a kiss to it. *Mates*—there would never be mistaking them as anything otherwise, no matter how strongly his lord father wished there were.

A brush of air touched Cerdwin's skin. He knew where Eldwyn would be without even looking. But he did. The male's expression was a heavy stare, a mixture of sorrow, grief, and guilt—and challenge, a warning to rein in the emotion Cerdwin knew burned in his eyes. Eldwyn knew him all too well. Cerdwin's jaw tightened as he squeezed his eyes closed, willing himself not to shift or light the grass on fire. A cool, soothing breeze wafted toward him—this one like the feeling of calm when the first stars spread across the night sky in Ozul—along with that damn mated scent. He opened his eyes to see that Eleonora had stepped away from her court and stopped directly in front of him.

She hadn't asked him to kneel when she'd staked her claim in front of his lord father—when Eldwyn and Cethin had sworn their loyalty. She wouldn't do that here, either. He knew her—this wasn't a test. It was a peace offering. Knew it as she brushed away the hot, angry tear streaking down his face, just as silent tears streamed down her own.

Eleonora didn't say a word, gave no command; she simply swept him into a hug. Through his anger, grief, and guilt, Cerdwin felt some of the familiarity between them—the way things had been in Ozul, before he'd returned to Aviva, before she'd come back and so much had changed between them. He gently squeezed back before she pulled away and took her place between the two males who'd so easily, so freely, sworn their loyalty to her.

A different kind of grief overcame Cerdwin then: it had been so simple for them to make that choice.

He watched as the court made their way down the path to the larger garden where the fallen soldiers would be honored. Their absence left space for the nobles who'd gathered to come forward and offer their sympathies, though Cerdwin didn't fail to notice the many eyes that followed Eleonora as she disappeared behind a large tree.

He shook his head and pulled himself back to his purpose. It didn't matter how hollow the nobles' words sounded. He was there to say goodbye to his sister.

Eldwyn

Cerdwin hadn't worn the uniform of the First Guard. Eldwyn heaved a sigh as he, Eleonora, and Cethin made their way to the larger space where the males under his command would be honored for their service. Families and friends of the fallen lined the foot-worn path. He inclined his head to each person as they passed, but Eleonora stopped walking, tears flowing freely down her cheeks as she took a crying female—the wife of one of his soldiers, Eldwyn recognized—into an embrace. He allowed the shield of air he'd placed around her and Cethin to drop slightly, just as he had when she'd approached Cerdwin. It was the only way he could really protect her here: magic.

Weapons weren't permitted in The Meadows—neither was violence of any kind—but he'd seen the anger mixing with the pain in Cerdwin's eyes when the male had beheld Cethin. Eleonora had handled that well, just as she was handling this well—a situation Eldwyn cursed himself for not thinking to prepare her for. But the lost princess was a natural queen.

He watched as she clasped the female's hands between hers, as their gazes met, her blue gray to the female's violet. A soothing quiet overtook them. He scented Eleonora's moonlit jasmine—with Cethin's salt and spice—around them. The female closed her eyes. Eleonora hugged her again fiercely—saying something even his wind couldn't make out—and stepped back. The female bowed to the queen with a small smile. Eleonora returned the gesture, surprising him, but he felt Cethin radiating pride next to him.

They continued down the path that way, with Eleonora stopping to comfort the people. She looked every inch a queen, the Light of Aviva setting the diamonds on her brow sparkling. But the light shifted as time passed. Eldwyn glanced up. The Light of Aviva overpowered everything, but he saw dark clouds gathering behind it—not clouds of true Darkness, but clouds threatening a summer storm.

Eleonora

She continued down the line of her people, going from one side to the other; spreading the calming energy of her Healing gift in the air; extending what comfort she could to the families of the fallen soldiers—especially the children. She hugged them the tightest. She knew it probably wasn't proper, but it was something she wanted to do.

She gave Eldwyn a quick look of gratitude for loosening the tight wall of air she knew he'd put around them the second they'd left the palace. These people—*her* people—had lost loved ones because of her. They'd likely lose more before the war ended—the war that hadn't even truly begun. So she wore her heart for each of them to see as she embraced them: to let them know who she was; that she felt their grief deeply; that their pain wouldn't go unanswered. Not all of them bowed. Not all of them showed an awareness that a queen offered them comfort. But she didn't care. This wasn't about her. This was about them.

Farther down the path, removed from the common folk, was Lord Arel. Though there was no formal separation, no defining line between status or class in The Meadows—except for the royal family, she supposed, musing over that detail—he'd managed to set himself apart, to set his daughter's empty casket apart. The nobility who'd entered The Meadows behind them—and long since passed them as she'd acknowledged each fallen soldier's family—stood around the male. She took a deep breath as she approached him.

"My lord," she said, inclining her head to him. "I am sorry for your loss." Lord Arel turned his attention from the noble he'd been speaking with and met her gaze. There was no real sorrow in his eyes—no tears. Just pain—pain layered over with malice. A small part of her was relieved to see it and know the lord for who he truly was. Another part of her was sad for him, the male who'd lost his wife, and now, his daughter.

He didn't speak, though she waited. But it didn't matter. Music to honor the fallen began to play.

Cethin

Cethin was going to kill the lord and bury him where he stood. It would be easy enough—they were already in a cemetery. There was no sadness, no regret in Lord Arel's eyes—no, there was nothing but rage and disdain in the lord's features. And all of it was directed at his mate. Cethin wished he'd been allowed to bring his weapons.

Easy, Eldwyn whispered in his ear. Cethin took a deep breath. Controlling his magic since becoming a fully-blooded Elf had been an easy task. Cethin wasn't sure why, but he wasn't about to complain. Controlling his emotions any time someone so much as looked at his mate wrong—that was far more complex.

She can handle herself, he told that ancient, primal part of him that wanted to rip the male who'd put her life in danger to shreds. Just as she'd handled herself beautifully on the path there, when he hadn't been able to do anything but watch in awe as she'd embraced each person who'd lost someone.

Fortunately for Lord Arel, music started before he could say anything that would damn him—or, rather, damn him further—in Cethin's eyes. Cethin took El's hand and brushed a kiss against it as she returned to his side. She gave him a small smile. Gods, she was beautiful. Even in a place of sorrow, in a sea of black, she was a light.

The Avivan army's musicians wove magic in the air with their playing; the music ebbed and flowed—as did the sounds of those the dead had left behind. It was startling to see those musicians—Alaric among them—trade their weapons for instruments. A few mourners pointed at the sky: it was an eerie shade of gold. Someone nearby whispered it was an omen from the Gods—their sorrow over those who'd been lost to the Otherworld bleeding into their world, especially the Healer.

It was almost time.

El took a deep breath beside him, and Cethin tightened his grip on her hand, watching as she reached for her locket. She peered over her shoulder at him and nodded.

The sky turned to silver.

Her other hand grasped his, and then she raised their joined hands, the petal of the *dianaflora* she'd taken from the cave between their closed palms.

Rain began to fall—not just any rain, but rain pulled from the tides of the sea.

Rain that brought healing.

Rain that brought hope.

It sent the site around them scattering into hundreds of rainbows, each made by that rain and the Light of Aviva, setting the Darkness, sorrow, and grief around them into new light and new color.

As the rain fell on the earth where the soldiers would have been buried—where Alanna would have found peace, where Sonia had been laid to rest—*dianaflora* sprung up from the ground.

Eldwyn

It was beautiful—absolutely beautiful, magical, and wonderful all at the same time, Eldwyn thought, as he took in the vibrant colors and flowers all around them. And it was all for them—from her.

Murmurs spread through the assembled crowd. Some fell to their knees, fists to their hearts as they looked toward where Eleonora and Cethin stood, hands still clasped and raised above them. Not all—especially amongst the nobility—but so, so many. Then the cry went out. "The Light of Aviva has returned! The Light of Aviva will restore hope!" Again and again the people called out—including more of the soldiers under his and Cerdwin's command. But Eleonora didn't seem fazed by it; nor, to his credit, did Cethin.

Eldwyn watched as Eleonora dropped her mate's hand and walked alone toward Alanna's empty coffin. She went to her knees—showing them all that this wasn't about her. This was about the fallen. The soldiers. The Healer. The lady's maid.

This was about her people.

He watched as Cethin joined her, bowing his head toward the symbol of the departed female, the female who'd given her essence so that he might live—and live fully—by his mate's side. A symbol of hope—and of change.

Eldwyn shifted his gaze to where Cerdwin had stepped into line with his father. The male's face was a difficult mask to read, but he could've sworn silver lined the Second Commander's eyes.

Cerdwin

He'd managed to bury the beast all day: through dressing in his family's house colors, through walking the streets of the city with so many eyes on him, through standing in the gardens of the dead with his lord father, through seeing him, through seeing her. Through seeing *them*.

Cerdwin's anger and fury—and the helplessness he'd felt, watching his twin's despair at not being allowed to help—had burned through his skin when his lady mother had died. He'd set so much furniture in his chambers aflame he'd had to live in nothing but an empty marble room for a night.

He didn't feel angry this time—wasn't furious in the same way he'd been then. It was as though his fire had gone out completely during the mourning service. And in its wake, all he knew was the beast—the lion.

The Meadows was empty after a day spent mourning the lost soldiers, the lady's maid, and his sister. There was no one to see the golden lion stalking through the *dianaflora* that was the queen's tribute.

No one except the silver wolf. Its fur glinted under the Light of Aviva as it trotted over to where the lion rested next to an ornate tombstone. The wolf brushed its nose up against the lion's as it sat next to it.

The two animals lay beside the tombstone all fake night in silent vigil, the wolf's paw resting atop the lion's.

He'd come. After everything that had happened—that hadn't happened, that might still happen, that would never happen—he'd come.

When the time stone showed daybreak, the golden lion let out a long, mournful sound. The silver wolf echoed it.

Chapter 41

She grimaced against the pain—she couldn't show weakness in front of any of them, especially her mate, who was already on edge. Besides, it had been her idea.

Eleonora sighed, turning her grimace into a sad smile as she reflected on the prior day. Leaving The Meadows had been easier than entering them. No one approached her or the males at her side. Instead, anyone they passed pressed their fists to their hearts. Not that she would've minded the hugs and tears she'd shared with them on the way in. They were her people. *Her* people.

The air had been warm and muggy from the rain she and Cethin had brought down together as they'd walked back to the palace. That rain—the *dianaflora*—had been the greatest honor she could think to bestow upon the mortal woman who had somehow ensured she'd be here, now; upon those who'd given their lives so that she might be restored to the throne; upon the life Alanna had given so that she and Cethin might share a life together.

She'd glanced to where her mate walked to her left, averting her gaze when his eyes found hers, tender emotion swelling. She'd almost been consumed by it in the cemetery when they'd joined their magic, when she'd allowed his power to freely flow with her own. It had felt so different compared to when she and Cerdwin had joined their magics—that had felt like a battle of wills. No, her power combined with Cethin's was like a never-ending melody and harmony. What they'd made together...that was another reason she'd averted her eyes, knowing full well what else they might create together in the future.

A few people wound through the streets, though most remained in The Meadows—to speak, to sing, to laugh, and to remember. So it had been a surprise when she'd seen a familiar face opening a door to a home on the cobblestone streets.

"Alaric?" she'd called out. The male had turned, and it was indeed the male she'd trained with in Cerdwin's camp—the one who had orchestrated the retreat on the mountainside. The first to swear his loyalty to her as queen.

"Your Grace," he'd sputtered, dropping to one knee, fist over his heart. But Eleonora had knelt, too, so they were knee to knee.

"You never need kneel before me, friend," she'd said with a smile, a smile he'd returned without hesitation. But when she'd grasped him by the shoulder, he'd winced. She hadn't seen him, not really, since they'd returned from the mountains. "Were you so gravely injured?" she'd inquired, but the male's expression had turned sheepish.

"No, Your—I mean, no, Eleonora, not injured, at least not in the mountains," he'd said as they'd both came to stand. He'd rolled up the sleeve of his black shirt, revealing three circles that formed a knot of sorts cast in black ink on his shoulder.

"A unity knot," Eldwyn had casually observed, and Alaric had nodded.

"All of the males who were on the mountain with you—and many more since who are part of Aviva's forces—have gotten them. A symbol of our dedication and loyalty to, well, you," Alaric had said. "A circle for you, a circle for your people, and a circle for our city."

"I want one," her mate had said before she could find the words. "But a lover's knot." He'd brushed a soft kiss to her fingertips. "A circle for you, a circle for me, and a circle for our mating bond—as strong a bond as yours is to your city and your people, Your Grace." She'd blushed, a strong warmth that had nothing to do with the weather seeping into her skin. "And I want it here," he'd added, pulling her hands to his heart, where that scar—and her claiming mark—would remain forever. "Where are they making them?" he'd asked, shifting his attention back to Alaric.

"I've been doing most of them myself," the male had admitted, "your...apologies, but what am I supposed to call you?"

Eleonora hadn't been able to help the laughter that escaped her as she looked between the two males. Both looked equally uncomfortable. "I suppose that's something we'll need to decide on at some point," she'd admitted, looking over her shoulder to Eldwyn for guidance.

"After the Lord's Council recognizes both of you," the First Commander had cut in, "Cethin will most likely be recognized as *His Highness*."

She'd stifled a giggle at the look of dread on her mate's face. He turned back to Alaric. "Just Cethin is fine."

Alaric had grinned. "Cethin it is. I would be honored to create yours. I've been inking them out of my home—here." He'd cocked his head toward the door he'd unlocked.

Cethin had squeezed her hand. "The sooner the better," he'd said.

"Tomorrow?" Alaric had questioned.

"Tomorrow," Cethin had said, making to steer her away.

"Hold on a moment," she'd called out. "I want one, too."

Cethin

Cethin gritted his teeth—not because of the pain from the tattoo that had been etched into his chest moments ago, the herbs in the ink crafted by a long-ago Healer—*or sadist*, he thought—slowing the Healing process so it would remain. It was the scent of his mate's blood—and the fact that she was lying on the table with her breasts exposed. He hadn't considered that once he'd said he wanted his tattoo over that scar and her mark that she would want hers in the exact same place. Which meant she was half naked in front of Alaric.

Cethin reined in the urge to strangle the male who stood over her, his needle moving quickly and easily through her flesh, more blood seeping up. A cool breeze washed over Cethin, jolting him back to his senses and warning him to just *not*. The only warning the First Commander would give him. Cethin cast his eyes to where the male stood by the door and glowered. Eldwyn simply glowered right back. The male had to know what effect seeing his mate's blood and body on display had on him. But Alaric was his soldier. Technically, Cethin supposed, he himself was Eldwyn's soldier, too—even though they'd both sworn themselves to El's First Guard. And, until she was officially recognized as queen, Eldwyn technically still outranked him—even if the mating bond was stronger than any rank.

Cethin had seen the simmering emotions he was feeling on El's face when he'd gotten his tattoo. He'd gripped her hand and looked into her eyes through the process, reassuring her that he was okay. She'd squeezed his hand back hard enough to shatter a mortal's bones and breathed an audible sigh of relief when Alaric had finished. Cethin had expected Eldwyn to go next, but the male had thrown him a sheepish look, explaining he'd already had his done. Alaric had chuckled softly in confirmation from where he'd cleaned the needles. So it'd been El next, though nothing could've fully prepared Cethin for it. And while Eldwyn had told him that Alaric wouldn't present any threat to her—or them—it didn't make Cethin any more comfortable with the situation. A situation that now included a male he had virtually no knowledge of beyond his competence on the battlefield and loyalty to Aviva's army seeing his mate's breasts. But Alaric worked steadily, all of his concentration on the task at hand. Cethin noted the male didn't glance once toward El's soft, peach-colored nipples, which were now pebbled in the cool air Eldwyn had sent through the space. He didn't scent any arousal from the male, either.

His mother was an artist, came Eldwyn's voice on the wind. *He took care of her after she became ill and his father left them. Learned more Healing magic than most males. He's seen the body in its most vulnerable form from a young age. He is kind and gentle, Cethin. You have nothing to fear from him.*

Something softened in Cethin's heart, but he still held his position, ready to attack, defend, provoke—whatever—should anything change.

Gods, why did this bond come with such intense feelings?

"All done," Alaric announced, and Cethin blew out a breath as El sat up and tugged the straps of the navy dress she'd worn back up.

"Are you alright?" he asked quietly, and she nodded—though she winced when the fabric brushed up against her freshly marked skin. Cethin growled.

She met his gaze, eyes full of stormy warning. "I'm fine," she said. Cethin couldn't help it: he lifted a hand to her face, brushed his thumb against her bottom lip. Her lips parted as her breathing slowed—

"We're about to have company," Eldwyn announced. Every part of Cethin that had been about to order both males out—one being the actual owner of the house—paused at the First Commander's tone and went back on alert. A knock sounded at the door. Eldwyn glanced back at them, then opened it. Despite sensing who was on the other side, Cethin didn't know why he was there.

Cerdwin's full frame came into view as the door swung open. "I have two pieces of news," he said as he strode into the space. The male's nostrils flared—he must've scented the blood—eyes going from El to Alaric to Cethin himself before settling on Eldwyn.

"The Lord's Council put your claim to a vote after the mourning service." Though his eyes didn't leave the First Commander's face, his words were for El alone.

"Your father—" she started.

"Had nothing to do with it." Cethin blinked, surprise rippling through him. "It was Lord Evailel," the male continued. Cethin looked at his mate—a flicker of realization fluttered across her face before it settled into the cool courtier's mask he'd seen Eldwyn occasionally wear, that Cerdwin wore often.

The air around them tightened—as if, as a court, they'd taken a collective breath. Cethin sensed the thrum of power filling the space: Eldwyn's, prepared to defend, should things go poorly; his own, readying for the same; his mate's, twisting and surging, as though it were about to fulfill a long-lost promise; and another—which he assumed was Alaric's—that felt like the shuddering warning of an avalanche. But no fire—not a single taste of ember or ash. Cethin stared at Cerdwin, but the male's eyes were fixed on El as he dropped to a knee.

"Eleonora, Queen of Aviva, the heir foretold to re-Bind the Balance and cast out the Darkness, Light of the People, and Honorary General of Aviva's forces. Your Grace—my Queen."

Eleonora

Cerdwin's words clanged through her in a powerful rush.

"Rise," she said, struggling to keep her voice even as she slid off the table. He stood.

She felt it from all of the males around her, then: the loyalty and honor radiating from Alaric; the hope and joy rippling from Eldwyn; the love and pride almost overwhelming her from her mate; and from Cerdwin—duty, duty and the yearning for the easy friendship from their time in Ozul, before everything had changed. That feeling stirred in her heart, and she willed it into her gaze as she took the Second Commander's hands in hers. Silver lined his eyes, but he held her gaze.

"I will make them pay," she said—and she would. She would drive every last bit of Darkness that had led to his sister's—her friend's—passing out of their world. She would cast every creature of Darkness into Hell for the piece of love and light they now both had to miss—for what they'd done to her mate; for what they'd done to her land, to her people, to her father. To her friend.

She sent her Healing gift through him, and Cerdwin closed his eyes. When he opened them again, the silver lining them was gone, replaced by something else—something foreboding. A chill ran up her spine.

"That is my other news," he said. "Darkness is coming here—and fast."

Tense silence filled the room after Cerdwin's announcements—quickly followed by Eldwyn moving them into action: the First Commander and Alaric would return to his camp, and Cerdwin to his, to arm themselves and issue orders; Eleonora and Cethin would go to the palace to do the same—well, Cethin would. Eleonora had a feeling they'd try to keep her safely ensconced behind the palace walls. The Commanders would meet them at the palace to discuss strategy, and Alaric would be in charge of the army until they returned.

Eldwyn shot her a look before he departed, and she silenced his question with a look. "You are the First Commander," she said, and he nodded. She didn't need her First Guard—she needed her First Commander, needed the males to see him as such and follow him onto the battlefield.

Eleonora and Cethin wove through the streets quickly—but she paused, just once, to see a great shadow looming from the center of the Endurnal Mountains, heading right for the middle of the city wall. Cethin tugged on her hand, urging her forward.

But she felt it: the panic of the people around her. Every instinct in her body, in her magic, urged her to soothe it, to give them light. She supposed it didn't matter if she used her power—the Darkness was already on its way, and she had no doubt the Noir were somewhere in that vast shadow. She suspected the only reason they hadn't come sooner was because she'd combined her power with Cethin's at the mourning service, making her harder to mark—to hunt.

What good was she to her people if she couldn't help them? Couldn't defend them? So Eleonora let a wave of her moon-kissed power ripple through the streets.

It would be alright—she'd make it so.

She barely registered the bows and curtseys that followed her through the palace as they aimed for their room. Cethin immediately went for the cache of weapons he'd stashed in one of the dressers. Her eyes flickered over the tense lines he carried in his muscles: worry for her people, concern for her, a readiness to savage the Darkness that wanted to spill over the walls and consume them all. Her heart twisted, stomach knotting, because she knew what she had to say was about to make his position a Hell of a lot more complicated—knew he sensed her shift in emotion when he walked over to where she'd dropped into a seated position at the edge of the bed. He brushed a soft kiss to her forehead, then her mouth. She closed her eyes and blurted, "I don't intend to be an honorary general."

Cethin stilled, hands on either side of her on the bed. "El," he said, voice low and edged with a warning that made her primal instincts flutter.

She opened her eyes. "I need to be out there. With them." *With you.*

"It won't be like the other times, El," he said, hardness settling into his features. "It won't be like any small skirmish you've seen—it won't even be like what happened on the mountain." A muscle ticked in his jaw. "This will be open war—a *real* battle. The first of many. And they are rough and long and no place for a queen."

"That didn't stop my mother," she snapped.

"Maybe it didn't," he agreed. "But she wasn't—"

"Wasn't what?" Eleonora hissed through her teeth.

Cethin stared right into her eyes, not backing down in the slightest. "She wasn't mated to your father, El. They were married, yes—claimed, maybe. But she wasn't his mate."

"And?" she asked, already knowing his answer, anger simmering in her blood.

"She wasn't his the way that you are mine."

Eleonora shoved him in the chest as she stood and drew herself to her full height. "And *you* are *mine*," she ground out, allowing silvery moonlit power to shine in her eyes. "We are equally matched. You do not make decisions for me."

Another emotion—hesitation, hurt, maybe guilt—flashed across his face. She stalked over to the dresser, pulled out the Avivan uniform she'd worn on the mountain, stripped off her gown, and pulled it on. She knew he watched every movement. Then Cethin quietly changed his own clothes, putting on the same uniform.

"El," he said quietly as she finished. "You know that's not what I meant. I only—"

A knock sounded at the door, followed by Eldwyn and Cerdwin entering the space. She turned away from him, buckling her blades to her sides.

"You intend to face battle," Eldwyn said—a careful statement, not a question.

"Yes," she said sharply. "Why?"

"Do you think it wise?"

She rose, fully intending to give him her newly minted queen's expression. But nothing of her friend or loyal guard shone on his face—no, this was the face of no one and nothing but the First Commander. "You all trained me," she seethed. "You've seen my magic. I have some control. I could *help*."

"You would be a liability." The words came from Cerdwin, and she pivoted to where he stood a step behind Eldwyn. "We need to be able to focus out there, Your Grace," he said smoothly, years of courtly manners making his voice sound like silk. "The three of us are sworn to you, but Eldwyn and I must serve as Commanders of your armies first." A sidelong glance at Cethin. "And, as Cethin is under our command as part of Aviva's army, he will need to focus as well—on his orders." She turned back in time to see her mate give the Second Commander a curt nod.

"Not to mention"—Cerdwin took a step forward—"you were only just recognized by the Lord's Council. You would be a distraction to the other males on the field. And"—he stepped closer, the lion flashing behind his eyes—"we will already need to keep someone back by your side because we do not know what enemies still linger at your back." It was the same warning Eldwyn had given her weeks ago.

"Not to mention," he added casually, "the Noir seem drawn to your power." She blinked. *How had he figured that out?* Even Eldwyn gave the male an appraising look.

"What do you mean by that?" Cethin asked. She felt his eyes on her, but Cerdwin's had her rooted to the spot.

"When she left Aviva," Cerdwin said, "the Noir were attacking the city. But as soon as her magic manifested, they knew right where she was—until she used her raw power on them. According to the various reports, of course."

"But they appeared twice when we were in Ozul," Cethin said.

"I would assume she was under duress both times."

"That light I thought I saw…" Cethin's voice trailed off, and she closed her eyes.

"Although I cannot explain why they came to the city a few weeks ago." Her cheeks heated. She opened her eyes to find that Cerdwin had stepped away, eyes now on Cethin, who'd come to stand by her side. "Ah," was all the Second Commander said.

"What about the changeling's camp?" Cethin asked quietly.

"I'd figured it out by then—or at least guessed," she mumbled. "I didn't use any of my magic when I came for you." Respect shone in her mate's eyes. "Yesterday, with the *dianaflora*…"

"Today couldn't have had anything to do with that magic," Eldwyn said sharply, and they both looked at him. "With the size and energy of the host, this was something pre-planned."

To her surprise—and relief—Cerdwin nodded his agreement. "They were already coming," the Second Commander said.

"But I did use my magic," she reminded them.

"But you didn't use it alone." They all looked at Eldwyn. "It's possible that using your magic in combination with another's disables whatever key the Noir have to track you."

She took a deep breath. "Then that's what I'll do out there."

Cethin opened his mouth—to object, or offer himself—when Cerdwin cut in. "That is what *we* will do out there."

Cerdwin

He'd made his decision the moment he'd seen the shadows rallying across the mountains. He'd known that Eleonora would want to fight. He'd also known that it was unlikely that Cethin would allow her to face the bloodshed that would undoubtedly arrive at their gates. So he'd made up his mind to reason with her. And, if that didn't work—which, of course, it hadn't—he would remain with her.

Cethin stared at him—wordlessly, for once—as Eleonora turned to him. "You know what our combined magic did on the mountainside," he said, watching the light rise in her ocean-colored eyes, kindling the fire back to life in his. "We could take out the Noir from the wall."

"I should—" Cethin cut in.

"You can't," Eldwyn said, and Cerdwin nodded.

"While your magic was able to take them out in an otherwise deserted hollow," he went on, reading the mix of emotions that flickered in the male's eyes—fear, anger, uncertainty—"we cannot risk you flooding the open space in the sands. Not with our males out there." Eldwyn murmured his agreement. Cethin's mouth formed a hard line.

"It's a valid plan," Eleonora said, but Cerdwin saw the way Cethin angled his body toward his mate—the protective stance, the unwillingness to leave her with anyone else.

"You mentioned having to watch for enemies—at her front, her back," the male said, fingers twitching toward a nasty-looking knife at his thigh. "What about enemies at her side?"

The queen whirled on her mate. "Cethin," she snarled. Cerdwin had known that this fight would come, too. Instead of saying anything, he removed the armor at his shoulder, tugged the undertunic down, and revealed the tattoo he'd had etched upon his skin: a unity knot, just as Alaric—and the majority of the males under his and Eldwyn's command—now bore.

"We can't continue fighting amongst ourselves," the First Commander said, words and gaze now firmly directed at Cethin. "Cerdwin stood up for her before his father. He brought us the news that the Lord's Council validated her claim. He alerted us to the Darkness making its way here, right now." Cethin stared back, and the lion in Cerdwin's head roared. "And, regardless of how we got to that place on the mountain," the First Commander continued, not backing down from the death stare the male was giving him, "he showed up for her. So, you need to decide right now, Cethin, if you are going to accept his loyalty to the queen. Not to your mate," he said, and Cerdwin felt Cethin's power rumble around the room, "but to the queen. Because that is who she is to all of us."

Cethin

He allowed some of his ocean-blessed power to rumble as a storm and wave around the room. *Not your mate. The queen.* At the end of the day, that was who she was: not just his mate, but their queen. *His* queen. Eldwyn's words had found their mark.

Cethin exhaled slowly as he pulled his power back and let her read every emotion on his face. Hers softened, nothing but love and tenderness in her eyes, as the storm passed. Only then did he look back at Cerdwin.

"On your life, Commander?"

Cerdwin bowed his head to Cethin. "On my life."

Chapter 42

Eldwyn

H e should've been used to it by now—the waiting.

The eerie silence of anticipation.

Eldwyn had seen skirmishes with the Dark King's forces before—had fought against them the day Eleonora had disappeared; had been a scout, a spy, or a soldier for most of his life. But sitting atop his horse in front the center city wall watching the impenetrable Darkness creep closer, preparing to face open battle on the sands—just as those who'd come before him over fifty years prior had faced open battle on a green meadow—no, this was something he'd never be used to.

They had lost that battle—the battle that had ended with the Breaking.

The battle that had ended with the loss of the king, Eleanora's father.

They would not lose a queen today.

Eldwyn looked to the front lines where he knew Cethin stood. Though the male had been on the front on the mountainside under false pretenses, he'd fought well there, despite what had happened at the end. Eldwyn had no doubt he would fight well again, but he would keep his word to his queen.

Eleonora had pulled him aside before she'd followed Cerdwin to the top of the wall and asked him to aid her mate, should it come to that. It had been an easy promise to make. Eldwyn briefly shifted his gaze to the wall—to where he knew Eleonora and Cerdwin had stationed themselves—then returned his attention to the Dark mass spreading in front of them.

Out here, Cerdwin was not his responsibility. Out here, they were not the lion and the wolf. Cerdwin was the Second Commander. He was the First. It was long past time he compartmentalized that.

Eldwyn hadn't pushed Cerdwin to talk about their night in quite some time, hadn't forced the issue of *them*. He knew how difficult it was for the male to be himself. But things had changed. Time had changed them.

Eleonora's return had changed everything.

"Hold the line," he barked as several horses in front of him shifted uneasily. The males chided their mounts to attention. This was what they'd trained for: weapons first, magic second, even against what was coming here, now, today.

He heard Alaric shout a similar command, steadying a few shaking males shielding their front lines. The soldier had taken on his new responsibilities with ease. Eldwyn had no doubt the male would continue rising amongst their ranks.

Cethin wasn't one of those apprehensive soldiers. After everything the male had experienced, he was a solid presence on the front. If anything—beyond Eldwyn, beyond Cerdwin—the queen's mate wouldn't allow their lines or the wall to fall.

Eldwyn wasn't foolish enough to think it didn't run deeper than their mating bond or the life oath. Cethin truly loved her. A conversation needed to happen after the battle—a conversation about the male officially becoming her consort through marriage.

Eldwyn sent a prayer to whoever might be listening: if they all made it out alive, he'd make sure that that happened.

Cethin

The Darkness took form. Thousands of soldiers—some human, some Elvish, plus some nastier looking creatures Cethin swore were created from a youngling's worst nightmares—were coming for the city behind him.

Coming for his mate.

His life-sworn.

His queen.

His El.

A mercenary's cold, killing calm filled Cethin as he drew blood from the first enemy soldier that ran into his line. Slick, black blood exploded from it, splashing his armor. Cethin smiled. He would kill anyone who came for his mate.

He snarled as he blocked a blow from another soldier attempting to stab him in his right side. Cethin pivoted, kicked them to the ground, and drove his sword straight through their neck. He smiled again as their screams turned into a gurgling noise, black blood flowing from their mouth.

Sensing another adversary at his back, Cethin yanked his blade free and whirled, ducking low and dodging the blade of a Dark creature he couldn't identify—

But that didn't mean he wasn't going to kill it.

He would kill all of them for her.

Cerdwin

Cerdwin scanned the eclipse of Darkness coming for the city—*his* city, the city his father had kept safe for over fifty years. He would continue to keep it safe.

Eleonora would keep it safe.

"Do you wish you were below?" came her voice from his side. Cerdwin turned to look at her, but her gaze was also on the impenetrable wall of Darkness sweeping toward the city.

"The strategy of where one is—with one's talents—is more important than where one wishes they were."

She turned and gave him an appraising look. "Then we will make our master plan count."

He could hear it now—the whispers and hisses coming from the Darkness. Figures took form on the sands below: mostly humans and Elves from what he could sense—thousands of them—and what looked like three Dark Commanders mounted on beastly steeds.

They were more prepared this time than they'd been on the mountainside, Cerdwin reminded himself. This plan would not bring about the same tragedy that one had.

He drew in a breath and looked toward where he knew three Healers were stationed behind their ranks below, ready to provide aid as quickly as possible. He vowed then and there that none of those Healers would die that day.

A soft breeze rustled the curls that had escaped his Commander's helmet. He leaned into that wind, purring in reply. Eldwyn would protect the Healers—would protect the queen. Would protect him, if it came to that. Cerdwin pulled himself out of the grief and sorrow he wanted to drown in and leaned into that feeling of companionship, of friendship—of fire.

The boom of wings startled Cerdwin from his reverie. Three Noir were visible above the army—and the birdlike creatures were headed for the wall.

"Ready?" Eleonora's voice was steady.

"Ready," he answered, gripping her hand and binding his magic to hers.

Eleonora

The first few seconds were a shock to her system: the flow of a different magic feeling its way into her body, her veins, flooding her with a different kind of power. It settled into her, then allowed her to draw it through her essence, her heart—the same as her own magic, though it wasn't as easy.

She felt the emotions flooding through Cerdwin's magic; though his pain and sorrow remained, there was also something she hadn't sensed from him that day on the mountainside: trust—and something that felt an awful lot like love. He turned inward at the same time she did. She met his eyes. They were simmering with his usual flame but etched in the silver of her moonlit magic. She knew hers would be the reverse if she could see them. Her body was the conduit; he was the tether that wouldn't let her burn out.

"Let them get a little closer," he said, and she could've sworn she heard it more in her mind than in her ears. She nodded. The beating of the Noir's wings, their hisses and snarls, the preternatural Darkness that oozed from them became clearer as the winged beasts approached their spot on the wall.

"Now," Cerdwin shouted. As one, they pivoted. She raised her hands and released a blast of silver and gold flame. The closest Noir shrieked and snarled, just as the one on the mountainside had. This one writhed and screamed—

Until it was nothing more than a wisp of black smoke on the wind. The two flanking it peeled off. Eleonora rallied their magics again.

But something in the air had shifted.

Eldwyn

"Fire!" A volley of arrows rained down on the ironclad enemy unit, striking them with fire magic—the only magic Eldwyn would allow this early in a battle. Most of Aviva's archers were blessed with the fire gift; others possessed the gift of wind. It was a decidedly deadly combination. The squad of enemy soldiers at the front was already down, though those behind them charged right overtop of their bodies, determined to smash Aviva's soldiers.

"Charge!" Eldwyn heard both Alaric and Cethin take up cries from where they held their lines. They could technically win, he summarized, surveying both armies—but his males would have to heed the endurance training they'd practiced. It would take time to push back an army of the enemy's size.

Push back—not defeat. They would not beat the entirety of the Dark King's forces present that day.

The Noir flew above them. Eldwyn recognized the heat and ice that blasted one out of the sky: Cerdwin and Eleonora. He let out a breath he hadn't realized he'd been holding.

"Fire!" he yelled again, and another volley of arrows shot into the Darkness. Eldwyn sent a spear of his air forward, searching for a whisper of Cethin's power. Even when the male wasn't using it, he could still sense it. Finding his queen's mate alive and unharmed, he let himself feel a moment of relief.

Suddenly, his magic paused, and he felt Cethin's do the same.

Cethin

There were different sounds in war: battle cries, jeers from the enemy, moans of the injured and dying on both sides. Cethin heard them all—had been one to sound a battle cry. Heard the hissing and cursing of the corrupted men and males he cut down. Listened to them die. Heard the shrieks of the Noir he could scent burning away in the sky above him.

But this scream was different. It was a scream of true fear. *Terror.* It was so potent he could taste it. He didn't take a moment to think about why before he pushed his way down the line, cutting down the enemy soldiers who'd made their way in between the Avivan soldiers still trying to hold it—though not very successfully now.

He quickly found the source of the screaming: an Avivan soldier was fighting one-on-one with an enemy soldier, and the other Avivan soldiers were giving them a wide berth.

"Get back in formation," Cethin snarled as he made his way to help the male.

The screams he'd heard became clearer, turning into words. "I don't want to hurt you," the Avivan soldier was yelling. "I don't want to kill you." The enemy soldier stayed on the attack. The Avivan soldier did everything he could to stay on the defensive without striking back—a strange position to take on the battlefield. Cethin stepped forward and cut the enemy soldier's head off. Silence shuddered around him—

Then, the Avivan soldier began screaming again. "He was one of us! He was one of us!"

Cethin swore as he swung his knife into the side of another enemy soldier who'd made their way through the still open line, then another.

"Close the Godsdamned line!" he shouted. The Avivan soldiers did—but slowly. Cethin sensed their dread, their hesitation. He toed the head over. Beneath the Darkness spreading over the male's face—for it was an Elvish male's head that rolled beneath his boot—Cethin recognized that face. He swore again. It was one of the males he'd fought beside in the mountains. But...that male had been cut down during the battle. The fear from the soldiers around Cethin took root in his gut.

What is it? Eldwyn asked on the wind.

"Some of the soldiers"—Cethin could barely get the words out—"some of the Dark King's soldiers are ours. Our fallen."

Cethin could've sworn the wind recoiled as he spoke—as he fought the fear that poked its head through his cold, battle-hardened demeanor.

How many more familiar faces would he see?

How many more would the others around him see—former brothers-in-arms, former friends, former lovers, former family—that they now had to kill?

A new terror gripped Cethin. He could not—*would not*—let that Darkness consume his mate. Gritting his teeth, he rejoined the fray.

Eldwyn

Horror roiled through Eldwyn's body at Cethin's words. The Dark King hadn't just taken their people and twisted them into something terrible: he'd also taken their dead—had *awoken* their dead—and turned their fallen against them.

"Hold the Godsdamned line!" Eldwyn let his power shudder through his forces—a direct order from the First Commander. "These are *not* the males you knew. These are *not* the males you fought beside. These are our fallen—taken by the Darkness. Do *not* hesitate. That's an order," he snapped, tossing every bit of dominant authority into his voice.

But it was too late. The front broke, and the Dark King's army rushed forward.

"Archers!" Eldwyn yelled over the clash of metal-on-metal that echoed from the front in a symphony of death. "Fire!"

But he knew it wouldn't be enough. They would all have to switch from weapons to magic—and soon.

Eleonora

Even from their position on the wall, she heard Eldwyn's order. And, from the look on Cerdwin's face, he had, too.

She was panting. Her magic wasn't at the strength it had been the day on the mountainside—she was still partially drained from using it with Cethin's to grow the *dianaflora*. And combining her magic with her mate's was different than combining it with Cerdwin's—she had already used more of her own magic than she'd anticipated. And now, hearing what was unfolding below…

Eleonora staggered, and felt warm arms wrap around her body. "Are you alright? Eleonora?" Cerdwin's voice was laced with concern.

"I'm fine," she replied, hearing her voice shake. "Did you…did you know?"

Cerdwin—flushed and sweaty, but steady—shook his head. "No," he spat. "I knew they had taken our people from the city. But this, to take our dead." His face swam. It took Eleonora a moment to realize that it wasn't her vision betraying her—it was Cerdwin's magic, his volatile anger creating chaos between his fire magic and his shifting.

She would not—could not—let this rattle her. "Cerdwin." The male was shaking. "Cerdwin," she spoke again, voice full of nothing but a queen's authority.

The pulsing of his body paused then. "I am sorry," he whispered.

"It's okay, just focus." She cast a quick glance behind them, noting where the Noir were hovering. "They'll approach again soon. We need to be ready—"

"No," he said, shaking his head. "I am sorry. For what happened before the mountainside."

Now Eleonora was shaking her head, tears flowing down her face as she gripped both of Cerdwin's hands in hers. "There is nothing to forgive," she whispered fiercely. She felt the shift in him then—like more of the grief and sorrow he carried flowed away, freeing up more of the duty and love she'd felt from him earlier—that she'd sensed from him in Ozul.

He opened his mouth to say something, then stopped. She watched as his eyes widened in a terror she didn't know he could feel as he looked over his shoulder.

To where a vast black hole eclipsed the Light of Aviva.

Chapter 43

Eleonora

*E*leonora. The voice was male. Smooth and dominating. Somehow familiar—and dripping with cruelty. There was no mouth that spoke, just a vast black hole that erupted before them, casting the battlefield below into shadow.

The Dark King had come.

Eleonora couldn't breathe, couldn't move, couldn't think, couldn't speak as Darkness blocked the Light of Aviva, blocked out her vision of her city, her people, the males fighting for her.

You could stop all of this right now, that voice said.

In another world, she could almost see, almost hear, Cerdwin pulling on her, yelling at her, but she couldn't feel him. He wouldn't be able to reach her.

The pain of your people—the Darkness lurched toward the city, pressing in closer to the sands—*the pain of your soldiers. The pain of your* mate. She felt as though hot irons were being pressed into her flesh, over her heart, where Cethin's claiming mark was.

Come, the Darkness beckoned. *Join me, and I promise, dear Eleonora, that all of this will end.*

In another world, she felt tears stream down her cheeks. She could end this—only she could end this. Spare her people, her friends, her mate, by giving her Light over to the Darkness. Something tugged at the outer edges of her mind. A memory—something Light.

She closed her eyes.

She could almost see it, that same battlefield. See so many enemy soldiers—more than she'd seen today—but with green grass beneath their feet. See Aviva's forces, fighting back, led by two figures in blindingly golden armor, one blazing as brightly as the sun itself.

Her mother.

She watched Darkness sweep in. Heard that same male voice, though she couldn't hear what it said—couldn't hear her mother's answer.

But she saw what it wrought: Darkness, every shadow, every soldier, gone by some invisible force. The Light of Aviva over the city. Sand where grass had once been.

And a cry—her mother's—as Queen Serenity knelt over a body.

Eleonora opened her eyes.

No, she told the voice of Darkness.

Then you will pay. The voice was colder now—harsher. *What I will bring down upon you next will be far worse than this.*

In that other world she could hear Cerdwin screaming her name. She closed her eyes again and let Light pour from her essence, her heart, her hands.

Then everything went blank.

Acknowledgements

What a wild ride it has been to get this story out into the world! I wouldn't have it any other way.

First, to my husband, my real life Cethin. Thank you for not letting me give up on my dream, even when I wanted to. To our daughter, who is my reason and motivation. You can do anything you want to do and be whoever you want to be.

To my incredible alpha reader and dear friend, Beth. I cannot begin to explain how grateful I am that you took a chance on reading this in its very (VERY) early stages. It means the world to me that you not only did so, but stuck around. Baffling choice, but appreciated all the same. And Nic. Sorry, she was mine first. But I'll share.

To my fabulous beta readers: Janet, Katie, Alexandra, Cassie, Shaunna, Ashly, Heather, Charlotte, and Andi. Between the live video reactions, wild theories, and most hilarious comments ever, the laughter, gasps, tears, and screaming, what a trip this has been. I love you all so much.

To my development editor, Callie, for helping me shape and mold this story while keeping its heart and integrity, and for the resources so I could make my next stories even better. To my proofreader, Kaitlin, for dealing with a thousand unnecessary commas and changing the word further to farther more times than I can count. I promise the next manuscript will be cleaner. And thank you for not judging me for spelling at least three different character's names wrong.

To Hope, for taking on proofreading the back cover blurb, Shaunna, for your marketing advice, and Heather, for helping me create the playlist. Thank you so much for your support.

To my cover artist, Dyonne, for taking my very (VERY) elementary sketch and turning it into something that had me sobbing in front of my computer screen. You are amazing. To my interior artist and dear friend, Brooke, for helping me bring these chapters to life through art.

To my street team, The Chaos Court. Being a debut indie author is absolutely terrifying sometimes. You made it less scary. Thank you. I appreciate all of you for everything you do. To the bookstagram community I've come to know and love, especially Dominique, for convincing me to start one, and The Very Secret Society of Soul Sisters for taking me in as one of their own. Thank you for being with me when I started my baby bookstagram, and for standing by my side when I transitioned it over to an indie author account. Your support is so appreciated. To the Book Babes/Bitches for being here with me every single step of the day, even if you didn't want to be (you're stuck with me now, sorry). I love you.

To my fellow indie authors, especially Lindsey, Courtney, AS, Willa, LeAnna, Justin, Dominique, and Bianca, who dealt with constant messages and voice notes. Ya'll are the real MVPs. Thank you for helping me navigate all of this.

To Dana, who always believed in me.

To everyone else I've met who's helped along the way, I appreciate you.

To you, the reader. Thank you.

And to my mom. I never knew you were a writer, too. I love you.

About the author

A. F. Schreiber is a former journalist and magazine writer turned author who enjoys creating immersive worlds with relatable characters. She mainly reads romantasy and dark romance. In addition to writing and reading, she's also a Swiftie with a slight hot cocoa addiction.

Connect with her on Instagram @_afschreiberauthor.

Also by

The Moon Cycle Series:

The Waxing Queen Part I

Coming Soon:

The Court, A Moon Cycle Series Novella
The Waxing Queen Part II
The Lady's Maid, A Moon Cycle Series Novella
and more to come...